Praise for
The Joyce Girl

"This is a hugely impressive debut."

—Lisa O'Kelly, literary editor at the *Observer* (UK)

"Here is a powerful portrait of a young woman yearning to be an artist, whose passion for life—and rage at being unable to fulfill her talent—burns from the pages."

—*Guardian* (UK)

"Abbs shows affection for Lucia [Joyce] in her debut novel, sympathetically reimagining her. . . . Lucia recalls her traumatic, nomadic childhood, her attempts to escape a claustrophobic family and striving to bring her own artistic expression to life through dance."

—*Irish Times*

"This intimate and absolutely splendid novel must top my recommendations as the best twentieth-century fiction of the year."

—Historical Novel Society

"One of those hidden gems of a novel . . . both sad and enthralling."

—*New Books Magazine*

"A haunting piece of historical fiction."

—The Mitford Society

THE

JOYCE GIRL

Also by Annabel Abbs

Frieda: The Original Lady Chatterley

THE

JOYCE

GIRL

A NOVEL OF JAZZ AGE PARIS

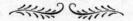

ANNABEL ABBS

wm

WILLIAM MORROW

An Imprint of HarperCollins*Publishers*

P.S.™ is a trademark of HarperCollins Publishers.

HarperCollins books may be purchased for educational, business, or sales promotional use. For information, please email the Special Markets Department at SPsales@harpercollins.com.

Originally published in the United Kingdom in 2016 by Impress Books.

FIRST U.S. EDITION

Designed by Diahann Sturge

Library of Congress Cataloging-in-Publication Data has been applied for.

ISBN 978-0-06-291287-9

20 21 22 23 24 LSC 10 9 8 7 6 5 4 3 2 1

To my husband, Matthew

There are sins or (let us call them as the world calls them) evil memories which are hidden away by man in the darkest places of the heart but they abide there and wait.

—James Joyce, Ulysses, 1922

SEPTEMBER 1934

KÜSNACHT, ZURICH

stand on the deck watching the trailing seams of white foam. Zurich recedes into the horizon and I wait for Küsnacht to appear ahead of me. On the banks the trees are shaking off their curling leaves. There's a shiver in the air and a thin odor of decay drifts across the lake.

I've been seeing him for three weeks, in his square shuttered house at Küsnacht. Three times a week I come by boat and sit with him. And still I haven't spoken. But today something inside me is stirring and my silence feels oppressive.

The lake is alight with autumn sun. Beside the ferry tiny fish flounce and turn, their spangled scales flashing like fallen stars. As I watch them, something begins to creep through the soles of my feet, up into my ankles, my calves. I feel it skim along my spine. My hips begin to sway; my fingers start to rap out a rhythm on the railing. As if my dull, plain body wants to be a thing of beauty again.

Today I shall speak. I shall answer his tiresome questions. And I shall tell him I must dance again. Yes, I must dance again . . .

* * *

DOCTOR JUNG STEEPLES his fingers in front of his mouth so the tips brush his neatly clipped moustache. "You shared a bedroom with your father until you were eighteen. How did you change your clothes?" His eyes are like small hoops of light that never leave my face.

"I slept in my clothes." I shift awkwardly, knowing what questions are coming next. And I'm sick of them. Sick and tired.

"Why did you not undress?" His words hang in the air as I pull my mink coat tight around my ribs. That eager little housemaid had tried to snatch it from me at the door. Kept telling me how warm the doctor's room was, how she'd laid the fire herself.

"Rats don't change for the night, do they?"

"Rats?" Doctor Jung pushes back his swivel chair and starts pacing the room. "I'm glad you've finally decided to talk, but you must explain yourself, Miss Joyce."

"We lived in hundreds of places . . . rooms . . . apartments.

Italy, Switzerland, Paris." Already I can feel my mouth stiff-ening, as though it's had enough of all this talk, enough of the doctor's endless questions. I run my tongue quickly over my upper lip, willing myself on. "We moved into Ro-biac Square when rich people started giving us money—my father's patrons. Before that my brother, Giorgio, called us migrant rats."

"And your father called it exile." Doctor Jung stoops, brings his face level with mine. And I wonder if he can see inside my empty, plundered soul, if he can see how they've robbed me and betrayed me.

"Tell me about *Ulysses*. I confess I fell asleep when I read it." He eases himself back into his chair, scribbles something in his notebook, turns his gaze back to me. "Banned for ob-scenity. How did it make you feel having a pornographer for a father?"

Outside, a cloud drifts across the sky and blocks out the sun. "*Ulysses* . . ." I echo, searching my moth-eaten mind for memories and clues. Fat blue spine . . . gold lettering . . . Mama snatching. "My mother saw me holding it once and took it from me. She said my father had a dirty mind and I could read it when I was married. Married!" I give a small, mirthless laugh.

"So, did you read it?"

"Of course. It's the greatest book ever written." I don't tell the doctor that I too found the plot dull, that the odd, unfa-miliar characters eluded me, that I never reached the "filthy bits" everyone spoke of. Instead I blurt out my question about Babbo, the question still gnawing at me after all these years. "Doctor, *is* my father a perverted lunatic?"

Doctor Jung looks at me through his gold-rimmed glasses. His eyes widen as the breath escapes noisily from his nostrils. There's a long silence during which he nods his head gently, as if expecting me to speak. "Why do you ask, Miss Joyce?"

My mink coat is now so tight around my body that my rib cage contracts and the air catches in my throat. "I saw it in a newspaper. They called him a perverted lunatic. They called *Ulysses* the most obscene book ever written." As I speak my voice detaches itself from my body and slips away, as though the words, the sounds, are nothing to do with me.

"Why do you think your father chose a chambermaid for his wife?" The doctor leans across his desk, pushes his glasses onto his forehead, prepares to inspect me again.

"He doesn't like intelligent women. He said that once." I don't tell him I know *exactly* why my father chose a chambermaid. There are some things that can't be spoken about. Not to fat Swiss men with pocket watches who are paid by the hour, like common prostitutes. Not to anyone.

Doctor Jung nods and chews thoughtfully on his thumb, always watching me, staring at me, trying to climb into my soul. Then he picks up his pen and I hear the nib rasping as he scribbles in his notebook. I stroke my mink coat, so soft, so comforting. Like a pet dog curled in my lap. Already Mama's face is dissolving in front of me, all of her fading away—her eyebrows like the feathers of a crow, her thin lips, her downy cheeks with their maze of broken veins. "I don't want to talk about her anymore. It was she who did this to me." I tap the side of my head three times with my index finger.

He stops writing and frowns for so long the muscles around his eyes twitch. "Tell me about your relationship with your father, before you shared a bedroom."

"He was always writing. He barely spoke to me until *Ulysses* was finished." I lower my lashes, look at my new shoes of softest Italian leather, feel my toes curling inside them. No need to say any more. Not yet . . .

"You were competing with a lot of people, real and imaginary, for his time." Doctor Jung's eyes are like pinwheels now, boring into my head.

"I suppose so." I run my fingers through the fur of my coat, teasing it out and pushing it against the grain as I think of my greedy siblings. All those characters wandering around Dublin. Yes, greedy siblings who had taken Babbo from me. I hold the doctor's gaze in a way I hope is bold and confident, but beneath my coat sweat is trickling slowly down my cleavage.

"What's the point of me being here?" I need to get away from his interminable questions. Time is running out. *Work in Progress* is still not finished. Babbo needs my help, my inspiration. What use am I incarcerated in Switzerland? My feet start jerking to and fro, desperate little jerks like gasps of breath.

"You are here at your father's request, Miss Joyce. But as you haven't spoken until today, we have a lot of catching up to do. Tell me about Giorgio." Doctor Jung laces his fingers together, watches me, waits.

And when he says my brother's name, I feel a surge of love. For ten years Giorgio and I were inseparable, like Siamese twins. I examine my hands, expecting to see the white imprints of his fingers from where he'd gripped me. To drag me away from the thin-ribbed cats I longed to adopt, to pull me up the steep streets of Trieste, to stop me falling from the omnibus. There are no marks, of course. Just the shiny puckered ghost of a scar on my thumb. But something else begins tugging and pulling at the edges of my memory. I pause, expecting it to swim slowly into focus. But it doesn't. Instead I feel a dull ache rising slowly from the base of my skull. I rub my temples for several long minutes as the silence seethes and swirls in my ears and the ache blooms in my brain.

The doctor looks at the fat gold pocket watch he keeps on his desk. "We're out of time, Miss Joyce. But I'd like you to write an account of your years in Robiac Square. Can you do that for me?"

"For *you*? I thought this talking cure was for *me*?"

"It's for me to help you." He speaks slowly, enunciating each word as if he's speaking to a child or an imbecile. He picks up the pocket watch and peers at it, pointedly. "Bring the first chapter of your memoir next time."

"Where should I start?"

"You are twenty-seven now?" He puts down his pocket watch and counts the fleshy fingers of one splayed hand with the other. "You said a Mr. Beckett was your first lover, is that right?" He nods encouragingly. "Start with him. Can you remember when you first saw him?"

"Wait," I say, closing my eyes as the memory floats toward me, bit by bit, struggling out of a shifting darkness. Faint at first . . . now bright and sharp. The smell of oysters and eau de parfum and Turkish cigarettes and cigar smoke. The popping of champagne corks, the cracking of ice in steel buckets, the chinking and clinking of glasses. I remember it all—the glare and rattle of the restaurant, Stella's turbaned head like a small yellow pumpkin, the damp heat of Emile's breath in my ear, the luminosity of Babbo's eyes as he toasted me, the exact words of Mama and Babbo. Oh yes . . . all those words. Of birth and marriage, of my talent and my future. Life had seemed to stretch out ahead of me then, all rosy and golden and shimmering with possibility.

I open my eyes. Doctor Jung has pushed back his chair and is standing at his desk tapping his fingers impatiently on the leather as if beating time to his pocket watch.

"I know where to start my memoir," I say. I shall start with the first stirrings of desire and ambition that pushed their way, like the greedy tendrils of a weed, into my young heart. Because that was the beginning. No matter what anyone else says, *that* was the beginning.

1

NOVEMBER 1928

PARIS

"Two geniuses in one family. Shall we be in competition?" Babbo turned the jeweled ring upon his finger, his rheumy eyes still on the *Paris Times*. He was looking at the photograph of me, scrutinizing it as if he'd never seen me before. "How beautiful you are, *mia bella bambina*. Your mother looked like that when we eloped."

"This is my favorite line, Babbo." I took the newspaper from him and read breathlessly from the review of my dance debut. "'When she reaches her full capacity for rhythmic dancing, James Joyce may yet be known as his daughter's father.'"

"What fierce and unadulterated ambition you have, Lucia. The next line is engraved upon my memory. Allow me." He started reciting in his thin reedy voice. "'Lucia Joyce is her father's daughter. She has James Joyce's enthusiasm, energy, and a not-yet-determined amount of his genius.'" He paused and put two tobacco-stained fingers to his freshly oiled hair. "You gave an astonishing performance. Such rhythm and evanescence . . . I thought of rainbows again." He closed his eyes briefly as if he were recalling the evening. Then his eyes snapped open. "What else does the incontrovertible *Paris Times* have to say about my progeny?"

"It says, 'Her performances have made her a name at the Théâtre des Champs-Élysées—home of avant-garde dance in Paris. She dances all day long; if not with her dance troupe, she is studying dance or dancing by herself. When she's not dancing, she's planning costumes, working out color schemes, designing color effects. To top it all, she speaks no fewer than four languages—fluently—and is tall, slender and remarkably graceful, with brown bobbed hair, blue eyes, and very clear skin. Such talent!'" I tossed the newspaper onto the sofa and began spinning around the parlor, turning in wide, emphatic circles. The applause was still ringing in my ears, the euphoria still tripping through my veins. I raised my arms and spun—past Babbo's beloved ancestral portraits in their gilt frames, around the stacks of Encyclopaedia Britannicas that doubled as stools when Babbo's Flatterers came to hear him read, past Mama's potted ferns.

"All of Paris is reading about me, Babbo. About *me*! And"—I paused and shook a finger at him—"*you* had better watch out!"

Babbo crossed his ankles and leaned lazily into his chair, watching me. Always watching me. "We shall dine at Michaud's tonight. We shall toast you until the wee hours, *mia bella bambina*. Invite your dancing American friend to grace us with her presence. And I'll invite Miss Steyn." He touched his hair again, smoothing it against his head with a sudden air of preoccupation. "And I suppose you'd better ask the young man who composed the music."

"Yes, let's ask Emile, Mr. Fernandez!" My heart gave a little skip as I rose on the balls of my feet and pivoted, once, twice, and then a third time before flopping onto the sofa. I glanced at Babbo. Had he seen the quickening of my pulse at the mention of Emile? But his eyes were closed and he was playing with his moustache, pressing the ends down with his index fingers. I wondered if he was thinking about Miss Stella Steyn, who had been illustrating his book, or about whether or not to wax his whiskers before we went to Michaud's.

"Did the newspaper not mention the composer—what was his name again?" Babbo opened his eyes and peered at me, his pupils swimming behind his fat spectacle lenses like black tadpoles in a jar of milk.

"Emile Fernandez," I repeated. Would he hear the soft inflection in my voice? While working on my premiere, Emile and I had become fond of each other and I wasn't sure how Babbo would react. He had always been very possessive where I was concerned. Both he and Mama muttered constantly about how things were done in Ireland. When I remonstrated that we were in Paris now, and every other dancer had hundreds of lovers, Babbo would sigh deeply, and Mama would lower her voice and say, "Strumpets, with not an ounce o' shame!"

"I'll telephone Miss Steyn and you can telephone Mr. Fernandez and your delightful dancing friend whose name escapes me." He put his hand to his throat and carefully adjusted his dimpled bow tie.

"Kitten," I said. And then I remembered how Mama and Babbo stubbornly called her Miss Neel. "You know, Miss Neel! How can you have forgotten her name? She's been my best friend for years."

"Kitten was bitten by an ill-starred bittern, bewitched by a catten after . . ." His voice trailed off as he dug into the pocket of his velvet jacket for a cigarette. And in the silence we heard the heavy tread of my mother on the stairs.

"I'm thinking it might be to our advantage not to read the review of your debut repeatedly to your mother." He stopped and closed his eyes again. "It is a peculiarity of hers, as you know." He placed a cigarette carefully between his lips and fumbled in his pocket. "Indulge me with a last twirl, *mia bella bambina.*"

I did a triple pirouette as quickly as I could. Mama didn't like me dancing in the parlor and I didn't want her angry words to mar my mood.

She bustled in with her arms full of parcels, her broad

chest heaving from climbing the five flights of stairs to our apartment. Babbo opened his eyes, blinked, and told her we were all going to Michaud's "for a wee celebration."

"D'ye mean to say there's some money comin' in the post?" I could see her scanning the room, making sure I hadn't meddled with the furniture as I did sometimes when she was out and Babbo asked me to dance for him.

"No, my mountain flower." He paused to light his cigarette. "Better than money. Lucia is the toast of Paris and we must toast her too. Tonight we shall be toasting and boasting."

Mama stood there, still holding all her bags. Only her eyes moved, narrowing until they were no more than slits. "Not your dancing again, Lucia? Sure it's wearing me out. You'll be putting me in an early grave. Along with the lift that's never working and all those stairs I'm having to climb."

I sensed the mood thicken, but I was used to Mama's martyred protestations and Babbo kept shooting me conspiratorial looks and winking at me when her head was turned. So I passed her the *Paris Times* and ignored her grumblings. "I'm going to be a famous dancer, Mama. Read it."

"That I will, Lucia, but I need to unpack me bags and have me some tea first. Look at these fine gloves, Jim." She dropped the parcels on the sofa, pulled a glossy white box from one, and started unrolling lengths of black tissue paper. The room suddenly felt cold, as though a sleeve of wind had blown through it. I put the *Paris Times* on the sofa and pulled my arms into my chest. Couldn't she be happy for me—just this once?

Babbo winked again at me then blew out a long plume of smoke. "They are indeed beautiful gloves. And nowhere will they look more elegant than 'round the stem of a glass of Michaud's most intoxicating champagne." He gestured to the newspaper on the sofa. "Read it, Nora. It describes the prodigious talents of our *bella bambina*. I am reminded of the proverb about the apple never falling far from the tree."

"Holy Mary, Mother o' God! You're like a pair o' chiselers who've been at the sweet jar." She sighed and looked at her new gloves. "Well, I'm not much in the mood for cooking and I suppose me gloves will be admired in Michaud's." She jabbed at the newspaper with her fingernail. "'Tis Giorgio who should be in here. Why is no one writing about our Giorgio?"

"They will, Nora. They will. Perhaps Lucia has had a Cassandra moment, a dream, about Giorgio?" Babbo looked expectantly at me, but before I could respond Mama cut in with a flurry of caustic comments about "daft omens" and "crazy Cassandras."

"Giorgio's time will come, but tonight we celebrate my rainbow girl." Babbo blew out a smoke ring, and I watched it shift and rise uncertainly before it broke away and disappeared into the air.

"What's all this about rainbow girls? Don't be telling me they—whoever they are—are seeing the future too?" Mama pushed her fingers fiercely into her new gloves.

"From my book . . . they rompride round in rout . . . for they are the florals . . . Nothing to worry your indomitable and imperious head about." Babbo stared up at the ceiling and sighed.

"Why can't you be writing a normal book, Jim? 'Tis sure to be the death o' me." She reached reluctantly for the *Paris Times* with her gloved hands. "Wear something colorful, Lucia. We don't want to be outshone by Miss Stella Steyn tonight. What page did you say?"

* * *

AS SOON AS the head waiter spotted us, he scurried forward, carving a path through the throng of people. Men kept stopping Babbo to greet him or ask about *Work in Progress*. Only Mama was allowed to know the real title of the book Babbo called his *Work in Progress*, and she had been sworn to secrecy.

As my parents exchanged greetings with other diners, Giorgio appeared behind me. "Sorry I'm late," he panted. "I had to wait hours for a tram. But I've seen the newspaper—what a stupendous review." He pulled me to him and kissed the side of my head. "What a clever little sister I have! Let's hope you make your fortune very soon, if only to pay for my singing lessons." He grimaced briefly and turned his face away.

"Let's hope so," I said, not wanting to brag. "Singing lessons not going well?"

"Not well enough to live up to Father's expectations." Giorgio fingered the starched collar of his shirt and I noticed there were lavender circles around his eyes and the odor of liquor on his breath. "I have to ask him for money every day and he always looks at me like a dog that hasn't been fed. Then he sighs in that disappointed way of his."

I touched his arm in sympathy. I hated seeing him so demoralized and I'd never smelled drink on him before. "When I start earning I can help."

But Giorgio didn't respond. Instead he said, "D'you remember Mr. and Mrs. Cuddle-Cake?"

I laughed. "Those parents we invented?"

His face broke into an expression of wistfulness. "I dreamed about them the other night. They finally came to adopt us and Mr. Cuddle-Cake taught me to ride a horse."

"It's a bit late for imaginary parents." I looked back at Mama and Babbo maneuvering their way through the crowded restaurant in the midst of a phalanx of black-and-white waiters.

"When we were children Mother and Father were never there. And now we're grown-up they won't leave us alone. Mr. and Mrs. Cuddle-Cake wouldn't have been like. that, would they?"

"No, but they weren't real." I didn't want to think about the past so I gave an exaggerated shrug and was about to remind him that Mama thought he was perfect and could do no wrong when he said, "Oh, look, everyone's here."

He pointed to a table in the window where Stella, Emile, and Kitten were sitting serenely among the gleaming cutlery and polished glasses. The chandelier lit up Emile's beaming face and I felt a little flutter in my chest. He'd pomaded his dark hair and put an orange lily in his buttonhole. He waved a hand at me and I saw the light catch on his diamond cuff link, sending a spray of rainbow-colored flashes across the table. Stella sat beside him, dressed in peacock-blue silk with three twisted ropes of amber beads that tumbled to her waist and a lemon-yellow turban with tassels that danced along her eyebrows. Babbo appeared silently behind us and examined her with the forensic eyes of a botanist inspecting an unfamiliar orchid.

"I wish I could dress like that," I whispered to Kitten as she pressed her lips to my cold cheeks. Stella had a bravado, a bohemian carelessness that I yearned for. Mama insisted on choosing and buying my clothes, and while they were always elegant and well-tailored, they never had the flamboyance of Stella's outfits.

"You don't need to worry about clothes, darling. Not after your debut and that review. I'm quite envious. Anyway, wait 'til you see what she's wearing below the waist! Tasseled harem pants—totally impractical if it rains." Kitten squeezed my hand affectionately. "But Giorgio doesn't look his usual carefree self?"

I dropped my voice and put my mouth to her ear. "He's worried about money and I think he's tired of being at the mercy of Babbo's patrons."

"It'll be fine when your pa can sell his book in America. But why's he staring at Stella like that?"

"She's illustrating a book for him, and you can be sure it's his book he's thinking about." I lowered my eyes and added, under my breath, "He's probably wondering how to describe her in Flemish or Latin or rhyming puns."

I slid onto the banquette next to Emile, felt the heat and sturdiness of his body next to mine. Around us swirled the sounds of talk and laughter, the jangling of bangles and beads, the scraping of chairs, the clattering of plates and glasses, the rattle of knives and forks. And in my head they became the applause from my debut, exhilarating and electrifying.

Babbo ordered champagne and oysters on ice, and as soon as our glasses were full, he pushed back his chair and stood up, gripping the table with a bony hand. "A toast to Lucia! Dancer, linguist, artist!"

"With her clear skin and blue eyes." Mama raised her glass, extending her neck and turning her head to the chandelier as she did so. I had the sudden thought that she was jealous of me. It was the briefest and most ludicrous of thoughts. But it was something in the angling of her neck beneath the light. As though she were making it clear my appearance had come from her. It struck me how rarely I saw Babbo's covetous eyes on her now, how rarely I saw him listening, in that fixed way of his, to the cadence of her speech. All that was reserved for me. I glanced across the table and there he was—glass aloft, blinking hard, his gaze swinging between me and Stella.

Meanwhile, the champagne fizzed in our glasses, the salt-green smell of oysters hovered above the table, small clouds of cigar smoke strayed from our neighboring diners who clapped and smiled at me. Emile's thigh pressed against mine, firm and full of certainty. And in that instant it seemed as though I could be happy forever and that no one could be happier than I was. I leaned into Emile and let my hand creep onto his leg.

"Where are you dancing next, Lucia? Will Josephine Baker have to vacate the stage for you?" Stella adjusted her turban then impaled an oyster on her fork and slipped it neatly into her mouth.

"She's a wild piece o' goods, that Mrs. Baker. Dancing naked with bananas. Shame on her!" Mama lifted her napkin and shook it out, as if she were hoping to shake away all discussion of Josephine Baker, the dancer who had taken Paris by storm with her risqué shows.

"They say she's making an absolute fortune," said Giorgio. The tip of his tongue curled from his mouth and rested briefly on his upper lip. "Apparently she's swapped the banana skirt for a small pink feather."

"She's naked but for a feather?" Kitten's eyes were wide with shock.

"She's a floozy, is what," said Mama, her nostrils flaring with contempt.

"She's a modern young woman and she's earning her own money. I say good for her." Stella raised her glass of champagne but quickly lowered it when she saw Mama glaring.

"She's had herself two husbands already and they say she has a lover now. What sort of a lady is that, I ask you?"

"That's why she can dance on stage wearing only a feather. If she wasn't married, it wouldn't be allowed," said Kitten quietly. "Pa says marriage is the only way a woman can be free, even today, even in Paris. All these liberated women, all these flappers—Pa says they're not truly free at all."

"Must feel pretty bloody liberating to dance in the nude." Giorgio snorted and ground out his cigarette. "Especially when you're earning a fortune from it. You can't be more free than that."

"What nonsense!" Stella, her eyes alight, stabbed at the air with the prongs of her fork. "Women now have a real chance for freedom. Look at all the women in Paris, painting and dancing and writing. They're not all married."

"Bravo, Stella," I cried, clapping my hands together. Stella had what Mama called "a tongue on her." It was yet another aspect of Stella I admired and envied. I was about to inter- ject with my own views on how free one could feel when lost in movement, how liberating it was to dance, whether you were rich *or* poor, clothed *or* unclothed, when Giorgio cut me short.

"They say she gets hundreds of marriage offers every week. Perhaps I should make an offer. What d'you say, Emile?" He turned to Emile and clapped him on the shoulder.

"I agree with Kitten. Marriage is the rock on which our society is built and the only way any of us can be free. That's how we Jews think. Marriage underpins everything. But I'm not sure that includes marriage to Mrs. Baker." Emile's hand had found mine beneath the tablecloth and he stroked my fingers with his thumb as he spoke. "What do you think, Mr. Joyce?"

Out of the corner of my eye I saw Mama squirming on her chair, staring at her glass of champagne. Babbo ran his fingers absentmindedly across his chin, smoothing and stroking his beard. "Marriage, religion . . . conventions and institutions. Shackles to be thrown off." He gazed fixedly at the plate of spent oyster shells in front of him.

"Take no notice o' Jim. Sure what would he be knowing about shackles." Mama gave a truncated sigh, as though exasperation had deprived her of breath halfway through. I shot Giorgio a questioning look but he was busy searching for his lighter, an unlit cigarette dangling from his lower lip.

"Freedom for women and the institution of marriage aren't incompatible. But no one can dispute the primacy of family. Look at you Joyces." Stella gestured across the table with its litter of bread crumbs and trails of ash and half-empty glasses. "Married for all these years, devoted to Lucia and Giorgio. Would they be so talented, so clever, if you hadn't married?"

"We'd be bastards in the gutter." Giorgio's mouth widened into a yawn, and as he stifled it with his fist he caught my eye and winked. "Instead we're rising stars on the stage, aren't we, Lucia?"

"Well, I'm o' the mind that Mrs. Josephine Baker should be locked up. Sure she'd be under lock and key in Ireland." Mama pushed away her glass and gave a tight shake of her head.

"And so would I, Nora. So would I." Babbo spoke into the knot of his tie so quietly that only I heard him, for then Emile leapt to his feet, crying, "Enough talk of gutters and prisons. Another toast to the talented and beautiful Lucia!" He lifted his glass and everyone shouted my name again.

That was when I saw *him*. He was standing in the street looking furtively through the window, so close his nose almost touched the glass. His eyes were bright and curious, and he seemed to be looking at Babbo, but then his gaze shifted to me. And in that split second something extraordinary happened. As he caught my eye a current of emotion passed between us. My heart jumped violently. Then he lowered his head, his shoulders curved forward, and disappeared up the boulevard. I felt Emile slide back onto the banquette, thrusting his leg against mine again.

"What *is* she looking at now? Lucia? Lucia? We're all toasting you and you're gawking out o' the window like someone possessed." Mama rolled her eyes despairingly.

Babbo frowned, put his champagne flute back on the table, and held up his palm. "Hush, Nora. She is having a clairvoyant moment. Quiet for my Cassandra!"

"Someone was staring at me through the window," I said, dazed and bewildered by the oddness of the experience, the intensity of those eyes, the sudden jolting of my heart. I gave a dismissive wave of my hand and turned gratefully to Emile, hoping to deter Babbo from any further talk of Cassandra.

"One of your new devotees, I'll be bound." Kitten laughed and squeezed my forearm. "He probably recognized you from the newspaper."

"Indeed, the price of fame. I know it only too well." Babbo

peered around the table, his spectacles flicking reflections of light from face to face. "You will have to bear it as best you can, Lucia. No doubt they will be queuing outside for your autograph."

Would he be outside? The man with the bird-bright eyes and the beaky nose and the cheekbones like fish knives? No. He had melted into the darkness. And everyone at the table was laughing at Babbo's wit. Everyone except Emile, whose lips were so close to my ear I could hear the smack of saliva in his mouth as he whispered, "You *will* have queues of followers. You will!"

And then Babbo started pronouncing on the indisputable link between dancing and visions, telling us about an obscure African tribe who danced until they saw the future. I knew his eyes were on me but I couldn't focus on his words.

"And they were half-naked too, I'll bet," said Mama in a thin, tepid voice. Everyone laughed again.

But all I could think of was the man staring at me through the window. I felt a strange sensation of restlessness spilling through me, as though something deep inside me was hatching.

And now, looking back from the Alps, where the air is starting to bite and claw at me, I see how right I was. Unlikely though it seemed at the time, something *was* hatching, unspooling low in my solar plexus. And this was where it started.

mile couldn't take his eyes off you last night." Kitten pushed herself up onto her toes until the muscles of her calves stood out like thick, twisted rope. "He'd be a terrific catch, Lucia."

"You mean because of his money?" I extended my leg, stretching until I felt my muscles pulling at my bones. Pale wintry sunlight sliced through the windows, throwing serrated shadows across the floor of the dance studio. Other dancers stretched and spun and examined their reflections in the mirrored wall as we waited for the dance master.

"Pa says the Fernandez family's worth a fortune. But I wasn't thinking of that. Ma says Emile could be the next Beethoven. Just imagine! He could compose entire symphonies for you." Kitten pushed back her neck, rolled her shoulders, and sighed longingly.

"He's very talented, but I'm not sure he's Beethoven," I said. Emile's cousin was Darius Milhaud, one of Paris's most celebrated composers, renowned for his stylish blending of classical and jazz. Emile longed to be like him and often talked animatedly about reconciling the rigor of Bach with the energy of jazz. What if Kitten's ma was right? I felt a small lump of pride lodge in my throat. "I do love working with him—he's one of the few composers happy to have his music governed by my choreography. Every other composer thinks choreography should play second fiddle." I shook out my hands in an exasperated way.

"Oh, I think it's more than work. And you know it." Kitten looked down the line of her nose at me, a knowing smile on her fashionably painted rosebud lips.

"I admit it—I'm very fond of him. He took me to the Bois de Boulogne last week in his new motor and kissed me for hours and hours." I recalled the rasp of his stubbly chin and the way his moustache had tickled my nose and how his hands had fumbled eagerly beneath my dress.

"Was it delicious, darling?" Kitten's head snapped back into position, her shoulders braced in readiness for my next confession. But then we heard the clatter of piano keys and the collective shuffle of feet as all the dancers turned. Monsieur Borlin, in a white three-piece suit, his hands in white kid gloves, swept into the room and rapped the silver tip of his cane against the side of the piano. I breathed out, relieved

I didn't have to disappoint Kitten, for Emile's dogged embraces had left me oddly cold and disconcerted. I'd wanted so much to feel like a brazen flapper. Instead I'd felt my blood cool and my insides curl up like a fist.

"Straight into third position," Monsieur Borlin commanded. "Reach open your arms . . . lift your palms . . . and extend."

"I have a hunch Emile might propose," Kitten whispered.

"Don't be silly! I'm poor, I've got a squint, and I'm not Jewish." I splayed out my fingers toward the ceiling, stretching until every muscle and sinew ached. But Kitten's words made my scalp tingle. Could Emile really feel that passionately about me? I thought of his huge house with its cream stone façade and its elaborate balconies at every blue-shuttered window. Of the artfully placed flowers and thickly daubed paintings his mother loved. Of his admiring aunts and sisters who fussed over me as if I were a new puppy. And I thought of Emile, his hands skimming the piano keys, his contented cheerfulness, his soft, loving eyes.

"Very nice, Miss Joyce, hold it there." Monsieur Borlin rapped on the floor with his cane. "Class! Please observe Miss Joyce. Note the position of her feet, how they hold her steady. Observe the elegance of her arms."

"I think you're wrong," hissed Kitten. "I think Emile's in love with you. And why shouldn't he be? You're beautiful, you're one of the most talented dancers in Paris, you're clever and kind. And your pa's the most celebrated writer in the world."

"First position . . . raise your arms, extending all the way through . . . push!" Monsieur Borlin bawled over the crashing chords of the pianist. "Now extend the left leg . . . Higher . . . Higher!" His cane struck the oil stove, making it spew out a column of black smoke. "And rotate!"

I could feel the muscles in my legs burning and the perspiration rising on my lip. And yet I loved this feeling, the tautness and control, the sense of every muscle at its perfect pitch, the way my teeming brain stilled in the effort.

"Emile would be impossible to turn down, darling." Kitten twisted her head to look at me. "He's so jolly, always smiling. He's rather handsome too, in a Jewish way."

"Jews don't marry gentiles and certainly not when her father's a well-known blasphemer without a penny to his name." I kept my eyes on my left foot as it pointed high into the air, willing it to stay steady and trying to avoid Kitten's stare as I pushed back the myriad thoughts that had begun to swarm inside my head.

"Perfect, Miss Joyce. Push out those toes, Miss Neel. Extend!" Monsieur Borlin raised his cane and tapped its silver tip on Kitten's left foot. "Keep extending, Miss Neel." When Monsieur Borlin had passed, Kitten lowered her voice again. "How's Giorgio? *He* certainly wasn't staring at *me* all night."

"He's exhausted from his singing lessons. Babbo's quite made up his mind that Giorgio is to be a famous opera singer. It's what Babbo wanted to do before he became a writer." I looked at my left foot, still hovering in the air, and wished Giorgio had chosen a different path. I still remembered the day we both enrolled at the same music school, a month after arriving in Paris. Babbo insisted on singing all the way there, even on the tram. A few months later I decided there were too many aspiring opera singers in the Joyce family and made my escape. But Giorgio had persisted, saying singing was the only thing he could do.

"I'll wager Giorgio's music master isn't half as demanding as Monsieur Borlin." Kitten slowly lowered her leg, her face pink and beaded with small pearls of sweat.

"Dancers, relax! Now we will work on improvisation. Imagine yourselves as cubist portraits. Make your bodies into squares, rectangles, lines. I want you to feel the joy, the spirit of Debussy's music, its subtle rhythms and its bold expressions." Monsieur Borlin gave a series of loud sniffs as if he were trying to keep a marble up his nose. "Listen closely to the geometry of the music. Mimic this in your movements. This is the beauty of free-form dance, of *modern* dance!"

I arched my back and reached for my ankles with my hands, flattening my ribs, my stomach, my chest. I could hear Monsieur Borlin shouting between sniffs. "A beautiful triangle, Miss Joyce. Dancers! If you are not indisposed, observe Miss Joyce's triangle!" He paced the room prodding and poking dancers with his cane and barking instructions. "Let the music flow through your limbs. It should inform your shapes and lines . . . That's very good, Miss Neel."

I breathed deeply and slowly and, with my forehead pressed against the floorboards, I thought about Emile and everything Kitten had said. Emile could never marry me, but

it was gratifying to be admired and the words "Madame Fernandez" sounded good on my tongue, shapely and elliptical.

And then I thought of the man with the bird-bright eyes,
and my heart soared and plunged. Should I tell Kitten I'd
been touched by premonition? She believed in my clairvoyant powers almost as much as Babbo. But even she would
think that ridiculous—the fleeting gaze of a complete
stranger! And I remembered the peculiar way my heart had
jumped. Many years before, when Babbo first claimed me
as his "Cassandra," Mama had grilled me on every aspect
of my "Cassandra moments." When I described the strange
physical sensations that accompanied each occasion, Babbo
had swiped his pewter paper knife through the air and said,
in a voice hoarse with emotion, "Won't you believe her now,
Nora?"

But I said nothing to Kitten. I didn't want to think about
my premonitions anymore. Sometimes they felt like stones
sitting on my chest. So I closed my eyes. Felt the music rippling through me. Heard the crack of Monsieur Borlin's cane
against the floor, the piano, the stove. Heard him sniffing
and proclaiming. Opened my eyes again.

"Margaret Morris from London is giving a movement
master class next weekend. Shall we go? Apparently she's all
the rage in England." Kitten peered at me from beneath her
armpit and for a second her eyes seemed silvery with tears.
But then she blinked and I wondered if it was only dust in
her eyes.

"I'd love that, Kitten. And I've got a new idea for a dance I want to choreograph. Can I show you after class?"

I thought about the new dance that was forming slowly in my mind. A Keats poem had inspired me and I wanted to include rainbows, and perhaps some tribal dancing, to help Babbo with his book. I wanted to create a frenzied dance of joy that would have the audience on the edges of their seats. It was an ambitious idea involving several dancers, each of whom would be dressed as a single rainbow stripe. I thought of weaving them together, pulling them into knots and strips of color, then scattering them across the stage where they would gently whirl like winged sycamore seeds falling to earth. I hadn't mentioned it to Emile but I hoped he'd write me another score, one heavy with the restless rhythm of several beating drums.

"Oh, yes, please! I don't know where you get all your ideas from. I never seem to have any." Her words were drowned out by the nasal voice of Monsieur Borlin telling us to "Breathe! Breathe! Do not forget to breathe!"

Yes, dancing was the answer. Whatever life might throw at us, we must keep dancing.

3

"You can take them a drink, Lucia. 'Tis after five." Mama passed me a cold bottle of white wine and two glasses. "He's been reading for nigh on two hours. He must be parched, the poor soul."

"Is it Mr. McGreevy or Mr. McAlmon?" I asked. For the last few weeks they had taken it in turns to read to Babbo in the afternoons. I hoped it was Mr. McGreevy. He didn't brag as much as Mr. McAlmon.

"Neither. Now get up and take this wine in, or they'll be slipping out to the Café Francis and we'll have lost them for the night."

"I can't move. I danced for eight hours today. We've been practicing for that film I told you about and I'm in agony. I limped all the way home." I gestured at my feet where small folds of skin hung like slivers of fungus.

"Oh, don't moan so. You've only yourself to blame. He's nice-looking." She paused and jerked her head in the direction of Babbo's study. "Irish. Speaks French and Italian and all. Not many Irishmen are doing that."

"What's his name?" I pulled myself up until I was perching on the edge of the sofa.

"Sure I can't remember. Your father has so many people hanging on his every word these days. God only knows where they all come from." She sighed, sat down, and started leafing through a fashion magazine. "If God himself came down to earth, he'd be in there typing up your father's book."

* * *

THE FLOOR OF Babbo's study was strewn with Irish newspapers. Books squatted in haphazard piles around the room. Babbo was wearing his white jacket that made him look like a dentist and sitting in his usual way, legs crossed, with the toes of his upper leg wedged under the foot of his lower leg. Opposite him, like a mirror image, sat a tall, thin man, his legs twisted into exactly the same position, reading aloud from Dante's *Inferno*.

I recognized him as soon as he looked up—the man at the restaurant window. I stared hard in case I'd been mistaken. But it was most certainly him. Only now his eyes were blue-green bottomless pools. He wore round, wire-rimmed spectacles identical to Babbo's, although with much thinner lenses, and a gray tweed suit. And when he looked at me, a frisson of recognition passed between us.

"Ah, white wine. Excellent." Babbo stood up and took the bottle and glasses from me. "This is my daughter, Lucia," he said, before turning to me and adding, "Mr. Beckett has just arrived from Germany. We must help settle him in, don't you agree?"

"Yes, of course. Where are you living, Mr. Beckett?" I tried to keep my voice even and measured but I could feel my ribs filling with air.

"At the university, the École Normale on the rue d'Ulm. I'm teaching there." He spoke with a soft Irish brogue that seemed to ripple around the room.

"Is it a nice place to stay?"

"The water is always cold and the kitchen is infested with cockroaches. But the library is magnificent and I have a bed and some shelves." His unblinking eyes held mine for a few seconds and then he looked down at his feet and I noticed his cheeks were suffused with color. Only later, when my own nerves had calmed, did I wonder if he too had been struck by overwhelming emotion at that first meeting.

"Don't be worrying about the cockroaches, Mr. Beckett. Paris is rife with places to eat. Why don't you dine with us tonight? We'll go to Fouquet's. Lucia, run and tell your mother we're going to Fouquet's and Mr. Beckett is to be our guest."

* * *

MAMA WRITHED AND twisted in front of the mirror. "This hat or the black one, Lucia?"

Her words floated across the air like vapor. I barely heard them as I stared out the window, eyes straining in the direction of the rue d'Ulm. The last few leaves clung to the boughs of the trees. And beneath them the streetlamps cast ragged circles of light onto the cobbled road. The smell of roasting chestnuts from the braziers on the rue de Grenelle seeped through the ill-fitting window frame, but I barely noticed that either. I moved as though in a dream, unable to feel the floor beneath my feet. All I saw, in every direction, was Mr. Beckett's face—his cheekbones in the bare branches of the trees, his eyes reflected in the darkening swell of the sky. My skin prickled all over and I felt light and tight at the same time. I said his name, wordlessly, again and again. Mr. Beckett. Mr. Beckett. Mr. Beckett.

"Lucia! What on earth's wrong with you? Aren't you hearing me? I might as well be talking to meself! Sure I've decided to wear the black hat. I think it goes better with me coat." Mama tucked some stray tendrils of hair behind her ears. "What are you staring at, girl? Find your hat and gloves!"

The door of Babbo's study opened and suddenly Mr. Beckett was standing in front of me smiling awkwardly, his eyes flickering around the hall, taking everything in: the Greek flag we kept pinned to the wall for luck; the photographs of ourselves, stern and solemn in our best clothes; the stacks of books waiting to be returned to Miss Beach's lending library. While Babbo and Mama went to look for Babbo's cane and hat, Mr. Beckett asked me about Fouquet's.

"Is it very smart? Am I suitably dressed?" There was a slight quaver in his voice, an apprehensiveness that didn't show on his face. I looked him up and down. His suit was threadbare at the knees and hung on him as though he were a coat hanger. His shirt was missing a button. His tie was knotted so tightly at his throat, he looked in danger of being garrotted.

"We a-always go there," I stuttered. "It's on the Champs-Élysées so we'll get a taxicab, I expect." I felt the color rising in my cheeks and my body fizzing. Why couldn't I master my body as I did when I danced? Why was I being so foolish? So tongue-tied?

"I have better suits at my rooms." Mr. Beckett lowered his eyes.

"You look grand," I said in a loud, exaggerated voice I hoped would drown out the thumping of my heart. "Just grand."

As I turned toward the front door I felt Beckett's eyes traveling up and down my body. Yes—it had been a good decision to wear my cherry-red dress with the tasseled hem. It showed off my dancer's shape and my long, slim legs and it made my breasts look fashionably small and flat.

And then he stepped toward the window and stood looking out, with his back to me, all stiff and upright. "You have a wonderful view of the Eiffel Tower, Miss Joyce."

I joined him at the window and together we looked out at

the lights of Paris. The city seemed to be winking and glittering with the lights of bars and restaurants, the quivering streetlamps, the bright streaks of motor car headlamps. And above them all, the lights of the Eiffel Tower leading our eyes heavenward. I was suddenly aware of the smell of Mr. Beckett's shaving soap and the warmth of his body next to mine. And my heart still knocking against my ribs.

"This is the advantage of living on the fifth floor," I said, and my voice seemed to bounce up the walls and across the ceiling.

"What a lot o' blather, Lucia! All those stairs I'm having to climb, with all the shopping, day in, day out." Mama and Babbo appeared behind us, their arms linked together.

"Ah, you're getting an eyeful of the Eiffel Tower, Mr. Beckett. Has Lucia told you about the time we climbed the awful Eiffel Tower?"

"No, she hasn't, sir." Mr. Beckett turned his face expectantly to mine.

I opened my mouth to speak but words fled me. Just as they had when Babbo and I stood at the top of the Eiffel Tower, clutching the handrail and looking down at the shrunken city. That same lurching, giddy feeling that washed over me then washed over me now, leaving me mute and shaky. Suddenly I wanted to reach out and touch Mr. Beckett, to hold on to him as I'd held on to Babbo that day, to grip Mr. Beckett's arm as I'd gripped my father's arm at the summit of the tower.

"I think of La Tour Eiffel as a skeleton, a cadaver, a carcass

looming over us," Babbo murmured, gesturing with his cigarette in the direction of the window.

"You do not, Jim," Mama said. "You never think of it. You
think only of Ireland and well you know it. Now, let's be going or there'll be no table. Lucia, close your mouth before you
swallow a fly. Oh, I do wish Giorgio was here. He's always
out these days. Always at his singing lessons. I'll ask him to
show you a bit o' Paris, Mr. Beckett."

And with that she pulled Babbo toward the door and down
the stairs. I looked at Mr. Beckett, my face hot. I thought I
saw the trace of a smile on his lips, but all he said was "After
you, Miss Joyce."

I felt the gnawing pain of the blister on my heel as it
rubbed against my shoe. But I thought of Mr. Beckett, just
behind me, and the pain receded almost immediately, as if
my blistered, callused feet had disappeared. Where had the
pain gone? Why were my feet no longer sore and aching? I
tried to focus on my heel, to feel the blister that only minutes earlier had throbbed and oozed. Nothing. I felt nothing.
Instead my feet seemed to flutter and float, following the
strikes of Babbo's metal-tipped cane on the stone steps.

That's when it came to me. A portent! An omen! I thought
back to Michaud's, where I'd first set eyes on Mr. Beckett
through the restaurant window. I recalled the tangle of
our gaze through the glass, the charge that had passed between us like electricity, the inexplicable jolting of my heart.
And hadn't Babbo said I was having a clairvoyant moment?
Hadn't he raised his hand, priest-like, to hush everyone?

He had sensed it too—the extraordinary force of that split second. I felt the hairs rise up on the back of my neck. Was Mr. Beckett to be my fate? Was my life to be woven into his?

* * *

AT FOUQUET'S THE waiters fussed over Babbo, elbowing each other out of the way so they might be the one who took his cane or hat, or guided him to his usual table, or presented him with the menu. Mr. Beckett looked at me with raised eyebrows and I took the opportunity to lean in and whisper, "He's famous for his generous tips . . . They always dance around him like performing monkeys."

Mr. Beckett's eyes widened.

"He has rich patrons," I explained. "We used to be very poor but now a rich American man and a rich English lady wire us money every month. So we can dine out whenever we want." I didn't tell him we spent our patron's money so effortlessly we kept having to ask for more.

Mr. Beckett looked around quickly and when he saw Mama and Babbo talking to another couple at the bar, he turned back to me and said, "Is that so, Miss Joyce?"

I nodded, ready to tell him all about Robiac Square, how splendid it was for Babbo to have his own study, for me to have my own bedroom, and how marvelous it was to have a telephone and electric lights and our own bath with brass taps, when he changed the subject abruptly. "Your father says you're a very talented dancer, Miss Joyce?"

"I dance all day, every day." I took off my hat and shook out my hair. The nervousness of earlier was fading now I suspected Mr. Beckett may be my fate, now I'd seen the hand of destiny at play. "I'm training to be a professional dancer. Dancing is the most divine thing in all the world. Do you dance at all, Mr. Beckett?"

He shook his head.

"I can teach you the Charleston. Or the Bunny Hug?" An image of Mr. Beckett in my arms flashed before me—his hand in mine, his skin against mine, our hips swiveling side by side, and the air between us sizzling and snapping like a forest fire. "I've taught all Babbo's friends to Charleston," I added, seeing the apprehensive expression on his face.

"Does Mr. Joyce do the Charleston too?" His eyes flicked back to Babbo, who was still talking to someone at the bar.

"He's more of an Irish jigger," I explained. "Don't assume you can't dance, Mr. Beckett. Anyone who can respond to music can dance. Do you like music?"

"I love music." Mr. Beckett cleared his throat and lowered his voice a fraction. "Please call me Sam."

"Oh, we're very formal in the Joyce household. Very Irish, I suppose. My father insists on it. But perhaps in private?"

Mr. Beckett, Sam, stared at me. Was he startled by my suggestion of being alone with him or by my parents' old-fashioned insistence on using a person's title?

"That's an idea." Nodding slowly, he pushed his spectacles up the bridge of his nose and I noticed that his cheeks had pinked again.

"Were you expecting my father to be more modern? Are you wondering why the Great Author can break the rules of fiction but not of etiquette, Mr. Beckett?" I dropped my voice and added, as an afterthought, "Sam." And the word sounded so delicious I repeated it silently in my head. Sam. Sam. Sam.

"I suppose I was," he said, and his gaze slid from me back to my parents, who were now weaving their way toward us, their arms still linked. It struck me then that, despite the shy intensity of his gaze, it also had a restless quality that had nothing to do with nerves.

"Oh, most people in Paris are very bohemian," I said breezily. "I'm sure you've heard all the stories. But my parents can't shake off their Irish upbringing." I didn't tell Mr. Beckett that they liked me to be home by nine o'clock and that Mama never let me go to funerals. I assumed these were Irish practices that he would be familiar with.

"How old are you, Miss Joyce, if you don't mind me asking?" Mr. Beckett's face was so close I felt his breath on my cheek, warm and dry like smoke.

"I'm twenty-one. And you?"

"Twenty-two," he replied. And his gaze sharpened—as if I had translucent skin and he was looking straight through to the blood skating in my veins.

Mama and Babbo appeared with an escort of waiters pulling out chairs, proffering menus, flourishing napkins, removing stray hats and scarves and gloves. No sooner had Babbo sat down than he turned to Mr. Beckett with a volley of questions about Dublin.

"Oh, here we go," Mama quipped. "Just don't get started on naming every wretched shop and bar on O'Connell Street. I can't be hearing all that again." She craned her head to see who had entered the restaurant. "Oh, look, Lucia, 'tis that famous actress. Mother o' God! Whatever is she wearing? Did you ever see anything so dowdy?"

I felt her elbow jabbing into my ribs but I didn't want to turn away from Mr. Beckett. I had no interest in the famous actress or what she was wearing. Mama's voice hissed in my ear, drowning Mr. Beckett's entirely. "Did you see her hat, Lucia? Some people have no idea how to dress. Peacock feathers . . . with her coloring . . . dear, oh dear." I strained to hear Mr. Beckett's voice. He and Babbo were huddled together on the banquette but the babble of other voices and the gossipy tongue of Mama in my ear blotted out their words.

I shrank in my chair, knowing exactly how the evening would go. So predictable. Babbo and his Irish compatriots reminiscing, drinking, reciting Irish poems, and, finally, singing Irish ballads or perhaps dancing an Irish jig. I felt exiled already. But I wasn't going to give up so easily. Not this time.

"I haven't been to Ireland for years," I interjected loudly. "I'd love to go back."

"It's not changed so much." Mr. Beckett fixed his eyes on mine and I felt as though I were being pulled into those blue-green eyes, spinning and falling.

I returned with a jolt, hearing the sharp voice of my

mother. "Don't be daft, Lucia. Ireland is a bog and a cesspit. Leave the blarney to your father. He can do that for the both of us."

"Come, Nora," Babbo chided. "It may be a land of barbarians with crucifixes, but it's no cesspit."

"A bunch of bigots and beggars!" Mama tossed her head. "Sure there's no going back now. You'd be arrested, Jim, and well you know it."

Babbo nodded glumly and Mr. Beckett shifted uncomfortably on the banquette. I tried to think of something to lighten the mood. But then Mama spotted another actress and began wheedling in my ear again and Babbo duly started reciting the name of every bar on O'Connell Street. I watched Mr. Beckett from beneath my lashes, observing the earnest look in his eyes and the solemn nodding of his head. And then his eyes strayed from Babbo's and met mine in a brief but uncompromising stare. And the air between us seemed to come alive—crackling, bristling, straining with tension. My fingers started to steal, unbidden, across the linen tablecloth. They crept toward Mr. Beckett, as if pulled by some invisible force.

"What about The Brazen Head, Mr. Beckett? Has that changed much?" Babbo's words sliced through the air, defusing the tension and breaking the peculiar magnetic charge that had taken control of my hands.

I flicked my fingers in the air, as if flicking away my father's question. "Tell us about your family, Mr. Beckett. We want to know all about you . . . if that's not too impertinent?"

Only later did I remember Emile. For a second I struggled to picture his face. And when I had it clearly before me, I felt so cruel and guilty I had to push it away. Far, far away.

* * *

IT WAS THE following evening that I learned of Babbo's intentions for Mr. Beckett. I was sitting in the kitchen while Mama bandaged my blistered feet. Another six hours of dancing had left them oozing a thick yellow pus and the insides of my dancing shoes were stained with blood.

Babbo appeared, a thin film of moisture on his spectacles and his bow tie crooked. "I can't go on like this," he announced plaintively.

"What is it now, Jim?" Mama gave the bandage a sharp tug.

"Ouch! Not too tight or I won't be able to get my pumps on tomorrow," I wailed.

"Mother o' God! You and your feet, your father and his eyes! I don't know if I'm coming or going. Where's Giorgio got to?" She looked up as if expecting Giorgio to walk through the door, but Giorgio hadn't been in all day. Or all night. I didn't tell Mama. I knew she wouldn't like it.

"I've spent the entire day on the telephone to lawyers. Pirated copies of *Ulysses* are being sold in England and America for forty pounds a copy." Babbo ran his hands distractedly through his hair.

"Well, we could do with the money, Jim. That's a lot o' money."

"But that's the point. We don't get a penny! Not a single penny. And they're riddled with errors. There's a man in America making a fortune from *my* work—my *mutilated* work." A note of petulance crept into Babbo's tone. He took off his glasses and wiped them with his silk handkerchief. His pink-veined eyes in their gray sockets suddenly looked tired and forlorn. "I'm a writer, not a lawyer. All this is making me feel vanquished in spirit. And now Mr. McAlmon says he's returning to America." Babbo put his glasses back on and sighed heavily. "Who will help me with my work, Nora?"

"Can't Mrs. Fancy Pants Fleischman help you? Or did she spend too much time gazing at you instead o' typing your work?" Mama gave the bandage another sharp tug and then started tying the ends into a knot.

"That's too tight," I protested. "I'll never get it off. I'll have swaddled feet for life."

"If you didn't do all this dancing we wouldn't be needing so much money. So stop your moaning, will you?" Mama stood up and started winding up the unused bandage in angry little jerks. I felt a stab of indignation. She never spoke to Giorgio like this and his singing lessons were far more expensive than my dance classes.

"No sense o' decency, that Mrs. Fancy Pants Fleischman with her Jewish brass and all." Mama snorted and lapsed into silence.

"Mrs. Fleischman has her uses," Babbo said. "She knows all the right people and is delighted, and wealthy enough, to work without remuneration."

"She's getting divorced, Jim. For goodness sake . . . 'tis a disgrace!"

"I can help you." I tentatively stretched out a bandaged foot. I didn't want Mrs. Fleischman back. There was something about her that unsettled me. The way she'd swanned into our home, sable coat over her shoulders, snakeskin bag on her wrist, a well-practiced smile on her crimson lips, pouting and purring and feigning an intelligence she didn't possess.

"You already do enough, Lucia, what with writing my letters and to-ing and fro-ing from the lending library. Perhaps if you did less dancing onstage. Perhaps if you just danced at home . . ." Babbo's voice trailed off.

"God save us! I can't have her under me feet all day. The pair of you, driving me plunging mad to be sure, with all your blather about omens and rainbow girls."

"You could do bookbinding, Lucia." Babbo leaned against the doorframe and stared into the space above my head, his thin fingers toying with his bow tie.

For a minute I thought he was joking. I waited for the little silvery chortle inviting me to join him in his mirth. Mama was busy filling up the kettle and laying out cups and saucers. No one spoke.

"Bookbinding?" I stood up and tried walking on my bound feet, hobbling up and down the kitchen. His words made no sense. Babbo loved my dancing. My dancing inspired him— everyone knew that. But would he prefer it if I were a bookbinder? Earning my own keep . . . Was that it? Or was it so that I could bind *his* books? I turned angrily toward him, my mouth choked with bitter words of accusation. But then it struck me. How stupid I'd been! He didn't want me to dance for anyone else. That's why he wanted me to dance at home and not onstage. He wanted me all for himself.

"Bookbinding is the perfect profession for a young lady. For a young lady determined to have a profession, that is." He coughed, a sort of punctuating cough as if to say *that* particular discussion was at an end. "No, Nora, I need the help of someone who will understand my work. McGreevy doesn't have enough time. He's always teaching now."

"'Tis a shame, to be sure. Mr. McGreevy's always so considerate. What about that Mr. Beckett? Can't he help?"

I felt my breath catch in my chest. In an instant my alarm at the prospect of bookbinding faded. I sat down and gripped the arms of the chair. Mr. Beckett at Robiac Square. Mr. Beckett working with Babbo. Was this another sign? The fates were surely throwing us together.

"Ah, yes, Mr. Beckett. The thought had crossed my mind. His work on Proust would have to be put to one side. And I can't pay him, of course." Babbo lit a cigarette, and in the flare of the match his face was brighter, his eyes clearer. "Yes, Mr. Beckett. Certainly able enough. Well-read. Erudite. Thoughtful. What did you think of him, Nora?"

"He didn't speak much, did he? Too busy hanging on your every word, like the rest of them." Mama pushed a cup of tea toward me. "What's the matter, Lucia? You look like you've seen a ghost. Have yourself some tea; it's good and strong."

"I liked Mr. Beckett," I said, trying to sound casual. "He's very clever, isn't he?"

"He didn't smile much. Very serious, to be sure," Mama continued. "Mr. McGreevy makes me laugh. He has a powerful sense of humor, does Mr. McGreevy, and such good manners. He always notices when I've had me hair done or got meself a new hat."

"I shall ask young Mr. Beckett. Indeed, I shall. Most would consider it a great honor, a great privilege, to help me with my work." Babbo's lips twitched as if he were suppressing a smile. "And if Lucia likes him, I'm sure we all will. Even if he lacks the charm and manners of our good friend Mr. McGreevy."

"Speaking o' charm, your composer friend was here today, looking for you, Lucia. All flustered he was, but I told him you were too busy dancing to be bothering about anyone else." Mama looked pointedly at me.

"Emile? Mr. Fernandez?" I waited for the tingle of excitement that usually accompanied Emile's name. But there was nothing. His gentle smiling face swam briefly before me and I heard the opening bars of his last composition, the one I had danced to so euphorically. But then they disappeared as quickly as they had come. I felt a prick of guilt, but a second later my thoughts swung back to Mr. Beckett. Mr. Sam Beckett at Robiac Square, every day. My fate, my destiny— how fast everything was moving!

"Sure, Mr. Fernandez. That's him. Smartly dressed he was too, in a suit o' Donegal tweed. These Jews have so much money to throw around." She got up heavily and moved to the sink with a long sigh. "When will you be asking Mr. Beckett to start work, Jim?"

"I'll walk to his rooms this instant. You'll need to come with me, Nora. My eyes are so bad today I can barely see a yard in front of me." He stood up and adjusted his waistcoat. "Will you join us, Lucia?"

I looked ruefully at my swollen feet in their layers of bandages.

"Don't be foolish, Jim. The girl can't walk! Put your feet up tonight, Lucia. You need to rest those feet o' yours or you'll not be dancing again. What about your tea, Jim?"

"No time. I must hire Mr. Beckett now. Strike while the iron is hot, Nora. I need Mr. Beckett at my beck and call. Will you find my hat and cane? Hurry, Nora. Hurry!" With his arms outstretched in front of him, Babbo lurched toward the door.

"Mother o' God! Can't I finish me tea?" Mama threw up her hands in exasperation. "Tell Giorgio there's a nice bit o' steak in the pantry, Lucia. And you're to fry it for him. With some onions and potatoes."

I listened to their departing steps, then limped to the stove and put the kettle back on. My brain was full of flip-flopping thoughts: excitement at the possibility of Mr. Beckett coming to work at Robiac Square; confusion at the thought of Emile; and a dull anger at Babbo's suggestion of bookbinding. Just so I couldn't dance for anyone else! What was it that made Mama and Babbo so uncomfortable when I performed in public? They loved the idea of Giorgio singing to an audience. But why didn't they feel the same way about me?

I had a sudden urge to dance. My feet were bound too thickly to contemplate any footwork, so I dropped to the ground and did some jazz floor work, my torso rolling and twisting, my legs scissoring through the air above me. By the time the kettle began its shrill whistle, I felt calmer. And as I measured out the tea leaves and filled the pot with boiling water, I could think of nothing but Mr. Beckett . . . Please, God, let Mr. Beckett come to Robiac Square. Please, God . . .

4

Kitten was the first person I confided in. We had just finished a two-hour rehearsal for the dance duet we were performing in Jean Renoir's new film. We collapsed onto a bench in the tiny changing room behind the dance studio and I began examining my raw feet.

Kitten peeled off her stockings with one hand while holding her nose with the other. The familiar smells of shoe glue and face grease and stale eau de cologne carried an undercurrent of something sharp and metallic. "These must be the smelliest dressing rooms in all of Paris. What is that disgusting smell?" I sniffed at the air. The odor of urine caught in my throat and I felt an involuntary spike of bile rise inside me. "I think it's the smell of piss . . . male piss." I cast around for a window that could be opened. Why did dressing rooms never have windows?

"Oh, that's too disgusting." Kitten kept her hand pegged to her nose.

"It reminds me of some of the places we lived in Trieste." I felt a shudder run through me and stopped abruptly. "Do you mind if we change in the studio? Everyone's gone and I've got something to tell you."

"I knew it!" Kitten looked triumphantly at me. "You're not the only clairvoyant one 'round here. I noticed it when you arrived with your stockings all rolled down like that. And late too. Not like you to arrive late, darling. Let's go back to the studio and you can tell me everything."

"Oh, Kitten, I was just waiting for the right time to tell you." We lugged our bags and coats back to the studio and squatted down beside the stove. I pressed my shoulder against hers, unable to keep my secret any longer. "I think I'm in love. I can't think about anything else. I had to walk in the Jardin du Luxembourg to calm myself, 'round and 'round the Medici Fountain. Did I dance very badly?"

"You danced with so much energy and radiance, I knew something simply marvelous must have happened to you. It's Emile Fernandez, isn't it?" Kitten tilted her face and regarded me for a long second. I shook my head, lips clamped tightly together to stop my secret from spilling out too fast and ruining the drama of the moment.

"Oh, you dark horse! How could you keep such a big secret from me?"

"I just met him, Kitten. Two nights ago. His name's Samuel Beckett. He likes to be called Sam but we call him Mr. Beckett. And he's wonderful!" I closed my eyes, dropped my head onto Kitten's shoulder, and sighed as I remembered the sharpness of his gaze, how it had enthralled and excited me.

"Fast work, darling! I forgive you for not telling me. But who is he?"

"It's faster than you think." I lifted my head and turned to face her. "I think we'll get married. Not right away, of course. But eventually."

Kitten gaped. "He's proposed? Already?"

"No, of course not. He has to fall in love with me first, but I have a funny feeling he will." I slid my foot up my thigh and pulled off a dancing shoe.

"You've had one of your clairvoyant experiences, I can tell." Kitten rubbed my back slowly, as if trying to cajole more information from me, and I suddenly saw how ridiculous it all sounded. I knew Babbo would understand. I could see it now: the fervent look in his eyes, his spidery fingers reaching determinedly for a crayon, his voice dropping in deference as he gently questioned me. But I had no intention of telling him. This was not something I wanted to read about, however cryptic or obscure, in his book.

"He was the man staring at me through Michaud's

window, the night we celebrated my review in the *Paris Times*." I licked my finger and dabbed at a bloodstain on the heel of my dancing shoe. "Now he's working for Babbo. And when I think of him my feet stop hurting. But last night I dreamed . . ." My voice faltered and I rubbed harder at the bloodstain.

"Yes?" Kitten gave my shoulder a little shake.

"I dreamed we were intimate, like man and wife, covered in sunlight." I didn't tell her how I woke up throbbing and aching at the thought. Nor did I tell her that I'd had to dance around my room for half an hour just to calm myself. Instead, I said, "I've never felt this sort of closeness to someone I barely know."

She gave a stagey gasp, as though what I'd told her was too fantastical to absorb. "But who is he? Where's he from?"

"He's Irish. He's got these mesmerizing eyes, the color of seawater but really bright and piercing."

"He sounds terribly exotic. What's he doing here?"

"Teaching English. But he only has one pupil at the moment. He's frightfully clever and he wants to be a great scholar. My mother's arranged for him to meet Giorgio tonight at the Café du Dôme for aperitifs. Can you come?" My heartbeat had quickened and already I could feel my body crackling and fizzing at the prospect of seeing Sam again.

"Right now? But I need to wash—and I haven't got anything to wear. And I need to rouge my cheeks. Can't I go home first?"

I looked at the clock on the wall. It was already six o'clock.

I stood up, ran my fingers through my newly bobbed hair, and smoothed down my dress. "No time. Come on, I'll tell you about him on the way."

"What about your stockings? Aren't you rolling them down again?"

"Giorgio might tell Mama and then I wouldn't hear the end of it. I was only trying it out." I gave a small shiver as I scooped up my bag and headed for the door.

"But they looked so daring," said Kitten in a disappointed voice. "I guess it is a bit cold now."

As we stepped out of the studio, we felt the snap of winter, a brittleness and sharpness in the air that made us pull our coats tightly around our bodies and tug our hats down over our ears. The boulevard Montparnasse was rousing itself for another night of revelry. The flower carts were heavy with thick bunches of red-berried holly and winter-flowering jasmine, and the smell of charred chestnut skins was everywhere. The sorrowful voices of street singers mingled with the cries of newspaper vendors and hawkers from the tobacco carts. The balloon sellers and the sheet-music vendors and the puppeteers were packing up and calling out to each other. The old women who sold shoelaces from up-ended umbrellas were stretching their limbs and yawning. The sword swallowers and fire breathers and jugglers were preparing for their evening acts. And everywhere people were spilling out of the bars as they ambled from one to another, looking for mislaid friends or somewhere cheaper to drink.

"I can't believe you're making me see Giorgio, dressed like

this." Kitten pointed down at her feet. Instead of her usual elegantly heeled shoes with their buckles and buttons, she was wearing her sensible brown Oxfords that she always walked home in after dance classes.

"He won't mind. You won't tell him about me and Mr. Beckett, will you?" I stopped to drop a few coins into the tin mug of a beggar crouching on the pavement, his wooden crutches lying across his knees. "Giorgio and Mama are a bit funny about Babbo calling me his 'Cassandra.' It is odd, though. I see him through a window staring at me, then he turns up at our house. And he's Irish and speaks fluent Italian, like us. And now he's coming to work for Babbo and he'll be at our house every day."

I looped my arm through Kitten's and drew her toward me. Ahead of us the warm lights of the Dôme streamed onto the boulevard. My pulse quickened and I took a deep breath of cold air.

"But do *all* your predictions come true? I mean every single one of them?" Kitten persisted.

I hesitated, unsure how to explain Babbo's certitude, his conviction about my clairvoyance. "They're not so much predictions as—as intuitions. Last Friday I woke up thinking about an old friend of ours from Zurich. We'd heard nothing from her for three years, but an hour later the postboy brought a letter from her saying she was coming to Paris." I chewed on my nail, thinking back to that morning. I'd woken with an odd tingling at the base of my spine and an image of Jeanne Wertenberg (who I hadn't thought of for at least a year) lodged inexplicably in my head. When her letter came, I told Babbo and was duly quizzed: How had she looked? What was she doing? Had she spoken? What was in the letter? How long did my spine tingle for? And then he'd closed his eyes and muttered about the mysterious workings of the somnolent mind.

"Sometimes they come as dreams." I stopped at the flower cart we were passing and buried my nose in the spears of yellow jasmine standing in enamel buckets.

"I know your dream about me came true. That was uncanny. Even Pa said so, and he's so cynical about most things." Kitten paused, as if recalling the experience. "D'you remember, Lucia? You dreamed I danced the lead role in *La création du monde* in Saint-Paul-de-Vence? And then I got the part."

"It's the vivid ones that come true, where I remember every detail, every smell and sound, and the colors are so bright it hurts my eyes. When I dreamed of me and Mr. Beckett naked, I could feel the heat of the sun on me, all golden, and the angles of his bones beneath me. And a strange ticking noise in the background, like a clock. You won't breathe a word, will you, Kitten?"

"Of course not, darling." Kitten turned and smiled at me. "But if you dream about me again, you will tell me, won't you? Even if it's horrible. Even if I'm in a coffin."

I unlinked my arm from hers and turned a few pirouettes as we passed the oyster sellers with their baskets and knives squatting on the terrace of the Dôme.

"I'm only a prophet of happiness, Kitten." But my words

were drowned out by the laughter and cries surging from the café as we pushed open the doors.

We spotted Giorgio and Mr. Beckett immediately. They were standing at the bar, blowing out long columns of cigarette smoke.

"Hello, flappers!" Giorgio pulled me to him and smacked a kiss on each of my cheeks. "I've been telling Mr. Beckett about the best jazz haunts in Paris, but turns out he's more of an instrumental man. Isn't that right, Mr. Beckett?" Giorgio paused to kiss Kitten and compliment her on her glowing complexion. Mr. Beckett stood shifting nervously from one foot to the other, puffing rapidly on his cigarette.

"We all kiss in Paris, Mr. Beckett," I said, feeling a warm flush rise up my throat. I stretched up and kissed him on each cheek, letting his stubble graze my lips and the smoke from his cigarette coil around my face. As I stepped back, I dipped my head, hoping Mr. Beckett wouldn't see my burning cheeks.

"Oh yes, it's the Paris way. I'm Kitten." She leaned across me and offered her cheek to Mr. Beckett. "It's one of the things I love about Paris," she added as she peeled off her gloves. "All the kissing! And if it's music you're after, Giorgio sings like an angel."

"Thank you, Kitten. These two do nothing but dance." Giorgio turned to Mr. Beckett, and as he gestured at us with his cigarette, I noticed the glimmer of its gold filter. These weren't his usual hand-rolled cigarettes and I wondered if he'd been paid for something. But before I could ask, he began talking again. "Day and night. Dancing, dancing, dancing. It drives Mother and Father mad."

"O body swayed to music, o brightening glance, how can we know the dancer from the dance?" Mr. Beckett's eyes were on me and I promptly forgot about Giorgio's good fortune.

I arched my brows. "Did you write that, Mr. Beckett?"

"I'm afraid not. It's an Irish poem I've been reading. Do you like poetry, Miss Joyce?"

"Of course. I'm just choreographing a new dance inspired by a Keats poem you might know." I hesitated, then saw the light spike encouragingly in his eyes and was about to continue when Giorgio interrupted.

"Tell him about Paris, Lucia. Tell him about the parties and the nightclubs. He needs more friends. He only knows us and Thomas McGreevy, and McGreevy's more mouse than man." Giorgio punched out his gold-tipped cigarette and called to the waiter for another round of martinis.

I turned to Mr. Beckett. "I'm so glad you accepted Babbo's job offer. He's been very unwell. Some days he can't see anything. He has to write with huge crayons and wear two pairs of glasses, one on top of the other. Light hurts his eyes, so you have to remember to keep the curtains closed."

"How will I read to him?" Mr. Beckett frowned.

"You have to sit by the window and open the curtains just a crack, so the light falls only on your book. That's what I do."

"It's a great honor to work for your father," he said gravely.

"I expect you'll be wanting to visit the salons. Babbo's been a couple of times, to Miss Stein's salon and to Miss

Barney's. All the great artists go there. I can get you an invitation if you want?"

"They're all lesbians! Why on earth would he want to go there? Unless he wants to observe wealthy Americans at play." Giorgio flipped open his lighter then snapped it shut. And I thought how bitter he sounded. But I said nothing. Bit my tongue. Rolled my eyes at Kitten, who suddenly looked tired and sad. And that was when I glanced down and noticed Giorgio's shoes. They had been polished so vigorously they seemed to radiate light.

"Who's been polishing your shoes, Giorgio?" I asked. Even Mama, in her maternal devotion to him, would never expend that much effort on his shoes.

He gave a childlike grin. "Never you mind, Lucia!" He turned to Mr. Beckett. "I'll show you the jazz clubs. Lucia can show you the bal musettes and the dance theaters and my father will show you the opera and the Seine. Did he mention his daily walks by the Seine? No, I thought not. He has to be accompanied—you'll get used to it."

"I'm not completely friendless." Mr. Beckett gave a tentative smile. "I've joined the university rugby team. As a scrum half."

"Oh, well done, Mr. Beckett!" Kitten clapped her hands together. "Are you keen on sports?"

Mr. Beckett nodded. "I played a lot of cricket back in Dublin. And tennis and golf. I even tried my hand at motorcycle racing and roller-skating." He gave an embarrassed cough as though he'd said too much.

Giorgio looked Mr. Beckett up and down. "Wouldn't have thought you've the right build for rugby."

I felt my heart miss a beat. What if Mr. Beckett—Sam— was injured or squashed to death in a rugby scrum? I looked anxiously at his thin body, noting the blades of his bones just visible beneath his suit.

"My lungs aren't great, it's true," he said at last, patting his chest and nodding pensively. He gave a rattling cough as if to prove the point.

"That'll be the Irish weather," said Giorgio, offering Mr. Beckett one of his gold-tipped cigarettes. "Your lungs will be fine here. When we were last in Ireland it rained every day. D'you remember, Lucia? Rain. And people trying to shoot us. And boiled potatoes full of black eyes. Damned awful place!"

I nodded, remembering the sounds of gunfire as Giorgio, Mama, and I sat on a train trying to escape the fighting that had broken out. Mama and I had thrown ourselves to the floor of the carriage but Giorgio had stayed bravely in his seat, saying he'd take the bullets for us.

"The countryside is beautiful, though." Mr. Beckett inhaled deeply on his cigarette, scooping out his cheeks. "They have these pink and green sunsets I've never seen anywhere else."

I tried to remember an Irish sunset but Kitten changed the subject with such haste, I blushingly forgot all about Ireland.

"Lucia is an amazing gymnast, aren't you, Lucia?" She nudged me in the back as if I were an actress who'd forgotten my lines and needed prompting. "In fact, she was a gymnast before she became a dancer. And she sings and plays the piano and she paints too, don't you, Lucia?"

"Lucia has so many talents, why she chose dancing is a mystery to us all." Giorgio looked at me and smiled like a proud parent, his chest all puffed up.

Mr. Beckett turned and stared at me, the light in his eyes brightening again. I flushed and shook my head awkwardly.

"And everyone knows she's Mr. Joyce's muse, don't they, Giorgio?" Kitten turned to Giorgio, nodding her head in an exaggerated manner. But Giorgio was waving to someone across the bar and didn't answer.

"I imagine you make a splendid muse," Mr. Beckett murmured, his eyes fastened on me as though I were an exotic butterfly he'd caught quite unexpectedly and didn't know what to do with.

"Time for me to show you the joys of Montmartre, Mr. Beckett. You flappers run along home. Tell Mother I'll be late, Lucia." Giorgio dropped his cigarette butt to the floor and stamped it out with the heel of his gleaming shoe.

"Can't we come with you?" I felt my stomach churn, cold and sour. Giorgio had never dismissed me like this before. It struck me then, quite suddenly, that our age-old bond was stretching and tearing at the edges, like a piece of fraying fabric. Had I been too caught up in my dancing to notice what was happening to Giorgio?

"Mother and Father wouldn't approve." He threw a stack

of five-franc notes carelessly onto the bar and something in the way he did it, the ease and nonchalance of it, made my stomach churn a second time. How different from all those times when the two of us had combed each other's pockets for coins, counting and shining each one, hurrying out to avoid the waiters' scowls because we couldn't leave a tip.

But then Mr. Beckett leaned toward me and kissed me on each cheek. And when I pulled back, he was grinning like a boy, so proud and triumphant I forgot about Giorgio.

"Gee, Mr. Beckett." Kitten stepped in front of me and raised her cheek expectantly. "Just like a Parisian gentleman now. I bet they don't do that in Ireland."

As he kissed Kitten's cheeks, Mr. Beckett kept his eyes on mine, until my heart was thumping so hard against my ribs I had to pull my gaze away for fear he would see the thumping reflected in my eyes.

"I'll see you tomorrow, Lucia," he said quietly, as Kitten and I pulled on our coats and hats. "Perhaps you'll tell me more about that dance you're choreographing? 'Take into the air my quiet breath' . . ."

"Oh," I said, flustered. "Yes, Keats. See you tomorrow."

As we made our way, arm in arm, to the tram stop, Kitten could talk of nothing but how Mr. Beckett had stared and stared at me. "Why didn't you tell him how marvelous you are, darling? You were far too modest!" She shook her head in a helpless gesture.

"Don't you think he's handsome?"

"Too bony and skinny for me. I like my men a little more filled out." She laughed. "D'you know who he reminded me of, though?"

"A Roman god? Lord Byron?" I gave a little skip as I thought of Mr. Beckett's hard, sinewy body, his face that looked as though it had been hewn from marble, his slicked-back hair still carrying the trails of his comb.

"He looked like your pa. If he changed his glasses and grew a little beard and got some more stylish clothes, he could be mistaken for your brother." Kitten giggled and then a shadow crossed her face. "Giorgio was odd tonight."

"Yes," I agreed, remembering the shine of Giorgio's shoes, the unusually thick twist of notes he'd left on the bar, his expensive cigarettes, his easy dismissal of me. But then Kitten's tram appeared, rattling and swaying down the boulevard Montparnasse, and saving me from any further discussion of Giorgio.

* * *

THE FOLLOWING MORNING, I was leaving for my dance class when Giorgio appeared in the kitchen yawning and wiping the sleep from his dark-circled eyes. "Off already?" he asked blearily.

"Yes, I'm late. How was Montmartre?" I pushed my dance shoes into my bag and skittered toward the door. I wanted to ask him a hundred questions but there wasn't time.

"It was good." Giorgio stretched and yawned again. "Beckett warms up after a few drinks. He's got quite a sense of humor when he's had a drop. And that reminds me, Lucia." He paused, plunged his hands into his pockets, and fumbled for his cigarettes. "You have an admirer."

I turned back from the door, my heart pumping like a piston. "Who?"

"That is something I cannot possibly divulge." He jammed a cigarette between his lips and began groping for his lighter. "Goddamnit! I left my lighter in that bloody bar!"

"Who?" I asked again.

"An admirer. That's all I'm saying." He staggered toward me and gave me a gentle shove. "You're going to be late, Lucia. You couldn't do a detour and pick up my lighter from Montmartre, could you?"

But I was gone, giddy and light-headed, skipping down the five flights of steps on the balls of my feet. And out into the clean, shining light of a day so bright with promise I whirled and spun all the way to my dance class.

A new fur coat, Miss Joyce?" Doctor Jung stands behind his polished desk, looking me up and down with his lizard eyes.

"Babbo bought it. I lost the other one." A tear squeezes at the corner of my eye. How could I have been so stupid! Babbo has enough to do without having to buy me replacement coats. If his great work is never completed, it will be my fault, all my fault . . . I lift the collar of my fox fur and bury my chin deep into its soft folds.

"No need to suffocate yourself, Miss Joyce. It's unlikely to blow away in here." The doctor crosses the room and closes the window, as if he thinks a gust of wind might rip the coat from my body.

"It didn't blow away!" I say indignantly. "I left it at the zoo. I was watching the bears, with that woman you're paying to spy on me, and I left it on a bench." I stop and look out the window, across the flat, glassy expanse of Lake Zurich. I can hear the shrill cry of the gulls and the faint chugging of the ferry coming toward the jetty.

"And how are you getting on with Madame Baynes?" Doctor Jung goes back to his desk and picks up the first chapters of my memoir.

"I know she's your spy. And I refuse to tell her my dreams. Anyway, what did you think of my story? Did you like it?" I fiddle nervously with the buttons on my coat, pushing them into their buttonholes and then tugging them out, one by one.

Doctor Jung nods. "I expected it to be more like your father's work."

I stop playing with my buttons and draw myself up, making myself as tall as possible. "That must be a compliment because we all know what you think of Babbo's work." My voice is icy as I remember how hurt Babbo had been when Doctor Jung publicly described *Ulysses* as cold and unfeeling and boring—and like a tapeworm. Yes, that was the word he'd used. "So, it's no tapeworm, Doctor?"

He flicks through the pages, nodding his head and sniffing noisily. "Where were you born, Miss Joyce?"

"I've already told you. In a pauper's hospital in Italy. Babbo was there too. Don't you want to ask about my story?"

"Your father watched the birth?" Doctor Jung's eyebrows rise up his forehead.

"Of course not! He was very sick in a different part of the hospital. My mother said he nearly died there."

The doctor pulls a handkerchief from his pocket and dabs ineffectually at his nose. "Did you know that you weren't nursed for very long, if at all, by your mother?"

I shrug. "So what?"

"But your brother was. Almost until you were born. Your father wrote that in the account he gave me. Does that make you feel anything, Miss Joyce?"

"Giorgio always had everything—that's just the way it was. My mother worships him. Babbo worships me." I shrug again. Why is Doctor Jung talking about my life as a baby? "My story," I persist. "Don't you have any questions?"

"I'm fascinated by the prophetic powers you touch on here." He taps his fat fingers on my manuscript. "Can you tell me more? Were there other occasions when you were able to see the future? Do you still see it?"

I pause and wonder whether to answer his questions. But then it strikes me that I have nothing left now. Nothing but my secrets. And he is being too eager, too greedy. "You must wait for the next installment. But don't expect your spy to tell you. I shall be extra careful not to let my secrets slip out." I don't tell him that nothing makes sense until I've shaped it in my memoir, until I've wrapped it in a skein of words. Instead I stand up and walk to the window, careful to keep my shoulders braced and my head very upright. Doctor Jung's manicured garden leads to the lake, where wild ducks and swans swim freely, sending out rippling cones of water. Overhead, the gulls jostle and swoop and dive.

"I don't want to be incarcerated anymore," I say, turning back to the room. "Babbo needs me. The future of literature depends on me." I think again of the caged bears at the zoo, how they'd prowled around their enclosure, their bodies limp and hopeless.

"You're making excellent progress, Miss Joyce, but this is only the beginning. Madame Baynes thinks you're less confused than we had thought. She finds you often lucid. And to have written this . . ." He pauses, picks up my manuscript, and flourishes it in the air. "You must have had many moments of clarity and recollection."

"When I start writing I remember everything. The darkness dissolves and it's as though it all happened yesterday." I begin to pace the room. I am so tired of sitting . . . sitting in consulting rooms and surgeries, sitting in cars and on benches, sitting in beds and at tables. Oh, how I want to move and dance again! Why can no one understand this?

"Please sit down." Doctor Jung's voice is strained and clipped.

"Did my father tell you how I loathe doctors?" I continue to pace the room, circling the doctor, looking at him from every angle. If the great Doctor Jung can walk around the room and examine me as though I'm a dead butterfly on a microscope slide, why can't I do the same to him?

"Yes, he did. How are you getting on with Doctor Naegeli?"

"He has taken so much blood from me that I must be empty now. He says I have constant leukocytes—a superabundance of white blood corpuscles. He is checking me for . . ." I don't want to say the word. Not to Doctor Jung. Not to anyone.

"For what, Miss Joyce?" The doctor's voice softens and he leans back in his chair so that his large stomach balloons in front of him. "You forget that I can ask Doctor Naegeli myself. Quite easily." He sniffs and wipes at his nostrils again.

"I'm not telling you!" I slump back into the armchair, pulling my coat into my ribs, hunching my shoulders. No doubt he will start on his old line of questioning again, about me and Babbo and all the bedrooms we shared. But he doesn't. Instead he asks me if I'm comfortable in Doctor Brunner's private sanatorium.

"It's like here." I gesture around the room, at the mahogany paneling and the oriental paintings on the clean white walls and the Mandala prints propped up on the mantelpiece. "Bourgeois," I add contemptuously.

"You don't feel comfortable here?"

"No. Only when I look out the window." I can't explain how the moneyed ease and comfort of the furnishings alienate me, how the thick velvet of the curtains and the polished parquet floor make me feel anxious and unwelcome, how they remind me of a certain Parisian apartment I'd rather forget.

"Miss Joyce . . ." Doctor Jung pauses and blows his nose so loudly I hear the snot bubbling from him. "You're twenty-seven and you have never lived away from your family. Even now, when you are with Madame Baynes in the sanatorium, I cannot prise you and your father apart. Contrary to all my instructions, he refuses to leave Switzerland." He pauses and inspects the contents of his handkerchief, as though Babbo may be lurking there. "Why did you never leave home?"

My eyes shift back to the window. "I used to imagine being Stella Steyn. I imagined her waking up every morning, putting on her green velvet coat and her hat with the orange feathers. No one telling her what to wear or what time to come home."

"Go on," urges the doctor, his gaping eyes trapping me in their bright beam.

"My friends went to nightclubs and had lovers. I went out to dinner with my parents. So, one day I asked Babbo if I could move out. I told him Mama hated me." I pause and close my eyes, willing the memory back. I can hear the doctor sniffling and clearing his throat, but after a few seconds I have the scene before me—Babbo's study, books everywhere, newspapers, magazines, comics, picture books, encyclopaedias, maps, dictionaries, fanned across the floor and stacked against the walls and tipping from the shelves. Babbo, head bowed over his desk. Silence but for the scraping of his pen. And me, stretching out my neck and arching my back as I prepared to dance.

"Babbo?"

"Yes?"

"I want to move out. I want my own place. Like my friends."

I rolled each shoulder back, first the right and then the left. "I'm nearly twenty-one!"

"I know, Lucia. You've asked us many times and our answer has always been no." He put down his pen and, from the corner of my eye, I saw him watching me.

"But why not? I'm the only dancer who still lives at home, except for Kitten." I rolled my spine down until my head hung loosely by my knees.

"They leap so looply as they link to light . . . linking and blinking to light and to flight. How does that sound?"

"Mama hates me and Giorgio's always singing with his choir and you're always writing." I felt the muscles behind my knees tauten as I placed my palms on the floor. I turned my head a fraction and looked through my legs at my father. He was watching me, his head cocked to one side, his face imperturbable and expressionless.

"Just a whisk brisk sly spry spink spank sprint of a thing . . . Will they like that, Lucia? Those philistines who mock me, who maim and mutilate my work." He sighed and turned back to his desk.

"I want my own life. I want to be more independent." I unrolled my spine, bringing myself up to a standing position. Then I pushed my head back until I saw nothing but the once-white ceiling, stained a dull beige from Babbo's cigarettes.

He fixed me with a single pink-veined eye. "How feline you are in that position . . . pussypussy plunderpussy . . ."

"It's nothing to do with you, Babbo. I'll come and visit, you know I will." I kept my eyes on the ceiling.

"In Ireland, nice girls don't live on their own. You stay with your mammy until you're married." The rasp of pen on paper started again.

"What's Ireland got to do with anything? This is Paris. And if Ireland was so wonderful, why did you and Mama elope and marry in Italy instead of Dublin?"

"Enough of your sauce. I need to get on with my work now. Run and post these letters for me . . . Pick, prick, pack, crack."

I slowly brought my neck and head back, enjoying the feeling of looseness in my muscles, but irritated by his words. I should have asked Mama. She wanted me out of the way. She found my dancing intrusive and unseemly. And when she saw Babbo watching me her eyes shrank and her face snapped shut. Yes, Mama would have agreed.

Babbo put down his pen again and looked at me thoughtfully. "Perhaps someone could live with you." He spoke very slowly, as if an idea was gradually forming in his mind.

"Who could live with me? You mean I could live with Stella Steyn or Kitten?" I tried to keep my voice calm.

"No, I do not mean that. I mean someone who could be like a mother to you."

"A mother? I don't need a mother. I'm old enough to *be* a mother!"

"I'm thinking of someone like . . ." He paused and looked

at me, as if deciding whether to continue or not. Then he shook his head quickly. "Run and post these letters, will you, Lucia?"

"Only if you tell me who you're thinking of."

"I'm thinking perhaps we could prevail on your aunt Eileen." He watched me carefully as he said this.

"I would love to live with Aunt Eileen again, but what about her children?"

"I'd pay her to live with you here. No doubt she needs the money." Babbo rubbed his goatee for a bit then turned back to his desk.

"Her children could come to Paris too," I said. "They're my cousins, after all."

"Oh no," he said quickly. "I couldn't afford that. But I could afford to put them in an Irish boarding school. I'll ask her when she comes, next week." And then his clawlike hand with its large ring had reached out for the letters on his desk. "Now go and post these, Lucia. And hurry back—I need you to dance for me again."

I open my eyes, blinking, bewildered. The faint odor of pond weed reminds me that I'm not in Paris about to dance for Babbo, but in Doctor Jung's study being watched and interrogated before he returns me to my spying nurse and the sanatorium with its barred windows.

"So what happened?" The doctor nods and smiles as if I'm a small child that has pleased him in some way.

"She agreed, but Babbo's family in Ireland got very angry and made her go back and look after her own children. You see, her children were still young and her husband had just shot himself." My voice trails off.

Doctor Jung frowns, his chin resting in his palm. "Your father asked his sister to look after you, a twenty-one-year-old woman, and leave her own newly orphaned children in a boarding school? Do I understand you correctly, Miss Joyce?"

I nod, and then the words tumble out of me, unbidden and uncontrollable. "My uncle shot himself while Aunt Eileen was staying with us. Babbo got the telegram but didn't tell her . . . He took her sightseeing instead. When she got home, to Trieste, my uncle had already been buried. She didn't believe he'd shot himself so she made them dig up his body." I can feel the plates of my skull grinding and the air wheezing in my throat. Why am I dragging up this memory?

"Was that the only time you tried to leave home?"

I sit, motionless and wordless, pulling thin strands of fox hair from my coat. How easily they come away . . . Soon my coat will be bald and hairless like an old man.

"Did your parents treat you like a child because you behaved like one?"

"Babbo needed me at home. He depended on me. You don't understand!"

"Because he was almost blind? He needed you to run errands, is that it, Miss Joyce? To take down his letters and collect his library books?" Doctor Jung stands up, pushes back his chair, moves toward me.

I shake my head vigorously. "I was his muse! He needed me for inspiration. You don't understand!"

"How did you know that?" He looms over me, swaying and sniffling.

"Everyone knew! People talked of it in the Montparnasse bars. He watched me all the time. Wait until his book comes out. You'll find me there—on every page!"

My head is throbbing, and inside my coat stray fox hairs are clinging to my damp skin. What if I'm wrong? What if I'm not in his book? What if he watched me dancing not for literary inspiration but for something lewd and disgusting? I struggle to stand up. I need air, oxygen. The doctor seems to have swelled and expanded until he's too big for the room, and I feel pushed to the edges, crushed by his presence, unable to breathe.

"I'll call the nurse to take you back to the sanatorium." He steers me gently toward the door, before adding, "Doctor Naegeli is dining here tonight. I won't forget to ask after your blood tests, Miss Joyce."

Doctor Naegeli. Dining here. Blood tests. His words roll around inside my head and suddenly I feel a surge of anger and my lungs fill with the ice-blue air of the mountains and the blood fizzes behind my eyes.

I spin around on the heel of my foot, the unexpected rush of fury making my voice rise. "In which case I'll tell you myself! I won't have you gossiping about me over your Swiss cheese!"

Doctor Jung reaches his arm around me, pushes open the

door, and propels me out. A dog barks incessantly some-where and the sound ricochets around the inside of my skull.

"Can I have no secrets? No privacy? Nothing that is mine—just mine!" I turn my back on the doctor, ashamed of my sudden fury. My memory of being in a straitjacket is still as sharp and bright as a knife. *I will not go back into a strait-jacket! I will not . . .*

"Of course, it is always possible that Doctor Naegeli will not tell me." Doctor Jung's voice is calm and soothing but I know he's placating me, lying to me.

"I will tell you myself!"

"An excellent idea." He runs his fat hand down my arm, as if he's stroking the haunch of a dog.

"Syphilis!" I spit out the hated word and take a deep breath. In the large airy hall with its view of the hills, the doctor seems diminished and I'm able to breathe again. "He is testing me for syphilis! They all think I have syphilis!"

"In which case, you must carry on with your memoir." He pats my shoulder. "And don't lose your new coat, Miss Joyce. Winter is coming and it gets very cold in the mountains."

5

DECEMBER 1928

PARIS

On Mr. Beckett's first day working for Babbo, I slipped out of my dance class early, hurried home, and positioned myself casually in the hall. I knew he would arrive punctually. Not only because he'd made plain his admiration for my father, but because there was something very precise about him. I couldn't quite put my finger on it, but I had a sense that Mr. Beckett appreciated order and exactitude. And no sooner had the clock chimed than the doorbell rang—and there he was, looking earnest and bright-eyed, a fat book clamped beneath his arm.

"Hello, Sam," I said, trying to sound calm.

"Good afternoon, Miss Joyce—Lucia." He stepped into the hall and stood there, staring at me.

"Have you brought that for Babbo?" I tilted my head in the direction of the book tucked under his elbow.

"*Great Expectations.* It's got a passage about the river Thames I want to read to your father." He stopped and looked over my shoulder at Babbo's study door as if he were willing it to open, like Aladdin's cave.

"Oh yes, he'll like that. Mama says if he mentions another river she'll go mad. He knows them all now, every river in the world. And when you're least expecting it, he starts reciting them, one after another."

"Is that so?" Mr. Beckett's eyes slid back to me and then back to Babbo's door.

I lowered my voice to a dramatic whisper. "The Nile . . . the Po . . . the Amazon . . . the Yangtze . . . the Mississippi . . . the Thames . . . the Avon . . . the Seine . . . Not to mention the greatest river of all—the Liffey!"

"Ah yes, the Liffey," echoed Mr. Beckett, his eyes flickering toward the clock.

"I forgot to tell you about Miss Beach's lending library when I saw you last week. She's the lady who published *Ulysses.* It's the best library and bookshop in Paris, Shakespeare and Company, on the rue de l'Odeon."

Mr. Beckett shuffled awkwardly as though he had pins and needles in his feet.

"We'd be nothing without her," I continued. "How are you enjoying the City of Light, Sam?"

Mr. Beckett looked nervously over my shoulder again. "I don't want to be late for your father. Shall I knock on his door?" He frowned as a crackling and unfamiliar voice floated toward us.

I laughed. "He's teaching himself Spanish by ear, from the gramophone. He had his Russian lesson with Mr. Ponisovsky this morning and now he's doing Spanish."

Mr. Beckett's eyes grew larger. "How many languages does he speak?"

"He's always learning new ones. Every holiday we go somewhere so he can research his book and he tries to learn the language. Flemish, Welsh, Provençal . . ." I rolled my eyes and shrugged helplessly as if to indicate the trials of living with a genius.

Mr. Beckett cleared his throat and looked at the clock again. I was about to regale him with stories of Babbo and me learning Dutch together when Mama appeared, scowling, her fingers glistening with soap suds.

"Lucia, show Mr. Beckett to the study. Now. Jim's been waiting these last five minutes. Mr. Beckett, go straight through." She flapped her soapy hands as though she were shooing off a pair of stray cats.

"He's listening to his Spanish," I protested. "Anyway, I'm telling Sam about Miss Beach's bookshop."

But Mr. Beckett had disappeared up the hall and was tapping on Babbo's study door. And Mama was glaring at me. "He's Mr. Beckett in this house," she said firmly. "Now for Heaven's sake, help me with this laundry. Your father's needing a clean pillowcase every night with his eyes pouring pus everywhere. And the pains in me stomach is half killing me.

Sure I could be dead tomorrow." She wiped her hands angrily on her apron and turned back to the kitchen.

An hour later she caught me hovering outside the study door, listening to Mr. Beckett's sonorous voice as he read aloud.

"What on earth are you doing now, girl? Earwigging, I'll bet." She shook her head despairingly.

"I'm waiting for them to finish so I can offer them a drink," I replied, indignant.

Finally, I heard the chairs scraping and Mr. Beckett saying he had to leave. My heart began its now-familiar gallop. I took a big breath to steady myself but Mama had started frying kidneys and the odor of meat fat stole into my lungs, making me feel faintly nauseous.

"Hello again." Mr. Beckett sounded both startled and pleased as he emerged from Babbo's study, looking visibly more relaxed than when he'd arrived.

"Did Babbo like Charles Dickens?"

"I think it was appreciated." He ran a cautious hand over his hair, letting it linger at the nape of his neck.

"How are your rooms? Do you need anything?" I stood as close to him as I dared, cursing Mama for frying kidneys at exactly the time when I could have been breathing in the smell of Mr. Beckett.

"Cold." He shivered slightly. "And I keep getting locked out at night."

"Locked out?"

"They lock the gates at eleven o'clock. I rarely make it

home in time so I have to jump over the railings." He gave
a shy smile that made him look like a boy and a man at the
same time.

I had a sudden urge to reach out and touch him, but instead I twisted my hands together and asked if I could help
him with his jumps. "As a dancer, I'm rather good at jumps," I
added, remembering Kitten's words about being less modest.

"Is that right?" He leaned his head forward and watched me
from under his lowered brows. For a minute I felt as though
I were swimming in his unblinking blue eyes—a strange
but not unpleasant sensation. And it struck me then that although he said very little, something in his eyes seemed to
reach out to me.

I gave a small chassé jump. "The most important thing is
landing. If you don't land properly you can strain your knees
and ankles. You need a powerful jump to get you over the
railings. A grand jeté might do it. Shall I demonstrate?"

Mr. Beckett shrank back against the wall as if he thought
I might accidentally kick him.

"Can't you get home before the gates close?" I could feel my
feet lifting of their own accord again. Our talk of jumping, in
the constrictive space of the hall, with its overpowering smell
of offal, was compelling me to move.

"I don't sleep so well at night. I have no choice but to jump."

"Insomnia?" I asked sympathetically, as I did a couple of
leg swings. "Or are you more of a night owl?"

"Both." He moved toward the front door and I felt my arms
instinctively stretching out after him. But then he turned

back to me, his hands gripping his copy of *Great Expectations* so tightly the veins stood out in blue ridges. "Would you like to come for tea in my rooms? In a fortnight's time?"

"That would be very nice, Mr. Beckett, Sam." I made a desperate effort to speak slowly and evenly, for I could feel the blood running hot and fast beneath my skin. And then he was gone and the hall was silent but for the ticking of the clock. I flung my arms into the air and spiraled to the parlor window, where I pressed my face to the glass and watched him leave the building and turn onto the rue de Grenelle. Monsieur Borlin's words about expressing our strongest emotions through dance filtered into my ears and I began glissading around the parlor, my arms whisking above my head.

"No dancing in me best parlor!" Mama's livid words cut through the air. But I didn't care. For once I didn't give a damn. I was going for tea with Sam Beckett and nothing she could do would stop me.

* * *

MR. BECKETT ARRIVED every day at five o'clock sharp. And every night after he left the flat, it was as though a light had gone out. I fumbled in the gloom for several minutes, adjusting to the space without him. It was a most peculiar and dismal feeling. But his invitation to have tea and the surety that our futures were to be entwined kept me cheerful.

A few evenings later, I was experiencing this peculiar

feeling of gloominess when the bell rang. Thinking it was
Mr. Beckett, back for a book or a forgotten scarf, I rushed to
the door. But it wasn't Mr. Beckett. It was Emile Fernandez.
My heart sank a fraction, but I hadn't seen Emile for a while
and I didn't want to hurt his feelings, so I switched on my
brightest smile, the one Babbo called my "shop-front smile."

Mama came into the hall, her hair brushed and re-coiled
and her lips glossy with fresh lipstick. "Good afternoon,
Mr. Fernandez. We haven't seen you in a month o' Sundays."
She was standing as tall as she could, with a very erect back
and her chin in the air.

"Forgive me. I've been busy composing a new opera,
Mrs. Joyce." Emile gave a small bow. "I trust you're in good
health?"

"I am not. I've been having terrible pains and Mr. Joyce's
eyes are hurting something awful. I don't know what's to
become o' him. Or me." Mama sighed dramatically. "Mrs.
Fleischman's coming in a minute to type up his crayon writing. But we've time for a cup of tea, haven't we, Lucia?"

Emile followed Mama and I into the parlor and waited
while we folded up the maps Babbo had spread out all over
the sofa.

"I don't know what it is with eyes in this family." Mama
straightened up and looked accusingly in my direction.

"We're worried Babbo could be blind by the end of the
year." I gestured to the now-cleared sofa. Emile stood gripping his hat with both hands and blinking hard. He was making me feel uneasy with his awkward twitching. I'd never

seen him like this before. "Please sit down," I said. "I want to hear about this new opera you're composing."

"Go and make us some tea, Lucia." Mama was about to lower herself into the rocking chair when the doorbell rang again. "Sure that'll be Mrs. Fleischman. Wait there, Lucia, in case Mrs. Fleischman is wanting some tea."

Emile perched on the edge of the sofa and ran his tongue over his lips while his fingers chewed at the brim of his hat.

I waited for him to tell me about his new opera but he didn't say anything and the silence became awkward. "Mama's not been feeling well," I said eventually. "She might have to go into hospital. The doctor thinks she may need surgery."

"I'm so sorry. That must be very hard for her," Emile agreed. "How are *you*, Lucia? Giorgio says you've been dancing constantly. Are you working on something new?" As he said the word "dancing," he gave a little flutter of his hands so they looked like thin fledgling birds.

"Yes," I said, relieved the silence was broken. "I'm trying to create a dance for my troupe, where they're transformed into rainbows. I want to have black oilcloth all over the stage and right across the ceiling. And maybe use neon lights to suggest the sun breaking through the stormy black of the oilcloth." I was about to ask Emile if he'd consider composing the score when I noticed a stricken expression on his face.

"You don't like the sound of my dance?" I asked, wounded.

"No, it's not that. But there's something I need to ask you." His fingers leapt from the hat on his knees to his striped cravat. He fidgeted with the folds and gulped loudly.

"Do you need something to eat?" I asked. He looked rather faint, as though he'd not eaten for a while. It was a look I'd seen often enough on my dancing friends and I knew what came next.

Emile's eyes opened wide in surprise. And he blurted out something so fast I couldn't understand it. When he saw my blank expression, he got up from the sofa and moved toward the door where I was still standing, waiting for Mama to return and give me Mrs. Fleischman's tea order. He dropped down on one knee and grabbed my hands in his. "Lucia, I want you to be my wife."

I stood, gaping wordlessly at him. In that instant, everything I knew about Emile flashed through my mind—his big house filled with sunlight and Persian rugs and grand pianos and hothouse flowers, his grandmother who sat in the ballroom all day wearing her diamonds, his celebrated composer cousin with his celebrated actress wife.

"Lucia? Lucia? What's the matter?"

"I'm s-sorry," I stammered. An image of Emile and I working together appeared before me, blotting out his handsome house and famous family. I saw myself gliding around his ballroom as his fingers bounded across the piano keys. I saw our heads bent over his score, me tapping out a rhythm with my foot and him swiping at the air with his pencil as if it were a conductor's baton. And Babbo applauding from the corner. This was the future I had predicted for myself. But the image ebbed, washed away by the ocean-blue eyes of Mr. Beckett, his bony brown hands, his fair hair swept back from his face as though a gust of Irish wind had set it there. Tears filled my eyes. I tried to stop thinking of Mr. Beckett but it was hopeless.

"I didn't mean to upset you." He gulped down the saliva in his throat and grabbed my hands again. "I thought you liked me . . . Giorgio said . . . Giorgio was sure . . ." He stopped, confused. We could hear Mama talking in the hall, her voice getting louder and louder as she led Mrs. Fleischman toward the parlor. I bit my lip and wiped my eyes hurriedly. I had to speak before she and Mrs. Fleischman came in.

"But you're Jewish, Emile," I blurted. "Now sit down and look as though nothing's happened. Quick. Before Mama comes in!"

Emile staggered back to the sofa, looking dazed and pained. "I didn't know you minded about that."

"*You* can't marry *me*—I'm not Jewish. Now sit down, quickly! Mama's coming!"

"But my family *wants* me to marry you. No one minds that you're not Jewish."

"I just can't, Emile." I shook my head and stepped back as Mama and Mrs. Fleischman appeared.

"Mr. Fernandez is going." I wanted to be kinder, but the words sprang, sharp and unrestrained, from my mouth.

Emile's face fell and his eyes clouded with hurt. "Goodbye, Mrs. Joyce. Goodbye, Lucia." He picked up his hat and cane, and shot me a final pleading look.

I stared at the floor, trying to make sense of everything. Why had I been so decisive? So callous? A second later I heard the front door close. And I knew Emile had gone, perhaps forever. Mama was looking at me curiously.

"He left sharpish. Wasn't he wanting tea, Lucia?" She turned to Mrs. Fleischman. "Why don't you go straight through to Jim. He's got plenty o' typing today, if you can possibly read it. It's the blue crayon. I don't know how you make head nor tail of it."

Mrs. Fleischman looked at me oddly, as though she could see the traces of tears on my face. "Are you all right, Lucia?" she asked, her voice rising and falling with feigned sympathy.

I didn't answer. Instead I stared at her dove-gray velvet dress, with its lace trim and tiny mother-of-pearl buttons. I saw the strings of pearls gleaming softly at her throat and the sable coat slung casually over her arm. I saw the poise and assurance that only money can buy. I shook my head and walked out.

* * *

IT WAS GIORGIO who first heard of Emile's proposal—and my refusal. A few days before I was due to have tea with Mr. Beckett, Giorgio stumbled into my bedroom. I was sitting at my dressing table in my nightdress, brushing my hair and thinking through the footwork for what I now called my Rainbow Dance. Kitten had danced a short sequence of it that afternoon, on a square of black oilcloth I'd sweet-talked from the fishmonger's wife. Although it had reflected the light perfectly, I was worried it might distract the dancers. Would it impede the footwork I was choreographing? How could I ensure it didn't slip during the performance? Pinned around my mirror were photographs of the dancers I most admired: Anna Pavlova; Isadora Duncan with her brother, Raymond, and her sister, Elizabeth; Madika; Vaslav Nijinsky; La Argentina. And my new heroine, the English dancer Margaret Morris. I cast my eye over them, as if for reassurance. And then Giorgio appeared, his face dark and bloated.

"I saw Emile tonight." He moved unsteadily toward me, one hand at his neck wrestling his tie loose.

I wanted to ask after Emile but Giorgio's expression didn't invite friendly curiosity so I said nothing and continued brushing my hair.

"He said he asked you to marry him and you turned him down. Is that right, Lucia?"

I nodded and opened my mouth to explain that I didn't love Emile. I knew Giorgio would understand because when we were younger we often made up love stories about Napoleon and Josephine and compared them to the romantic elopement of Mama and Babbo. But before I could speak, Giorgio staggered toward me, drops of spittle falling from his mouth onto my bare arm.

"Are you mad? Do you know how rich the Fernandez family are? How rich you could be? How rich *we* could be?" His words were slurred and the smell of liquor and sweat hung around him like a noxious cloud. "So what's wrong? It can't be Emile. Everyone likes Emile."

I shook my head, bewildered by the barely supressed rage and disappointment in Giorgio's voice.

"You think you're going to get other offers? Is that it? Better offers, perhaps?" He snorted with contempt. "Oh, come on, Lucia! Have you forgotten the war? Have you forgotten how few men are left?"

I opened my mouth to protest, but before I could draw breath Giorgio started a new line of questioning. "D'you know how many beautiful girls would marry Emile at the drop of a hat? Rich Jewish girls without squints. He could have any girl he wants!" He snatched at the knot of his tie and pulled it savagely. "You had a chance to escape, to bring real money into the house. His family could have helped in so many ways. Did you even think about that?" Giorgio's hot breath kept hitting me in angry bursts. But then his voice softened. "It's not too late to change your mind. I could tell him it was all a mistake and you've had second thoughts. Wouldn't you like to have everything you've ever dreamed of?"

I shook my head again, miserably. I wanted to ask how Emile was, to ask if I'd lost his friendship forever. But Giorgio's aggression had unsettled me, so I thought of Mr. Beckett's face and clung to it like a drowning man clutching at a passing branch.

"You could have fur coats and a motor car with a chauffeur. Think how the Fernandez family could help Father! Emile's family could help us *all* in so many ways." He paused and I knew he was thinking not just of the Fernandez money but of how Emile's musical connections could help *his* singing career. After a long minute he said, in a wheedling voice, "It might not be too late. We can tell Emile you've changed your mind."

"I can't marry Emile," I whispered.

"Why ever not?" Giorgio's voice rose and hardened. He started stamping around my room, the heels of his shoes slamming into the floor. "What's-wrong-with-Emile?"

"Nothing's wrong with Emile. I just don't love him." I dragged the brush so vigorously through my hair, I felt its bristles clawing at my scalp.

"This is preposterous! Have you forgotten everything we went through? All those years without enough to eat, living in those filthy rooms, traipsing from one flea-ridden bed to another." Giorgio stopped pacing and came to my stool. He crouched down and fixed his eyes on mine and his look became milder, kinder, as if he were recalling the intimacy and friendship we once had. My mind blinked back to the past, to those dull, dismal days when Mama took in washing and Babbo taught and wrote all day and drank all night—and Giorgio and I spent hour after hour listening to the mice in the walls and playing dominoes. When I lost, I'd throw the dominoes across the floor in a spasm of rage, and Giorgio would pick them up and lay them out and let me win the next game. Where was that Giorgio now?

He leaned in toward me and I smelled the brandy on his breath. And something shifted in one of the dark anonymous cavities of my memory. I shuddered and pulled back. But he tipped toward me again. "D'you remember the old days in Zurich, Lucia? When Mother and Father went out drinking and left us behind, like pigs in a sty? D'you remember when you nearly fell over the balcony while we were shouting at them?"

Giorgio's words pulled me back with such clarity that for a second I thought we were in our old Zurich apartment. I shook my head forcefully. I didn't want to think about the past. The past was over. Finished . . .

"I saved your life."

I put the hairbrush down and looked sideways at him. Why was he reminding me of this? Was it some ploy of his to remind me of the poverty we once lived in, the poverty we could so easily return to?

"I thought I'd lost you over that balcony, Lucia." Giorgio dropped his hand onto my knee and let it linger there. For a minute I wondered if I should be honest with him, ignore the growing breach between us and tell him about Mr. Beckett.

But then his stare turned to hostile curiosity. "It's someone else, isn't it? That's the reason you turned down poor old Emile. I can see it on your face. You're waiting for another offer!" He stood, triumphant and smug. "So who is it, Lucia? Who *exactly* are you saving yourself for?"

I shook my head. I didn't know what to say. I wanted my old Giorgio back. And I wanted the new, inebriated Giorgio to go. Something about him frightened me.

"I just hope he's rich." His tone was bitter, as though he'd been duped in some way.

I gripped the hairbrush so hard my knuckles ached. "Why does everything have to be about money! What about love? Don't you remember how we used to talk about falling in love? What's happened to you, Giorgio?"

He reeled toward the door. "Because money is all there is! Our poverty was so humiliating, so shameful. It haunts me, Lucia. It haunts me." He turned back into the room, and through the dimness I saw his eyes, glazed with alcohol and dark with fear. "The way Father begs for money. He thinks it's fine to take other people's money and fritter it away. But I find it so demeaning!"

A cry of wordless sympathy rose in my throat. But then Giorgio moved shakily toward me again. "We aren't geniuses. We won't have patrons like Father does. Couldn't you pretend to love Emile? Aristocrats manage it. They marry for money; they breed. They don't give a damn about love!"

My mouth fell open. "You think I should marry Emile without loving him? Just for his money?"

"And for his—his connections!" he hissed. "To help us all. Do you really want to be the family errand girl forever?" He turned and lurched toward the door.

"I'm a dancer," I exclaimed, shocked at his disregard and his cruel words. "I'm going to be successful. I help Babbo because he's unwell and he needs me. That doesn't mean I'm the family errand girl!" The photographs of my dancing idols looked back at me, urging me on. "My dancing helps him, you know that. And it's the most important thing in my life."

Giorgio snorted angrily, making flecks of spit form at the

corner of his mouth. "I was thinking of all those letters you
write for him, the endless bloody errands. Emile offered you
a way out and you stupidly turned it down. How could you be
so selfish!" He turned toward me and stood swaying in the
doorway. "Think about it, Lucia!"

And it was only then I remembered his earlier words, his
jibes about my secret admirer. And I felt my body deflate.
Had my secret admirer been Emile all along? Or dare I still
hope it was Mr. Beckett?

"My secret admirer," I croaked, but the words mangled in
my throat and all I heard was the slamming of my bedroom
door and Giorgio's furious footsteps in the hall.

* * *

THAT NIGHT I dreamed of Ireland. Green and slick with rain.
And Mr. Beckett, his mouth like a ripe plum and his hair
standing up from his head like a crown. He was calling to
me from a sea mist so thick and wild I saw nothing but the
blue flames of his eyes. And then his disembodied face came
to me, floating through the salty air. Pausing. Hovering in
the damp folds of mist. Calling me to him. I heard his breath
coming in great gulps as though he were battling with the
mist, as though it were forcing its way into his eyes and nose
and mouth, sucking and oozing into his throat and lungs
and heart, suffocating him. I called his name, over and over.
I reached out for him, stretching my arms into the swirling
mist. But I was too late and the mist had pulled him back

and was clinging to him like a ghostly mantle, taking him
further and further away, taking him out to sea. And I was
left standing on the damp grass, calling his name, again and
again. And hearing my echo blown back to me.

I looked around and everything was rinsed clean and
green and the mist was gone. Mr. Beckett was standing beside me, his hand on the small of my back. And out to sea was
a small figure clinging to a piano.

"Wave to Emile," instructed Mr. Beckett, and I felt his fingers crawling over my back. "Wave, Lucia! You must always
wave to drowning men." And Mr. Beckett's voice was so imperious, so commanding that I waved. But the man and his
piano had gone and the sea was as flat and shining as glass.

~~~~~

6

Mr. Beckett had bought tiny macarons, lemon, pistachio, and rose, which he served straight from the box. He made Lapsang Souchong tea and poured it into chipped cups, over thin discs of lemon that he cut with a pocket knife. We sat in his little sitting room on a sofa with springs that groaned and complained whenever we moved. In the corner, a stove belched out sporadic puffs of smoke, giving the whole place a gentle odor of burning.

"It's rather bare. Why don't you buy some cushions or a rug? Or some paintings?" I surveyed the room again, noting the plain gray walls with their peeling paint, the meager shelves where Mr. Beckett had stacked his books in alphabetical order, the condensation that bloomed on the window.

"There's a thought." Mr. Beckett fingered the collar of his shirt, pulling it from his neck in small jerks.

"Doesn't your mother have anything she could lend you? Even an old blanket over this sofa, although cushions would be nicer. Look, it's almost worn out." I pointed to the threadbare fabric that covered the sofa and through which tufts of horsehair and coils of metallic spring threatened to burst forth at any moment. "And pictures. You need some pictures to brighten up your walls. It's like a monk's cell in here."

Mr. Beckett was silent for a few seconds as he looked around his room in an observational manner, almost as though he hadn't seen it before.

"You said your parents have a big house. Don't they have some pictures of Ireland they could give you? Wouldn't it be lovely to wake up and look at Ireland?" I sighed dreamily. "Tell me about your house again, and your big garden and your dogs and chickens." I loved hearing about Mr. Beckett's childhood home. The very normal-ness of it thrilled me. Already I could picture myself there, scattering corn to the chickens and picking apples from the orchard. "Tell me about your dogs again. What type were they?"

"Kerry Blues were the breed we usually had." Mr. Beckett looked wistful for a moment and then offered me the box of macarons.

"What were their names?"

"We had . . . um . . . Bumble . . . and Badger . . . and Wolf . . . and, er . . . Mac. My mother prefers dogs to people." He took off his glasses and wiped them with the hem of his jumper in a distracted sort of way.

"And your father built the house you were born in? And they still live there? You only ever lived in one house?"

Mr. Beckett nodded.

"I want to know all about it! Tell me everything." I put my teacup down carefully on the upturned wooden crate that Mr. Beckett was using as a coffee table and then tucked myself into the sofa while the springs creaked beneath me.

"I've already told you."

"Tell me again. Tell me about your walks in the mountains with your father. And tell me about your mother. I want to know all about her." I almost added, "Because one day she'll be my mother-in-law," but I realized that would sound presumptuous and stopped just in time to see Mr. Beckett flinch slightly.

"She likes donkeys." He hesitated, almost as though he couldn't think of anything else to say. "Dogs and donkeys." He looked down at the spectacles lying in his lap, and it struck me then that perhaps he'd come to Paris to get away from his mother, away from Ireland. Not unlike Babbo. I decided not to press him on the subject of his family.

"Tell me about your garden again. The lemon verbena growing 'round the porch and the daffodils and the roses. We've never had a garden." I gave another pensive sigh. "What's your earliest memory, Sam? Is it lying in your basket under the shade of an apple tree?"

"No," he said shortly. "In the womb. I remember being in

the womb." The sofa squeaked and groaned as Mr. Beckett shifted around uneasily. He put his glasses back on and then picked up the macaron box again and offered it to me.

"What was it like? The womb." I took a pale-green macaron and began nibbling at the edges, conscious of Mr. Beckett trying to get comfortable and wishing he'd relax a bit more.

"Terrible. Dark and suffocating."

"Really? Did anything else happen in there? Could you hear sounds from outside? Or smell anything?" I leaned forward eagerly, wondering if Mr. Beckett was also gifted with second sight.

"I don't remember any smells. But I heard voices. I heard my parents talking and the sounds of china and knives and forks." His hands were curled up in a tight ball in his lap.

"How extraordinary. What were they saying? Could you make out the words?"

"Not clearly." He uncurled his fists and reached for his cigarettes. He took one out of the packet and tapped it several times before putting it between his lips, where it dangled for a few bemused seconds.

"You must tell Babbo," I said eventually. "He'd be fascinated."

"I was born on Good Friday," Mr. Beckett added. "Friday the thirteenth, as it happens." He lit a match and held the quivering flame to his cigarette, inhaling hard as he did so.

"Really? You'd better not tell Babbo that. He's very superstitious and his mother died on the thirteenth." I sat and looked at Mr. Beckett as the full weight of his words washed over me. Born on Good Friday, on Friday the thirteenth, with memories of being in his mother's womb. He too carried the burden of expectation and history on his shoulders. He too was special in some way, unlike others, marked from birth.

"Tell me about yourself, Lucia." Mr. Beckett blew out a jet of smoke and then coughed for several seconds. "All your travels, growing up with your father . . ."

"Yes, so many travels and so many houses, but none with a porch." I smiled my poster smile. I had no intention of souring the mood by discussing *my* childhood memories. I tossed my head as if to cast off my past. But Mr. Beckett persisted, wanting to know which cities had most inspired my father and where I'd gone to school.

"Oh, here and there. Eight different schools, or was it nine? Or ten? I don't remember. Three in Trieste, two in Zurich, one in Locarno, two more in Paris. Almost one a year." I bit hard into a macaron. I could still remember those first days in new schools in new cities, my small hand gripping Giorgio's, the sprawl of new faces speaking in unfamiliar tongues, the hollow feeling in my stomach.

"It can't have been easy," Mr. Beckett said gently. He was looking at me with such tenderness that for a minute I considered telling him everything, unburdening myself of all those memories that lurked, tightly spooled inside me. But instead I swallowed down my macaron and brushed a stray crumb from my dress and said nothing.

"Which language do you like best?" He got up and put

some more coal in the stove, filling the room with a thick cloud of smoke.

"When it's just the four of us, we speak Italian. When Babbo's Irish friends come over, we speak English. And Giorgio and I speak German if we don't want Babbo's friends to understand us. And naturally we speak French when we're out and about in Paris. But I like Italian best. Babbo calls it the language of love." I said the word "love" very loudly so he'd hear it over the rattling of the coal scuttle.

Mr. Beckett loped back to the sofa, his face rosy—although whether that was from the heat of the stove or from the thought of love, I couldn't tell. "Truly polyglot. I envy you that. I've been teaching myself German, the language of philosophy. Is your father fluent in German?" He sat down again, adjusting himself between the protrusions of horse-hair and erupting springs, and wiping at the glow on his face.

"Yes," I said. But I was tired of talking about Babbo, so I added, "It's Saint Lucia's day today, did you know that?" I reached out and took a pale-pink macaron from the box, biting into it as daintily as I could.

"Saint Lucia's day?" Mr. Beckett crossed and uncrossed his long, thin legs, reminding me suddenly of a cricket or a grasshopper, all angles and lines.

"Ironic, really. She's the patron saint for the blind, and Babbo's almost blind and Giorgio's got to wear glasses now and I—I have an—an eye impediment." I stopped and looked away. Why had I said that? Why had I drawn attention to my squint like that? I had no choice now but to tell him about it.

And whenever he looked at me, from then on, he'd see nothing but my swerving eyeball.

"Do you?" I felt Mr. Beckett's eyes burning into me.

"You haven't noticed? 'Strabismus' is the medical term. Babbo says I can have an operation on it." I tilted my face toward the light slanting through the window and pointed to my left eye. "I got it from my mother but hers is very mild and no one notices it."

Mr. Beckett put his cup of tea down, placed his cigarette carefully on the edge of the ashtray and looked at me from under his thick brows, his head cocked like a bird's. "I hadn't noticed, but now that you mention it . . ."

"What d'you think, Sam? Should I have the operation? So many of Babbo's operations haven't worked. And it's so expensive."

"I think you look . . ." He paused and picked up his tea. I heard the stutter of the cup on the saucer. "Beautiful," he said at length.

I was so surprised, so startled, that I dropped the macaron I was holding and then began scrabbling on the floor for it, trying to hide my confusion and excitement. I don't think Mr. Beckett had intended to be so direct, because he also became quite flustered and slopped half his tea into his saucer.

I could feel my face growing scarlet and the heat rising through me. I was glad my macaron had rolled away, glad of the excuse to kneel down and reach under the sofa and hide my blushes. Beautiful! Mr. Beckett thought I was beautiful! Everything was suddenly going around and around in my head, as though someone had put a spoon inside my skull and was stirring and stirring. As I reached out my hand, dislodging a veil of dust, I realized he kept his work under the sofa. Instead of finding my macaron, I could feel stacks of fat envelopes wedged beneath the spilling springs. The word "beautiful" was still ringing in my ears, but the dust under the sofa was distracting me, getting into my lungs and making my throat dry and tickly. I could hear Mr. Beckett coughing and asking if I was all right, telling me not to worry about the macaron. I got up from my knees and smoothed down my dress and brushed the dust from my arms.

"I think the macaron is still under there somewhere," I said, before giving an awkward little laugh. "I didn't want to mess up your—your work."

"Leave it for the mice." He thrust the macaron box at me but kept his eyes lowered. I could see the color fading from his cheekbones, his thick eyebrows flaring like the wings of a bird, his hooked nose like the beak of an owl. And his narrow body, so ill at ease and awkward as he shifted around on the sofa. I wished he would just take me in his arms and pull me into him. I swallowed hard and brushed down my dress again, as if to brush away my yearning and his discomfort and our mutual timidity. Oh, why couldn't I be more like a Parisian flapper! Why couldn't I be alluring and bold, like my fellow dancers, like Stella? I cursed my parents for wrapping me up in their Irish morals. And then it dawned on me that Mr. Beckett must be suffering from the same constraints, and I felt a stab of sympathy.

I shook my head at the box of macarons he was still holding toward me. "Are you going back to Ireland for Christmas, Sam?"

"Briefly." He put the macaron box on a pile of books, before adding, "And then I might go to my aunt and uncle in Germany."

"Don't stay away too long, will you? Mama's going into hospital in January. The doctor thinks she might have cancer. We're all rather worried, and Babbo will need you to help him." I retrieved my coat and gloves from Mr. Beckett's desk and tried to put aside my concerns about Mama. "Babbo's taking us out to dinner tonight to celebrate Saint Lucia's day."

"Oh!" Mr. Beckett had regained his composure and was watching me calmly, unblinkingly, as I pulled on my gloves.

"She had her eyes gouged out by soldiers, but after they killed her, her eyes were miraculously replaced with perfect new ones." I wondered if I should tell him that Saint Lucia was clairvoyant, that she had seen the future in her dreams— and that I too sometimes saw the future in *my* dreams. No, now was not the time, I decided.

"Ah yes, I remember now. She refused to obey her husband." Mr. Beckett moved toward the door and held it open for me. Smells of frying onions floated down the corridor and I could hear the sound of running water and a lavatory flushing in the shared bathroom next door.

I lowered my voice. "And they had her defiled in a brothel. All rather gruesome."

Mr. Beckett looked sideways for a second. How sensitive he was! But of course—he'd come from Ireland where such things were never spoken of. "Babbo also named me after Lucia di Lammermore from the Donizetti opera," I added, quickly changing the subject.

"What happened to her?" Mr. Beckett led the way into the corridor and toward the big wooden doors that opened onto the rue d'Ulm. The air was colder in the corridor, and behind the mask of frying onions, I could smell damp and mildew.

"She went mad and killed herself." I pulled my coat around me in readiness for the evening air. "Betrayed by her brother. Then her lover kills himself too, so they can be reunited in Heaven. It's very sad, but the music's wonderful. It's one of my favorite operas."

"I'll look out for it, then." Mr. Beckett nodded to the concierge, who was sitting wrapped in a blanket reading a newspaper. He pushed open the heavy wooden door that led out toward the street and I felt the sharp evening air on my face.

"You must come with us. I'll find out when it's next coming to the Palais Garnier."

I leaned up and kissed him on both cheeks. And as I did so, I breathed in his smell and let the warmth of his cheeks linger on my lips. And all the while I heard his voice saying "I think you're beautiful," over and over—and over again.

And all the way home I heard nothing—not the clattering of trams nor the blasts of motorcar horns, not the orchestras tuning up in the music halls nor the cries of the newspaper vendors—nothing but the sound of his words, his glorious words, again and again. My secret admirer, after all . . .

* * *

A WEEK LATER something wonderful happened. I was in Monsieur Borlin's studio, with its peculiar porthole windows that looked up to the Sacré-Coeur, and its uneven floorboards that whined as you walked on them. Our class had ended, but Monsieur Borlin knew Mama didn't like me dancing at home, so if he had no further classes he always let me stay behind and practice.

Today I was working on my Rainbow Dance, trying to figure out how to synchronize a few of the more complicated sequences. I'd described it to Babbo the previous evening and he'd become very enthused, making me demonstrate some of the bolder moves and exclaiming at their novelty and verve—until Mama appeared and insisted I put some clothes on and behave like a lady. But as I leaned against the barre, some old words of Babbo's about looping and linking to light played over and over in my head. From the porthole above, a frugal shaft of light fell across the floor in a tremulous stripe. I shimmied toward it, swept my arms up and bent my torso into a perfect arc.

"Ah, Miss Joyce. I'm glad I've caught you. I thought you might have left." Monsieur Borlin stood in the doorway smoothing the front of his waistcoat with his gloved hands and peering at me through his monocle.

I straightened up and brought my arms to my sides. There was something about his expression that piqued me. Besides which, he rarely made small talk.

"Sit down." He pulled a scalloped fan from his breast pocket and gestured at the gold wicker chair beside the piano.

"But that's your chair, monsieur." I moved uncertainly toward it. No one ever sat in the gold wicker chair except him.

"I shall be sitting all night at the Théâtre des Champs-Élysées."

I sat on the edge of his chair, wondering what he was about to tell me. What could be so terrible I needed to be sitting down? It crossed my mind he was about to dismiss me from his classes. He was notorious for throwing out pupils who displayed no talent or discipline. I felt my muscles stiffen.

"I have taken the liberty of entering you for the International Festival of Dance in April. It's short notice but I have no doubt you are up to the challenge."

"What?" I frowned. Me? Had I misheard him?

"Let me be frank. You are my most talented student. Modern dance is the alphabet of the inexpressible, and you understand this, Miss Joyce." He opened his fan and fluttered it in front of his face while I considered his words.

"What do I have to do?"

"You will dance two solos, for which you will also do the choreography, costumes, and staging. You have the talent to win, Miss Joyce." He snapped his fan shut and began painting at the air with it. "Dancers are the pioneers of a new dawn of art. I see it embodied in you. The way you move so freely, so eloquently, and yet with utter control. How did you master that?"

"My background's in gymnastics," I said lamely, wishing I had a more distinguished history to refer to.

"I can see that. On occasion you are more acrobatic than balletic. But that's not what I refer to. Dancing is the writing of the body and you instinctively understand this. I sense in you, Miss Joyce, a raw emotion ordered into something potentially quite extraordinary. It's a gift, Miss Joyce, a gift." He stuck his fan back into his pocket and screwed up his monocled eye.

"Thank you, monsieur." I wanted to sing out in triumph but my voice was a dazed stutter. I wanted to circle the room in vast leaps, to dance out of the studio and up to the Sacré-Coeur where all of Paris would see me turning and spinning. I wanted to cry out to the moon and the stars, "I have talent! Monsieur Borlin says I have talent!"

"Three months and then you will compete with the very best dancers from across the globe. The judges are yet to be confirmed, but rest assured they will be the world's most eminent dancers." He gave a succession of small sniffs and turned to leave. "Lock up when you go, Miss Joyce, and put the key in its usual place."

As soon as Monsieur Borlin left, I did the highest toe-touch jump I could muster. Again and again I jumped. I had to start

planning my competition dances but my head was too muddled and my heart was too full—and I only wanted to dance.
I cartwheeled across the studio, three, four, five times. And
then back again. Suddenly my tunic felt too heavy, too hot.
My canvas dance shoes felt constrictive and tight. I kicked off
my shoes and threw off my tunic so that I was barefoot and
wearing only my dance knickers and a vest. The cooling air of
the studio licked at my arms and legs. The stove had gone out
but I felt scalded, and for one crazy moment I thought about
stripping off all my clothes and dancing naked.

Instead I backflipped across the room. And as my feet flew
over my head I heard a cough. Taken aback, I landed clumsily,
stumbling against the barre. I felt a flush racing up my neck
and wished I'd kept my tunic on. No doubt Monsieur Borlin
had dropped his fan. Or perhaps his monocle had fallen out.
But it wasn't Monsieur Borlin. It was Mr. Beckett.

"I'll wait outside." His voice was rough-edged, as if he had
a throat full of embers. "Your father said you'd be here. And
I was passing."

My insides cringed as I looked down at my large dance
knickers, but Mr. Beckett had discreetly withdrawn and I
could hear the floorboards shifting in the corridor.

"Please don't worry," I called out as I slipped my tunic
over my head and grabbed my dress from the barre. "I don't
normally dance in my undergarments, but I was very hot and
I've had some wonderful news."

"Oh?" Beckett cleared his throat again.

"My dance teacher has entered me for the biggest modern

dance competition in Europe. I'm nervous and excited and happy and scared all at once."

"Congratulations," he called through the doorframe.

"He thinks I have real talent." Even as I repeated Monsieur Borlin's words, I heard my voice quaver. Had he really said that?

"Mr. Joyce has been telling me so. I-I wanted to see for myself."

"I'm fully dressed now. You can come in." I shook out the hem of my dress and pushed back the hair from my face. "Would you like to see a bit of my Rainbow Dance? It's not finished but I'm creating it with Babbo in mind."

"Could I?" Mr. Beckett appeared slowly from behind the door.

I nodded, wondering if I should take my dress off and dance in my tunic. But I heard Mama's tongue in my ear and decided against it.

"Imagine the music and imagine I'm one of six dancers. And imagine I'm in some sort of rainbow costume." I stood in first position, slid back my right leg, and then began the opening sequence. Sheering across the studio. Pivoting and gliding. Swooping and soaring. An ephemeral arch of color, swaying and dissolving. Flashes of imprisoned light. Trembling loops of movement. A wind-washed rainbow, my bands of color shivering and melting. I crouched and twisted. Needles of rain, spiked and hard. I stretched and spread my fingers, soft rays of warm sunlight. I was a swath of luminous color. I was the gold-skinned weaver of the wind. Sun-spangled sovereign of the cosmos.

"That's as far as I've got." I waited for Mr. Beckett's verdict, suddenly feeling nervous and unsure. What had come over me? Monsieur Borlin's praise had gone to my head!

"Incredible," he said, stupefied. "I had no idea . . . Mr. Joyce said you were good but . . ." He shook his head as if lost for words.

I paused, unsure what to say next. But then my mouth opened of its own accord and I blurted out something so bold, so flirtatious, it was as if a Parisian flapper had taken possession of my vocal cords. "I'd love to teach you to dance, Sam."

There was a wordless moment while I stared at the floorboards and waited for him to blush and politely decline. But he didn't. To my surprise, he said, "I'd like that too. Very much." He gave me one of his long, hard stares—as if he were looking straight through me, to my palpitating heart, the air trapped in my lungs, the hot blood springing in my veins.

I tried to modulate my voice so he wouldn't see how elated I was. "We should start with the Charleston. Everyone in Paris does the Charleston."

"Very well. The Charleston it will be." He gave a half smile and gestured at the windows. Darts of rain were hitting the glass with a spitting sound. "I ought to go. I'm on my way to Montmartre."

"I can't teach you until after my dance competition. Can you wait until then?"

"I think so." And there was a timorous tone to his voice that I couldn't decipher.

We parted ways outside the studio. When I got to the end of the street, I looked back for a last glimpse of him. He was climbing the steps toward the Sacré-Coeur, his hair spreading out in the wind like a small ruffled halo. My thoughts immediately turned back to dancing, to Monsieur Borlin's words, to the festival, to Charlestoning with Mr. Beckett. How was I to do it all?

7

When Mr. Beckett returned from his Christmas break, Giorgio and I had already moved out of Robiac Square to stay with Mrs. Helen Fleischman. Her husband was away; Mama was in the hospital and Mrs. Fleischman had offered to look after us, saying she would be "like a mother" to us. Babbo had accepted with an alacrity that took me by such surprise, all my words about Giorgio being twenty-three and me being twenty-one died on my tongue. I hoped Giorgio might put up more of a fight and convince Babbo we were quite capable of living alone at Robiac Square for a few weeks. But he didn't. Instead he nodded and mumbled something about Mrs. Fleischman's generosity.

"Why didn't you insist on staying at Robiac Square?"

I asked Giorgio later. "I thought you were tired of Babbo treating us like children. And you know I can't stand Mrs. Fleischman."

"Why would I want to stay here without Mother? At least Mrs. Fleischman has a houseful of servants." And with that Giorgio had slapped the tip of his cane against the doorframe and marched out.

So our apartment at Robiac Square was shut up, and Giorgio and I packed our suitcases and headed to Mrs. Fleischman's apartment on rue Huysmans. Spacious and sumptuous, it was quite unlike our homely flat. Canary-yellow silk curtains framed the tall windows. Oriental rugs in muted ochers and emeralds lay neatly on the parquet floors. The walls were lined, on one side, with oil paintings in gilded frames and, on the other, with thick shelves of leather-bound books. The thin winter light streamed in and fell in pleats on the polished antique furniture, the collections of fine porcelain bowls, and the carefully placed bronze sculptures. Every room smelled of freshly polished shoes and Mrs. Fleischman's eau de cologne. Housemaids flitted silently from one room to another, removing a dead flower, closing a window, placing a log on a fire. Even the maids were perfect, their hair pulled tightly back from their scrubbed faces, their black-and-white uniforms starched, their tiny feet in glossy black slippers.

Babbo refused to be away from Mama while she had her operation. He moved into the hospital, taking all his books and papers with him. Mr. Beckett spent most of his time running between the hospital and Robiac Square and Miss Beach's lending library, finding misplaced books and papers or returning encyclopaedias and dictionaries that Babbo no longer needed. I yearned to see him, but Mrs. Fleischman kept our evenings full, with theater outings and dinners and "socials" that I found unutterably dull but which Giorgio found riveting.

During the days I danced and danced, preparing for the International Festival of Dance. Monsieur Borlin made me perform my solos for him every day, and I was determined to be a finalist. Babbo had already invited Mr. Beckett to join him. And knowing I was to dance in front of Mr. Beckett had given a new impetus to my practice. As I stretched and sprang, I imagined Mr. Beckett's admiring eyes upon me, and his long, thin hands clapping with such vigor he'd be unable to write for days. Babbo warned me that Mama might not be well enough to attend after her operation, and although that saddened me, I couldn't help remembering all the performances she'd watched, always squinting into the audience to see who was there, her eyes small and hard like coins, her hands resolutely clasped in her lap. No—this performance would be different. Mr. Beckett would be there!

* * *

AS I PRACTICED early one Sunday morning, I became aware of something that unsettled me, that tossed a shadow over my new bloom. I was standing with my hand on the back of a chair practicing my pliés, pushing down through my thighs until I felt every muscle taut and contained. I let go of the chair and raised both arms above my head, counting my breath as I did so. I paused, head back, arms outstretched. I could hear nothing but my breathing, even and controlled. Every sinew was still and at perfect pitch. As I held the pose I imagined Monsieur Borlin and Mr. Beckett watching me.

It was then that I heard laughter, muffled and smothered, from the room next door. Giorgio's room. I held my breath and waited. The laughter stopped. I exhaled, my nose wrinkled in confusion. Was I imagining things? Perhaps Giorgio had gone out and the maids were sharing a joke as they tidied his room and made his bed. I looked at the clock. Half past seven. Not like Giorgio to be up so early. Not like Giorgio at all. He and Mrs. Fleischman and some of her friends had had a late night at the jazz clubs in Montmartre.

I took hold of the back of the chair again and thrust one leg out, before raising it in front of me as high as I could. I then swung my upturned leg out and back, releasing my arms as I did so—my own variation of a turn en attitude. I began counting my breath in and out again. It was coming faster now, in little gulps, and I could feel a faint fluttering in my muscles. And then I heard it again. The distinctive sound of laughter, Giorgio's laughter, intermingled with furtive giggling. Someone was in Giorgio's room. Did he have a maid in there? A woman he'd picked up in Montmartre? Surely he wouldn't bring a whore back to Mrs. Fleischman's apartment?

I padded down the hall to Giorgio's room and knocked

softly on the door. Giorgio opened it slightly, his body wrapped around the door so I couldn't see beyond him. Was he—was he—naked? He raised his eyebrows inquiringly.

"Giorgio? Are you all right?"

"I'm busy. I'm getting dressed." He tried to close the door but I felt a surge of unexpected and inarticulate hatred, as if hundreds of furious firecrackers were exploding in my head. I knew he was lying to me, and in that moment I loathed him.

"I don't believe you," I shouted, putting my foot between the door and the frame so he couldn't close the door without trapping my foot.

"Oh, Lucia, grow up! I'll be out in a minute." He nudged the door purposefully against my dancing shoe.

"What are you doing in there?" Out of the corner of my eye I glimpsed the black and white of a maid, head bowed, scurrying silently down the hall behind me. But even that didn't bring me to my senses and snap me from the ungovernable emotions sweeping through me.

"I'm getting dressed!" Giorgio's face was black with rage. "Now bugger off!"

I withdrew my foot from the door, and Giorgio slammed it in my face. Dazed and unable to move, I stood there with my eyes fixed on the door handle. And then it opened again and there was Mrs. Helen Fleischman in her violet cashmere dressing gown, smiling her serpent smile and beckoning me in.

"Sit down, Lucia." She gestured to a chair.

Speechless and stiff with anger, I moved toward the chair, noting the clothes strewn across the floor, the bed with its covers flung back, the salty odor that hung in the air. Giorgio had pulled on a dressing gown and was sitting on the bed glaring at me.

"I'm sorry we didn't tell you." Mrs. Fleischman coughed delicately and fiddled with the sash of her dressing gown. "But with your mother in hospital and . . ."

Another spark of rage exploded inside me. Blinding light flashed behind my eyes. My lungs rattled with the effort of each breath. How long had this been going on? All this deceit and treachery—behind my back, behind Babbo's back, behind Mama's back. Mrs. Fancy Pants Fleischman pretending to look after us while she seduced Giorgio.

"You're married. You're old enough to be our mother!" I jabbed my finger at her with undisguised ferocity. "You've got a husband! You've got a child! You've got money! You've got everything! Why do you have to take Giorgio?"

"My marriage is over, Lucia. It's all just a formality now, the divorce, I mean. And I'm not old enough to be your mother. Not quite." She gave an embarrassed gulp of laughter.

"Mama and Babbo won't like this. They won't approve and you know it, Giorgio." I paused and turned to Giorgio, who had lit a cigarette and was now pulling hard on it. My eyes cut back to Mrs. Fleischman. "Babbo doesn't need you. There are hundreds of women out there who want to type his man-uscripts and read to him. He doesn't need you."

"You may be right, Lucia, but we haven't done anything

wrong, have we, Giorgio?" Helen turned to Giorgio, who exhaled a thin jet of cigarette smoke and grunted.

"You're married and you've got a child! And you're too old! And now you're trying to take Giorgio because you couldn't get Babbo. Just because you've got lots of money you think you can do what you like."

"Lucia!" Giorgio stabbed me with his eyes. "Don't be so bloody rude! What's got into you?"

I ignored him. "I know why you started working for my father. I saw you batting your eyes and trying to touch his hand when you took his papers off him. I saw it all. I could see what you were trying to do. Worming your way into our lives. Wanting a little bit of 'genius Joyce' all for yourself. You didn't fool me!" I could hear my voice rising, becoming louder and shriller, as if someone else was speaking, someone full of bitterness and savagery. "And now you're buying Giorgio with your filthy American money. Just because you couldn't bribe my father away!"

"Actually," said Mrs. Fleischman tersely, "it was the other way 'round. But I don't think we should talk about that. Giorgio and I just want to calm things down so we can all carry on living sensibly together until your parents get back from the hospital. So why don't we be grown up about this?" She was standing proprietorially over Giorgio as he sat stooped on the edge of the bed, dragging furiously on his gold-filtered cigarette.

"You can start by apologizing to Helen." Giorgio was talking more calmly now, but his face was still a cold mask of rage.

"I'm sorry if you feel betrayed." Mrs. Fleischman's manicured hands moved distractedly from the cord of her dressing gown to the pearls at her neck. "As soon as your parents
are home you can go back to Robiac Square. But we need to
let your mother's operation go ahead first. Until then we're
just going to have to muddle along."

I glowered at Giorgio. "And who's going to tell them about
you two?"

"I will, when I'm ready. It's really nothing to do with you."

I stumbled to the door, slamming it behind me. Once in my
room, I fell onto the bed, choking back my bitter sobs. For I
knew that Giorgio had gone. That whatever it was that had
stitched us so tightly together had gone. Mrs. Fleischman
was to blame, of course. She had persuaded Giorgio to lie
to me, to deceive Mama and Babbo. The air around me was
no longer heavy with beeswax and perfume. Now it seemed
thin and white and tarnished. But as my sobs subsided, it
struck me I was wrong—and that it wasn't necessarily
Mrs. Fleischman who had seduced Giorgio. What if Giorgio had seduced Mrs. Fleischman? A shiver of anxiety ran
through me. Had I gotten everything wrong? Was he, coldly
and deliberately, using her for his own ends? His words of the
previous month, when I turned down Emile, surfaced reluctantly in my memory. He had accused me of being mad and
selfish. Was I? Was this my fault? No! I shook my head so
hard my eyes popped. This, I told myself, was Mrs. Fleischman's fault. Anything else was unthinkable . . .

OCTOBER 1934

KÜSNACHT, ZURICH

'm not interested in your brother." Doctor Jung bats at the
air with his hand, as if flicking away a fly. "It's your father
who is the problem."

"Babbo's not a problem. He's the only one who understands me, the only person who has stuck with me through
this—this crise de nerfs." I try to move my chair away, but
it's too heavy. Doctor Jung has seated himself in the adjacent
armchair and pulled it so close to mine I can smell the sour-
ness of his breath.

"And why is that, Miss Joyce? Why is that?" He edges his
chair closer and I try again to move my chair away. When it
doesn't move, I shrink into the back of the chair until I'm sure
I must be about to disappear into the upholstery.

"Because only he loves me now!"

Doctor Jung gets up angrily from his chair and begins pacing around the room, sighing and scowling at me. "We need transference. Your father needs to leave Zurich; he needs to leave you. Until you can transfer your feelings for him to me, I cannot help you. And him hanging around in Zurich, watching over you, is not helping."

"He *has* left," I say, stroking my fur coat, wishing the doctor would stop shouting at me, stop pecking and plucking at my secrets.

"No he hasn't!" Doctor Jung walks to his desk and picks up my manuscript. "This," he says, giving it a derisory shake, "is pointless unless your father stops interfering with your treatment."

I flinch. I have spent hours and hours, days and days, writing the story of my life, and now the great Doctor Jung tells me it's "pointless."

"So Madame Baynes has been spying on me again, has she?"

"She is not a spy." The doctor sighs heavily and eases his large thighs into his swivel chair. "She is helping you. She is helping me. Everyone has seen your father in Zurich. He is well known, Miss Joyce." He writes something laboriously in his notebook and then slaps it closed and gets up again.

I stare out the window at the silvery winter sky and the looming hills. How did it come to this? How is it that Giorgio is in New York, about to sing on the wireless? That he has a chauffeur and a wife and a son? How is it that I, who had so much more talent, who worked so diligently, am sitting here being hectored by a fat Swiss man with a pocket watch . . . being spied on . . . friendless and hopeless . . . incarcerated. How did this come to be?

Doctor Jung follows the direction of my gaze. "You like the hills, Miss Joyce? What do they make you think of? Your father?"

I frown. "My father? Is that all you can think of?"

"I shall insist he leave Zurich. I have no choice now." He spins slowly in his swivel chair, keeping his eyes fixed on me.

I shrug. "You can do what you like. I don't care anymore."

"Miss Joyce." The doctor hesitates and drums his fingers menacingly on his notebook. "I think this is a way of getting your father's attention. By pretending to be in need of psychiatric help, you are forcing him to pay attention to you."

I pause to think about his words. Does he mean that I am *pretending* to feel the way I do? That the empty spaces inside my head, that the fear and hopelessness that so often grip me now . . . are feigned? *Just to get Babbo's attention?*

His voice softens. "The sort of attention he paid you when you shared a bedroom, perhaps?"

I stare at him, speechless, my fingers frozen against my fur coat.

"I see I have dumbfounded you, Miss Joyce. Well, if you'd rather talk about your brother, I suppose it won't do any harm. Why *were* you so upset about his dalliance with

Mrs. Fleischman?" Doctor Jung prods my manuscript with a fat forefinger.

I blink hard, blinking away his stupid theories. Then I close my eyes and imagine Giorgio. And he struggles slowly into focus, like a person coming up from the ocean. His body as thin as a strap, his long, gangly legs, his swept-back hair, and owlish spectacles—the very image of Babbo, everyone said that. I begin stroking my fur coat again, keeping the pressure of my fingertips firm and even. "Because something had changed. We'd been so inseparable, the best of friends. For twenty years we'd done everything together, looked after each other at every new school, played together when we had no friends. Even Babbo said the love between us was an out-of-the-ordinary love." I pause and look at Doctor Jung.

"Go on, Miss Joyce."

"I thought I'd let him down—not marrying Emile. I thought he was trying to save the family finances by becoming Mrs. Fleischman's lover and getting her money and her connections."

"Exactly as you were supposed to do with Emile Fernandez?"

"Yes." I nod miserably. Dear, kind Emile . . . always cheerful and smiling. Why hadn't I married him? Why had I gotten everything so very wrong?

Doctor Jung gets up and begins pacing again, his large hands swinging loosely at his sides. "I never get any exercise so I'm very glad to walk up and down. I apologize if you find it distracting, Miss Joyce. But back to Giorgio. Was he jealous of your feelings for Mr. Beckett? Was Mrs. Fleischman his revenge?"

I close my eyes briefly, summoning back those memories that only last week had been as sharp and clear as glass. "He didn't know at that stage. Only Kitten knew about me and Mr. Beckett."

Doctor Jung circles me, his hands now pushed deep into his pockets.

"It was all about money," I continue. "I noticed—in Paris and Zurich and Trieste—that rich people are different. They move differently, more upright, more graceful. Mrs. Fleischman had a certain poise that neither I nor Mama had. Giorgio saw this too."

"None of your problems are anything to do with money," the doctor says bluntly. "Stop buggering around and blaming other things. Your father didn't let a lack of money stop him, did he?"

I wince at his words. This isn't the first time Doctor Jung has become aggressive and rude to me. "They even talk differently, rich people. Their voices are fuller and rounder and louder. Have you noticed that, Doctor?"

But he isn't looking at me. He's peering down at the floor, by my feet, at my lower calves. "Are you wearing anything under that fur coat, Miss Joyce?"

"Of course!" I draw myself up to my full height and lift my

chin. Who does he think he is? I don't tell him that I'm naked beneath my coat. Naked but for my French knickers. I feel the furry hem of my coat brush against the skin of my bare legs. How good it feels! How free! Is this the only freedom left me now? A picture of Mama's blurred face floats before me. How angry she would be—how shamed—if she could see me now. Not properly attired. A strumpet!

"Excuse me a minute, Miss Joyce." The doctor moves toward the door and opens it. "I'll be back in a moment."

The instant Doctor Jung leaves the room I go to his desk. His leather-bound notebook is lying there, whispering to me, calling to me, begging me to open it. He could be back any second. And if he catches me, there's no knowing what he might do. Send me back to the lunatic asylum? Put me in a straitjacket? Bind me to Madame Baynes?

I open the notebook, gingerly at first, my eyes flickering from the book to the door, ready to spring back into my chair. I riffle through until I come to the final page. It bears one word. A single word in the doctor's scrappy, shredded handwriting, the nib pushed so hard against the paper it's almost broken through. Big scratchy letters, right across the center. What does it say?

I hear his footsteps, soft on the scrubbed flagstones of the hall. He's at the door. I see the handle turn. Quickly, I close the notebook and skitter to my chair.

In that fleeting glimpse, I saw a word, but it makes no sense. I need more time. I need to see it again. But the doctor's striding to his desk, his eyes bright with purpose. He picks up his notebook, locks it in the drawer of his mahogany desk, and slips the key into his pocket.

The word I saw, was it "insect"? Does he think I'm an insect? Spineless? Not enough backbone to leave home. Is that it? I perch on the edge of my chair, baffled and bewildered. Insect? Am I nothing but an insect now?

8

FEBRUARY 1929

PARIS

They're arguing about money," I whispered, stepping closer to Mr. Beckett in the dim hallway. The angry voices of Babbo and Giorgio drifted through Babbo's open study door and down the hall to where Mr. Beckett and I hovered.

"Should I go?" Mr. Beckett took a step back toward the front door.

"He thinks, because he's a genius, that other people should pay for everything. But it never seems to be quite enough. I've suggested not dining out every night but Mama won't hear of it—even though I've offered to do all the shopping and cooking. And I'm sure we could spend less on clothes. The lady who pays for all this lives like a puritan." I looked conspicuously at my new shoes with their rows of mother-of-pearl buttons and their carved heels.

"All the great artists had patrons." Mr. Beckett's voice was barely audible.

But Giorgio's voice had risen almost to a shout. "So why did you give four collectors' copies of *Ulysses* to Mother's doctors? Four of them! The leather-bound ones! How will they become collectors' books if you hand them out willy-nilly?"

"Those doctors looked after your mother exceptionally well." Babbo's tone was clipped and dry.

"And they were well paid for that. The American Hospital is twice the price of the local hospital."

We heard Babbo sigh wearily in response. Mr. Beckett's eyes darted to the front door, but I put my hand calmly on his arm and said, "They've nearly finished. Just give them a minute and then I'll take you through."

"Or leave them in the family—that's the alternative." Giorgio's voice was strident.

"Ah, your inheritance. Is that what this is all about, Giorgio?"

"Of course not!" snapped Giorgio. "I'm just thinking of you and Mama. You need to be less generous and you need to charge more. Do you know what Picasso is charging for his little pictures these days? You're his equivalent but you're paid a pittance. And look how hard you work, every day from morning 'til night. For what?"

"So tell me, Giorgio, what is Monsieur Picasso selling his paintings for?" Babbo couldn't conceal his eager curiosity.

"Apparently he sold some small picture of his current mistress to Gertrude Stein for five hundred dollars last week." Giorgio paused.

I eyed Mr. Beckett from beneath my lashes. The air was thick with his discomfort and I wondered if I should release him. But something prevented me. It was as if I wanted him to see us as we were, the famous Joyces stripped back to the bone. And greedy Giorgio fighting for the only thing he seemed to care about now.

Giorgio started again, his voice swelling with indignation. "But since then he's been boasting that it only took him four hours to paint. Four hours! You work ten times as hard for a fraction of the money. Surely you're as great—no, greater than Pablo Picasso? Everyone says you're a genius. So why aren't you decently paid? Your words will last forever in the minds of millions. They'll change lives. But Picasso's pictures will sit on someone's wall and be appreciated by . . . by . . . Gertrude Stein!" He spat out her name as though it were a fly that had flown into his mouth.

"I have no intention of pandering to Miss Stein but I accept your point about my value. How does one put a price on that?"

"I think we should start with the chapters of *Work in Progress* the Black Sun Press is publishing. What have they offered you?"

"One thousand dollars. Not much to Picasso, I imagine."

"That would be eight hours of Picasso's time. Eight hours! And how long have you slaved over those words, Father?" Giorgio's voice had risen again, shot through with barely stifled outrage.

"It's my life's work, Giorgio. My whole life is in there. I have nothing left."

"Quite. You must insist on double or treble what they've offered you. You should never take someone's first offer. Never!"

"But they've been so kind to me. Did I tell you about the giant light bulb they had specially made so I could see the text? And they still magnified it so I didn't have to strain my eyes with the editing. When you've had your books rejected by as many publishers as I have, you appreciate these little touches of kindness."

"That was the past, Father. Before your talents were recognized. Now you must model yourself on Picasso. He clearly has no inhibitions about demanding what is rightfully his. *You* must ask for what is rightfully *yours*. Get a pen and I'll write to the Black Sun Press asking for two thousand dollars. And when they try and negotiate—which they will—we are not going to budge. Understand, Father?"

"I think I should go." Mr. Beckett was edging up the hall, toward the front door.

"Oh no, Sam, Babbo will be ready for you now. I'll show you in." I grabbed his hand, his thin, bony hand, and pulled him toward Babbo's study, calling out, "Babbo! Mr. Beckett is here!"

"Come in, Mr. Beckett." Babbo's head appeared around the study door, his eye patch clamped to his head beneath his spectacles. "Giorgio is just writing a letter for me. Come out of that dim hall and into the light. Close the curtains, would you, Lucia?" In the silence I heard the scratching of Giorgio's nib and Mr. Beckett clearing his throat.

"Dim," said Babbo, thoughtfully. "Dim. Dumb. Done. Damn."

Mr. Beckett cleared his throat again, a little louder this time.

"Lucia, are you done with holding dumbfounded Mr. Beckett's damn hand?"

"Oh, I'm so sorry!" I dropped Mr. Beckett's hand in a flustered way, and moved toward the curtains. I pulled them together, leaving just enough space for light to fall on whatever book Mr. Beckett would read that evening.

"I think . . ." Babbo paused and straightened his eye patch. "It's time to drop the 'Mr.' Don't you agree, Lucia?"

I turned back into the room, a vertiginous joy rushing through me. "Oh yes, Babbo. Mr. Beckett is almost family now!"

"From this day on, you are to be Beckett in this house. Just Beckett." Babbo got up from his chair and offered his outstretched hand to Mr. Beckett.

"That's a great honor, sir." Mr. Beckett stood there smiling, his eyes shining in the gloom. Then he thrust his hand out and shook Babbo's hand, and I did a little pirouette, carefully avoiding the towers of books and maps and newspapers that lay across the floor.

Babbo sat down again, nodding and fiddling with the bow tie that sat at his throat like an impaled butterfly. "Shut the door behind you, Lucia . . . From swerve of shore to bend of bay. What do you think of that, Beckett?"

My mouth curled into a smile as I closed the door. Babbo had never called anyone by anything but Mr. or Mrs., except immediate family. Even his favorite Flatterers were "Mr. This" and "Miss That." And now Mr. Beckett was to be Beckett—plain Beckett. Was this another omen? Another sign that we were meant to be together? A presage of my future as Mrs. Beckett?

9

~~~~~

APRIL 1929

PARIS

For all of March and April I did nothing but dance and stitch. I was blistered all over. My feet ached from dancing all day, and my fingers were red and raw from sewing all night. There were only two weeks to go before the International Festival of Dance, at the Bal Bullier in Montparnasse, and I was starting to tingle with anticipation.

I'd thought long and hard about my performance. Babbo had wanted me to do a dance of the river Liffey. I knew the Liffey was an important part of *Work in Progress*, but for some reason I didn't want it to be the central theme of my choreography. Eventually I'd decided to dance as a mermaid, appeasing Babbo by suggesting I came from the watery depths of his beloved Dublin Bay.

I designed and made a costume of blue, green, and silver sequined moiré that would transform me from Lucia, daughter of James Joyce, into Lucia, dancing fish and writhing mermaid. I would have scales and fins and gills but also long braids of seaweedy hair tumbling to my waist. I made the fins from pigeon feathers I'd collected in the Jardin du Luxembourg and dyed a luminous briny blue. On my head would be a skullcap of scales into which I could tuck my hair.

Whenever I pricked my finger or accidentally tugged the thread so it cut into my skin, I closed my eyes and imagined myself onstage, glittering and sparkling as I dived and leapt and twisted and turned. I imagined the enthralled shouts and cries of an ecstatic audience. I imagined the eyes of Beckett upon me, wild and thrilling. I imagined Monsieur Borlin waving his fan and shouting, "My most talented pupil!" And Babbo, standing, his hands sore from clapping, his throat parched from cheering.

Mama was still recuperating after her surgery and so we spent most evenings sitting together in companionable silence, listening to the rasping of Babbo's pen and the rising and falling of Giorgio's voice as he practiced. Giorgio was to make his singing debut, his first solo recital, the week before my performance. Mama and Babbo were so enthused about Giorgio's concert, so anxious that nothing should affect his voice, that I was left to dance and sew in peace. If only Mama knew about Mrs. Fleischman, I thought. But I had no intention of revealing his secret.

One Sunday morning, as I sat in the parlor sewing my mermaid cap, carefully pulling the needle through the stiff, shiny fabric, Beckett arrived to walk in the Bois de Boulogne with Babbo.

"Are you joining us?" He slid his long, thin body onto the sofa beside me. Mama was brushing Babbo's coat in the hall and Babbo was hunting for his scarf and gloves.

"I can't, Sam." I gave the needle a sharp tug. "I have so much sewing to do and I need to practice my routine again. I haven't practiced at all this morning."

"Oh." Beckett looked at me. No—not looked, he stared at me for far longer than was polite, and my heart began to skip and my blood began to bound under my skin.

"The Bois de Boulogne will be beautiful now—the daffodils and crocuses and catkins. Not as beautiful as Ireland, of course, but it'll cheer Babbo up all the same. We've been rather cooped up recently." I pushed the needle slowly through the fabric, aware of Beckett's eyes burning into me. "What have you been up to, Sam?"

"Not much," he replied, guardedly. "Tell me about your dance. Mr. Joyce says you refused to dance the river Liffey."

"I've only seen it once, and it was so dirty and covered with filthy hovering fog. I couldn't. Not even for Babbo. Is he terribly disappointed?"

"He's stoical. What is your dance?"

"It's a secret. Only Babbo knows. But I'll tell you this— one of my legs will be completely naked," I said, lifting my eyes and coolly meeting his gaze. "I'm not telling you any more than that. It's going to be a surprise."

"Naked?" he repeated.

"Just my leg. So that the other looks like a tail." I was about to say, again, that it was a secret and he'd have to wait for the big night, when he reached out and ran his fingers down the side of my face and along my jawbone, as if he was quickly tracing a line there. The surprise of it made me give a little mewling sound, but when I turned toward him he'd drawn back his hand with such haste I wondered if I'd dreamed it. And then Babbo appeared in the doorway, cane in hand, asking if Beckett was ready.

"Yes, sir," said Beckett, jumping to his feet. He moved toward the door and only then did he turn back and look at me. And I knew I hadn't dreamed it. His eyes had a hungry, abandoned look, like the eyes of a beggar child. He gave one of his half smiles and said, "I'll see you next week, at Giorgio's concert."

I nodded and tried to concentrate on the movement of my needle. But as soon as I heard the front door close, I threw my sewing to the floor and began spinning and twirling around the parlor, my arms wide and my head back. Oh—that touch! The roughened tips of his fingers on my cheek. The charge of emotion that had coursed between us. And soon I would be teaching him to dance, holding him in my arms, feeling his body sway against mine. I wrapped my arms around myself and swooped past the window. Wild euphoria washed over me, as it had at my last performance. And it struck me that being in love with Beckett was not dissimilar to dancing— the breathless sense of invincibility, the feeling of time and space falling away.

"Lucia! What are you doing? You know you're not to dance in me best parlor!" Mama stood in the doorway, her arms folded on her chest. "Giorgio needs peace for his vocal exercises, so stop this dancing right now! And why is your bedroom full of old slices of potato?"

"Oh, Mama," I said, breathlessly. "I've just experienced a moment of utter perfection."

"Some of us are trying to recover from surgery." She scowled. "So that's enough 'utter perfection' for one day. Now clear up the potato from your bedroom and get on with your sewing."

"It's for my eye." I slung myself back onto the sofa and ran my fingers down the side of my face, exactly where Beckett's fingers had been. "Kitten said I should put cold slices of potato on my squinty eye. It's an ancient remedy."

"What hogwash!" Mama came into the parlor, picked up my sewing from the floor, and gave it to me. "And you better stop thinking about your eye right now. How can we be paying for you to have surgery when we're begging money for your father's eye operations?"

"Have you ever had a moment of pure joy, Mama?" I asked, running my fingers down my left cheek again.

"Sweet Jesus! All this dancin' onstage is makin' you vain and selfish, Lucia."

"Have you?" I persisted. "You must have had a single second of complete bliss. When you met Babbo?" I reached for a cushion and hugged it suggestively to me.

"You know nothin' about the real world!" To my surprise, Mama's eyes were blazing. She yanked the cushion from me and began beating it with her hand. "You know nothin' about men! You know nothin' about what I had to do to keep this family together! And you have the gall to talk to me of bliss!"

I shrank back into the sofa, wounded and speechless.

"I've seen you moonin' over Mr. Beckett. And you need to be forgettin' about"—she paused and then spat out her next words—"joy and bliss and perfection." She whacked the cushion so hard it shot out a thick flare of dust. "Men are animals with appetites. Just remember that when you're smirkin' about 'pure joy.'"

"Why are you always so horrible?" I shouted, tears pushing at the corners of my eyes.

"I've worked bloody hard to raise you nicely. And look at you! Paradin' 'round in front of your father—and on a public stage—half-naked. In Ireland, only strumpets prance onstage with no corsets and their legs showin'." She punched the cushion again and then flung it on the sofa. "And all this blarney with visions! In Ireland, only crazy nuns have visions. So you better make your mind up—are you a nun or a whore? Or is it Joan of Arc you are?"

"Babbo understands. Just because you've no creative spirit, no genius. You're nothing but a chambermaid. I don't know why he ever married you!" I leapt from the sofa and hurled the cushion at her. How could she be so hateful! I rubbed my eyes with my knuckles, as a tear rolled down my cheek.

"Oh, I could have been a dancer, all right! If I hadn't been beaten, and taken from school, and put out to work changin' filthy sheets!" She stooped for the cushion, but as she did so, she gave a cry of anguish.

"Mama? Are you all right?" I rushed toward her. She had eased herself down onto the edge of the sofa.

"Yes, yes, Lucia. That I am. 'Tis a pain from the surgery." She clutched her abdomen and I wondered if I should apologize. I'd never spoken to her like that before.

"Sorry, Mama." I looked at my hands, and as I did so all her words came back to me. Strumpet. Whore. That's what she thought of me. She hated me. My dancing—the thing I loved best—was a source of shame to her. I waited for her to apologize. Surely a mother should apologize for saying things like that?

A hush fell over the room. And then she heaved herself up from the sofa and shuffled out, saying she was going to lie down.

I tried to think about the touch of Beckett's fingers on my face. I tried to relive the moment his eyes met mine, that moment of utter perfection. But it was too late. Mama had ruined it.

* * *

I DIDN'T WANT Mama's angry words festering inside me while I practiced, so I tried to forget what she'd said. I put it down to her still being in pain after her surgery. And when that wasn't convincing enough, I told myself she was traumatized at having lost her womb. Finally, I told myself she was jealous. But to no avail. Her words repeated on me as if I'd eaten rancid food, disrupting the rhythm of my dance and upsetting the smooth sequence of movements I was trying to master. It wasn't her accusations that plagued me but her cryptic reference to the things she'd done to keep our family together. What had she meant?

I could tell she was still cross with me because she sniffed ostentatiously whenever I referred to my dance. And if I mentioned Beckett, she scowled and turned away. But she said nothing—and I knew it was because she didn't want to upset Giorgio. The air at Robiac Square was crackling with tension because of his debut at the Studio Scientifique de la Voix, where he had been studying Voice with the acclaimed Professor Cunelli.

When the evening of Giorgio's debut finally arrived, his nerves were thoroughly shredded. Mama and I tiptoed around him while he stood in front of the mirror running through his scales.

As he sang, Babbo (who had almost been a professional tenor and still fancied himself one after a few drinks) made his views very clear. Every time Giorgio hit a wrong note my father let out an unnecessarily loud sigh. If he was in Giorgio's line of sight, he'd shake his head with theatrical abandon. As I danced, I reflected on this and realized that Babbo had rarely forbidden Giorgio anything. Instead he sighed and looked mournful or used carefully chosen words that made his desires implicit and incontrovertible. Sometimes he sat in stony disapproving silence, his wordlessness speaking volumes. It was different with my dancing, of course. For me, he stroked his little beard or played with the end of his moustache, always nodding and tapping his foot, sometimes humming and clapping the rhythm, or scratching down a few words in his notebook.

And now every time Babbo sighed, Giorgio stiffened. Which made his voice creak like an old rocking chair. Eventually Mama came in and told Babbo to go and get changed, to put on his flowered waistcoat and his jacket with the purple silk lining.

"And you, Lucia. You can be changing into that new frock I bought you. Mr. Beckett will be here any minute." Mama took Babbo's arm and steered him out of the room. Giorgio immediately collapsed onto the sofa, where he lay prostrate, with a cushion over his face.

"What if my voice doesn't come out right? What if my throat seizes up? What if I get my nervous cough? Oh God! Why am I doing this? Why?" Giorgio pushed the cushion from his face and looked at me despairingly. Then he swung his body around until he was sitting upright and ran his hands through his hair before remembering Mama had oiled it in readiness for his performance. He seemed so vulnerable and frightened I felt a rush of pity for him. He was like my old Giorgio again, Giorgio before he became money obsessed and Mrs. Fleischman obsessed.

"You'll be fine." I sat beside him, took his oily hand in mine, and stroked the marbles of his knuckles with my thumb. There was a distinct undertone of liquor on his breath, which worried me. Monsieur Borlin told us repeatedly never to drink before a performance, not even to calm our nerves. But then I thought of Babbo, who always sang perfectly after guzzling several bottles of wine.

"I won't! Father's completely unnerved me. Help me, Lucia! You've done far more of this stage stuff than me." He sniffed and blinked and for a horrible moment I thought he was about to cry.

"Take lots of deep breaths before you go onstage and imagine you're singing to me. Or to Mama."

"Is that what you do?" Giorgio's voice wobbled.

"Yes, that's how Monsieur Borlin taught us to conquer our nerves. He also told us to imagine the audience naked."

"Urgh!" He shuddered. "That might be a step too far. Imagining Father and Mother naked."

We laughed, and briefly, fleetingly, it was like old times, when we were the best and closest of friends. Before Mrs. Fleischman stole him away. Would she be there tonight? I wondered. No, surely not. Surely he wouldn't risk exposing their affair tonight. Not on his big night. Or perhaps she'd slip into the back row and then slip out before she was spotted. And thinking of her reminded me that Beckett was coming. I felt a delicious shudder of excitement run down my spine.

"The truth is I'm not the sort of singer Babbo wants me to be." Giorgio pulled his hand from mine and stood up awkwardly.

"You'll be fine," I repeated.

He shook his head. "You're a great dancer and I'm a second-rate singer. And any fool can see that." He pressed his fingers against his mouth as if he didn't want to talk anymore. And as he did so, I smelled the drink on him again.

"Just remember my tip," I said. "Promise?"

* * *

BY THE TIME we were all sitting on the hard wooden chairs at Professor Cunelli's studio, I was so overwrought I could barely sit still. I tried to think about the ambitious footwork I'd choreographed for the finale of my mermaid dance, running my feet through it under the chair. But even that couldn't distract me. Beckett sensed my jitteriness and pressed my forearm reassuringly.

"Don't worry, he has a wonderful voice," he murmured.

"For the love o' God, will you sit still, Lucia," Mama hissed. "I can't concentrate and your chair squeaks every time you wriggle. Sure he's only singing. You're more likely to distract him with your carryings-on." She glowered at me, then rearranged her hat and looked around the audience to see who was there. I followed her gaze, expecting to see Mrs. Fleischman in her sable coat. But there was no sign of her. Perhaps Giorgio had asked her to stay away, either for the sake of his nerves or to preserve his dignity in the event of any vocal humiliation.

By the time Giorgio appeared, I was ready to explode with worry, convinced he'd drunk himself into a stupor backstage. As he announced the two pieces by Handel he was to sing, my hand shot out and grabbed Beckett's. I reddened when I realized what I'd done, but it was too late by then, so I squeezed hard and prayed that Giorgio's debut would be faultless. I knew my hand was clammy and damp but I didn't care.

Giorgio cleared his throat, nodded to the pianist, and opened his mouth. His first note warbled slightly and he stopped. The pianist stopped. My fingers dug into the soft cushions of Beckett's palm. Giorgio cleared his throat again. He nodded to the pianist and opened his mouth. But instead of singing, he gave a small yodeling sound, then a little spluttering cough. Babbo and Mama were both sitting rigidly, like a pair of chisels. I gripped Beckett's hand even harder and prayed silently for Giorgio. Professor Cunelli appeared on the stage with a glass of water. Giorgio drank it, handed the glass back, and cleared his throat again. He looked out into the audience, and surprisingly, I saw a glimmer of a smile on his face. He gulped, nodded to the pianist, and opened his mouth. And this time there was no fissure in his voice, no irritating nervous cough—just beautiful deep notes, one after another, filling the studio until the air throbbed.

When he finished and the applause had died away, Beckett showed me his palm, marked with a line of red crescents.

"My nails?" I asked, horrified.

Beckett laughed and then showed his hand to Babbo. I heard the word "stigmata" as the two of them chortled like schoolboys.

Relieved that Giorgio's performance had been a success, I shifted my chair closer to Beckett's. He was too busy chuckling with Babbo to notice, so I sat quietly, relishing the warmth of his thigh, its clean muscular hardness against mine. There was something reassuring, comforting, about his physical proximity. Bizarrely, the words of Kitten's pa floated into my head. Only married women are truly free. And I wondered if this was what he meant . . . that love provides the scaffolding of life. Would Babbo have written his masterpieces without Mama? But if that's what Kitten's pa had meant, why hadn't he said "only married *people* are truly free"?

Giorgio's arrival put an end to my musings. After much back-slapping from Babbo and hugging from Mama, she asked him why he'd smiled at the audience after drinking his glass of water.

"Lucia told me to imagine the audience naked." He grinned as he fished for his cigarettes. "So I did. And if that doesn't get you going, I don't know what will."

"Where are we dining tonight, Jim?" asked Mama, leading the way out of Professor Cunelli's studio and onto the boulevard.

"Fouquet's." Babbo turned and raised his cane in the direction of the Champs-Élysées, letting it swish through the air like a samurai sword. "For a continuation of the celebration of Giorgio's oration."

"How about peroration, Mr. Joyce?" suggested Beckett.

"Ah, I think recitation might be more exact, technically." Babbo turned to Beckett and clapped a clawlike hand on his shoulder. "Beckett, you understand me so completely I am beginning to wonder if some sinister form of witchcraft is afoot."

"Which craft might that be, sir?" Beckett asked with mock curiosity.

"Has elle sinned, perchance?" And Babbo chuckled with such unbridled glee I found myself chuckling too, although I had no idea what the two of them were talking about.

"In God's name, will you two never stop this blather?" Mama linked her arm through Babbo's, smiling even as her eyes rolled up into her head.

Beside us the lights from the barges and fishing boats reflected on the black water of the Seine, moving and rippling in the evening air. Pale shreds of mist hung above the river and on the far bank a brace of ducks stood, their heads twisted into their feathery bodies. I thought about my mermaid dance, the way I planned to thrash and flick my tail. Perhaps it was too forceful. Perhaps I should move more like mist. Floating and drifting.

"It's mesmerizing, isn't it?" Beckett was at my shoulder, following my gaze.

Yes, I thought. That's how I want my dance to be. Mesmerizing.

* * *

KITTEN RUSHED INTO the dance studio, laughing and panting and waving a piece of paper at me. The Bal Bullier competition was just a few days away, and I was practicing day and night.

"It's the final list of judges, Lucia!"

I stayed where I was, rooted to the spot and mute.

"Charles de Saint-Cyr *and* Emile Vuillermoz!"

Both were highly respected dance critics and I felt a tremor of excitement run through me.

"But wait for the rest." Kitten paused dramatically and then reeled off the names of some of the most eminent artists in Paris. "Uday Shankar, Marie Kummer, Djennil Annik, the musician Tristan Klingsor. But there's one more." She posed like a statue, eyes wide.

"Who?"

"Madika! The final judge is Madika!"

My legs felt weak beneath me, as if they'd turned to ribbons. I slipped to the floor, steadying myself with my hands. My heart was stammering—with nerves and anticipation and fear. "Madika," I repeated in a whisper. I could see her now, looking over me from my bedroom wall. Anna Pavlova on one side of her and Isadora Duncan on the other. "She's everything I want to be. I can't believe she's going to watch me. You know she trained as a classical ballerina and gave it up to retrain as a modern dancer, don't you?"

"Yes, yes—I know all about Madika," said Kitten impatiently. "This is your chance, Lucia."

I shook my head apprehensively. "I'm not good enough,

Kitten. What if I can't do it? What if she hates my dance? Or my costume? Or everything?"

"She won't, darling." Kitten squeezed my hand. "You're the best. Just dance for Madika. Forget the audience, forget everything, just dance for her."

"Sam's coming and lots of Babbo's friends. And Stella Steyn. I don't want to let anyone down." Waves of anxiety were starting to wash over me. "Oh, Kitten, I had no idea the judges were going to be so celebrated." I put my head in my hands, suddenly overcome with dread.

Kitten knelt down beside me and put her arm around my shoulders. "You're one of the best amateur dancers in Paris. You can do this. Remember what the newspaper said about you? Remember what you told your father last year? Remember how you told him you'd have your name headlined on the front page before him? Well, that's because you're a great dancer and a great choreographer. Now, would it help if I watched your 'secret' dance? No one need know. What's the music?"

"All right. I'll feel better when I dance. The music's over there."

As Kitten moved toward the gramophone, I crouched on the floor, closed my eyes, and twisted into my starting position. Four long, deep breaths. Oxygen moving through my body like seawater. Limbs and breath fusing. Water circling and surging around me. To the opening bars of *Feu Follet*, I was, once again, mercurial queen of the briny underworld, spirit of the oceans, empress of a salt-green sea.

Five minutes later, Kitten was clapping her hands loudly and shouting, "Encore!"

* * *

THE BAL BULLIER was cavernous and high-ceilinged. Hot bright lights threw their beams directly onto my spangled body as I lay curled on the stage floor, listening to the audience talking and laughing behind the heavy velvet curtains. I had already performed twice. And each time I was announced as one of the winners. As I accepted my award and curtsied to the crowd, I heard Babbo's cheers rising above the auditorium, and saw Monsieur Borlin waving his gloves from the box where he sat with his lover, Monsieur de Maré. But I hadn't felt the usual glow of success, because I knew the most difficult competition was yet to come.

So now there were only six of us left to compete in the final and most demanding round. This was the dance I'd practiced, hour after hour. My mermaid dance. Only Kitten and Monsieur Borlin had seen it. Of course Kitten had been fulsome in her praise. But Monsieur Borlin had nibbled the end of his fan and said, "Very ambitious, Miss Joyce. Very bold and very brave." His words made me wonder if perhaps I'd extended myself too far.

As I lay there, I imagined myself as a mermaid. I saw my tail meandering behind me, felt its firm, fleshy weight in the waves. I imagined the ocean chewing and slurping at my scales, the salt collecting in my grainy hair, the crush and crackling of shells beneath my hands. And I breathed, as slowly and steadily as I could. I shut out all thoughts of the audience, the judges, my rival contestants. I was no longer Lucia, daughter, sister, errand girl. I was a mermaid who had bloomed from the wind-bridled sea.

The orchestra started and the curtains swished softly as they drew back. I slowly unfurled myself before springing into a series of leaps and vaults, my head thrown back, my arms scissoring through the air.

The stage lights were so dazzling that when I looked out to the audience, I saw nothing but darkness. A black ocean waiting for me. The music swelled, filling the hall as I spun across the stage, chin tilted upward, back arched, fingers splayed. I was a flying fish, diving and swooping before I arced and twirled through the air. I was a mermaid, pouncing and plunging. I was half seabird and half eel, my arms fluttering and rippling, my head lowered as I sprang across the stage.

As the music crashed to a finale, I slumped to the floor to finish as I'd started, suddenly tense and anxious. Had the audience liked it? Would the judges appreciate the gymnastic element? The intricate footwork? The complex varying rhythms? I waited for the final chord, and as it faded out, the sound of clapping hands and stamping feet erupted in the hall, and my worries slipped away. I lay on the stage, my heart thumping in my ears, and waited for the applause to end. But it didn't. For a full two minutes (Babbo timed it on his pocket watch) the audience applauded and shouted and drummed the soles of their shoes on the floorboards. The pigeon-feather fins were cutting into my skin but I barely felt them, such was the surge of euphoria sweeping through me. When Kitten called me from the wings, I stumbled across the stage and fell into her arms.

"Darling, you were electric!" she cried. "Electric!"

* * *

BACKSTAGE, THE AIRLESS dressing room was thick with tension. Six of us had made it to the finals: a Norwegian, a Greek, three French dancers, and me. We exchanged hesitant smiles and fidgeted with our costumes, our hair, the odds and ends littering the dressing tables. The Norwegian dancer made a great show of stretching out her muscles, while the Greek girl sucked on the end of her plait. No one talked. We could hear the audience shouting at the judges to hurry up. Their cries and the stomping of their feet grew louder. The Greek girl's plait-sucking turned to gnawing. I offered her a toffee from my bag, but she gestured to her stomach and waved it away. The orchestra began tuning up as if preparing for the next concert. We eyed each other nervously. What was going on? Why were the judges being so slow?

Finally, we heard the strains of a Beethoven piece. The audience quieted and we tapped our feet impatiently, wishing the judges would get on with it. The longer we waited the more I wanted to win. I'd never felt so consumed by ambition, and the rawness of my desire startled and unnerved me.

More than anything I craved a word of praise from Madika. But I wanted something else too. What was it? Recognition? Validation? And in that nail-biting second, it came to me. I wanted to win so I could dance forever. So Babbo would never mention bookbinding again. So Mr. Beckett would know my place was on the stage. So Mama would never call me a strumpet or a whore.

A fanfare of trumpets sliced through the air. We ran our fingers over our hair, wiped the perspiration from our faces, and smoothed the creases from our costumes. The Greek girl put her hands over her ears, saying she couldn't bear to leave the dressing room. I took her hand and led her to the wings, where we'd been told to wait while the judges announced their verdict.

They sat in an ominous row at the end of the stage. I could just make out Madika, her hair piled high on her head and large gold hoops in her ears. Even the angle of her neck was graceful.

The head judge stood up. The audience was so quiet I could hear the Greek girl chewing on her plait. He shuffled some papers in front of him, gave an important-sounding cough, and began his announcement. My body braced itself, as if I were about to walk on very thin ice.

"An impossible decision, *messieurs et mesdames.* But we have reached a conclusion." He paused and surveyed the audience. "In third place, Agata Giannoulis from Athens."

My heart leapt. Would I be first? I'd had longer applause than Agata. I'd had longer applause than anyone. I drew the plait from her mouth and hugged her as the audience clapped demurely.

"In second place . . ." He paused and looked down at his papers as if he'd forgotten who to announce. I felt the air stealing out of my lungs. The crowd was getting restless again and some had begun waving their programs at the judging panel. "In second place," he repeated, "is Lucia Joyce from Paris."

My heart sank. Second place meant no praise from Madika. Second place meant I wasn't good enough. It meant I'd let Monsieur Borlin down. And Babbo. And what about Mr. Beckett? I felt the crush of disappointment. My dance master had been right. The choreography was too ambitious, too bold for someone as pedestrian as me. Agata was jumping up and down, trying to put her arms around my neck. I heard the judge announce the winner but I didn't catch her name. One of the French girls bounded out onto the stage, her lavish hair flicking in my eyes as she rushed past.

As she curtsied, the judge announced her name again, Mademoiselle Janine Solane. I waited for an eruption of applause, for flowers and programs to be thrown onto the stage. Nothing happened. Janine was about to do a second curtsy when something stopped her. She turned to the judges in confusion. I pricked my ears . . . I could hear my name. Who was calling me? Confused, I turned to Agata. She smiled and pointed to the audience. I craned my neck to look out into the darkness. The crowd was on their feet, shouting, heckling. My name. They were calling my name. What else were they saying? I strained to hear the words. And then I caught them: "Lucia! *L'Irlandaise! Un peu de justice, messieurs!*"

Agata pushed me onto the stage. Before I knew what had happened, I was back under the bright lights, bewildered— and intoxicated. Janine had retreated to the wings opposite, and the judges were standing behind their long table, shrugging and gesticulating.

My mermaid's tail prevented me curtsying so I gave a low bow. Tulip heads and daffodils rained down on me. And in the audience I saw Babbo waving his cane, and Monsieur Borlin leaning dangerously over the edge of his box, blowing me kisses. And I wanted the moment to last forever and ever.

It was only later that I read the lead judge's assessment of me in the press: *The only contestant with the makings of a professional dancer . . . Subtle and barbaric . . . A remarkable artist!*

* * *

IT WAS HOT and oppressive in the dressing room. Costumes lay crumpled on the floor, scarves and wigs slung carelessly over chairs. The smell of sweat and face grease and leather dancing shoes and unwashed feet had intensified now we were changing. The dancers were scrubbing makeup from faces, brushing out hair, searching for clothes, when a sudden silence fell across the room. I looked up and saw Madika picking her way through the discarded outfits strewn here and there. All eyes were on her as she walked straight past Janine Solane, winner of the International Festival of Dance, and stopped in front of my dressing table. She was dressed entirely in black, except for several long strands of pearls yoked together, with a tassel made of hundreds of tiny seed pearls that dangled at her waist.

"Quite a triumph, Miss Joyce. You should have won, of course. The audience made that perfectly clear." She spoke in heavily accented English but made no attempt to lower her voice. "There is a fashion for negroid dancing and we are all guilty of falling for fashion, are we not?"

"Th-thank you," I stammered, overcome by the presence of my idol and heroine.

"Perhaps slightly too acrobatic. Otherwise faultless, technically. You are a fugitive from classical ballet, like myself, perhaps?" Her dark eyes were appraising me, inspecting my feet then my legs, arms, and chest.

"No, madame. I started dancing at the Jacques-Dalcroze Institute and then I trained with Raymond Duncan." My voice trailed off as I saw the light dull in Madika's eyes.

"Oh, him!" she said contemptuously. "His sister, Isadora, was the real genius, of course. He has done something for rhythmic dancing, I suppose. Where else have you danced?"

"Now I train with Monsieur Borlin and with Elizabeth Duncan, Madame. And I'm doing a few workshops with Margaret Morris." I wondered if I should tell her about my dance troupe, but Madika started talking again.

"You have natural talent. Possibly genius. You must enter next year's Festival of Dance." She hesitated, fingering her pearls. "I will train you. I admit I am surprised you have had no classical training. It is generally considered a good thing. Give me your left foot." To my surprise, she knelt down, twisted my foot, and inspected my arch.

Then she stood up, nodding vigorously. "Sometimes the modernists ignore the debt we owe to ballet. I myself am fleeing tradition but I cannot ignore its benefit in building a strong physical foundation. Do not worry. If you train with me, you will win next year's competition. Let me know." She thrust a card into my hand and was gone, leaving me open-mouthed.

* * *

BABBO WAS BESIDE himself with excitement—and fury. He whisked us to a celebratory dinner at the Closerie des Lilas, opposite the Bal Bullier. Mama wasn't there. An hour before my performance, she'd complained of pains in her abdomen and retired to bed. Babbo said she was "revivifying herself after her recent attack of nerves." He was referring, of course, to Giorgio's debut, which had resulted in a surfeit of nervous tension at Robiac Square that had quite exhausted Mama. I'd felt hurt at first, but later I wondered if her absence—the lack of accusatory eyes in the audience—had improved my dancing.

So there we were, eight of us, around a table heaving with platters of discarded oyster shells and cleanly picked chicken bones. We drank glass after glass of champagne while Babbo berated the judges' decision and repeated, several times, the words of the audience as they heckled. Every time he said, *"Nous reclamons l'Irlandaise!"* he chuckled to himself. Because Mama wasn't present with her usual vigilant eye on the bottles, Babbo drank quickly, gulping down champagne as if it were water.

Madika's words followed me from the dressing room to the restaurant, where I repeated them to Beckett. He, like Babbo, was puffed up with pride and pleasure for me. But something in what she said irked me. Her lightning inspection of my foot had disturbed me. The aftertaste of her flattering words was slightly sour and cast a gauzy shadow over my night of triumph.

"You should have won," Beckett said for the tenth time. "You were magnificent. Everyone thought so."

"Thank you, Sam!" I felt my face glowing and my jaw beginning to ache from smiling.

"You were extraordinary. So, are you going to train with the madwoman?"

"Her name's Madika. And she's my idol." I playfully slapped Beckett's forearm. "Of course I'm going to train with her. She's a terrific dancer."

"Will you have to leave Paris?" My smile faded. It hadn't occurred to me I might have to leave to train with Madika. How could I leave Paris now? How could I leave Beckett?

"Well, I mean, she's Hungarian, isn't she?" Beckett reached for his champagne glass, and as he did so, his hand grazed mine. A charge ran through my body and I involuntarily snatched my hand away as though I'd been stung. Beckett gave me a skewed look and I wondered how much champagne he'd drunk. He was rarely this talkative.

"Yes, she's Hungarian, but she works here. Paris is the dance center of the world. We're forging a whole new philosophy of movement, of rhythm. And I want to be part of that." My words spilled out, making me sound like Babbo's apostles, with all their fervor and passion. "Isn't that right?" I called out to Kitten, who was deep in conversation with Stella at the other end of the table.

"We Irish girls can do anything!" shouted Stella, brandishing her feather boa above her head.

"*Vive l'Irlandaise!*" Kitten winked at me as she held her glass aloft.

"*La plus belle Irlandaise.*" Beckett looked at me over the top of his glass. I moved closer to him, aware of his leg against mine, his hip against mine, his arm against mine. He'd barely talked to anyone that evening except me and Babbo. Indeed, he'd barely drawn his eyes from me all evening. But then Babbo began pulling at my sleeve and indicating his watch. "Your mother—the v-venerable and imperious Mrs. Joyce—is alone at home waiting for us and for your news," he said, his voice heavy with drink. He stood up and pushed back his chair, and Beckett did the same.

"She should have come," I said, irritated.

"She's still recuperating," Babbo chided, before belching softly. I refused to be cross or bitter. It was *my* night, so I turned to Beckett and we latched eyes for a second.

As Babbo headed toward the door, pressing coins indiscriminately into the waiters' palms, Beckett reached out and took my hand. Giddy with champagne, I fell toward him. There were chairs and table corners butting up against us, waiters and diners pushing past us. I heard people calling for more wine, hollering for their bill, shouting goodbyes and au revoirs, the scraping of chairs and tables and the clunk of empty bottles being cleared away—and from far off the mournful sound of an accordion.

Beckett put his hands on either side of my face and brought his mouth toward mine. But in a flash he had pulled back and was coughing and blinking and gesticulating.

"Yes, Babbo's waiting," I agreed, soothingly. "He won't see anything. He's talking to the waiters and he's half-blind anyway." I put my arm out toward Beckett and was about to pull him back to me, when his words broke through the hubbub around us.

"Behind you," he rasped, pointing over my shoulder. "That man—he wants you."

I turned back to where Babbo's table of guests were still drinking and laughing. And standing there, watching me, was Emile Fernandez.

"Forgive me, Lucia, I just wanted to say congratulations." Emile ran his tongue quickly over his upper lip. "I've never seen such exquisite dancing." He lifted his hat to me and turned abruptly toward the door. I watched him snaking through the mass of tables, slipping past Babbo, and disappearing into the night.

"I'm sorry," said Beckett, looking awkwardly at his shoes. "Did you want to be alone with him?"

"He's just an old friend." I picked up my gloves from the table and began easing my fingers into the ends. My previous feelings of elation were now barbed with guilt. Poor Emile! How sad he had looked. I wondered if I should pull Beckett back to me or perhaps fall against his chest. But the moment had passed. Babbo was waving his cane at us from the front door and Emile's sorrowful face kept reappearing in my mind's eye.

When we got to the front door, Beckett touched my arm gently and said, "I'm looking forward to our dancing lesson. Good night, dancing mermaid." And once again I was lost, completely lost.

* * *

THE NEXT MORNING, I woke late, my head woolly from the previous night's champagne. Almost immediately the sound of applause and the cries of the heckling crowds came back to me and I smiled as I stretched out under my blanket. I recalled the conversation with Beckett over dinner, the feel of his hand on mine, his admiring glances that seemed to take in my whole body, his attempt to kiss me, his parting words—affectionate and intimate. I remembered Madika's words, her proposal to train me for the next International Festival of Dance. And then I remembered her question about whether

I had been classically trained, and it was as if a small dark cloud had appeared in a bright summer sky.

A few minutes later the cloud cleared, and my future was suddenly obvious. Of course! Why hadn't I realized this? Hadn't she said I was like a building with shaky foundations? Well, perhaps not quite. But that was clearly what she had implied. The foundations were not in place. And without foundations I would be nothing. I would be little more than a rootless tree blowing in the wind.

And as the image of a rootless tree appeared in my mind's eye, a recent dream flashed before me. A chestnut tree under a restless sky. Its boughs dragging in the air. Its gnarled roots creeping over a single nameless grave. I clutched at the memory. Was this an omen? A sign that I needed deeper roots? I'd ignored the dream at the time. Such a sliver of a dream it had been. So flimsy and indecipherable and without the vividness and bright colors I associated with my clair-voyant dreams. But now I realized this snatch of a dream was telling me something. Was it telling me that without well-grounded roots I might die? Was that it? Was this eerie image a sign that my spirit might die if I didn't anchor my dancing in classical ballet?

I leapt out of bed, threw on my dance tunic, tugged a brush through my hair, and ran through the apartment, down the five flights of stairs, out into Robiac Square, and down the rue de Grenelle. Past the concierges scrubbing doorsteps on their knees, past the butchers and bakers winding down their awnings, past the fat fishmonger heaving slippery eels from wooden crates, past the white-aproned waiters laying out rows of chairs on the sidewalk, past the musty shop where I bought my first dancing shoes. I ran all the way to the Seine. Cyclists rang their bells at me, horns beeped, motor cars swerved, a caped gendarme blew his whistle, flocks of pigeons rose into the air. But on I ran. Along the edge of the Seine, past the booksellers setting up their stalls, past the flower carts where the air was thick and heavy with the scent of hyacinths, past the caged birds where the immured parrots flapped and shrieked.

I ran until I got to the rue de Sèvres, where I stopped to smooth down my dress and wipe the sweat from my face. I knew where her academy was, and although it was too early for classes, I knew enough of Madame Egorova to guess she'd be there, preparing for her pupils, tidying the studio, dabbing at the mirrors with a handkerchief. I pushed open the door, climbed several flights of stairs, and there at the top was her studio. This was it! The best place to train as a ballerina in all of France. And there she was, Madame Egorova, standing in front of a mirror and pulling her hair into a knot.

* * *

"YOU'RE DOING WHAT?" Kitten could barely hide her incredulity.

"Training as a ballerina," I repeated, pushing a cup of tea toward her.

"So you won't be training with Madika?"

"No. I have to master the principles first. It was Madika who made me see that." It seemed very clear to me and I couldn't understand why Kitten was being so stupid.

"But that's what Zelda Fitzgerald's doing. You must have heard what people are saying about her. You don't think you're too old?" Kitten dropped a cube of sugar into her tea and stirred it, watching me from beneath her lashes.

"Of course I'm not too old! I'm much younger than Mrs. Fitzgerald. Madame Egorova danced with the Ballets Russes and Diaghilev and Nijinsky—she knows what she's doing."

"Yes, I know that." Kitten's voice was a trifle sharp. "*She* knows what *she's* doing, but do you? Everyone says you have a gift for dancing, but for rhythmic dancing, for modern dance. It's completely different." Kitten pulled her lips into a thin line and shook her head as if I were an idiot.

I explained to Kitten that I was like a wonderful building without foundations. And then I pointed out the window toward the Eiffel Tower as if to make my point.

"Tosh!" Kitten tossed her head. "Do you know how terribly hard she'll make you work? Do you have any idea of the hours and hours she'll expect you to practice?"

I was taken aback by the vehemence of Kitten's views. She was still stirring her tea, scraping the spoon around and around the bottom of her cup, as though she might find something there that would confirm her words. "What do your parents say?"

"Oh, they don't care. Their minds are on other things at the moment. Babbo has a book of essays coming out, and

Mama's planning some big trip for him, or else she's waiting hand and foot on Giorgio. I think they're pleased I'm going to be out of their way. Anyway, it's too late now—I've already told Madika I won't train with her this year. And she thinks it's a good idea. She's offered to have me back after I've done a year of ballet."

"Have you had one of your Cassandra moments? Is that why you're so determined this is the right course?"

"No," I said, toying with my necklace. I didn't want to share my strange dream of a tree and a grave with Kitten when she was in such a hostile mood. She'd probably interpret it in an entirely different way. She might even say it was a sign of impending death if I *did* take up ballet.

"Well, I think it's a mistake. I'm sorry, but I do." Kitten took the teaspoon out of her tea and laid it carefully in the saucer. After a few minutes of jagged silence, she continued, "But I'm your friend so I'll support you whatever you do. What about the dance troupe—will you carry on dancing with us?"

"I will if I can but I can't make any promises. Madame Egorova made it very clear what she expects from me." My voice trailed off as I recalled the meeting with Madame, her dark glittering eyes like polished pebbles, her hair pulled back so tightly I could see the stretched line of her scalp. Madame had demanded "no less than six hours a day, every day, here in my studio." I hadn't balked. I had been dancing for six years, often for hours and hours every day. Her pebble eyes flashing, Madame had talked of "the need to subdue the body" and said I must prepare "to push my body beyond its physical limits." She had mentioned the word "discipline" at least five times. I decided not to repeat any of this to Kitten.

"Did you see Zelda Fitzgerald there?" asked Kitten. "Do you know her?" Mrs. Fitzgerald was notorious for her American glamour and her tempestuous marriage to an American writer. There was always something in her life to gossip about, and Kitten, being a fellow American, always had the latest gossip.

"Madame said Mrs. Fitzgerald was training with her." I hesitated, trying to recall what I knew of the Fitzgeralds. "I think my parents had dinner with them once. Yes, Mr. Fitzgerald wanted to throw himself out a window. I think they must be a bit crazy. Are they crazy? I've not read any of his books—no time for reading! Too much dancing to do. Anyway, she's much older than me, but Madame didn't seem to think that was a problem." I took a long mouthful of tea, steeling myself for another round of Kitten's condemnation.

"Apparently she's dancing for eight hours a day and she's become completely obsessed. Ma says she was an awfully good child ballerina back in Alabama." Kitten looked pointedly at me. "Did you ever do ballet?"

"You know I didn't," I said. "You just said you'd support me, whatever I did."

"I just think you're more of a gymnast, an acrobat. I'm sorry, darling." Kitten pulled me toward her and hugged me. "I know you'll be wonderful at whatever you set your mind to. I'm just not as brave as you, not as adventurous." She heaved a sigh and then added, "Speaking of such, how is your adventure in love going?"

"Oh, Kitten." I grabbed her hands in mine. "It's Beckett that's given me the confidence to do this."

"He thinks you should train as a ballerina?" Kitten's eyebrows shot up into her fringe.

"No, silly! But my love for him and his love for me. I feel as though I could take anything on. Knowing he's there for me, that someone really cares for me. I can't explain it. You need to fall in love, Kitten." I pressed her hands in mine and wished I was more articulate, wished I could explain how the prospect of imminent liberation was impelling me forward, urging me on, giving me courage and audacity.

"You're so lucky." Kitten turned to gaze wistfully out the parlor window. "You have a world-famous writer as a pa, a tall, handsome man in love with you, and now Madika wants to turn you into a celebrated dancer."

"It's not all wonderful." I paused and swallowed. "Giorgio has taken up with a married woman who's old enough to be his mother. No one knows. But I thought you should. I'm so sorry, Kitten."

"I knew he wasn't interested in me. A girl knows these things." She squeezed my hand. "But you're still as close as you were?"

"No," I said, biting my lip. "I don't think he's forgiven me for not marrying Emile. And I don't like the woman he's having an affair with." I lowered my voice. "She tried to have an affair with Babbo while she was working for him. Right here, under Mama's nose."

"Your pa would never do that! He can't live without your ma. What's she like, Giorgio's new flame?"

"Old. Her face looks like an overbaked apple. But she's very, very rich. Her father made millions selling pots and pans in America and now she's spending it on Giorgio. It'll kill Mama." I shook my head dejectedly. "She hates divorced women and she's always been besotted with Giorgio."

"Well, don't worry about me. I've got a few men wanting to take me out." She stood up and shook out her skirt, before adding, "It's you I'm worried about. I don't want you to dance yourself into an early grave, as my ma would say."

"My mind is made up." I pushed myself up onto the balls of my feet and pirouetted, arms outstretched. "I want proper foundations."

10

JUNE 1929

PARIS

The coach was thick with cigarette smoke and babble. Everyone who wasn't inhaling on a cigarette was talking. The sun sloped through the windows, adding to the sense of excitement.

"Madame Egorova's going to go mad when I don't turn up," I hissed to Mama, who was sitting beside me, inspecting her nails and complaining about the lack of air. "I shouldn't be here. I should be dancing." I paused and listened to the conversation from the seats behind me. But Beckett still hadn't spoken. All I could hear was Mr. McGreevy talking and talking.

"Sure, Lucia, we've been through this. 'Tis Jim's big day and he wants his family with him. One day off from the dancing won't hurt you." Mama turned away and looked out the window.

"Dancers don't take days off. Don't you understand that?" I ground my teeth with exasperation. "Where exactly are we going? Will I be able to practice there?"

"'Tis Miss Beach's idea, you know that, Lucia. So stop blaming me. Your father says she's found us a place we can eat, near Versailles, and it's called Hotel Bloom or Hotel Leopold or something like that. God only knows how long she spent looking for it. 'Tis lucky it's only in Versailles, not Timbuktu."

Yes, good old Miss Beach! Where would we be without Miss Beach? Without her bookshop and her lending library and her endless free credit—and her devotion to Babbo. It was Miss Beach's idea to celebrate the French publication of *Ulysses* on the day *Ulysses* is set. She organized the coach and the invites. She made sure all the French translators of *Ulysses* were there and that all of Babbo's Flatterers were invited to her so-called Déjeuner *Ulysse*. Annoyingly, this included Mrs. Fleischman, whose garrulous voice I could hear as she ingratiated herself with the other acolytes on the coach.

As Mama turned back to the window, I took the opportunity to lean around and check on Beckett. I had been so busy at my classes I'd barely seen him since my dance competition. And when I wasn't dancing, I was planning our Charleston lesson—choosing the music, working on my instructional tone, trying to fathom out how to get Mama and Babbo out of the house for an entire afternoon.

There he sat, as beautiful and taciturn as ever, smoking and nodding while Mr. McGreevy held forth. Would he try and kiss me again today? Could I find a way for us to be alone? Away from the watchful eyes of Mama and Babbo, away from the prying eyes of the Flatterers, away from the snoopings of Giorgio and Mrs. Fleischman. If I had to miss a dance class with Madame, there could only be one good reason—progress with Beckett.

At Hotel Leopold we had a long table reserved in the restaurant. I was determined to sit next to Beckett, so I let him take his seat first. Then I elbowed my way around the table in pursuit, jostling Mr. McGreevy aside and pushing Miss Beach so hard her straw hat fell across her face. But I was too late. Helen Fleischman slid quietly into the seat next to Beckett and put her gold beaded handbag on the adjacent empty seat. She was looking around for someone, in that imperious chin-lifted way rich people have. I saw her catch Giorgio's eye. She gave a small fluttering wave that made her diamond rings flash in the light, and beckoned him over.

I spent all of lunch trapped between two of Babbo's Flatterers. They talked across me most of the time, only including me when they started guessing the real title of *Work in Progress*. Predictably, they wanted to know if I had any inkling of what it might be.

"No!" I shouted. Several people looked up from their soup. Mama shot me a warning glance. I gripped my spoon and took a deep breath. I had sacrificed a day with Madame

Egorova to sit on a coach with my mother, to be ignored by two amphibious aging men, and to be muscled out by Helen Fleischman. Every time I looked down the table, to the seat *I* was supposed to occupy, I saw Mrs. Fleischman simpering and pouting at Giorgio or laughing hysterically at something Beckett had said. I was surprised, because Beckett didn't say much normally. Even Babbo described him as "a man of few words." But on this day he was clearly cracking joke after joke, judging by Mrs. Fleischman's endless cackling. I had to get to him. I had to rescue him from her scheming ways, before he was blinded by the flaring of her diamonds.

After lunch we all lined up for a photograph. Babbo was obviously the centerpiece, with Miss Beach behind him. I was just positioning myself behind Mama when Mrs. Fleischman barged in front of me and leaned heavily on a tall male Flatterer, almost obliterating me from view. Furious, I raised my hand and yanked a piece of her hair that had become uncoiled from her chignon. I was so shocked at my own temerity that when she turned around and saw my expression, she didn't believe it was me.

Instead she said, "Did you see that, Lucia? Someone pulled my hair!"

"Shocking," I agreed, and looked pointedly at the famous poet standing next to me. The photographer started shouting at us, telling us to stand still and face the camera. I looked around anxiously for Beckett, but he was nowhere to be seen.

Eventually, we headed back to the coach for the return trip to Paris, and I noticed Beckett was still missing. "Babbo," I said, tugging on his jacket. "Beckett's not here. We can't go without him."

Babbo squinted at the queue of Flatterers lining up by the coach. Mrs. Fleischman stood at the front, her lips pulled back to flaunt her buffed pink gums and china-white teeth. Giorgio lounged beside her, complacently blowing smoke rings over her head.

"Mr. McGreevy is missing too," Babbo said. "Go and extricate them from the bar. Tell them if they don't come now they will be ingloriously abandoned."

"The bar?" I looked blankly at him.

"You will find them at the bar." A knowing smile drifted across his face. "They are Irish, Lucia. They are fond of a drop."

The hotel bar was empty. The waiter suggested I try the café around the corner, the one in the square with red-and-white checked tablecloths. He indicated the direction and I hurried off, wondering whether this would be my chance for an amorous encounter with Beckett. Already I could feel my heart beating a little faster in expectation.

The café was empty. There was a bar at the end where the proprietor, in a dirty white apron, was pouring brandy into balloon glasses. I heard Beckett and Mr. McGreevy before I saw them. They were singing an Irish song, loudly and out of time. I turned the corner of the café (which was an odd L-shape) and there they both were, slumped onto a table, singing into the tablecloth. Disappointment shivered through me.

Beckett stopped singing and raised his head from the table. "When can we dance, lovely Lucia? Lucia . . . lovely Lucia!"

"Garçon! Où sont les cognacs?" demanded Mr. McGreevy.

"The coach is leaving," I said, petulantly. I hadn't seen Beckett drunk before and I wasn't sure what to do. Of course Babbo often used to reel home drunk in the fickle hours of early morning. I'd waken to the sound of crashing furniture as he fell over tables and chairs. I'd hear his metal-tipped cane flailing against the wooden floor. And I'd hear him singing Irish ballads—always Irish ballads. And my mother puffing with labor and vexation as she steered him into the bedroom.

"Are you coming?" I stood by their table, my arms crossed on my chest like Mama when Babbo had been drinking.

"Not until you kiss me, lovely Lucia. Not until you show me how to Charleston. You promised." Beckett dropped his head back onto the table but quickly lifted it when the proprietor brought over the two glasses of brandy.

"Do you think that's sensible? To be drinking more brandy?" I decided now would not be the right time to advance our romance. His eyes seemed glazed and unfocused, and his body loose and floppy like a rag doll. Was Mama right after all? Were all Irishmen drunks? No, I refused to believe this of Beckett. Today was an aberration. Mr. Mc-Greevy had led him astray. Beckett couldn't hold his drink. He wasn't used to it.

Mr. McGreevy had already gulped down his brandy and

was tunelessly humming to himself. Beckett lifted his glass to his mouth and tipped the contents directly down his throat. "Come on, Lucia, just one kiss . . . Just one little kiss!" He lurched toward me. Terrified he was going to fall and crack his skull open, I widened my arms and let him fall into them, glad I had the strength of a dancer. His body felt wiry and sinewy but limp. I could feel his head lolling against my breasts. As he leaned on me, I felt the sharp juts of his hip bones against my stomach. I'd waited so long for a moment like this, but instead of excitement I felt nothing more than the exertion of trying to keep him off the floor. I was attempting to negotiate his body onto a chair when I heard my mother's heels clicking and her voice calling me.

"Sweet Jesus! What's goin' on here?" She looked around, startled. "Right, gentlemen. 'Tis time to go." She slapped Mr. McGreevy's face and then grabbed Beckett's armpits and dragged him from the café to the coach. "Always the same, bloody Irishmen. Let this be a lesson to you, Lucia. What is it with men and the drink? And Irishmen—the worst o' the lot!"

I could see the faces watching us through the coach window as my mother and I, grimacing, pulled Beckett along the ground. Mr. McGreevy stumbled after us, mopping clumsily at his face with a handkerchief and singing. Babbo and Giorgio were laughing and pointing, but I could see the distaste and outrage on other faces, and Miss Beach was looking distinctly sour.

Mama made Beckett sit next to her. He leaned against the

window, his eyes closed, mumbling about the dancing lesson I'd promised him. Every now and then his voice would rise into a whine and I'd hear him say my name and the word "Charleston." Mama had her arms tightly folded on her chest and sat glowering until twenty minutes into the journey when Beckett stopped muttering, opened his eyes, and started bellowing at the coach driver to stop.

"What on earth is wrong now?" demanded Mama.

"Call of nature, Mrs. Joyce. Stop the coach!"

She stood up and swayed down the aisle to the driver. He nodded and, a minute later, pulled into a small village. Beckett tried to stand up but fell back into his seat.

Mama shook her head despairingly and pulled him up by his wrists. She maneuvered him down the aisle and shoved him unceremoniously out of the coach. "Good riddance!" She spoke so loudly several Flatterers started nudging each other and smirking.

As she made her way back to her seat, the driver started the engine and headed out onto the main road. I assumed he was finding somewhere to turn around, but then it dawned on me we were on the road back to Paris—and the coach was accelerating.

"Stop!" I shouted. "We've left Mr. Beckett behind. We need to go back for him." Even though Beckett's intoxication had disappointed me, I'd seen enough drunkenness to know it was temporary. And that *my* Mr. Beckett, *my fate*, would be returned to himself as soon as the liquor wore off.

"Oh, Lucia, do be quiet! He's making a fool of himself and he's best doing that where no one can see him. Anyway, no one's wanting him here. I honestly thought he was going to be sick on me new dress." Mama smoothed the creases carelessly out of her dress as she spoke.

"But . . . but . . . he doesn't know where he is. He might not have any money. We can't just leave him. What if something happens to him?"

"Oh, stop your wailing, child!" Mama rolled her eyes to Heaven as she settled herself comfortably into her seat. Then she lowered her voice and added, "For shame! Leading him on like that when he's had a drop too much."

My mouth fell open and hung there, in a stiff circle. Words of retribution clawed in my throat. But no sound came out. I heard Babbo's friends laughing and making jokes about Beckett. I heard Sylvia Beach telling Babbo how lucky he was to have a wife like Mama. I heard the Flatterers placing bets on how long it would take Beckett to get back to Paris. I heard the coach driver whistling. But all this was nothing to Mama's words playing over and over in my head. Something in her words made me feel dirty, sleazy. Something in her words made my gut twist, hot and sharp. Had I done something wrong?

"Don't fret so." Mama's voice was low and mollifying now. "He'll be 'round tomorrow, you'll see. But you must stop mooning over him, that's all I meant." She reached over and squeezed my hand. I looked at her, surprised at this unfamiliar gesture of affection. Then she said something I'd never heard her say before. And even now, all these years later, I wonder if I misheard her.

"You're quite the beauty now, Lucia. 'Tis a worry to me, you being so like your father." She made a series of clicking sounds with her tongue, then added, "But don't be fretting about Mr. Beckett. Sure he's a grown man and can look after himself."

She was right, of course. The next day, at five o'clock, Beckett arrived to read to Babbo. I was waiting for him, lurking near the front door, desperate to know he was all right. He apologized immediately and sheepishly asked if he was still welcome at Robiac Square. I noticed he was carrying himself differently. His shoulders were stooped, his head bowed, as if under the weight of ignominy.

I smiled with relief. "I'm just pleased you've returned safely, Mr. Beckett—Sam."

"Oh, it didn't take long. I sobered up and walked back. I didn't drink so much in Ireland." He looked at his feet and chewed his lower lip. "Groups make me nervous. I'm no good in a crowd. I only meant to drink until my nerves calmed. I must apologize to your mother." Two spots of color appeared in his cheeks and I realized that, in this sparse confession, he was opening himself up to me. He'd never talked so explicitly about his feelings before.

"Mama thinks all Irishmen are drunkards. You've seen what a beady eye she keeps on Babbo." I pointed toward the kitchen, trying to keep my voice matter-of-fact. "She's in there."

As Beckett headed off in search of Mama, I recalled his request for a kiss. With his tongue loosened by liquor, he had begged me for a kiss, for a dance. And now, finally, he was revealing his deepest emotions and fears. In that moment I didn't merely hear his words, I felt them. I rose onto my toes and spun down the hall, my silk skirt spilling out around me, my arms weaving through the gloamy light. "He loves me," I whispered to our lucky Greek flag. "He loves me!"

* * *

I WAS LEAVING Madame Egorova's studio, a few days later, when I bumped into Mrs. Fitzgerald, wild-eyed and flustered.

"The Joyce girl?" she drawled, her eyes swiveling in every direction. "James Joyce's daughter? I'm Zelda Fitzgerald. I heard you were dancing here."

"I've just started." I took a deep breath. The air was heavy with the smell of lime flowers, which were dropping their sticky sap all over Paris. And Madame Egorova's studio had been stuffy and airless.

"Your parents had dinner with us last year." Mrs. Fitzgerald craned her head, looking over my shoulder as she spoke. For a minute I wondered if she was speaking to someone behind me. "Did they tell you about it?"

I nodded.

"Scott—that's my husband—offered to jump out the window in honor of your pa. He sure worships your pa. The great James Joyce!" Mrs. Fitzgerald started rummaging in her handbag. "What's it like being the daughter of a genius?"

"It's fine—mostly." My voice trailed off. Mrs. Fitzgerald was so fidgety she was making me nervous.

"Yeah, but you're just a daughter, right? I hate being married to a genius, although Scott's only an aspiring genius. Of course, I'm intending to be a genius ballerina." Things were spilling out of Mrs. Fitzgerald's handbag and onto the pavement. A silver lipstick tube rolled toward the gutter, but when I bent and moved toward it, she told me to leave it, that she never liked it anyway.

"You must come over one day. Perhaps we could practice together? We're off to Cannes next month but we'll be back. Madame Egorova is furious, of course!" Mrs. Fitzgerald laughed shrilly. "Do come, won't you?" And she was gone, her gold chiffon scarf trailing behind her like a streamer.

There were so many questions I wanted to ask Mrs. Fitzgerald, but it was only afterward I realized how tongue-tied I'd been in her presence and how her nervous energy had unsettled me. As I walked home, I reflected on her question. Being the daughter of a genius, I thought, is like being a sapling that has taken root too closely to an ancient plane tree. The sapling's spindly roots burrow down for water, but the plane tree's roots are deeper, thirstier. The sapling grows tall and thin in its bid for light, but the plane tree, with its broad canopy, takes most of the sunshine for itself. Come autumn, the plane tree drops its abundant leaves, and the sapling is buried beneath them.

I couldn't stop thinking about my analogy. I felt a burning need to discuss it with someone but knew Giorgio wouldn't understand. Since our moment of renewed intimacy on the night of his debut, Mrs. Fleischman had reappropriated him. And he had reverted to his new persona: cold and materialistic. I needed someone else familiar with the workings of the Joyce family.

When Beckett came to read to Babbo that afternoon, I was waiting in the hall for him. He looked surprised to see me, my hand on the door handle before he'd even rung the bell. I grabbed his hand and told him about my encounter with Mrs. Fitzgerald.

"Fitzgerald is a good Irish name," he said.

"You must have heard all the stories about them," I rattled on. "They used to have lots of parties and she wears beautiful clothes and Kitten says they did crazy things in New York that made it into the newspapers. And now we're training together with Madame."

"I've seen Mr. Fitzgerald in Miss Beach's bookshop," Beckett said.

"Anyway, she asked me what it was like being the daughter of a genius and I've come up with a rather good analogy—me a sapling and Babbo an ancient plane tree."

"Aren't all children like saplings and all parents like plane trees?" A shadow flickered over Beckett's face. "Isn't that why we have to leave them?"

I frowned. Was he trying to tell me something? Was it time for me to leave home? To marry, perhaps?

"You can look at it another way," he said, lowering his voice as if we were sharing a secret.

"What other way?"

"The leaves of the plane tree die and fall around the sapling, turning into compost, which nourishes the sapling and helps it grow." He hesitated and the skin between his eyebrows pleated. "And when lashing rain and ferocious thunderstorms come, the plane tree protects the young tree, perhaps even saving its life. And when the woodcutter comes, he has no interest in the sapling, only in the plane tree, which will make excellent floorboards."

Was Beckett laughing at me? I peered through the paltry light of the hall and saw his grave eyes, his unsmiling mouth, and his furrowed forehead. I realized I was still holding his hand, gripping it tightly as if he might try to escape. "But if the plane tree comes down, surely it'll break the sapling in two?"

"Only if it falls directly onto it. And as the sapling is so small, it could easily miss. Is the sapling an offspring of the plane tree or a seed floated in on the wind?" Beckett made no effort to extricate his hand from mine, and I could feel his blunt thumbnail cutting into my palm.

"Oh—offspring. Child of plane tree."

"Ah," he said. "Genius sapling of genius tree, perhaps?"

I could hear my mother advancing and calling, "Lucia, are you showing Mr. Beckett in? Jim's got a pile as high as the Eiffel Tower that needs reading, if you please."

"Sam," I whispered urgently. "Can we have tea next week?"

"Sunday," he said, easing his hand out of my grip. "The two saplings shall have tea away from the plane trees. Have you canceled my dance lesson after my disgraceful manners the other day?" He rubbed at the bridge of his nose, his neck mottling with color.

"Of course not. But your room's too small. I need to find a time when I can clear enough space in the parlor." At the thought of him in my arms (finally), a lightness came over me. I felt as if I could rise into the air like a balloon. I put a hand on his arm as if to keep me tethered to the earth. "I promise I haven't forgotten."

* * *

IT WAS WHILE I waited for tea with Beckett that a dance began to form in my mind's eye—a sequence of movements based on a sapling and a plane tree. As I walked through the Jardin du Luxembourg I looked closely at the swaying boughs and the trembling leaves. I watched the scudding of the clouds and the way rain spattered on the boating lake. I found an old chestnut tree and stroked its warped bark. How could I turn the solidity of an ancient tree into dance? When I passed the Seine, I noted the ebb and flow of the water. That too would be part of my choreography.

As soon as I got home I took notes and made quick sketches of what I'd seen. I wanted to incorporate ballet, eurhythmics, flamenco, and jazz. I wondered if Mrs. Fitzgerald might like to dance it with me. Or perhaps Kitten. And could I ask Emile to compose a score for me?

Although I was undecided about who was to dance and who was to compose the music, my mind was resolutely made up as to how the dance would end. The sapling must die. I had an image of the grand finale as a slow dance of death, leaving the sapling prostrate and motionless while the plane tree remained triumphantly upright. And yet I didn't envisage this as a battle played out in movement. It was to be a slow struggle, where nothing was obvious until the end. Would it work? Could I do it?

* * *

THIS TIME BECKETT had bought madeleines, which he insisted we dip into cups of lime blossom tea.

"Proust," he explained. "It brought back his childhood memories."

But I didn't want to think about my childhood memories, so I settled myself between the protesting springs of his old sofa and asked if he had anything interesting to tell me. The green shutters of his window were wide open and beyond I could see a huge chestnut tree in full bloom, its pink blossoms hanging like lanterns among the foliage.

"Yes, I'm about to have my first story published." He topped up my cup of lime tisane, edging a little closer as he did so.

"Congratulations! I didn't know you wrote."

"I've been writing prose and poems these last few months.

Your father's inspired me, and so has being here in Paris." He cleared his throat, then added, "I want to be a writer."

"That sounds wonderful!" I felt a thrill run over me. Our destinies seemed to be drawing closer, colliding in unforeseen ways. For a brief, crazy second, I imagined myself as his muse. Was that what my Cassandra moment had been about? Was I to be his muse rather than his wife? Or was I to be both? I batted the idea away. I needed to concentrate on what he was saying.

"I'll finish my study of Proust and try and get my contract at the École renewed for another year. And then I'll beg my mother for some more money." He dipped his madeleine into his tisane and stared gloomily at it.

"What if she won't give you any?"

He must have heard the anxiety in my voice, because he laughed. "I'll have to write a novel and find a publisher fast. Having a story accepted by a magazine makes me think it might be possible."

"What sort of writing? What sort of stories? Ones with plots and characters?"

He laughed again. "I doubt it. Thankfully your father has freed us from those particular tyrants."

"So what will you write about?" I smiled sweetly to hide my racing thoughts. Would he write about me? About my dancing? About love?

"I don't know . . . isolation, loneliness, suffering, decay, madness."

"Oh, Sam, that sounds terrible! Will anyone want to read

it?" My smile wavered. How could I be a muse for any of those?

"They're common enough themes." He took a quick, nervous sip of his tisane and then put the cup and saucer carefully on the complete set of Shakespeare he used as a side table. "I want to get below the surface . . . explore the voids in people's lives . . . I want to show how life can be so precious and yet so worthless. I'll put some humor in so it's not too sad."

"So precious and yet so worthless," I repeated slowly, feeling the pulse of his words on my tongue. Perhaps I could help him with the precious bits, I thought.

"I've become possessed by the rhythm of words, and patterns, and echoes. Your father's influence." He paused and stared into the space between us.

I picked up a notebook he'd left on the floor beside the sofa. "Your writing? Can I read something?" I felt an intense curiosity to see how he wrote. Would it be like *Work in Progress*—full of puns and rhymes and abstruse joined-up words that made no sense?

"That's just my notes." Beckett's fingers darted toward me, as if to snatch it away. But I'd already opened it and was perusing the scrupulously listed words and phrases, many accompanied by a fastidious tick:

- Flattening flatulence
- A double-handed divisible deluge
- Dotter daughter doter dotage

- Poodlenozzling, foxrotting filth
- Hairy hoary whore-less nights
- The rising spinning soundlessness

I tried to keep my face blank as I scanned the page. His writing seemed identical to Babbo's. Beckett's fingers had closed around the notebook, and in his restrained and polite way, he was attempting to pull it from me.

"Are these from *Work in Progress?*"

"They're phrases I've come across that I like. Some are my own. Can I have it back, please?" He shifted on the sofa, making the springs rise and fall in rusty jerks.

I released my grip on his notebook. He hurriedly pushed it under the sofa, presumably with the rest of his work and the huge dusty bundles of letters he kept there. But my appetite had been whetted.

"What were the ticks for?"

"I tick a phrase when I've used it. So I don't use it twice."

"I liked 'the rising spinning soundlessness.' I could dance to that." I could see the words snaking through the air between us like something living and breathing. Something voluptuous, sinuous. It struck me then that perhaps our destiny was to work together. And nothing to do with marriage. Would I choreograph dances from his stories and poems? Would he compose words for me in the way Emile had composed music for me? Were we being propelled together for the sake of art rather than love? But then I remembered my dream of us naked and I recalled all those little moments of physical intimacy. And I remembered how disinterested, almost repelled, I'd felt by Emile's gropings in the Bois—and how different I felt with Beckett.

"Could you now?"

"Yes, I think so. Can I see the story you've had accepted? Perhaps I could turn it into a dance."

"I'll show you when it's published." He thrust the plate of madeleines at me with one hand while his other hand wiped at the sheen on his pink face. "I don't much like talking about myself. Or my work. Tell me what you've been doing."

"I'm exhausted." I lay back against the sofa and closed my eyes. "Giorgio's out so much I'm having to do everything for Mama and Babbo. Yesterday I danced for six hours, then I had to dine out with them when all I wanted to do was take a bath and go to bed. And then, when we got home, I had to write to Babbo's eye surgeon for him, even though I could hardly keep my own eyes open."

"Can't your mother help?" The shimmer and color faded from Beckett's face as he visibly relaxed now the tussle over his notebook was finished. He draped his long body across the sofa and turned his head toward me. In this respect he's entirely unlike Babbo, I thought with relief. My father loved to talk about his own work and was most at ease when he did so, preferably with an audience of Flatterers. Thank goodness I wouldn't have to compete with an army of sycophants for Beckett.

"She's virtually illiterate." I nearly told him about Mama's list of Things to Do I'd spotted the other day—how beneath "get apples" she'd written "colleckt ulisses." But a sudden stab of embarrassment stopped me. "She had no education," I explained.

"Is that so? None at all?" Beckett passed me the plate of madeleines again and nodded sympathetically.

"My parents don't understand what a privilege it is to be a pupil of Madame Egorova." I took a madeleine and examined it. There was something about the shape of it, the deep grooves through its yellow crumb, that made me think of dancing again. I put it on my saucer, frowning. This was becoming ridiculous. I was seeing movement in everything. Even in cake. Was there something wrong with me? Did Kitten look at a pork chop and see a potential dance?

"Madame Egorova?" prompted Beckett.

"Oh yes. All the Ballets Russes dancers still come to her for lessons. She hardly takes any new pupils unless she thinks they have real talent."

"She danced with Nijinksy, you said?" Beckett reached for his packet of cigarettes and put one carefully between his lips.

"Yes, before he went mad and got locked up." There was silence while I sipped at my lime tisane and Beckett lit his cigarette. "Babbo keeps saying I can take up bookbinding if it gets too much. I thought they'd prefer me doing ballet. I assumed it was more acceptable in Ireland than modern dance. But now I think they just don't like me dancing in public. I think it shames them in some way. Babbo enjoyed my success at first, but I get the feeling that's changing. It's crossed my

mind that ballet doesn't intrigue him in the way that rhythmic dancing does. And that's why he's losing interest—in me,
in my dancing."

"It's certainly not as expressive. Or . . . or . . . as sensual."
Beckett gave an embarrassed cough.

"Don't women dance in Ireland?"

"Oh, they jig—you know, country dancing. The odd waltz,
perhaps. But Isadora Duncan would never have danced in
Dublin. And Josephine Baker would be locked up." His words
came out with wraiths of smoke that screened his face. He
batted them away and added, "Your father and I have a very
strong sense of Ireland within us but we both despise the
ethos of the place. And the Irish can be very cruel."

I nodded. I wanted to ask him if it was true, what Mama
had said, that only strumpets danced in Ireland. But I couldn't
work out how to phrase it, so I said nothing.

"Your father . . . what does he think of me?" Beckett faltered as a tube of ash fell from his cigarette onto his shirt. He
brushed it off but kept his eyes lowered.

I paused, surprised. "Babbo thinks of you as a son," I said
eventually, in what I hoped was a reassuring tone.

"Mr. Joyce told me he loved no one except his family. Is
that true?" Beckett took a long inhale and then let the smoke
drift out through his nostrils.

I nodded. "He's only ever friends with someone for a reason. He told me that. He doesn't really have friends, only
Flatterers. That's what I call all the people who fawn over
him." I picked up my madeleine and nibbled at the edge. What

an odd conversation, I thought. Why is Beckett so concerned about my father? Always asking me about him, always so anxious to know his views. And now I find his writing is just like Babbo's too. I looked sideways at him. He was lying back against the sofa, blowing smoke rings slowly into the air. He seemed brooding and slightly morose, and I wondered what I could say to bring back the earlier mood of cheerfulness.

"We're off to England for the summer," I said, changing the subject. And then I remembered that I hadn't told Madame Egorova yet. How was I going to tell Madame Egorova? "Madame's going to kill me! Perhaps I should refuse to go."

"Oh no—you have to go." Beckett looked at me from under his brows. "Your father needs you. He really is the genius everyone says he is."

I chewed absently on my thumbnail. "Have you seen me in his book, Sam?"

"I assumed Anna Livia Plurabelle was based partly on you. And Issy, of course. He's been working on some lines about dancing rainbow girls too. And he refers to dancing all the way through."

"And because of that, I have to do what he wants? Go where he wants?"

"Oh no," said Beckett quickly. "I only meant, in my inept way, that you're integral to his work. I didn't mean you should be . . . sacrificed." He took the cigarette from his mouth and carefully placed it in the ashtray where it sat, sending its coils of smoke into the room.

I was about to give a nonchalant shrug, a what-can-you-do sort of gesture, when it finally happened. Without warning Beckett lurched across the sofa and pressed his face against mine, his lips against my lips. I felt the contours of his body against me and the taste of cigarette smoke in my mouth. I tried to free my arms so that I could wrap them around him, show him that my desire was as great as his—but my hands were pinioned beneath him. And some odd sense of impending disaster stopped me from pulling them free. Instead I writhed as though I was trying to escape. Beckett drew back.

"Oh God—I'm so sorry, Lucia." He jumped up from the sofa, grabbed his still-smoking cigarette butt from the ashtray, and took a deep drag.

"No, it's fine," I spluttered, unsure what to do next. Oh, why wasn't I more accomplished at this sort of thing? Why was I such a schoolgirl? Why didn't I just reach out, throw my arms around his neck, and pull him to me? What was it that made me so awkward, so resistant to his touch?

"I'll walk you home." Beckett moved toward the door, blushing ferociously.

I was about to interject, to tell him I felt the same way, that our destinies were to be together, when there was a sharp knock on the door and Mr. McGreevy's head appeared.

"Ah, good afternoon, Miss Joyce. Are you off? I'll join you, I'm walking your way. Precisely your way—I'm dining with your parents tonight. I'll see her home, Beckett. You can get on with Proust. Oh, and I have these for you." Mr. McGreevy fumbled in his pocket. "These were the very reason I was knocking. The concierge couldn't find you earlier so I said I'd deliver them personally."

While Mr. McGreevy searched his pockets, I patted my hair and straightened my dress and tried to calm my nerves. Beckett's face was still pink and his spectacles were awry as he stood twitching by the door.

Mr. McGreevy pulled a narrow sheaf of letters from his inside pocket. "More letters from your aunt in Germany. She has beautiful handwriting." He presented them to Beckett with a small theatrical bow. "Come, Miss Joyce, let us go, then, you and I."

As I left, Beckett leaned in stiffly to kiss me on the cheek, as he always did now. Mr. McGreevy was already walking down the corridor, so I took the opportunity to swiftly turn my face so that Beckett's lips brushed mine. He colored and apologized and moved his lips back to my cheek—as though *he'd* made the mistake, not me. Oh, how I wanted to be held and kissed by him again!

"I think I've found a time for our dancing lesson, before we leave for England," I whispered. I could hear Mr. McGreevy calling me from the corridor.

Beckett looked at the letters in his hand. "When were you thinking of?"

"Next week. Tuesday afternoon." I knew my parents were going to a matinee then and Giorgio had choir practice, so the house would be empty. "Can you come?" I had to see him before we left. I had to have him in my arms before we left. If not, I would stay in Paris, refuse to accompany Mama and

Babbo to England. I would stay here, in Paris, with Beckett and Madame Egorova. At least until Beckett left for Germany.

"McGreevy's calling." Beckett jerked his head in the direction of the corridor. "I'll see you next Tuesday."

As I walked home, I closed my ears to Mr. McGreevy's prattlings and thought only of Sam. My awkwardness had spoiled the moment—again. I had to find a way to show him how I felt. I had to conquer my nerves and overcome his shyness. Together, we had to throw off our Irish inhibitions. I slid one leg forward, twirled, and then pushed up into an impromptu fan kick. Mr. McGreevy looked at me, startled, but I took no notice. How good it felt to move and stretch and spin after being folded up on Beckett's sagging sofa for hours. And then it struck me. It struck me so forcibly I felt like a moth blinded by sudden brightness. Our dancing lesson! If we danced, we could be different beings—free, spontaneous, abandoned, shameless.

I thought of my dream, remembered the patina of his golden-white skin, the feel of it against me, the heat of him, the way his hands had run across my breasts and thighs, the light that had fallen over our tangled naked bodies. Yes, I would make it happen. By hook or by crook, I would make it happen.

11

JULY 1929

PARIS

Beckett and I stood in the parlor surveying the room. Everyone was out, and the house, liberated from Mama's heavy-boned movements and Babbo's aggrieved sighing, had acquired a lightness, an airiness, that made it perfect for our first dancing lesson.

"I prefer it like this." Beckett nodded stiffly at my morning's work: the overstuffed furniture pushed to the sides of the room, the gaudy Chinese rug twisted up and shoved under the sofa, the potted ferns hidden behind the door, the piano rolled back against the wall, the chintz curtains fully opened. I'd pushed the shutters flat against the outside wall and a fragile blue sky was just visible, its light falling in a rectangular block across the wooden floor.

"You don't like my mother's parlor?" I spoke with mock indignation, wondering if he'd seen inside some of Paris's more fashionable apartments. Stella had a zebra-skin rug and whimsical painted lampshades in her rooms, and Mrs. Fleischman was redecorating her apartment in the latest art deco style with black walls and mirrors everywhere.

"I like light." Beckett stared at the window and then added, "And emptiness."

I thought of his austere rooms and his alphabetically ordered bookshelves. "So you prefer a room naked?" I looked directly, brazenly, at him and saw a blush rise up his throat. He'd pushed his hands into his trouser pockets but I could see his knuckles twitching through the fabric.

"I like things tidy and ordered." He looked down at the floor and his feet gave an odd little shuffle. Then his gaze slid back to me. "Is this what you wear in your dance classes?"

I nodded and wondered if I should make a joke about the big dance knickers he'd glimpsed me wearing in Monsieur Borlin's studio. Instead I lifted the short diaphanous skirt to show how freely my legs could move in my dance tunic. "Monsieur Borlin likes to be able to see our bodies clearly. So he can prod our muscles if they're not straining enough. But I wouldn't normally wear stockings—they're for the sake of my modesty." But Beckett wasn't listening. He was staring at my legs, his face pink.

"Are you ready to Charleston, then? I can't believe it's taken us so long. I don't know how you've survived in Paris without being able to dance." I hoped my chatter would put him at ease. "I told Babbo I was teaching you to dance and he's so looking forward to seeing you Charleston. He's a good dancer but he never managed to get the hang of it. Not that it's difficult. Anyone can do it. I've taught all his Flatterers, although most of them had no rhythm at all. And you need energy—lots of energy." I paused and looked thoughtfully at Beckett. He had moved to the wall and was leaning against it. I couldn't tell if this was his recovery position after viewing my legs or his usual state of torpor. His insomnia often made him lethargic—he'd told me that himself. And although I loved the languor of his movements, it occurred to me I'd chosen entirely the wrong dance for him. "We could do something slower, if you'd prefer? A waltz?"

"Oh no," he said quickly. "I'm a bit nervous, I'll admit. But I want to Charleston."

I offered him Babbo's silver cigarette case, thinking a smoke would help him relax. I had to get him dancing, but how was I to do it if he was too awkward and shy to learn a few basic steps? I snatched a look at him—he was grappling with the cigarette case, his cheeks still flared with color. I decided to put a record on the gramophone. Everyone relaxed to music.

I wound up the gramophone and put the needle carefully on the rim of the record. The air filled with crackling and a second later the beating and rippling of drums and pianos erupted into the room. Immediately my body began swaying, my feet tapping, my arms swinging. Who wouldn't want to dance to music like this? But when I turned around, Beckett

looked more stricken than ever, puffing agitatedly on his cigarette. I glanced at his feet. They were sure to be tapping out
the rhythm on the floor. But no, they weren't. Not a patter.

And then I had an idea, a brain wave. Why hadn't I thought
of it before?

"I'll be back in a minute, Sam. Try and let the music move
through you. Get a feel for the rhythm." I scurried toward
the door, turning back to add, "The Charleston's very fast."
Which was a stupid thing to say, because everyone knew the
Charleston was a fast dance. But his nervousness had affected
me. It had crept under my skin and made me edgy.

I went into Babbo's study and scanned his bookshelves.
Which book would he have chosen this week? I thought back
to what I'd heard and seen him reading. Yes—he'd been
browsing through a Norwegian dictionary. I remembered
it clearly because he'd muttered about the sparseness of the
Nordic vocabularies and asked if I knew any Norwegians in
Paris.

I found the shelf where he kept his collection of reference
books. The Norwegian dictionary was tellingly protruding
from its slot. I pulled the book out. And there it was—Babbo's beloved bottle of Irish whiskey.

"I think this might help." I sauntered back into the parlor
flourishing the bottle. Beckett was standing exactly where
I'd left him, tatters of cigarette smoke coming from his
mouth. I don't think his feet had moved an inch, in spite of
the music bouncing around the room. But when he saw the

bottle, he smiled. Not his usual half smile but a smile that swept up everything inside him and made his eyes spin with relief.

"I'll replace it later." I took an emboldening swig straight from the bottle, coughed as it caught in my throat, and then offered it to him.

His face sank. "I can't drink your father's best whiskey." He made a crablike retreat toward the door.

"Oh no, it's not Babbo's. It's Giorgio's. He won't be back for days. It'll relax you, Sam."

"Well, if it's Giorgio's . . . and if you let me buy him another one . . ." He took the bottle and tipped it down his throat. He wiped the neck clean with his ink-smudged fingers and passed it back to me. I put it on the piano, hoping he wouldn't be too tight to dance now. I remembered how we'd had to drag him from the café at Babbo's book launch, the heavy feeling of his head between my breasts. I didn't want him inebriated, just sufficiently relaxed to dance.

"Shall we start, then? Use the music to get a feel for the rhythm." I put a hand on each of his arms, maneuvering him into position. He felt like wood beneath my touch. So I retrieved the bottle of whiskey and thrust it at him. "Finish it, Sam. You need to be really loose for this dance."

His eyes widened. "All of it?"

"I'll have some and then you finish it." I gulped encouragingly from the bottle until the room, in all its unfamiliar bareness, staggered around me. I could feel the alcohol catch in my throat like burning coals. I tried to muffle my choking cough with my hand. I didn't want him to think I'd never had whiskey before.

Beckett saved the last few mouthfuls for me. This time he didn't wipe the mouth of the bottle. I felt the damp warmth where his lips had been and then put the tip of my tongue to the rim. But all I could taste was the sharp heat of the whiskey.

Everything changed after that. The liquor flooded my brain as I tried to dredge up all the instructional words I'd rehearsed for so long. But the words didn't come. They crawled around my larynx, lurking at the base of my throat, silently forming and re-forming. I could feel them scraping at my vocal cords . . . "Anyone can Charleston, Sam" . . . "Start with your feet shoulder width apart, Sam" . . . I could see the words in my mind's eye. But my tongue was paralyzed.

"Language has failed us," Beckett said suddenly, as if he knew exactly what I was experiencing. "A piece of music can move you in an instant. To tears even. A painting too. Look at what can be conveyed with a single brushstroke. But not words. Words have failed us."

I nodded in agreement and tried to check the alignment of his feet and hands. Everything seemed to be blurring and meandering around me.

"Dancing, movement—they speak to us directly. Like a painting. Like music."

While the whiskey rendered me mute, it had the opposite

effect on Beckett. He had shed his cloak of brooding shyness. His hands fluttered in the air. His cigarette burned unnoticed between his fingers. His left foot began beating out the rhythm of the music. "Most words are lies, Lucia. How can we understand human existence with words? How can we understand human existence at all?"

And with that peculiar question, my voice returned to me and the room stopped tilting.

"We dance, of course."

"Perhaps we do. Dancing is more honest than words." He moved toward the piano and I thought he was after the empty whiskey bottle. Instead he picked up Giorgio's metronome and put it squarely in the center of the empty floor. I felt anticipation fluttering in the pit of my stomach. While I had become light-headed and vague with alcohol, he had become bold and purposeful.

"What's that for?" I enunciated my words very carefully to disguise any slurring and to mask the excitement that was growing inside me.

"To help with the rhythm. I thought we could start without music." He was rolling up his sleeves now.

"You want to dance to a metronome?" I blinked, baffled.

"Yes." He went to the gramophone and lifted the arm. The room fell silent. "If we dance without music, we'll hear other sounds too."

"Other sounds?"

"The sliding of our feet on the floor, the creaking of my

bones. I've a bone in my ankle that cracks in certain positions." His voice petered out as he crouched and fiddled with
the metronome.

He'll hear my breath, I thought. He'll hear my heart. And
I will hear his. Was that his intention? How beguiling he
was! I stared down at the curve and knots of his spine beneath his shirt, at the soft hairs on the back of his neck, at the
freckles on his forearms. I was about to reach out and touch
him, when he looked up at me and asked, "Can you teach me
without music?"

"Yes, yes, of course." I dragged my eyes from his crouching body. Damn the whiskey! Where were all those lines I'd
practiced for so long?

Beckett stood up. The metronome was ticking loudly. "I
think that's the right time. How should I start?"

"With the hands." I held mine up in front of my shoulders, palms facing out. Concentrate! I must teach Beckett
to dance! Babbo was waiting to see him Charleston. "Good.
Now swing them like this, up and down, making sure your
shoulders swing too." I could feel the whiskey and the music
running through me, making every bone in my body seem as
supple and curling as ribbon.

He swung his arms and grinned.

"Still too stiff in the shoulders." I brushed at his shoulders,
felt the arc of them melting into the moist heat of my hands.
"Looser. Breath out." He exhaled and I felt his shoulders
drop. "That's good. Now try swinging them again."

"You see what I mean, Lucia. About words. How inadequate they are. I know your father believes in the absolute power of words. But this . . . dancing . . . this is true . . . trustworthy." His soft Irish brogue was more marked now. I felt it fold around me. Folding itself over and around me until I heard nothing else. Not the metronome, not the heels of our shoes against the floor, not the beating of my heart.

Beckett stopped swinging his hands and began fumbling with the top button of his shirt. "It's a bit warm. Would you mind if I undid a few buttons?"

I tried to speak, to tell him of course I didn't mind, but for some reason words fled me again. So I shook my head instead.

The metronome ticked away while his fingers fumbled at his buttons. And then the most peculiar thing happened. My fingers, the very fingers that had just brushed his shoulders with professional nonchalance, crept toward his throat. Beckett had managed to work the first button free of its buttonhole and was now wrestling with the second button. His clavicles protruded sharply from the frayed collar of his shirt. Between them was a small hollow like a freckled seashell. My fingers drifted to that dip, that hollow at the base of his throat. First the tip of my index finger stole into the hollow and stroked its sunburned center. Then my middle finger followed. Then my wedding finger. Then my little finger. Until each fingertip had drawn a small curve through the curl between his collarbones.

I watched my disembodied fingers as though they belonged to someone else. In the silence all I could hear was

Beckett's breath and the relentless ticking of the metronome. And then, quite suddenly, the button with which he'd been struggling flew across the room and rolled across the bare floorboards and under the sofa.

It was as if a hypnotist had clicked his fingers. I stepped away awkwardly and tried to resume a more instructional pose. My cheeks burned. Beckett shifted and I wondered if he was going to try and reclaim his shirt button from beneath the sofa. But he didn't. He just stood there, blushing.

"I'll get it later." His voice had an odd scratched quality. And something about it made my brain disconnect from my body again. I felt the thread that seemed to run between us. I felt it tug at me, drawing me toward him. He stood in exactly the same place, blinking and appearing to search for words.

"You think this is more honest?" I put my hands on his forearms. Turned him to me. Tilted my face toward his. Waited to be kissed.

"The metronome . . ." We heard the metronome skim over the floor as our feet knocked it.

"Forget it." I lifted my face higher. Pushed myself onto my toes.

"Your parents . . ."

"Out for hours." I put my hands on either side of his face. Felt the rasp of his stubble. Pulled his face toward me. Touched my lips to his. Smelled the whiskey and tobacco on his breath. Felt the thrill of liberation.

Beckett pulled back. "What time is your father home?"

His arms shook uncertainly at his sides as if he wanted to clasp me to him, but could not.

"Out for hours and hours." I wrapped my arms around his waist. Brazenly pulled him back to me. Felt the bony slightness of him. Pressed my ear to his chest. Heard his heart thudding. Raised my face. Let my lips skim over his. Warm. Soft. Not quite yielding.

I pressed my mouth more firmly against his. Felt the flutter of his lips. The gradual opening of his mouth. And suddenly he was kissing me. Pushing his mouth hard against mine. As if his concern about the metronome and his anxiety about Babbo returning had slipped away. His lips moved from my mouth to my neck, to behind my ear. Back to my mouth.

But then he pulled away. "Your mother?" His breath kept catching in his throat. He gestured jerkily at the door.

"Everyone's out," I whispered.

"I think . . . perhaps . . . the dance . . . they will want to see me Charleston . . ." His eyes flickered to the wall of Babbo's ancestral portraits.

"If the portraits are bothering you, we can go to my bedroom." I took his hand and tried to draw him toward the door.

"If they find me in your bedroom . . ." Beckett held back, and in the silence of the parlor I heard the beating of his heart, and it seemed to me our hearts beat in unison.

I turned toward him. "No one's here. No one at all." A second later our mouths were clinging together, his tongue searching my mouth, my throat. I felt the sharpness of his hips, ran my fingers down the plunge of his back, felt the lines and points of his bones, the long stretch of his limbs.

Beckett's mouth moved back to my neck. Crooned into my ear. I strained to hear his words over the heaviness of our breath. ". . . beautiful . . . your body more perfect than . . . but I . . . the whiskey . . ." I couldn't catch all his words. Our breathing and sighing were too fulsome. And the empty room seemed to echo with it.

I began undoing the buttons of his shirt. Tugging at his belt. Urging him toward the floor. Toward that block of sunlight that beckoned so enticingly. We would make love right there. Our own golden bed of light.

I peeled off a stocking. Tossed it away. Hurled Beckett's belt with such wild abandon its buckle clattered against the metronome. Pressed myself to him. Felt the press of him against my hips, my ribs, my stomach. Felt his hands seeking out my breasts. Felt my nipples spring up at the brush of his fingertips. All the while encouraging him to the floor, to that slice of light that called so urgently to me.

* * *

WE WERE ON the floor when it happened. I had eased Beckett deftly into that oblong of syrupy afternoon light that lay across the parlor floor. I thought of it later as our wedding bed. But that was much later. Our arms were twined around each other, our fingers exploring and searching and fumbling. His shirt and my dance tunic lay puddled on the floor beside us. His belt and one of my stockings twisted like slumbering snakes across the sofa. He was still whispering in my ear, concerned about my honor and my parents. Even in the throes of passion, he was gallant and gentlemanly.

Beckett heard it first. I felt him stiffen. Then he leapt to his feet, pulling up his trousers, groping for his shirt, searching his pockets for his spectacles.

"Quick! Your dress!" He grabbed at my dance tunic and threw it at me.

My ears pricked. And then I heard it too. The heavy tread on the stairs. Her voice, vinegary and plaintive. The *tap, tap, tap* of a cane on the hall floor. And then Babbo's voice, as clear as a bell.

"Are you here, Beckett? Have you mastered the art of Charlestoning yet? I told you any old Charlie can Charleston. Where are they, Nora?"

Beckett was shaking so badly he couldn't do up his buttons or thread his belt. His face was hot and glistening. A tic had taken hold in the lid of his left eye.

"If she's fiddled with me best parlor, I'll be having words with her. Now give me your cane, Jim. Before I trip over it meself."

Part of me wanted to stay there, on that rug of sunlight, my thighs and stomach exposed, my hair tangled, my clothes littering Mama's precious parlor. Part of me wanted to be seen, almost naked, in Beckett's arms. And in that moment, for no reason I can explain, I thought of all those nights sharing a bedroom with Mama and Babbo. My hands over my ears, night after night, hating the sound of their bones grinding beneath the sheet, their muzzled panting, the grunting of the bedsprings.

But Beckett's terror was so palpable I had no choice. I leapt up, yanked my tunic over my head, and reached for my stocking. And then I heard the door squeaking on its hinges.

Mama stood there, a look of weary distaste on her face. She threw up her hands and turned her head toward the hall. "Jim, go and put the kettle on! I'll be right down. Mr. Beckett's not here!"

We heard Babbo's voice, thin with disappointment. "Is there to be no entertainment, then? Have I returned replete with words of approbation and adulation to no effect?" And then the fading rap of his cane as he moved toward the kitchen.

Mama shut the parlor door. Her eyes sharpened to points. She crossed her arms and stood very straight. "I never much liked you, Mr. Beckett. I always thought you were secretive. And a Holy Joe at that, looking down your Protestant nose at me." Her voice hissed like water on hot coals.

I closed my jaws tight and carried on rolling up my stocking and adjusting my garter. Beckett said nothing. He had managed to do up his belt but his unbuttoned shirt hung from his shoulders.

"With your fancy Foxrock airs, all high and mighty, thinking me nothing more than a Dublin chambermaid. Only for

Jim, I'd throw you out. But Jim needs you and he likes you well enough, so we'll say no more."

I looked at Beckett, waiting for him to reassure Mama of his honorable intentions, to placate her with his declarations of love for me. But he said nothing. Just stood there with an expression as blank and inaccessible as stone.

So I spoke up, unabashedly shaking out my tunic as I did so. "We were just dancing, Mama. There's no need to be so rude to Mr. Beckett. I should remind you that Babbo relies entirely on Mr. Beckett now."

Mama's eyes blazed. She snorted with outrage. "Dancing—my foot! Don't think I don't know mischief when I see it. And in me best parlor!"

I turned to Beckett again, searching his face for some sign of emotion. Why didn't he say something? Why didn't he tell her we were lovers now? Or if he wasn't ready to admit it, why didn't he deny her allegations of mischief? She might believe him. Possibly.

But Beckett didn't look at me. He gaped at Mama, his left eyelid twitching feverishly, his fingers still scrabbling at his shirt buttons.

I decided to be bold, to confess all. "Mama, Mr. Beckett and I are—"

"Sweet Jesus! I don't want to hear another word. Mr. Beckett, get down the stairs while Jim's making tea. Don't let him hear you. Lucia, I want me best parlor put back like it was. Now. And for God's sake, put some proper clothes on!"

She opened the door and flapped her hands at Beckett. "Well, get on with it, Mr. Beckett. He won't be all day making tea. Or would you rather be doing the Charleston for him?" She narrowed her eyes. "I thought not."

And with that, Beckett slunk out. I waited for him to turn back, to shoot me a final look of tenderness, but he didn't. He sloped out, wordless and hunched.

I didn't care. I could still feel the burn of him on me, the press of him, the taste of him. My fingers still tingled with the touch of his skin, the peaks and hollows of him, the sharp precipices of his hips against mine, the freckled dip at the base of his throat. I put my fingertips to my mouth. Sucked hard. Smiled to myself.

"Mother o' Mary—what sort o' trollop are you? I told you to stop moonin' at him! I told you to stop leadin' him on! Now, put me parlor back. This instant. 'Tis lucky Jim is as blind as a bat." She turned to go. I started heaving the sofa back into place, hoping I'd find Beckett's missing button. It would be my keepsake, my trophy. But then Mama turned her head sharply. "You didn't let him go all the way for sure?"

"What's it to you?" I feigned an indifferent shrug.

"He wouldn't have done that. Not an Irish boy from Foxrock. Not with you. Tell me he didn't." And her eyes pooled with tears. "Oh, Lucia, tell me he didn't."

I shook my head. "He didn't do anything. There'll be no bastard in the family, so don't worry, Mama." I knew she couldn't bear the taint of scandal. Not in the family. She'd never seen anything disgraceful in Babbo's writing, even when *Ulysses* was banned for obscenity. Of course, there'd been no scandal in Paris. *Ulysses* sat proudly in the windows of all the best bookshops, making Mama glow with pleasure. And that was all she saw. But a scandal in the family—that was different.

She exhaled loudly. "'Tis a good thing. Now, don't let him touch you again. Marriage first and mischief later. And no more dancing with him. I don't trust that Mr. Beckett. Always lounging, he is. Never looks me in the eye. Shifty and sly for sure."

I felt a quiver of rage and indignation. "He's not sly. He does look people in the eye! That's not fair—"

"Oh, I know he's looking in *your* eyes whenever he gets the chance. If only Mr. McGreevy were still here. He never looked down his nose at me. He knows I'm Mrs. Joyce who dines out every night. A proper Catholic gentleman is Mr. McGreevy. He would never have laid a finger on you. Never!"

"I think you should know." I paused, took a long breath. I would tell her the truth about Beckett and me. I would take her into my confidence. "We feel things for each other."

"And so do mating pigs. I can't be listening to another word of this." She walked toward the door, her chin jutting furiously in the air. But then her head snapped sharply toward the piano. I felt my insides cringing. I knew she'd seen it. I busied myself with the curtains. Pulling them half shut. Fussing with the folds.

"Mother o' Mary! Is that your father's secret whiskey? The bottle he thinks I'm knowing nothing about. Is it now?"

Babbo's peevish voice floated through the open door. "Nora? Nora? The kettle has boiled. Where are you?"

"If you didn't steal this from behind the Norway dictionary, I'm a dead dog." Two red spots flared in Mama's cheeks as she moved toward the piano and picked up the empty bottle. "Was it your idea—to steal your father's whiskey? Did you lead Mr. Beckett on with a wee drop?"

I shook my head. My mouth suddenly tasted dry and rusty. My temples were starting to throb. All my energy had drained away.

"Now, get this room in order and change out o' that strumpet's outfit. We'll keep this quiet, the two of us. But promise me you'll leave Mr. Beckett to your father? Promise me that?"

"Yes, Mama." I could feel my humiliation congealing around me. I wanted my mother to go. Something about her anger, my shame, the heat of the room, the way it all bled together, sickened me. My stomach rolled and churned as her accusations thrummed in the air. Leading him on. Mating pigs. Strumpet. Trollop. I felt the floor sucking at my feet, as though I were mired in something foul and noxious. And when I looked for the golden block of sunlight where Beckett and I had experienced such passion, it was gone.

I picked up a fern in its brass pot and hoisted it onto the coffee table. And when I heard the door close, I put my hand on its stem and snapped the furled leaves clean from the root.

* * *

"I SAID THIS would be hard, Lucia. I said you must be committed." Madame Egorova drummed her nails on the lid of the piano.

I lowered my eyes as I mumbled an apology.

"You miss another day of class two weeks ago. And now you want miss all your lessons for ten weeks. That is correct? Ten weeks!" She shook her head, incredulous.

"No," I pleaded. "I don't *want* to miss my lessons. But it was my father's book launch—I had to go. And now they're insisting I go with them to England." I could hear how ridiculous, how weak and ill-disciplined I must sound to Madame. Recalling Beckett's words about *Work in Progress*, I tried to explain. "My father is James Joyce, the author. He's writing a great novel and dance is an important part of it. He likes me to dance for him, for inspiration. And he and my mother have been very ill. I have to help them."

"I do not care who is your father or where you are taking holidays. This is nothing to me. If you want train in classical ballet, you give your life. Everything!"

I could feel my cheeks reddening and my eyes stinging.

"You make commitment to ballet, Lucia. I give you place in my studio, in *my* classes, with me." Madame stabbed a bony finger into her chest. "This is not little hobby you stop and start when you want. This is ballet."

"Madame, dance is my whole life! It's all I've done for the last six years." I wiped angrily at a tear rolling down my nose.

"Bah! Rhythmic dancing is not ballet. If you want do modern dance, go back to Madika. Be like her—traitor to ballet!

But here"—she paused, sweeping out her arm to indicate the empty studio—"here you must be like Mrs. Fitzgerald; arrive when I open and leave only when I close."

"Yes," I whispered. "That's what I want."

"Tell your parents you must stay here, until I close the studio in August."

I shook my head despondently. How could I explain the impossibility of such a conversation? How could I tell Madame that my father thought it enough for a woman to be able to write a letter with elegance and put up an umbrella with ease? That although he had once celebrated my successes, something had changed now. That although he liked me to dance privately for him, he didn't like me flaunting myself onstage. That my mother thought women who danced were little more than prostitutes. How could I tell her all this? How was I to explain such things to Madame Lubov Egorova, who had danced with the Russian Imperial Ballet and then with the Ballets Russes, with Diaghilev and Nijinksy? How could she possibly understand?

"Everything is booked." I didn't tell her that the ferry, the train, the multiple hotels were all booked ages ago, without my knowledge, without my consent. Of course, my parents never entertained a shred of doubt that I wouldn't accompany them, and their servile friends, on a trip to research Babbo's book, to record *his* voice reading *his* work, to meet the people *he* needs—to further *his* position. I felt resentment mounting inside me. Why did they always assume I would accompany them? Why did they never ask?

"Can I telephone to Madame Joyce?" Madame Egorova's voice softened.

"No!" I blurted out, unable to conceal the panic in my voice. I knew exactly what would happen. Mama would cruelly mimic Madame's Russian accent. I could hear her now, sniggering, laughing, not just at Madame's accent but at her misguided belief in me. I could see her pirouetting in the kitchen, saying, "Only strumpets dance like this in Ireland."

And Babbo would be hurt and upset. The Flatterers would point at me and whisper. They would accuse me of denying him the muse he needs to write. Even Beckett said I had to go, that I was vital to *Work in Progress*. And at the thought of Beckett, a subdued smile crept over my lips. I could still feel him in my arms, the taste of his breath on my tongue.

"Why do you smile?" Madame looked at me, displeased. "It is not funny. I have done it for other girls. Sometimes the parents do not understand and it is necessary to explain about talent. It would never be necessary in Russia, of course. Do I need to explain to Monsieur and Madame Joyce?"

I shook my head, no longer thinking of Beckett, no longer smiling.

"You need commitment, Lucia. If you cannot be strong with your family, it is possible you do not have the strength to be ballerina." Madame reached out and put her hand gently on my forearm. "Ballet is not easy choice. Great physical and mental fortitude are required."

"I'll ask Babbo if I can stay. And if not, I'll find a dance teacher in Torquay and practice every day. Thank you, Madame." I curtsied but I couldn't look at her. I didn't want her to see the thickening veil of tears in my eyes. Even thoughts of Beckett couldn't console me. All the way home Madame's words played through my head. I *had* to tell Babbo that I couldn't accompany him to England. I *had* to stay in Paris.

* * *

"WHY DID NO one tell me we're sailing tomorrow?" My voice was shrill with panic. "I thought we were going next week."

"No, *mia bambina*. Your mother has been packing for months, such is her eagerness. We've always known our departure was tomorrow." As he spoke, Babbo waved his hand, as if dismissing me, the huge stone on his ring glinting as it caught the light. He was sitting calmly in front of his wall of portraits—oil paintings of himself, his father, and his grandfather in their carved frames.

"But why didn't I know? Why didn't anyone tell me? I can't go tomorrow!"

"We have all known, *mia bambina*. Your mother, who is a veritable rock in this household, has packed your trunk for you." Babbo caressed his newly shaved chin in a distracted way. "You have been preoccupied, I fear. Your attentions elsewhere."

It was Giorgio who'd told me we were leaving the following day. And that Babbo's Flattering friends, Mr. and Mrs. Gilbert, were coming. Oh, and Helen Fleischman too. He mentioned it in passing, saying Mrs. Fleischman had always planned to join us, and hadn't I known? And then he put his finger to his lips, expecting me to keep his sordid little secret.

When I nodded, quiescently, he had the cheek to say, "Everyone knows we're leaving tomorrow." I looked at him in disbelief, before shaking my head so frantically I felt myself go dizzy. He made me sit down while he got me a glass of water and called Babbo. And now here I was, in the parlor with my father, trying desperately to compose myself, to stay calm.

"I can't go! Madame says I must stay and dance. I have to stay in Paris." I felt a howl of rage and despair rising inside me. I had to keep it at bay. I had to stay calm. "And why is Mrs. Fleischman going?"

"Calm yourself, Lucia." Babbo's lenses on his new concave glasses were so thick his eyes resembled a bullfrog's, huge and bulging. "Mrs. Fleischman is coming to help me and your mother."

"With her Louis Vuitton trunks and her swagger and her supercilious airs," I burst out. Babbo gave me an odd look but said nothing, so I carried on, marching around the parlor, my fingers clutching and plucking at chairs and shelves and curtains. "I can't go, Babbo. I have to dance. Madame wants me in Paris."

"As long as you know how to walk into a room, that is all that matters, Lucia." His eyes skimmed the portraits behind him, as if he were speaking to his illustrious ancestors. "Your mother knows how to walk into a room. Just observe her."

"But I can't go to London, or Torquay! Can't you hear what I'm saying?" I took deep breaths and counted between them, remembering my dance teacher's words for conquering stage fright. For that was how I felt—full of dread and terror. No Madame. No Beckett. No time to say goodbye to Beckett. I hadn't set eyes on him since our moments of intimacy, our almost-lovemaking. I needed to reassure him that Babbo didn't know, that Mama had promised to keep it secret, that I still yearned for him.

"I hear you, *mia bambina*, but we need you. My eyes . . . you know I need help with everything now . . . you've seen how your mother has to cut up my food. And she's still recovering from her illness. She needs you too. Everything's reserved. We're booked into the grandest hotel in Torquay, where your idol, Napoleon, laid his battle-broken head."

"Napoleon hasn't been my idol for ten years! And Mrs. Fleischman can cut up your food," I growled.

"She's not coming out until later. You and I will have ample time to discuss your dreams, your Cassandra moments. I know you've had some, Lucia. I can tell by the brilliance of your eyes. They have been shining like pearls recently."

I ignored him. "What about the Gilberts? And everyone else you're meeting in England? It's lucky I've learned from my mother how to walk into a room, isn't it?" I spoke with such unconcealed bitterness that Babbo looked away, his eyes creeping back to the portraits behind him.

"Oh, Lucia. There's no pleasing you." He sighed heavily. "This is an important trip for all of us. I'm seeing publishers, I'm being recorded, Miss Weaver—my most important patron on whom we're reliant for money, I should remind you—is coming to stay. Without Miss Weaver there would be no dance classes." He moved to the wall and straightened the portrait of his father. "Ah, cleft by a crooked crack. I can't have a crooked father in my house . . . There was a crooked man and he walked a crooked mile . . . Can you recall the next line, Lucia?"

"What about my dancing, Babbo?"

"You can dance every day in the hotel. Did he find a crooked sixpence? Against a crooked stile? I believe so." He stepped back, tilted his head, and peered myopically at the portrait of his father.

"I do have to dance every day, Babbo. No one understands—I *have* to dance!" I felt another rush of anger. Why does he, who has to write every day, not understand that *I* have to dance every day?

"Well, that's settled, then—you can dance in the hotel. And when we return, you can recommence at the ballet school." He patted my hand, his eyes traveling slowly over his wall of portraits. "No one in my family needs to work. You can all be ladies and gentlemen of leisure now."

"I—don't—want—to—be—a—lady—of—leisure," I said through gritted teeth. "I—have—to—dance!"

"I know, I know," Babbo said soothingly. "I'm only saying that you have the choice. Your mother and I didn't have that, but you do. Guess what?"

I knew he was about to change the subject, that he'd had

enough of listening to me. I opened my mouth to remonstrate, but as I did so I had another overwhelming urge to shake my head, to shake it until I was too giddy to stand, to shake myself into oblivion. I remembered Giorgio's earlier expression of distaste and alarm, and somehow this stopped me, like the brake on a speeding motorcar. "Yes, Babbo?"

"Picasso has refused to paint me. Apparently the great master is 'too busy.' Can you believe it?" I could see Babbo was piqued. I wanted to tell him I didn't care, I didn't give a damn. But my anger frightened me and I wanted to restrain the furious voice inside me.

So I took a deep breath and said, with feigned composure, "So who will paint you for the frontispiece of your next book, Babbo?"

"I'm thinking of asking Brancusi," he said, taking his eyes from me and gazing at his beloved wall of portraits again. "Yes, I think Brancusi could do it."

And that was that? You just went with them to England?"
Doctor Jung sits very close to me, my manuscript on
his lap.

"Part of me wanted to go." I stare at my hands as if they
hold the answers. The pink puckered scar on my thumb looks
back blankly at me. "There were things I hadn't told Madame Egorova."

"Like what?"

"I couldn't tell her that I no longer had the energy to fight.
Her teaching was wearing me down . . . her classes were un-
relentingly physical . . . they were so demanding . . . and all
that practice! It was beginning to exhaust me."

The doctor nods encouragingly.

"It was as if she was asking me to take on yet another battle. My life felt like a constant struggle—with my parents—their beliefs, their expectations." I run my hand across my face. Just talking of these things is making me tired.

"Had you always felt like that?"

"No. But I was starting to see things differently, more clearly. There was something pernicious going on and I was beginning to catch glimpses of it."

"I think we may be getting somewhere, Miss Joyce. You are most articulate today. What was it you were beginning to see?" Doctor Jung rises from his chair and starts his customary pacing.

"I'd like to walk too, Doctor," I say, rising from my chair and moving toward the window. Today the hills are blue and veiled in mist. I hear the sound of a door slamming and a dog yapping, and above the lake, gulls are wheeling and fighting. "I was beginning to see another side to our life at Robiac Square."

"Go on, Miss Joyce." The doctor comes and stands beside me, his eyes following mine to the hills beyond the lake.

"I was beginning to see that we were all spokes in Babbo's wheel. That we were all part of his story. And that if nothing happened, I would be trapped there. Trapped in his imaginary world."

"And this frightened you?"

"Yes. Mama was happy buying clothes and dining out every night. Giorgio had Mrs. Fleischman's money to appease him. But I—I wanted more." I stop suddenly, as I recall my past ambition. And it occurs to me that perhaps my craving for recognition disgusted my parents somehow. I swat at the air, pushing this unpleasant thought away.

"Shall we take a turn around the room, Miss Joyce?" Doctor Jung offers me his arm and I take it. Such a large arm, like the trunk of a tree.

"I felt my stamina leaching from me. I was very tired and kept pulling and straining muscles. And I had this feeling ballet didn't interest or inspire Babbo, and that he was casting me off like an outgrown piece of clothing." I fall into step beside the doctor, my bitten nails gripping his sleeve. And for a few seconds my mind floats to a faraway place. How formless and shapeless life is when you're in its midst, how murky and chaotic. It is only now, and with the help of my memoir and the doctor's interrogations, that I can understand and shape all that has happened to me. The thought pulls me back to Beckett.

"My love for Beckett kept me going. It made me see things I hadn't seen before. The way Babbo pulled us into his world, the way we all revolved 'round him. It was Beckett who made me see all this."

"How?" The doctor paces slowly toward a picture of a mandala hanging on the wall, me in tow, the hem of my satin dress trailing on the floor behind us.

"I saw it happening to him. Falling in love had opened my eyes. I can't explain it." My voice trails off as I remember Babbo's words of the previous evening. Over dinner, I had shared a recent dream with him in which Beckett and I were together, in London. In the dream we walked through Hyde Park while magpies swooped around us. I hadn't remembered much—the smell of green sap in the air, the diving of the birds. And Beckett's blue eyes, but with a weight behind them, as though I had stumbled beyond the blue sea and reached a vast landscape of mudflats. When I finished recounting my dream, I looked at Babbo. He was blinking hard and I saw his lashes were wet with tears. He told me Beckett had left Ireland to take a talking cure in London. Now. Doing the same thing as I am. At the same time. And for a minute I wondered if our destinies were still entwined. But Babbo said not. He said I had to let Beckett go.

"What did you see happening to Mr. Beckett?" Doctor Jung points to the framed mandala. "Look in there, it might help you."

I peer into the jewel-colored image, but all I can see are repeating whirls like writhing serpents. Where is Beckett? Where are my memories? The shifting darkness is coming for me, closing over me. I clutch at the doctor's arm, panicked.

He eases me into the armchair. "Deep breaths, Miss Joyce. Take your time."

I sit with my head in my hands, breathing deeply and slowly, feeling the oxygen dragging reluctantly into my lungs.

"What did you see happening to Mr. Beckett?" He repeats his question deliberately and loudly, gesturing into the mandala again.

"He was becoming obsessed with Babbo." I frown, trying to make sense of my flailing thoughts, my disintegrating memories. "I could see Giorgio making his escape with Mrs. Fleischman. And Beckett falling into his place. Babbo thought very highly of him. He was starting to see him as a—a son."

"And that would have made Mr. Beckett like a brother to you?" The doctor's voice is suddenly so soft I have to strain to hear him.

I ignore his question. There's a chill creeping through me and I wish I had my fur coat on.

"Where is my fur coat, Doctor?"

"You didn't bring it today, Miss Joyce. Have you lost it again?"

I bridle at his words. "No!"

"So. You tried to tell your father you couldn't go to England. But you still went?"

"I know what you're thinking." I recall with sudden clarity the word in his notebook. "You're thinking I had no backbone, no spine. That I just keeled over and did as they bid. You're thinking I'm no better than an—an insect!"

"Indeed I am not, Miss Joyce. I am merely trying to understand your motives. Did you say goodbye to Mr. Beckett?"

"Not in person. Not sapling to sapling." I smile to myself at our old joke. "There was no time. But I telephoned him at the university. He said I should go. He said Babbo needed me. He said I was Babbo's muse and no genius should be denied his muse." I stand up, suddenly needing to feel taller, needing to unfold my guts and push back my shoulder blades. "And he said Babbo was in constant pain. In his eyes. His stomach. And too blind to be unaccompanied—and that it was too much for my mother. You see, he cared very much for my father."

Doctor Jung clasps his hands behind his back and looks at me, as though he's examining a favorite painting in a gallery. "So your beloved Beckett was prepared to sacrifice you too? Even after what had passed between you?"

"He said he'd write to me. That he'd be in Paris when I got back." I recall his voice, how it had reached to me down the telephone wires, comforting and consoling. I sink back into the armchair, suddenly drained and wearied and cold. Why didn't I bring my fur coat? Why did I come in evening dress?

"Do you like my frock, Doctor?" I spread out my legs so he can see the full width of the skirt, the swathes of red satin that have been used to make this exquisite evening gown.

He looks at his pocket watch. "Why not wear evening dress at eleven thirty A.M.? Indeed, why not?"

"It's for my father. To inspire him. A final inspiration before he leaves Zurich." I stand up and give a little twirl, so that the skirt spills out around me. "I will dance again, won't I, Doctor? I mean proper dancing, not just jigging with Babbo. I want to dance onstage again, like I used to." I triple-step past his desk, swinging my hips and clicking my fingers to create a beat.

"Anything is possible, Miss Joyce."

"I have to go now. Babbo and I are lunching together. Then

we have an appointment with Doctor Naegeli. The blood tests I told you about." I stop dancing and reach for my hat.

"Ah yes, the syphilis tests. I wish you luck, Miss Joyce." He walks with me toward the door. As he puts his hand on the door handle, he turns to me and says, "I *can* cure you, Miss Joyce. Of that I am certain. I *can* cure you."

12

AUGUST 1929

ENGLAND

It was in Torquay that Beckett haunted me most. When I looked at the cliffs, I saw his craggy face. And when I watched the sea from my window, I was reminded of his eyes and the line of his collarbones. I watched the gray water and imagined the arc of his white-gold body splitting the waves. When Babbo brought me a pale-pink freckled shell, I ran my fingers through its interior, remembered the dip at the base of Beckett's throat, how it had inflamed me with love and desire.

When I wasn't thinking of Beckett, I was longing to dance. I looked at the curved spine of the bay with its sweep of golden sand and wished it would stop raining so I could dance barefoot from end to end. I watched the foaming seahorses and churning waves and thought about composing a ballet in which I would perform a drowning sailor saved by white-maned seahorses. I studied the shifting colors of the ocean and promised myself I'd sketch out costumes in oyster blue, as soon as I'd helped Mama to settle in.

But the pleasure I took in these small fantasies came to an end one damp afternoon when Mrs. Fleischman arrived. I was looking out the window of the suite I was sharing with Mama and Babbo. Giorgio had gone to meet Mrs. Fleischman at the station, and the two of them returned in a taxicab. They stepped out and loitered at the front of the hotel, presumably waiting for her trunks and hatboxes. I could see Giorgio twirling his cane and looking very pleased with himself, and Mrs. Fleischman looking coy and haughty at the same time. She had on a Chanel dress that clung to every roll of well-nourished flesh and draped expensively over her vigorous hips. I watched her open her handbag, take out her purse, and give Giorgio a wad of what I assumed were English pound notes. Mama was fussing around the suite, asking "Is Giorgio back yet?" and I could hear Babbo's crayon scraping as he wrote.

"They've just arrived," I said, gesturing vaguely at the gray sky. "She's wearing a Chanel dress." Immediately I regretted my words.

Mama rushed to the window, craning over my shoulder to see Mrs. Fleischman's outfit. She began fiddling with the window latch, all the time staring greedily down at the hotel entrance. And at that very moment I saw something that made me wince and blanch. Because Mama saw it too.

Giorgio stood there, flicking through the notes Mrs. Fleischman had given him as though he was counting them or checking they were the right currency. Then she twisted around her rolled parasol and hooked its ivory handle into the top pocket of Giorgio's jacket. Mama gasped. "What on earth is she doing? She'll ruin his new jacket!"

I wanted to push Mama away, but it was too late. Besides which, I had frozen. I couldn't move. I couldn't even blink. So the two of us watched in horror as Mrs. Fleischman pulled Giorgio to her using her parasol. Even Giorgio looked faintly surprised, and I saw him gesture up at our window. But it was too late. She had pulled him to her, unhooked the parasol, and put her arms around his neck. And now she was nuzzling his neck and had her hands inside his jacket in such an intimate and familiar way that nothing I said could have excused or explained it.

"Sweet Jesus! Blessed Mother o' Mary! How long has this been goin' on?" Mama turned to me, her top lip curled in disgust. "Jim—come quick! Giorgio and Mrs. Fleischman are . . . are . . ." She gave a small strangled cry.

Babbo hobbled to the window and peered out. "Are what?"

"Lovers," I said with a grim satisfaction. For once, Mama would turn her displeasure on Giorgio rather than me. For once, I had done nothing wrong. This time Giorgio would be in trouble. And Mrs. Fleischman too. Big trouble! I silently thanked Mrs. Fleischman for being so indiscreet.

"Oh," said Babbo blandly. "I can't see anything. Are they fornicating on the hotel steps?"

"This is no laughin' matter," choked Mama. "She's my age and she's married and she has a babby!"

"But she is rich." Babbo coughed delicately and began polishing his glasses with his handkerchief, bunching it tightly between his spidery fingers.

"What does that matter? She's snared our Giorgio!"

"No doubt he will tire of her monetary charms."

"And her wrinkles and her saggin' flesh," added Mama bitterly.

"Indeed, Nora. Paris is full of charming young ladies. I suggest we let it run its course."

"If you think I'm not sayin' anything, you're wrong. I'll not have any mischief here, in this hotel, under me own nose." Mama gave a stifled sob and rubbed angrily at her eyes with her fists. "My Giorgio! 'Tis why he's been out so much and never at home. And her all done up like a dog's dinner! Oh, my Giorgio!"

"She has a husband and a son to contend with too. No doubt Giorgio will tire of the competition." Babbo put a consoling hand on Mama's arm and tried to guide her away from the window. But she refused to move and kept wiping her eyes and looking down at the hotel steps where Mrs. Fleischman now had her head on Giorgio's chest as though she were a doctor listening to his heartbeat.

"Nothin' but an old tart! A strumpet . . . Mutton dressed as lamb. Not an ounce o' shame!" She took Babbo's handkerchief from him and pressed it to her red, watery eyes.

"Now, now. It will run its course. Let's not interfere, Nora. We forget he is twenty-three."

But then Mama seemed to notice my presence, and she turned on me viciously. "All this goin' on behind me back and you knew it! You knew it!"

"Hush, Nora. My Cassandra may have had a premonition, but that doesn't mean it is her fault Giorgio is dallying with Mrs. Fleischman. If indeed he is." Babbo made soothing motions with his hands, stroking at the air. But his words only made Mama angrier than ever.

"So how long has this been goin' on, Cassandra?" She sneered. "And what exactly have they been doin'? Have they copulated? Have they?"

"Nora!"

"She pulled the wool over me eyes. She's lied to me. Me own daughter! Tell me, Cassandra—have they fucked?"

"Nora—calm yourself." And Babbo's words were so sharp and commanding that Mama fell against his chest with a low, ragged moan. I drew back, shocked and confounded by the harshness of her words. My blood had stopped moving and turned to ice, and I could feel my teeth biting down on my tongue. And inside me, I felt something tugging, plucking at my intestines . . . her rage, the image of Giorgio copulating, fucking. My stomach started to churn.

"She is upset," Babbo mouthed to me over Mama's weeping head. "Go and warn your brother."

* * *

MRS. FLEISCHMAN STAYED for five days, and during that time Mama preserved a cold hauteur. At meal times she fretted ostentatiously over Giorgio, making sure he ate enough, checking the waiters kept his glass topped up, fetching his cigarettes when he left them in his room, picking up his napkin when it slipped to the floor. But toward Mrs. Fleischman her air of frigid aversion didn't change. And her silence said everything. Giorgio left early with Mrs. Fleischman, saying he had an unexpected singing competition to prepare for. A lie, but I couldn't blame him. Toward me, Mama maintained her sense of wounded betrayal. But she didn't call me Cassandra again, and she never, ever used the word "fuck" again. Not in my presence.

By then the weather had cleared up, and I longed to get out and dance on the beach. But every time I tried to slip off on my own, Babbo or Mama or their Flattering friends would call out for me. I was needed to help Mama choose a hat or to accompany Mrs. Flatterer along the seafront. Please could I read to Babbo or escort him to the beach to take the air, or pop to the post office with a parcel? These endless, tiresome errands infuriated me, but on the few occasions when I protested, Mama snapped at me, and Babbo begged me to be gentle with her, blaming the huge shock she'd suffered over the discovery of Giorgio's affair.

Mama was convinced that a good long break was exactly what I needed and repeated this to anyone who'd listen, while issuing a constant stream of orders and instructions to me. All I could think was that I needed a break from her and her endless errands. I barely had time to write to Beckett, although he sent me several postcards from Germany. And then Babbo fell over a wall and I had to keep him company on the beach while he lay there playing with the pebbles and asking, over and over, if I'd had any premonitions of him tumbling from a wall. When he suggested I dance on the sand in my bathing costume, I tried a few pliés and ran my feet through their positions. But in his most piteous voice, he said, "What about your Isadora Duncan dancing?" I wasn't in the mood, so I helped him arrange pebbles in tight whorls instead. Emir's turbans, he called them.

Slowly, inexorably, my muscles slackened and my strength diminished. My body was atrophying. And at the back of my mind, Madame's parting words lay festering. What had she meant when she said if I couldn't be strong with my family, I may not have the strength for ballet? It was only after several sleepless nights that I suddenly understood Madame's words. In her veiled Russian way, she was trying to tell me I didn't have the talent or the physical strength for classical ballet. On the train home I experienced another moment of clarity and decision. I had to prove Madame wrong. And there was only one way to do this. I had to remove myself from the suffocating, clawing influence of my family. It was time to realize my destiny, to take control of my fate. It was time to marry.

* * *

IT WAS MARVELOUS to be back in Paris. After the damp, gray beaches of England, I could barely contain my joy at returning to the city I now thought of as home. The boulevards were strewn with the hollow, spiked shells of fallen chestnuts, and the leaves on the trees were starting to bronze and curl. And yet the city gave an impression of rebelliousness, as if it didn't give a damn whether winter was coming or not.

It even felt good to be back at Robiac Square, tinkering on the piano, dancing in front of my full-length mirror, sleeping in my own bed, eating breakfast with my hair unbrushed. Beckett appeared most afternoons, and it seemed to me that his piercing eyes lingered a little longer and our hallway chats were a little more intimate. As if our tumblings in the parlor had awakened something in him. Only when Mama was around did he revert to his old stooping and shy self.

"I can't live out of a suitcase," I explained one afternoon, shortly after we'd returned. Beckett had arrived earlier than expected so I'd managed to steer him into the parlor for a quick cup of English Breakfast tea. "Mama and Babbo love staying in hotels. They love packing and unpacking and moving from place to place, ferry to train to motorcar to hotel."

"And you don't?" Beckett sat perched on the edge of the

sofa, three volumes of Shakespeare carefully aligned on his lap.

"They do it with such ease, so effortlessly. I hate the endless packing and unpacking and not knowing what the next hotel will be. It makes dancing impossible. Babbo can write on trains and ferries, but I can't practice, can I? And I loathe all the dressing up." I gave a deep sigh, threw myself dramatically back against the sofa, stared at the ceiling.

"Dressing up?"

"Having to dress for breakfast, having to dress for dinner. Always having to look the part. I don't want my life to be so . . . so unsettled. Or so much about appearances." I twisted my head to look at Beckett. He'd started to dress like Babbo. He'd bought a pair of patent leather shoes with pointed toes, like Babbo's. They were too small for him. I could tell they pinched his toes. Dancers spot things like that.

"Oh, I see." Beckett leaned forward, dropped a cube of sugar into his tea, and stirred it thoughtfully.

"I need space to dance. Preferably the same space each day. And a gramophone and my dance shoes. Mama doesn't understand that." I shrugged hopelessly. I wanted to give Beckett some idea of the life I hoped to have as Mrs. Beckett. It was important he understood the requirements of a dancer.

I pulled myself up and edged closer to him. "I feel much better now I'm home, and with you, and dancing again. My equilibrium is quite restored!"

"Madame Egorova welcomed you back, then?" Beckett's gaze shifted beyond me to Babbo's wall of portraits.

"Yes, but I know she's watching me closely. And I'm practicing like crazy." I looked at him again. He needed to know I had no intention of giving up my dancing. He needed to know that, as Mrs. Beckett, I would continue to dance. I didn't want a life like Mama's—sorting laundry and buying shoes and having my hair waved. No, I was a dancer and that was that. But Beckett was staring intensely at Babbo's ancestral portraits, as if to imprint them on his memory.

"Although Mama and Babbo had me running hither and thither, my days felt quite empty without dance. I don't think it's good for me—not to dance." I said this very emphatically. It wasn't only that Beckett needed to be clear about the future Mrs. Beckett's requirements. It was also that two months without dance had helped me articulate its importance in my life, and I wanted to sound out my thoughts on Beckett. I knew he would understand. "Dance gives my life purpose and meaning, of course. But it's more than that. When I dance I experience myself differently. As a different person, as different people."

But Beckett didn't seem to hear. I saw his eyes darting toward Babbo's study door and back to the Shakespeare plays cradled in his lap. Then he said, "Did your father enjoy England?"

I didn't pursue the topic of my dancing. I could see he had something on his mind. "Oh, he sat in pubs listening to the conversations of strangers, and he worked on his book, and saw another eye doctor in London, and played with a lot of pebbles on the beach."

"Pebbles?" Beckett's gaze swiveled back to me.

"You know—stones. The hotel in Torquay was like a palace. It had its own orchestra and an electric lift. They loved it—you know how they like the grand style. Mama hasn't stopped talking about it. I preferred Cambridge. Babbo made a recording of himself there, reading from *Work in Progress.*" I paused and gave a clipped laugh. "Someone described his voice as 'liquid and soft with undercurrents of gurgle.'"

"Did they now?" Beckett chuckled into his teacup.

"Enough about us. How were your aunt and uncle?"

"Fine." He coughed lightly. "Your father's asked me to translate some of *Work in Progress* into French."

My heart gave a little skip. "Babbo thinks you're wonderful, Sam. So you'll be here more than ever?"

Beckett nodded and then sank into a brooding silence, staring despondently into his tea.

"I can help you. It won't be easy to translate, but we'll manage." I stretched out and gave his forearm a reassuring squeeze, relieved to discover what was on his mind.

"You're very kind, Lucia. Very sweet." He ran his hand across his face. Oh, how I wanted to reach out and take him in my arms. He seemed so tired all of a sudden, as if the prospect of translating Babbo's work was weighing him down. "I have to go back to Ireland next week," he added. "I have to sort out the renewal of my contract and see my parents."

"When will you be back?" I took a sip of tea, leaned over him so my breasts brushed his chest, put my teacup down on the table, and sat back. Beckett blinked and swallowed so extravagantly his Adam's apple rippled in his throat.

"November."

And then Babbo appeared, his eyes all red and oozing. Mr. Beckett leapt up and the two of them sloped off into the study.

I picked up Beckett's teacup and put my lips to the rim, exactly where his lips had been. How right it felt! How happy I was to be back in Paris, with Beckett, with Madame Egorova. I would miss Beckett when he returned to Ireland, of course. But that gave me more time to perfect my marital plans, to make them foolproof and flawless. Yes, everything was edging forward perfectly.

* * *

I NOTICED THE heavy perfume of the roses first, and then their color, yellow like marzipan. Only when I was close enough to touch them did I see Mrs. Fitzgerald peering out from behind, her eyes wheeling up and down the stairs. I was just leaving Madame Egorova's studio and Mrs. Fitzgerald was arriving, holding her huge bouquet like a shield in front of her face.

"What beautiful roses," I exclaimed.

"Oh, these are for Madame. I bring her a gift every day. Usually flowers but not always." Mrs. Fitzgerald's voice was gushing and breathless. "I can't bear to think of the great

Madame Lubov Egorova living in poverty. I just can't bear it! She's the Princess Troubetsky, don't you know?"

I nodded, nonplussed.

"And now she lives in poverty. Have you been to her tiny house? She has no bathroom! I just can't bear to think of her like that!" Mrs. Fitzgerald was blinking hard behind her roses, as though she were fighting back tears.

"How are your classes going, Mrs. Fitzgerald?"

"Look at this, Lucia! Just look at this." She thrust the roses at me. "Here—hold these! You gotta see this. You really gotta see this." She slipped off her embroidered pumps, unpeeled a stocking from one leg, and waved her foot at me. Her toenails were so infected with nail fungus they looked like miniature oyster shells, ridged and discolored. And on her little toe was a septic corn, red and angry, leaking thick blond pus. "I dance for eight hours a day. Eight hours, Lucia. Other dancers in my classes are dancing until the blood pours out of their ballet shoes."

Mrs. Fitzgerald saw me recoil. It wasn't that I was squeamish—a weeping corn and nail fungus were nothing I hadn't seen before. Rather it was her manner. As though she was trying to frighten me in some way. She put her stocking and shoe back on, then snatched the roses from me.

"Madame demands total dedication," she continued, her American drawl lifting and dipping as she spoke. "You can't be a ballerina without it. I do nothing but dance and sleep now. If you really want to dance, that's the sacrifice you gotta make." She looked around the stairwell constantly as she spoke, as though she was checking to make sure no one was listening. And then she lowered her voice and beckoned me to her until I was so close all I could smell were the yellow roses.

"But I'm not too old—don't let anyone tell you that. I've been invited to join the San Carlo Opera Ballet Company in Naples. With a solo role in *Aida* as my debut! What d'you think?" There was an exultant light in her eyes, making them shine almost unnaturally through the roses.

"Will you go?"

She shook her head. "Oh no! Scott has forbidden it. He says it's out of the question." She paused, her face wistful for a second. "I'll wait for a role with the Ballets Russes. My dream is to dance with the Ballets Russes. They had their talent scouts here last week." Her feverish eyes flickered around the stairwell again. "I think they spotted me, Lucia! I must go. Madame will be waiting." And she was gone, skittering up the stairs, clutching her beautiful yellow roses.

As I walked home, I kept thinking about her infected corn. And the implicit meaning of her words—about her husband forbidding her to take the job of ballerina with the prestigious San Carlo Opera Ballet Company. I should have been inspired by Mrs. Fitzgerald's success. But I barely thought of this. I thought only of Mr. Fitzgerald's insistence that she turn down the chance to dance in *Aida*. I thought of her acquiescence and it filled me with foreboding. Perhaps married women were no more liberated than unmarried women. Perhaps my marriage plan was not as foolproof as I thought . . .

* * *

TWO WEEKS AFTER my meeting with Mrs. Fitzgerald, a letter arrived, throwing me into disarray and shattering my equilibrium once again.

Mama, Babbo, and I were having breakfast, Babbo crunching noisily on his toast while Mama scraped out the bottom of the jam jar with a pickle spoon. I carefully prised open the envelope with a paperknife, assuming it was from one of my childhood friends. A letter fell out, on paper as thin as silk, and written in an unfamiliar hand. I read it quickly and at first I couldn't believe it. So I read it again and then again, until my fingers were shaking with excitement. It was from Isadora Duncan's sister, Elizabeth Duncan, whose dancing school I attended every summer.

"Who's that letter from?" Mama demanded. "You've been reading it long enough."

Babbo glanced up, muttering, "A letter to a king about a treasure from a cat."

Mama rolled her eyes. "Who's it from, Lucia?"

I didn't tell her it was from Elizabeth Duncan, offering me a job as a professional dance teacher at her school in Darmstadt, teaching German girls modern dance and movement. All I could think was that I, who was treated as a child by so many, was being offered a real job—with payment.

"I can choose my own clothes," I shouted. My first teaching job. My first proper job offer!

"What in God's name are you talking about now, Lucia?

Is that from one o' your Zurich friends?" Mama leaned to-ward me, as if to snatch the letter from my hand. I drew back, pressing it against my chest.

"You need some new clothes, Lucia. That nightgown is torn at the hem, and you know we don't like you having breakfast in your nightwear. Sure you're letting yourself go. Why haven't you brushed your hair yet?"

"It's a job offer!" I shouted, jubilantly waving the letter in front of Babbo and ignoring Mama. "Mrs. Duncan wants me to teach at her dance school in Germany. She's offering me a salary."

Babbo looked up, his eyes wide with surprise. Mama put her slice of toast down and stared at me.

"She wants me to start in four weeks. I'll live in the dance school with her and the other teachers and I can come back for Christmas." My voice petered out. Mama's face was black. Babbo's eyes, magnified by his thick lenses, were numb. His mouth twisted as though he wanted to speak but couldn't find the words.

"Show me that letter," demanded Mama, reaching out for it again.

I passed it to her. She read it silently and then offered it to Babbo.

"I can't possibly read this, Nora," he said in a very quiet voice, putting the letter back on the table.

"'Tis out o' the question." Mama's lips were pursed, her arms tightly folded across her chest. "Your father is almost a blind man. He needs you here. Giorgio's no use—he's always off with Mrs. Fancy Pants Fleischman. If you go, it'll kill your father, that it will."

"What about your ballet?" Babbo's voice was distant, as though he were speaking from the end of a long tunnel. The purple crescents beneath his eyes darkened.

"This offer means I'm a good dancer, I'm good enough to teach. I can always come back to Paris afterward."

"But you won't be a ballet dancer?" Babbo took his spectacles off, rubbed his rheumy eyes, pressed his eyelids closed.

"I . . . I suppose I can't do both. But I can pick up the ballet again—I'm not too old."

"Sure this is ridiculous." Mama pushed back her chair noisily. "The whole dance thing is ridiculous. It's what rich girls do so they can walk with airs and graces, as your father knows only too well. So let's be putting a stop to this job talk—right now. You're not Anna Pavlova and you never will be." She stood up and started stacking the plates with such anger I could barely hear Babbo over the crashing of crockery and the clanging of cutlery.

"It would be very hard for us, Lucia. Darmstadt is a long way." Babbo passed the letter back to me, his hand trembling.

"'Tis bloody selfish. How can your father finish his book without you here? He's been working on it for seven years. Seven years! Our job is to help him, not to waltz off without a care in the world."

"If it's more money you want, we'll give you more. If you want to choose your own clothes, I'm sure your mother will let you, won't you, Nora?"

Mama tossed her head with contempt but said nothing. She was screwing the lids back onto the jam pots with such vehemence, I put a hand protectively to my throat.

"This isn't about clothes or money," I whispered, shrinking beneath the full force of Mama's outrage and Babbo's hurt.

"Well, and what is it about, then?" Mama put her hands on her hips and glared at me.

"It's about me—my life. My . . . my . . . independence. I want to dance."

"Yes, yes, it's always about you, Lucia. You'll get your independence soon enough, when we both keel over dead from your selfish ways. Talk some sense into her, Jim." Mama walked out, slamming the door behind her with such vigor the teacups rattled in their saucers.

Babbo and I sat silently staring at the curling toast in the silver toast rack. The very silence seemed to resonate with Babbo's fear and anxiety.

"You can see how distressed your mother is, Lucia. It would be insufferable for her to be alone with me for months on end. And here in Paris you can come to the theater with us and watch all the best dance and ballet."

"I don't want to watch it—I want to do it. I'm a dancer. A good dancer!"

"Your mother thinks dancing onstage makes you nervous." Babbo paused and ran his hands over his hair. "You might find bookbinding more calming, more suited to your disposition."

"Oh yes! Bookbinding!" I gave a hollow laugh. Why did it always come back to bookbinding? Why could they not see the value of dance?

"Or . . . or drawing. You could illustrate my work." There was a peculiar light in Babbo's pink-veined eyes, as though this idea had just come to him, an epiphany that would solve everything. He leaned across the table and took my hand. "Can you imagine that, *mia bella bambina*? You and me working together? I'll hire you a drawing teacher. I know just the man." He smiled broadly as though our conversation about my job offer had never happened.

I looked at him blankly, speechless. I couldn't understand how, in such a short time, we had moved from discussing my prospects as a dance teacher to arranging drawing lessons. I was so stunned I couldn't find words to answer him.

He stood up and cleared his throat. "I'll telephone Alexander . . . Mr. Calder today. And I'll ask Miss Steyn to show you 'round the art galleries. Your mother thinks it would be good for you to have friends who aren't dancers." Babbo nodded his head energetically as he left the room. At the door, he suddenly turned back and added, "And, of course, Beckett is here in Paris. I doubt he could endure Darmstadt." I heard his study door open and close. Then I heard the front door shut as my mother went out. Silence.

I found a sheet of paper and a pen. I wrote and posted my reply to Elizabeth Duncan that very morning.

* * *

I COULDN'T SLEEP that night. It wasn't just the storm rag-
ing outside, but the litany of questions that taunted me
and nagged at me. Questions about my own fortitude,
my determination, my inability to "be strong with my
family" as Madame Egorova had put it. I thought too of
Mrs. Fitzgerald's dedication to ballet in the face of
Mr. Fitzgerald's opposition. And then more questions—
about Giorgio and Mrs. Fleischman, about Babbo's book
and my role as his muse, about Mama's hostility, and, of
course, about Beckett. By deciding not to go to Darmstadt,
at least I had more time with Beckett. Surely my parents
couldn't stop me from marrying him? And when we married, would he also try and stop my dancing? Would I be
able to stand up to my beloved Beckett? These questions
plagued me, tormented me, until finally the wind died
down and I fell into a fitful sleep.

The next morning, as I was stretching at the barre after
my ballet class, Madame Egorova beckoned me over to the
corner of the studio. She was sitting on the piano stool, her
small hands folded neatly in her lap and her hair pulled back
so severely the corners of her eyes reached into her hairline.
The pianist had just left and the other dancers were untying
their ballet shoes, shaking out their hair, and ambling toward the dressing room.

"Lucia, this is your third month here, yes?"

I nodded warily. "Yes, Madame." No doubt she'd noticed
the stiffness of my body at the barre. The anxious thoughts
of last night had exhausted me, interfering with my sense of

rhythm and depleting my energy. I lifted my chin and tried to inject a little lightness into my body.

"You are not working hard enough." She tapped her foot impatiently on the floor. "I have been watching you. I know you did not practice on your holidays."

"I'm sorry, Madame. I had to look after my parents. My father fell over a wall." My voice trailed into stunned silence.

"You did not have energy today, Lucia. You were . . . flagging. Yes, flagging." She screwed up her glittering black eyes and stared at me.

"I didn't sleep well last night. I know I'm still catching up from the summer, but I want to carry on. I'm committed to ballet, Madame." I looked down at my feet still in their ballet shoes, the ribbons lying in limp pools beside them.

"Did you think about what I said before you left, Lucia?"

"Y-yes, Madame," I stuttered. "I want to prove I can do it. I'm just tired today and my muscles are very sore. I'm sorry, Madame."

"You have fallen behind, Lucia. Ballerinas do not have holidays. They dance until they are this far from death." She held up her thumb and index finger to reveal a sliver of light between them. "You must go down a class. You will dance with the children."

I felt the blood draining from my face. My legs started quaking.

"Did you hear what I said, Lucia?" Madame was looking at me with concern. "You are not feeling well?"

I shook my head dumbly. The studio seemed to be tilting

and my lungs felt drained of air. I heard her telling me to lie on the floor. I felt her hands on my arms, gently pushing me down.

"And breathe deeply, Lucia. Lie still and breathe."

The room was spinning as I felt my body crumple and slip to the floor. When I came around, Madame was leaning over me, distorted and huge, as though reflected in a fish-eye mirror.

"You fainted," she said. I sat up slowly. How weakened I was. How frail. For a second I didn't know where I was. But then everything swam back into focus. I was in an empty dance studio with a wall of mirrors and a barre and windows that looked out on treetops. Curling yellowed leaves were floating down and hitting the grime-streaked glass. Above the trees, a weak autumnal sun struggled behind a blanket of dirty gray cloud. The sounds of traffic rose from the street below—bleating motorcar horns, squealing tires, the clatter of horse hooves and cart wheels, bicycle bells and the piercing note of a gendarme's whistle.

"Are you eating? You dancers never eat." Madame fished some violet creams out of a bag and gave them to me. "A gift from Mrs. Fitzgerald. Now I have to teach. You must stay here until you are strong enough to go home."

Dazed, I nodded and closed my eyes again. Her words reverberated around the studio, skidding off the mirrors, slurring across the floorboards, slinking along the barre—"You must go down a class . . .You will dance with the children." She has seen the truth about me, I thought. She has found me out. That I cannot dance, that I have no discipline, that my body is all wrong for ballet, that I am a child and should be taught with children. I'm not a dancer—I'm a fraud. And Madame has found me out. How stupid and arrogant I'd been. To think I could master ballet. To think I had any talent at all. Had I ever been able to dance? Had I ever possessed a single speck of talent? Babbo too had seen the truth. That was why he wanted me to take up bookbinding. I imagined myself dancing with the little girls, their curious stares stalking me around the studio. No—not dancing, but lumbering, large and ungainly. I heard them whispering about my squint. I saw them pointing at my overgrown breasts, my too-big hips, my legs that won't turn out properly, my oversized feet with their calluses and corns. All of me monstrous and grotesque.

Slowly I stood up. Said goodbye to the studio. Walked down the hall. Down the seven flights of stairs. Into the tiny lobby. I found a sheet of paper and a pen and wrote a short letter to Madame Egorova, thanking her for all she had done. Put it in an envelope. Wrote her name on the front. Marked it "Private." Left it on the side table, propped against a vase of wilting chrysanthemums.

It was only when I reached the Jardin du Luxembourg that tears started to trickle down my face and the enormity of my decision hit me, like a blast of icy air. I stumbled home and spent the next fortnight crying in my room. Mama left trays of food outside my door. Babbo called through the keyhole, begging to know what was wrong. Eventually I answered him, my voice smothered in its own sobs.

"I don't have the physique to be a ballet dancer. I've wasted my talent. And now I can't go back. I've thrown away years and years of hard work. My life's over. And no one understands. That's why I'm crying. Now leave me alone!"

This may be the last day of the year when I can get out in my little sailboat, Miss Joyce." Doctor Jung has watched me walk down the long tree-lined path to the door of his house and is now ushering me through the garden toward the small boathouse on the edge of the lake. "I only take out my favorite patients." He pauses and smiles at me. "The ones I can trust not to throw themselves overboard."

"What makes you think I won't do that?" I take his hand and step into the sailboat, relieved I'm not wearing evening dress today.

"We will sail out onto the lake and then continue our conversation. I have your memoir right here." He taps the pocket of his jacket.

"How different everything looks from the water." I look back at the green shutters and the iron trellis work on the windows of his large, square house. The trees on the bank are in full autumn color now—copper and bronze and gold. On the lake, boats and ferries cut white foaming furrows through the water while black-headed gulls wheel and turn above us.

"Yes, you see things quite differently from here." The doctor pulls out my manuscript and puts it on the bench beside him where I watch the wind lick at it. "Don't worry, Miss Joyce, it won't blow away." He fiddles with the sails and then puts a large stone on my memoir.

"Where would you like to start today? Doctor Naegeli, perhaps?" He pulls a rope toward him and then loosens it as the boat starts to turn. I look up toward Zurich, lying like a scab at the end of the lake.

"I told Babbo any syphilis was my fault—only my fault. For things I'd done. Bad things."

"And what did your father say?"

"He said it was all his fault. But I don't believe him. He's so good, so pure."

Doctor Jung frowned. "Tell me about all the illnesses your father's had. And about his eyes. He's almost blind, you say?"

"He gets recurrent attacks of iritis. His irises swell up. Doctors wanted him to take arsenic, but that can kill you and he knew someone who went into a coma after taking it. But he also gets conjunctivitus and glaucoma and something called episcleritus and something else called blep . . . blep." I put my hand to my temple. Why can't I remember the name?

"Blepharitis?"

"Yes. And fatigue and nervous exhaustion. Babbo says he deserves it all, on account of his many iniquities, but I think it's my fault." I look up, past the doctor, at the hills rising in waves behind Zurich.

"No, Miss Joyce. It's not your fault." Doctor Jung lowers his voice, as if he's talking to himself. "Arsenic. Boils . . . Does he get boils? Loss of appetite?"

"Yes, sometimes. But the good news, Doctor, is that Professor Naegeli found no sign of syphilis in my blood."

"Ah, so now it's down to psychoanalysis to cure you. We need to uncover your pathogenic secrets."

"Pathogenic?"

"Deeply repressed secrets. Things that have happened to you and been locked away and are now making you ill. Things you must face up to." Even out here on the water, his eyes probe me mercilessly.

"But if they're locked away, how can I face up to them?"

"Keep writing down your dreams. The dream is a little hidden door in the innermost secret recess of the psyche. Better still, paint them or draw them. Can you do that?" He strokes his moustache, watches me.

"What did you think of my memoir, Doctor?"

"Why did you turn down the job as dance teacher?"

"Babbo needed me. Not to accompany him like a blind man's dog, but to provide substance and inspiration for his book. My dancing was a source of revelation to him."

"You stayed to continue as his muse?"

"I never spoke of being a muse. I knew my mother wouldn't like it. But all the time I was growing up, Babbo's eyes were on me, watching me, examining me. That was why I slept in my clothes." I hesitate. Shiver. Coldness is spreading slowly through my chest as though the temperature of my blood has suddenly fallen.

"Pray continue, Miss Joyce."

Beyond the white sail a heron dives and surfaces with a small fish flailing in its beak.

"Sometimes I thought his eyes were covetous. His head would perch sideways, like a bird's, and I knew he wasn't just watching but listening and recording." I see the heron fly to the bank, disappear in the trees.

"No doubt, he was interested in what you had to say, like any good parent." Doctor Jung leans out of the boat, scoops up a handful of water and drinks noisily from his cupped palm.

"Oh no! I was never under any illusion about that. He thought my words, or the rhythm of them, might be useful. He thought my dreams could help him too, especially when he started writing about the dark night of the soul. *Work in Progress* is a dream, you see. He uses everything around him, everything that inspires him."

Doctor Jung dries his hand on his handkerchief. "When did you first know you were your father's muse?"

I look over the edge of the boat at the water, so green and clear I can see tiny fish meandering around us, their scales glimmering as they catch the light. When did I discover I was Babbo's muse? Yes, that was it. The evening at Robiac Square when Babbo gave his first reading from *Work in Progress*. I was seventeen. He invited several of his Flatterers to come and hear the few pages it had taken him a thousand hours to write. Everyone had sat at Babbo's feet while he read, their faces uplifted as if in supplication. I flitted in and out serving drinks and helping my mother prepare the food we were to eat afterward. She stayed out of earshot, saying she had "heard it all before." I remember the melodious quality of his words and his thin, high voice rising and falling. But then, with a jolt of awareness, I realized he was talking about me, he had written about me and I was part of what was surely to be the greatest novel ever written. My gut twisted. I had to stop myself from crying out, "But that's me! That's mine!" I'd felt a peculiar and inexplicable sense of violation, as though he had taken something from me.

I don't tell Doctor Jung this. Instead I say, "He used my words. Kitten said I was lucky to be a muse." I run my fingers through the cool green water. I'm starting to feel tired and weary. All this talk of muses. What has being Babbo's muse done for me? It has imprisoned me, manacled me to him. And yet it's all I have left now. Everything else has fallen away.

"It's true. Many artists have muses and it's generally considered a great honor." He pushes his wire-framed glasses up onto his forehead and watches me.

"My father is a genius, as great as Rabelais or Dante."

I push back my shoulders, letting the lake air wrap itself around me. "He's fêted wherever he goes."

"Do you envy that?"

I say nothing. Sometimes I remember the swell of pride and the glow of success, the prolonged applause and the cries of appreciation that followed so many of my performances— at the Bal Bullier, at the Théâtre des Champs-Élysées, at the Théâtre du Vieux-Colombier. And yes, it felt good.

"So why did you give up ballet, Miss Joyce?"

"It was too hard. Kitten had been right all along. I was too old for ballet." I pause and look over the edge of the boat, where I catch sight of my reflection in the water. My face looks back at me, shimmying and undulating. And for a confused second, I wonder if I'm dancing again. "I discovered a new form of dance, one that didn't involve going onstage. One that helped people. Have you heard of the Margaret Morris Movement? It was my vocation, really, my dancing destiny. Kitten and I had done a few of her weekend classes, but then Babbo found out she was setting up a school in Paris." I look pointedly at the shore. The boat is starting to rock and sway, jumbling my memories, throwing them against each other until they blur and distort. "Take me back to the jetty," I say imperiously. "You'll have to wait for the next chapter."

"Have you had any more clairvoyant experiences, Miss Joyce?" The doctor moves across the boat and his shifting weight causes it to change direction, so that we're now heading back toward the bank.

I hesitate, and for a few seconds the bottom of the boat seems to suck at my feet as if the boat itself is anchoring me, protecting me from its own pitching and rolling. And I remember last night's dream in which I and Mrs. Fitzgerald and Mrs. Fleischman and Nijinsky sat in a circle wearing straitjackets and weaving baskets from boughs of willow that glowed like jewels. "No," I say, closing my fingers tightly around the side of the boat. "Nothing."

"We are making excellent progress. Now your father has left Zurich, there is no obstacle to your cure." Doctor Jung pulls a rope toward him and the white sail swings violently to one side. "Duck, Miss Joyce."

And as I duck, I decide not to tell him Babbo is still in Zurich, secretly ensconced in the Carlton-Elite Hotel at the huge expense of his patron. No—that is our secret and I will not tell Doctor Jung.

13

OCTOBER 1929

PARIS

Mia bella bambina?" Babbo's voice came through the key-hole of my bedroom door, where I sat in bed wrapped in blankets.

"Go away!"

"I have hired the redoubtable and formidable Mr. Calder, Mr. Alexander Calder, to teach you drawing."

I didn't reply. Instead I pulled the blanket tighter around my hunched shoulders. I didn't want to draw. I wanted to dance. I *needed* to dance, to move.

"I think you will like him, Lucia."

"Is he Irish?" I called, my voice deadened by the blanket that covered my mouth.

"Unlock your door, *mia bella bambina,* and I will reveal all."

"Does Mama like him?"

"No, but that is no impediment."

I lifted my head, letting the blanket fall from my face and shoulders.

"Mr. Calder will instruct you, and then you and I will work together. And Miss Steyn has agreed to show you 'round the picture galleries. Now will you deign to open your door?"

I shook off the blanket and cupped my hands around my mouth. There was to be no misunderstanding about my next request. Locked away in my room, I'd spent many hours in front of my mirror and it had become obvious that my squint was hindering my grand plan of marriage. The strabismus had to go. "Only if you pay for surgery on my eye!"

"I will talk to Doctor Borsch and see what can be done. I promise. Will you unlock your door now?"

I got out of bed, moved to the door, and crouched down so that my mouth was against the iron-rimmed keyhole. "I'm not ready to throw away my talent, Babbo. And I don't want to do bookbinding!"

"I have found somewhere for you to dance, *mia bella bambina*. Please open the door."

"Who with?" I could smell Babbo through the keyhole. Disinfectant and tobacco. Mama must have been dousing one of his abscesses or bathing his eyes. I felt a pang of guilt.

"Miss Margaret Morris has opened a training school not five minutes from here. I have secured you a place."

"Margaret Morris from London?" I stood up, raised my

head, and turned to the window. Light was pushing at the shutters, and outside, crows were cawing in the trees.

"She thinks you will make an excellent teacher of her movement. And I have a letter from Beckett asking after you."

And then I heard Mama's heels coming determinedly toward the door and her voice barking at Babbo: "Leave this to me, Jim. You know nothing about your daughter and nothing about women." She started hammering on the door with the flat of her hand.

"You've been lounging in that bed for nigh on two weeks, Lucia. It's our twenty-fifth wedding anniversary tonight and Miss Beach has arranged us a party. We want you there. Your father's agreed to all your daft demands and I've bought you a new dress."

I moved back from the door, straightened my spine until I was standing tall. Yes, I thought. A fortnight is long enough. I've work to do. Beckett will be returning from Ireland soon. And I need to dance.

"What sort of dress?" I called back.

"You'll love it . . . green silk, dropped waistline, sequined hem. Open the door and I'll bring it in, that I will."

* * *

STELLA STEYN AND I stood in front of a self-portrait by Chardin, in the Louvre. She told me it would make the perfect starting point for our "Discourses on Art." I tried to focus on the picture, on the painter's lined face, the bright blue fabric around his head, but my eyes kept flicking to the oil painting beside it. In the oil painting was a dead pheasant strung up over a table of artichokes, apples, and wineglasses. My eyes met the eyes of the pheasant and for a second it was as though something passed between us.

"Chardin was a very slow painter." Stella's warbling voice pulled me back from the dead bird. "He painted only a very few paintings each year, three or four on average. This self-portrait, he did in his seventies, when he was so blind he couldn't mix oil paints anymore, so he had to use pastels." Stella examined the picture, her eyes just a few inches from the frame.

I tilted my head to one side and then to the other and looked at the portrait. I took a step back and then a step forward, trying to see what it was she found so captivating. Then my eyes darted back to the pheasant again.

"He was a master of still lifes and portraits. Look at how he's captured the light, Lucia." She gestured at the side of Chardin's self-portrait. "And look at his use of color. Even with pastels he's created texture and vibrant hues. Look at the peacock blue on the band 'round his head scarf." Stella gave a sigh replete with contentment. I stared into the glazed eyes of the dangling pheasant.

"Lucia?" She looked at me curiously and pointed to the self-portrait. "Have a closer look."

I narrowed my eyes and tried to focus on Chardin. The

blue band adorning his head was the exact color of Babbo's new smoking jacket. But then my gaze slid back to the pheasant. Something seemed to be moving at the back of its eyes . . . an iridescent light.

"And look at his expression, Lucia, and the way he's dressed. What does that tell you about him?" Stella looked at me with raised eyebrows.

I turned my back on the pheasant. "He looks kind," I said. I could feel the pheasant's eyes boring into my spine.

"Yes, I agree," Stella enthused. "He paints with such feeling. There's no pomposity, is there? There's a humility and an honesty in his face. He never left Paris. He found everything he needed right here."

"Perhaps that isn't so strange," I said. To live in one place, to be born and to die looking at the same vista, hearing the same familiar sounds—a life of repetition, familiarity, constancy. I thought of Beckett's childhood stories, of the garden, orchards, and house his father built. Of how these things cheered me but seemed to repel Beckett. And then I turned back to the pheasant, and its eyes were still upon me, watching me.

"Why d'you keep looking at that picture, Lucia?" Stella sounded snappish.

"I'm not," I lied. "I'm thinking about what you said. About living in one place. Is this the first time you've left Dublin?"

"I was delighted to leave Dublin." Stella turned back to Chardin's self-portrait as though she were talking to him, not me. "Paris is the place to be if you're an artist. Anyway,

I'm not staying here much longer. I've applied to study at the Bauhaus in Germany." She gave a little skip of excitement.

"Oh," I said flatly. I wanted to look at the dead pheasant again, to peer into its eyes, to fathom the light that flickered so peculiarly behind its irises. But I didn't want Stella to think me strange or to tell Babbo that I hadn't behaved in her "Discourse on Art."

"Oh, not just yet, Lucia." She reached out and grabbed my hand. "Don't look so sad. There's lots of time for you to teach me French and me to show you paintings. This is going to be so much fun!"

Stella turned her head back to Chardin's self-portrait and began examining it again, sighing happily as she did so. I turned my head back to the pheasant and our eyes met again.

"Has your father found you a drawing instructor yet?" she asked.

"Oh yes, I've had my first lesson with Mr. Calder."

"Sandy Calder?" There was a splutter in her voice as though I'd said something shocking.

"Yes, he does the amazing mechanical circus. Have you seen it?"

"No," she said, an expression of surprise and confusion on her face.

"Well, I'll take you. Why are you looking at me like that?"

"I know Sandy Calder. He's not a serious artist. He's an engineer." Stella's tone was scornful. "You need to be learning from nature, studying life drawing and painting from models. It seems so flippant to hire him as your drawing master. I must admit I'm very surprised."

"Oh, I rather like him." I tried to suppress the smile his name brought involuntarily to my lips. "He makes me laugh."

"I believe he's engaged to someone in America." Stella looked at me through little screwed-up eyes as though she were examining another painting. "So perhaps he won't be in Paris for much longer."

"He keeps asking me to go to the Coupole with him, so I doubt he's engaged. Of course I won't be unfaithful to Beckett."

"And how is Mr. Beckett?"

"He's in Dublin. We're expecting him back any minute. Of course, Mama doesn't want me to marry an Irishman. She's made that very clear." I rolled my eyes dramatically.

"But *she* did. *She* married an Irishman."

"Yes, well, that's different. Or maybe that's why she doesn't want me to marry one. She thinks they're all drunks."

"Perhaps she doesn't want you to marry a writer with no prospects?"

"Sometimes I don't think she wants me to marry anyone. I don't know what she wants. I know she doesn't want me to dance—she's made that abundantly clear. But when I'm married, I'll dance onstage again. You'll see!" And I thought of my marriage plan and felt my hands curling resolutely into fists.

"You must carry on. You're a marvelous dancer." Stella beamed at me.

"Oh, I haven't given up entirely. I'm training with Margaret Morris to teach her method of movement. It's dance with a practical purpose." I unclenched my fists and put my hands together, fanning out my fingers and rippling them from side to side. "This hand position's called the river."

"How is that practical?" She looked inquiringly at me.

"Miss Morris believes how we move can help children, women in childbirth, physically handicapped people, invalids." Then I lowered my voice and pulled Stella toward me. "What d'you think of my left eye? Look closely, as an artist would. What d'you see?"

Stella looked startled, and I could see her fumbling for words, as if she wasn't sure what to say.

"Babbo's promised me an operation to correct my squint. I think it could be the answer to my prayers." I pushed my palms together and raised my eyes to the ceiling.

"May I ask what you're praying for, Lucia?"

"If my eye was normal, perhaps I could go back to performing again. And it would be easier for Beckett to propose."

"What *are* you talking about?" She stared at me.

"He might be concerned about having children with a squint. He might not want a wife with crossed eyes. Appearances are very important to men." I looked at Stella, and for the first time that morning, I noticed how she looked, what she wore. I saw her black hair in glossy ringlets, her round face, her dark eyes like two black marbles, her arched eyebrows that sat like two obedient black caterpillars above her eyes. She wore a striking outfit in bottle green, with an orange scarf knotted at her throat and a cloche hat to which she had fastened a small bunch of silk flowers, again in vibrant orange. Why hadn't I noticed the boldness and elegance of her outfit earlier? Why had I been so obsessively distracted by the inert eyes of a dead pheasant?

"I think your cast is part of you. It gives you a vulnerability that's rather endearing. I think if a man loved you, he wouldn't mind it." Stella spoke very slowly, as though she was thinking about each word as she chose it.

"Well, I hate it! I can't wait 'til it's gone!" Two old ladies at the other end of the gallery turned and looked at me. Stella gently took my elbow and steered me toward the next room, but not before I'd turned back for a last look at the dead pheasant hanging ignominiously from its ropes.

My lips moved wordlessly. "What are you trying to tell me?" I didn't wait for an answer—I didn't want Stella to report back to Babbo on my idiosyncratic behavior in her "discourse."

"Can you manage another painting or would you rather go home, Lucia?"

I took a deep breath. Why was Stella talking to me as if I were a child? Or an invalid? "Of course I can look at another painting. But I want to look at a painting of hands. Long, thin hands. Male hands . . ."

"Hands?" Stella frowned and gave me an odd stare.

"Yes, bare hands." I didn't tell her about Beckett's hands, the sculpted beauty of his wrists, his knuckles, his tapering fingers. I didn't tell her that I couldn't stop thinking about his hands, those beautiful hands that had held me, fondled me, burned themselves onto my skin. No—that was all mine, and I wouldn't share it with anyone.

14

NOVEMBER 1929

PARIS

By the time Beckett returned to Paris, it was late November and the days had turned dank and cold. While he'd been away, Babbo had become utterly possessed by an Irish opera singer called John O'Sullivan. He was an elderly and cranky man, bitter at his lack of recognition after so many years touring the world's opera houses. But he was in Paris to sing in *William Tell*, and Babbo was determined everyone should see him and acknowledge his vocal "genius."

I was enlisted to write invitations to everyone we knew. Perhaps "invitation" was the wrong word, for as I sat at his desk, pen in hand, it seemed to me that I was writing begging letters—begging, beseeching, cajoling all our friends, all Babbo's Flatterers, anyone we knew in Paris, every journalist Babbo had ever met—to buy tickets to *William Tell*. When I asked him why we were putting so much time and effort into the career of John O'Sullivan, he said it was to help Giorgio's career.

Babbo paced the shadowy room dictating to me: "John O'Sullivan—no, drop the *O*—just say John Sullivan for the love of music—has the greatest human voice I have ever heard." He paused, took off his glasses, and rubbed his swollen eyes.

"You want me to write that? The greatest voice you've ever heard?"

"Lucia, please don't question what I'm writing. It makes me lose my thread." Babbo shook his head impatiently and put his glasses back on. "I do not believe—are you writing this, Lucia?—there can have existed in the past a greater tenor than his, and as for the future, I think it doubtful that human ears"—he paused, groping for the right words—"will ever hear such another until the Archangel Michael sings his grand aria in the last act."

I took down his words dutifully in my most elegant hand-writing, meticulously looping the *g*'s and adding a little flourish to the *s*'s. Babbo bowed his head, resting his forehead in his ringed hand. Then he lifted his head and pointed a yellowed finger at me.

"Are you ready for the next paragraph?"

I nodded, completely absorbed now in perfecting each letter, embellishing where I could with curlicues and whorls.

He started pacing again, feeling his way around the two

chairs, his hands outstretched to avoid collisions. *"William Tell* follows the same theme as *Ulysses*—a father's search for a son and a son's search for a father. Please join us for a champagne dinner, with John Sullivan, after the performance. There . . . I think that'll do."

Three hours later and my hand ached. So too did my back from stooping over Babbo's desk. Two blisters were ballooning, one on the tip of my index finger and one on the corner of my thumb. I surveyed the pile of envelopes in front of me—well over forty. As I uncurled my back and stretched out my neck and shoulders, I heard Babbo on the telephone talking about John Sullivan, his voice rising with excitement.

"You must come. He can reach high Cs with the greatest of ease. No other tenor in the world can do that." There was a long pause and then Babbo was off again, eulogizing, praising, beseeching. His enthusiasm bubbled out of him like champagne from a bottle. But I couldn't share it. Indeed, it filled me with disquiet for I realized this had nothing to do with helping Giorgio's career. Why wasn't I asked to write forty invitations to Giorgio's debut in April? I thought of Sullivan—grumpy, *old* Sullivan who had come to dinner and only spoken in French and hectored everyone and bickered with his wife. I thought, with a spasm of pain, of Giorgio, who was dutifully living out Babbo's unlived life as an opera singer. For a measly five hundred francs a month singing in the choir at the American Cathedral on Avenue George V. I lay down on the couch and sucked my blistered finger. Babbo was still talking on the telephone, his splintered voice floating through the apartment. "John Sullivan . . . Yes, John Sullivan. You have to come and you must write something. He's been overlooked entirely . . . Yes, persecuted . . . exactly."

And then it hit me. Why had no one written forty invitations to see *me* dance at the Bal Bullier? Or the Théâtre des Champs-Élysées? Or the Théâtre du Vieux-Colombier? Why had Babbo not enlisted his army of Flatterers to applaud vigorously for me? To demand encores for me? To write articles extolling my dancing? Where were the reporters and photographers that he was so assiduously courting for John Sullivan? Why did Babbo prefer quarrelsome old Sullivan to me?

And without warning, before I had time to stamp it out, a blast of fury rose inside me, closed over me.

I tried to crush it, but I couldn't. I've relived that moment a hundred times, a thousand times, since then. Although I was alone in Babbo's study, I felt the presence of someone else. Someone violent and desperate. As if the shadow that usually stretched behind me had come to fiendish life and stolen into my body. I closed my eyes and willed it away. But it slunk back, dark and ugly.

I pulled myself up from the couch, closed my eyes, and began circling Babbo's study, trying to rid myself of this *thing*. I twisted and turned, crouched and leapt, and when Babbo came in, I was whirling like a Turkish dervish, my eyes frenzied and my heart pounding. Books and papers spewed from the shelves. Pictures and photographs skewed from their hooks. The electric light swung dizzily from the ceiling.

"Lucia!" Babbo stood in the doorway, his body rigid with shock. I continued spinning, knocking over an empty wine bottle and an ashtray. Billows of ash rose from the floor as I kicked the ashtray away. Papers skittered into the corners of the room. Books tumbled.

"What—what are you doing?" He gaped at me.

The furious person inside me started fading, shrinking and diminishing like a vulture disappearing into the horizon. But then it hovered, not quite out of view. So I danced on, spinning with abandon, oblivious to Babbo, oblivious to the papers and books underfoot, oblivious to the empty wine bottle spiraling perilously across the floor. My arms outstretched, fingers splayed, palms open skyward. I threw my head back, arched my spine, and orbited the books and papers and cigarette butts that now lay scattered across the study.

Babbo hadn't moved from the doorway, but suddenly, as quick as a flash, he darted into the room and snatched up the spinning wine bottle from under my feet. Then he retreated to the doorway where he stood, clutching the bottle and staring at me. He made no effort to retrieve his writing, his precious sheets of crayoning.

"Lucia?" There was a tremor in his voice. I was gliding by then, bending gracefully to avoid the chairs, the desk, the spilled papers, the books that sprawled promiscuously across the floor. Babbo moved gingerly, cautiously, toward me, his clawlike hands easing in my direction.

"It's all right. I'm just dancing." I curtsied so low my knees grazed the rug.

Babbo, his arms still outstretched, one hand still clutching the wine bottle, stared at me. He looked confused, as though he didn't know who I was. "Is . . . is that what you're learning at the . . . the Margaret Morris school?"

I panted slightly as I bent to pick up his papers. "We do a lot of improvisation. Sorry about your work. I'll try and put it back in order."

"It's of no importance. I can sort it out." He got down on his knees, put down the wine bottle, and tentatively reached out his hands to feel for the books I'd knocked over. Slowly, he started putting them back into piles, his eyes straining through his spectacles.

"What about the invitations you've been writing, Lucia? Are they all right?"

I looked at Babbo's desk. The invitations, in their thick cream envelopes, were still there in a neat stack, stamped, addressed, and ready to be posted.

"Yes," I replied shortly.

"Good. They need to be posted as soon as possible. I mustn't fail John O'Sullivan. Ah, John Sullivan. I think I'm right to insist he drops the *O*. Rolls more easily off the tongue, easier for the newspapermen to spell. Would you mind running them to the post box, *mia bambina*?"

* * *

BABBO NEVER MENTIONED my wild dance. Not even to Mama. His obsession with John Sullivan grew until he could talk of no one and nothing else. Even his Flatterers were mystified by his efforts to promote John Sullivan. Beckett was not only perplexed but indignant that Sullivan was so lacking in gratitude. Together, Beckett and I huddled in the hall at Robiac Square and complained about Sullivan and how much of our time he was consuming. Sometimes we made jokes at his expense, and I discovered that Beckett, normally so grave and serious, had an acerbic wit. Mama banned any mention of John Sullivan's name so Babbo was very careful not to say anything in front of her. But he showed no restraint with anyone else.

One good thing came from Babbo's obsession: a new intimacy between me and Beckett. Our shared dislike of the querulous graying tenor became a private "anti–John Sullivan alliance"—yet another thing that bound Beckett to me. One evening, a fortnight after his return from Ireland, we were corralled into attending yet another John Sullivan opera. Halfway through, as we were both stifling yawns, Beckett shifted in his seat, pushing his thigh hard against mine. His warmth spread into me like a hot-water bottle. I moved closer to him until it felt as though our bodies were melting into each other. I could smell his distinctive odor—tobacco and typewriter ribbon and soap. Then I felt the brush of his fingers against mine. His hand, his beautiful hand, fluttered onto my knee and lay there in the dark. It was five months since we'd almost made love on the parlor floor, and I remembered vividly the taste of his mouth, the feel of his skin, the heat and press of him upon me. But I also remembered Mama's words: marriage first and mischief afterward. I decided, just this once, to take her advice.

So after a few minutes, I picked up his hand and placed it very gently back on his own knee. And then I sat staring at his hands—the fingernails, the joints, the tendons and veins lying like spaghetti under his skin. I didn't look up again until Sullivan minced onto the stage for his final bow, and Babbo burst into yet another flurry of applause.

"Sam?" I whispered, as I clapped limply.

"Yes?" Beckett had pulled away in his seat so that we were no longer joined like Siamese twins.

"I have a date for my eye operation. I will be starting 1930 with new eyes. No more squint. No more strabismus!"

"Oh." Beckett continued his half-hearted applause while John Sullivan strutted around the stage like a puffed-up cockerel.

"All romance is off until then, Sam." I peered into his face, searching for signs of hurt or disappointment. But before I could decipher his expression, I felt the tip of Babbo's cane butting into my shoulder.

"Astonishing! Incomparable! The man is a consummate genius. Beckett, did you count the high Cs?"

"No, Mr. Joyce."

"Will you dine with us, Beckett? We're taking Sullivan to

the Café de la Paix for champagne and cold chicken." Babbo drew his opera cloak around his shoulders with an elaborate flourish.

"I can't tonight, sir. I have to pack. I leave for Germany tomorrow to stay with my aunt and uncle."

As we shuffled from our seats, I looked again at Beckett's inscrutable unsmiling face. Had he misunderstood my rejection? Had I pained him with my new strategy? I watched him wind his scarf around his neck and follow Babbo out of the opera house. And I reminded myself that Beckett was my destiny, and soon I would be free to love and dance for the rest of my life.

15

⬿⬿⬿⬿⬿

FEBRUARY 1930

PARIS

After my eye operation, I lay on the couch for a week, my head wrapped in bandages. Babbo took time out of his John Sullivan campaign to tend to me, bringing sweets and pastries to cheer me up. Even Mama was exemplary in her solicitude and bought me a new hat to show off my new eyes.

When the bandages came off, Kitten and Stella appeared with bunches of hothouse flowers. They both inspected my new eye and declared it a miracle. Babbo danced an Irish jig and sang me a song about "the lass with the lovely eyes," and Mama huffed and puffed and said if this didn't put a stop to my complaining she didn't know what would. Giorgio bought me a bottle of perfume, which he must have taken from Mrs. Fleischman's dressing table because it wasn't quite full. Most important of all, Beckett brought me a book. He had written a message inside that read, *What better use for eyes than reading. Much Love, Sam.* Frankly, I could think of several better uses for eyes, but I didn't mention that. After he'd disappeared into Babbo's study, Mama read his message and tut-tutted, rolling her gimlet eyes and shaking her head all at the same time. I read the two words, "Much Love," over and over again. And my heart sang.

When Beckett came out of Babbo's study one night, I was waiting for him in the hall. I passed him his coat, brazenly fixing him with my new eyes. I felt quite extraordinary, free and unshackled, as if I'd been released from an evil spell. His desire for me—and mine for him—was palpable. The air hummed with it. And then Babbo appeared silently behind us, waving a book in the air. Beckett leapt away from me as if he'd been stung by a hornet. I just laughed. He'd made himself perfectly clear and that was enough for me.

All that evening I smiled to myself. Babbo didn't notice— he was too engrossed in his work, wearing his eye patch *and* two pairs of spectacles, one on top of another. But Mama commented several times as she leafed through her magazine, asking me to "share the joke." I just sat there sketching (and smiling), preparing for my next art lesson with Sandy. With two perfect eyes, the possibilities ahead of me seemed endless, infinite. I couldn't stop the words "Mrs. Beckett" echoing inside me. And each time I said them to myself, I smiled. Suddenly I saw myself back onstage, dancing to spellbound audiences, their rapturous applause punctuated with the cries of "Encore, Mrs. Samuel Beckett!"

Of course, it took my mother to bring me down to earth. She kept telling me not to get too far ahead of myself, that my checkup with Doctor Collinson would confirm everything. Babbo, however, shared my jubilation. He was amazed at how quickly the operation was performed—and with what success.

When I saw Doctor Collinson, he looked at my eye from every angle and through a hundred different devices and glasses. Then he declared himself satisfied and asked me to come back for a final checkup in a month's time. Mama and I stopped for coffee and cake to celebrate, and I very nearly told her about my marriage plans, but something made me stop and talk about the weather instead.

A week later, as I was washing the dishes and thinking about a new dance routine, Mama suddenly stopped prattling midsentence and stared at me. I thought she was about to scold me for not listening to her, but she didn't. She just carried on staring. Staring at my left eye. She brought her face right up to mine and gripped my shoulders so I couldn't move. I could tell from the expression on her face that something had happened to my eye. And then she shouted out to Babbo, "Jim, it's rolling again!" Her words hit me like a boulder. Of course Babbo couldn't see anything. He peered into my eye, pronounced it perfect, and hurried back to his study.

But it was too late. What had she meant? Had my squint

returned? Had the operation been a failure? Mama became evasive and said she'd probably been mistaken. She gave me a slice of seed cake and a cup of sweet tea in her best wedding china, with the pink rosebuds on it. When I'd calmed myself, I decided to undertake my own examination with a mirror and a ruler.

As I stared into the mirror, trying to measure the distance between my pupil and the inner corner of my new eye, I saw something wasn't right. From time to time, the pupil and the iris appeared to slide, very gradually, toward my nose. I recalled Doctor Collinson's words at the outset, that these operations are not always successful, and I thought of Babbo's many eye operations and how few of them had worked. And finally I thought of Mrs. Samuel Beckett, in her wedding dress, her eyes crossed, squinting, deformed and sullied.

* * *

WHEN SANDY ARRIVED on our doorstep for my first drawing lesson, Mama turned him away thinking he was a salesman. He came on an orange bicycle, wearing a wool suit in broad orange and brown stripes, with a straw boater on his head. Balanced on the handlebars of his bicycle was a battered leather suitcase. Mama opened the door and then shut it firmly in his face. Unfazed, Sandy simply rang the doorbell again and laughed when Mama shouted out the window that she didn't want to buy anything. Babbo had to be cajoled out of his study to identify Sandy. And only then was he allowed in. When he insisted on conducting my drawing lessons from the kitchen table, Mama threw up her hands in outrage. Sandy just smiled and used all his American charm on her, before opening his suitcase and revealing some of the miniature circus he carried everywhere with him.

I loved his little sculptures. I picked them up and turned them over in my palm, relishing the feel of them—metallic, cold, and spiky, or cushioned, soft, and plump. I loved the way each dancer, acrobat, and animal moved and turned, some in strange staccato jerks, others fluidly, like ribbons blowing in wind. I loved Sandy's enthusiasm, the excitement with which he talked about "mechanical movement" and "composing motions." And I adored his tales of drunken parties. As he showed me how to sketch an acrobat tipping from a trapeze, he told me about all the parties he'd been to that week and the antics of his wild friends. If the parties had been dull, he'd reminisce about the times his circus had gone wrong—when the gramophone didn't work in Berlin, when the head of the lion fell off in New York, the Left Bank theater where he forgot to turn up. Each anecdote was accompanied by deep bellows of laughter. Sandy was immune to feelings of shame, embarrassment, and regret.

* * *

AND SO IT was Sandy who first told me the rumors. We were sitting side by side in the kitchen at Robiac Square. In front of us was a little metal sculpture of an acrobat whose limbs swayed in the breeze. Sandy wanted me to draw it as it moved.

"Just blow on it and watch how its arms swing." Sandy grinned as he dangled the metal figure in front of me.

I took in a deep gulp of air and blew. Its arms and legs swung wildly for a second, and then its head fell off, dropping onto the table with a tinny clunk before rolling away. Sandy leaned back in his chair and laughed and laughed, his huge frame quivering, the ends of his long moustache shaking.

"Did you do that on purpose?" I asked indignantly.

"No—I swear to God I didn't!" Sandy was still laughing, his eyes bright and brimming with amusement. "But I'm mighty glad it got decapitated here and not in my circus show." He picked up the miniature head and tried to reattach it to the metal frame, but his fingers were so large he couldn't twist the wire thread that joined the two parts.

"Let me do it. I have smaller fingers." As I took the tiny sculpture from him, I brushed the tips of his fingers with mine and felt an unexpected prickle of excitement. Snatching my hand back, I concentrated on mending the metal acrobat. Sandy was still chuckling, still watching me. And then he said something that startled and surprised me.

"So how long have you and Sam Beckett been engaged?"

"Engaged?" I asked, my eyes focused on the metal acrobat. I felt confused and intoxicated at the same time. Why did he think Beckett and I were engaged? Had Beckett been making his intentions known to others before me? Was he on the verge of proposing? And then it occurred to me that perhaps, obscurely and mysteriously, we *were* engaged and everyone knew but me. The tacit understanding between Beckett and me, the growing intimacy between him and my family, the almost daily interchanges at the door, the brushing of hands and the pressing of thighs in restaurants, theaters, cinemas, his stroking of my breasts and thighs, my hand at the fork of his trousers and around his buttocks—our almost-lovemaking on the parlor floor—could this be an unspoken engagement? Was this how it was done in Ireland?

"People were talking about it at the Coupole last night. Everyone in Paris is talking about it. I was surprised you hadn't told me." Sandy looked quizzically at me. "Everyone's seen him out with you and your parents. People say he's always at your house."

As I twisted the head of the figurine onto its body, my fingers trembled and a tightness in my chest caused my breath to quicken. Everything Sandy said was true. Beckett *did* come every day. The four of us *were* often out together. And I'd seen the fire in Beckett's eyes when he looked at me, when he touched me in passing. I remembered his fingers on my face, his hand on my knee, the way he'd fallen with me into that golden slice of afternoon light. Sandy scrutinized my flushing face, waiting for a response.

"Yes, that's all true . . . Could it be . . . could it be . . ." I hesitated. My voice sounded stilted and unsure. And then I blurted out the question, wild and crazy as it sounded. "Could it be that we're engaged but I . . . but I'm not aware of it?"

I expected Sandy to laugh, but he didn't. Instead he said,

"Yeah, it's possible, I guess. Not back home where I come from. It's still done the old-fashioned way there—marriage proposal, engagement ring, setting the wedding date. But in Paris it's different. Anything goes here. I guess there would have been some discussion of marriage between the two of you or between Beckett and your pa."

Would Beckett speak to Babbo without speaking to me? Surely Babbo would have told me? I felt the hope of an assumed engagement ebbing. For seventeen months Beckett had been coming to our home, accompanying me out, exchanging glances and words. How easy it would have been to slip into an engagement as one slips between the sheets at night, wordlessly, with easy familiarity. For a minute I imagined an engagement, tacit and assumed, where no bended knee was required, no stiff and awkward proposal, no discussion of dowries or "paternal permission" or wedding dates, no formal engagement party. I imagined Beckett saying to his friends, "Of course we're engaged—isn't it obvious?"

Sandy grinned again. "I don't really know Sam Beckett but he seems kinda reserved. Sounds to me like he's working up to a proposal. If he marries you, he's a mighty lucky man." His eyes lingered on me for longer than was polite. "You better start drawing, Lucia." He took the mended figurine from me and passed me a piece of paper and a pencil. "I want you to have a go at drawing her as she moves. I'll blow on her and you watch how she moves. Think of her as kinetic sculpture."

But I couldn't concentrate on the floating limbs of the figurine. All I could think of was Mrs. Samuel Beckett. Soon I was to be Mrs. Samuel Beckett, holding Beckett's beautiful long, thin hands in mine for the rest of my life.

"Have a go, Lucia. Start with her hair. Lucia? Lucia?" Sandy boomed across the table, but I ignored him. My heart was too full to speak.

* * *

SANDY FOUND MY family life perplexing. I knew this because the only time he didn't smile was when he asked me questions about my family. He asked why my parents wouldn't let me go to parties with him. He wanted to know why I had to be home by nine o'clock. He asked why Babbo wrote only about Ireland but never went there. He was particularly confused by the conventionality of our home—the bourgeois furniture, Babbo's ancestral portraits, and his strict adherence to routine. He was bemused by Babbo's dislike of the nightspots where the artists of Paris congregated. He found the intimacy of my family life unorthodox and odd. I tried, falteringly, to answer his questions, but usually I couldn't, so I just reiterated that Babbo was hard at work on the dark night of the soul (which is how he described his *Work in Progress* to the Flatterers), and that I was an important muse for him. Sometimes Sandy asked me why I didn't leave home, why I didn't embrace the revolutionary and artistic fervor of Paris, why I didn't enjoy the freedom that Paris offered.

"It's not like this in America, Lucia. Or in England. They ban books there, like your pa's. Back home they're still painting horses standing in fields and you have to get married before you can kiss someone. Damn it—you can't even have a drink! All the great writers and artists have left. Paris is where everything's happening. If you're a woman back home, you're expected to marry and get breeding. That's why Gertrude Stein, Djuna Barnes, Sylvia Beach—that's why they're all here. They've escaped!" Sandy's eyes sparkled and his moustache twitched. "It doesn't seem right that you're here where everyone's creating, exploring, breaking down the boundaries, experimenting, and yet you're sitting in Fouquet's with your parents looking out for movie stars."

"It's not like that, Sandy," I said haltingly. "My mother looks out for movie stars because she loves the movies. Babbo likes the waiters there, and the food. He's a serious writer. He doesn't want to sit up all night with you lot. And he hates Gertrude Stein."

Sandy guffawed with laughter and then turned to me, suddenly serious again. "But you, Lucia. Everyone tells me what a great dancer you were. You speak four languages. You sing like an angel. You draw like an angel too—goddamnit!" He picked up one of my pen-and-ink drawings of a jumping dog and let it flutter before my eyes.

"I'm still dancing." I stepped back from the table, performed a perfect toe-touch jump, shimmied for a few seconds. "And I have plans. Big plans."

Sandy looked at me curiously. "You should get out more. Everyone's in Paris to be free and have fun, and you're living like a nun in a convent. You're too talented to spend your life as someone else's muse, wife, call it what you will. Anyway, Paris is changing and you need to grab what's left while you can."

I was grateful to Sandy, grateful for his belief in me. But how could I explain the invisible thread that bound me to Babbo? How could I explain the responsibilities I carried as muse? Or how these both repelled and attracted me?

Instead I agreed to take Kitten and Stella to see Sandy's circus on the weekend.

* * *

AS WE WALKED along the gravel paths in the Jardin du Luxembourg, all three of us had a spring in our step. And not just in anticipation of Sandy's circus. Stella was excited because *Paris Montparnasse* had published a second article about her, with copies of her paintings of local street scenes. Kitten was chirpy because she had a new beau. I was particularly happy because Beckett had given me a lover's gift the previous evening, while we were dining out *en famille.* I knew something was up because he stared at me all night, even while he was talking to Babbo. He was normally very deferential when Babbo spoke, like all the Flatterers. But last night his eyes had kept flicking back to me. Just as we were leaving Fouquet's, he gave me a copy of Dante's *Divina Commedia*, beautifully bound in blue leather with the title embossed in gold.

"This is for you, Lucia," he said. I knew how much it meant to him—he and Babbo were both obsessed with Dante.

And I knew exactly what he was saying in his silent, cryptic way. Dante is the poet of love; Italian is the language of love. He was trying to tell me he loved me. I was so overcome I couldn't speak. Afterward, as we all walked down the Champs-Élysées, I hooked my arm into his and walked very slowly so we lagged a good way behind Mama and Babbo. I told him about the pheasant's eyes in the Louvre, how they had followed me, trying to tell me something. And I told him how I kept dreaming of his hands. I had almost summoned up the courage to tell him I loved him, when Mama started shouting for help.

"For the love of Mary, give me a hand! Jim's fainted clean away!" She was standing amid a small knot of people, Babbo's limp body in her arms. His hat had rolled onto the pavement, and his cane had fallen loosely against his body, where it rested like a third leg. I unlinked my arm from Beckett's and we both ran toward her. Beckett helped us drag him to a bench, where he started to blink and convulse.

"He saw two nuns, just over there." Mama pointed across the Champs-Élysées. "He started shaking like a leaf, and I prepared meself for one of his turns, but then he looked down and there was a big rat scuttling down the gutter. That was it! He fainted dead away. Thank the Lord you were coming behind!"

"That's a double dose of bad luck, two nuns *and* a rat crossing his path," I explained, catching sight of Beckett's perplexed expression.

"Get away—all of you!" Mama flapped her hands at the

motley crowd of onlookers. "This'll bring on an eye attack tomorrow, that it will." She gave Babbo a small slap on his cheek. "Pull yourself together, Jim. Find us a taxicab, will you, Mr. Beckett? Pick up his hat and cane, Lucia."

And that was how the evening ended. But I had Beckett's book in my handbag, and if that wasn't a sign of his love, I didn't know what was.

As Kitten, Stella, and I walked through the park, past ranks of early pink tulips and tightly clipped box hedges, I told them about Beckett's gift. Kitten squeezed my arm and trilled, "Oh, darling, Le Tout Paris is talking of your engagement with Sam Beckett."

"Be careful what you wish for," Stella added, her face unsmiling. I ignored her. Irishwomen are always wary of Irishmen, according to Mama.

When we arrived at Sandy's studio, there was already a queue of people waiting to buy tickets. We pushed past, climbed the stairs, and nudged open the studio door. Sandy was crouched on the floor laying out his circus. There was a ring constructed from blocks of wood, and inside the ring were tiny rugs and strips of red carpet, a full-length trapeze and a miniature seesaw. The ring was festooned with brightly colored flags and bunting. Lying on the floor of the circus was the circus master in a black jacket, his black felt hat askew. To one side of the ring were Sandy's five suitcases, out of which spilled tiny wool lions, clowns with gaping mouths, trapeze artists with metal hooks for fingers—none of them any bigger than my hand.

Around the ring, which was slightly larger than a full-brimmed lady's hat, were upturned boxes and wine crates for the audience to sit on. Handwritten posters announcing *Cirque Calder—25 Francs* were pasted to the walls and the door. Squatting beside Sandy was a red-haired man fiddling with the gramophone. I looked sideways at Kitten and Stella. They were staring, bright-eyed and entranced, at Sandy's miniature circus. I felt a surge of pride as I waved at Sandy, indicating my two friends with a jerk of my thumb.

"I've brought Kitten and Stella," I said. "Can we do anything to help?"

Sandy jumped up and kissed Kitten and Stella on both cheeks. "Pleased to meet you. Real glad you could make it. I've mislaid the sword-swallower's sword, but once I've found it, we're ready to go. I've gotten a whole new act today. The trapeze artist's gonna fall off and reveal all. I hope you ladies won't be offended?"

"Of course not, Sandy," I said, trying to sound as nonchalant and blasé as I could. "We're all modern girls now."

As we took our seats, Kitten and Stella bombarded me with questions. Kitten wanted to know if Sandy was any relation of Stirling Calder, who made some huge sculpture in Philadelphia, and where in America he was from, and how old he was, and was he married. Stella wanted to know if he did his own sewing and stitching, and where he found his materials. Their questions made me see how little I knew Sandy. We talked mainly about his social life or my home life, or he talked of motion, space, velocity, and volume.

"I'll ask him all your questions at my next lesson, I promise. But he's definitely not married. He's *very* single." I gave
Kitten a knowing look before reminding her that she had her
own beau and explaining that Sandy was rather keen on me
and kept asking me out.

"But *we* know your heart belongs to Mr. Beckett," Kitten
whispered in my ear. "Sandy's very handsome, though."

As Sandy announced *Le Grand Cirque Calder*, everyone
stopped talking and the upturned crates stopped scraping.
The gramophone started playing a march and Sandy maneuvered his circus master into the front of the ring. After that
came a succession of acts, some done by hand (Sandy pushing, pulling, blowing, lifting, and dropping his little people)
and some done using motors and elaborate pulley systems
he'd rigged together. For an hour we watched miniature con-
tortionists, fire eaters, lions and lion tamers, while Sandy
provided a commentary in halting French. When the lion
appeared, Sandy stopped his commentary and roared with
gusto. Kitten couldn't stop smiling, clapping loudly and enthusiastically after every act. Stella kept tilting her head from
one side to the other, trying to fathom how Sandy made his
figures move. I sat, straight-backed and proud, like a mother
watching her precocious but talented child.

During the interval, Stella jumped up to examine the
tightrope and trapezes from which hung the little trapeze
artists with their clawlike hooks. When she came back, she
said, "It's fascinating and so clever. You can tell he's an engineer."

"He retrained as a painter," I said defensively. "He's just as talented at painting and drawing. You should see his pen-and-ink sketches of animals. I'm learning so much from him."

Stella looked at me doubtfully. "But this is what he's brilliant at, understanding how to use movement and space. And color—look at the bunting! What else does he do?"

"He's made wire sculptures of Joan Miró and Josephine Baker," I said uncertainly. "He calls them his wire portraits. And I think he had an exhibition in New York last year. Or was it the year before?"

In the second half of Sandy's *Grand Cirque Calder*, we watched, spellbound, as a clown blew up a balloon. Sandy had attached a rubber tube to the back of the clown and blew through this himself. As the balloon expanded, an acrobat was sent flying and everyone clapped and laughed with delight. After this came wild horses that looked like soft toys on wheels, accompanied by a cowboy and a dancing girl. As Sandy pulled a hidden lever, the horses bucked and pranced, tipping the girl into the ring and flipping the cowboy high into the air. The audience became noisier and more raucous, and by the time Sandy's new act started, some of the men were stamping their feet and cheering in anticipation. When the delicate dancer finally tumbled from the trapeze, she fell headfirst and her skirt rose up, revealing two tiny buttocks, after which there was such a cacophony of applause that Sandy had to end the circus before a riot broke out.

We walked back to the tram stop, laughing and giggling. But just as we turned onto the boulevard Montparnasse,

Stella soured my mood by asking about Beckett. She wanted to know why I hadn't invited him to Sandy's circus and why Paris was discussing our engagement before we had. Kitten leapt to my defense. "Mr. Beckett's obviously been discussing his plans but not found the right moment to propose yet."

"He seems so reserved. Not the sort of man to tell everyone else first." Stella looked straight ahead, her eyes fixed on the horizon.

"That's exactly it," Kitten said. "He's so darned shy, he hasn't plucked up the courage yet. I think you need to help him along, Lucia."

"What d'you mean?" Stella turned and frowned at Kitten.

"I think Lucia should help him overcome his shyness. It's never going to happen if he's always with Mr. and Mrs. Joyce."

"You think I need to be alone with him?" I asked slowly. I'd never told Kitten about my whiskey-fueled dance lesson with Beckett. I didn't think she would approve. And after Mama, I couldn't face any more disapproval.

"I sure do! How can the poor man propose with your pa watching his every move? He can't even kiss you!"

"But you *have* been alone together, haven't you? You're not *always* with your parents?" Stella kept her eyes fixed on the end of the road.

Kitten nudged me in the ribs and mouthed something to me that I couldn't decipher, but the light in her eyes suggested it was something amusing, a joke at Stella's expense, perhaps.

"It's not easy. We *are* mostly with my parents these days. And he's a gentleman. An Irish gentleman."

"Oh, there's no question of his *desires*!" Kitten rolled her eyes. "I've seen how he looks at you, Lucia. He's just terribly shy. Any girl can see that. He doesn't want to be turned down. You need to give him some more encouragement. It must be so intimidating for him, you being the daughter of a genius. I'm terrified of your pa!"

"Mr. Joyce is very intimidating—that's true." Stella nodded. "But would Sam Beckett feel as intimidated as we do? After all, he's very clever and he's a man."

"Beckett worships Babbo, but everyone does. Everyone except my mother, who just scolds him." I hesitated. "Yes, perhaps that makes it hard for Beckett. It's as though I'm the daughter of the Lord God himself."

"Yes!" Kitten was wide-eyed and enthusiastic. "Of course! Imagine how daunting that must be. Poor Sam Beckett. I feel sorry for him. When I bring a new beau home, it's so easy. Pa's just a boring banker. But your father must have such high expectations of a fiancé. They'd need to be so clever, so well-read."

"But Sam Beckett *is* clever and well-read, so he wouldn't need to worry about that, would he?" Stella sounded vaguely mocking, and the twists and turns of her words confused me.

"It would still be intimidating. That's the point. Don't take any notice of Stella . . . she's just jealous!" Kitten squeezed my arm and beamed at me. Shocked, I looked at Stella and saw her face flushing pink, her chin tilted defiantly toward the sky.

"Are you, Stella?" I asked.

"He's too Irish for me," she said brusquely, a flush spreading down her long neck and into her turquoise-and-crimson scarf. Kitten elbowed me in the ribs again. I stared at Stella. Ahead of us was the boulevard Montparnasse: news vendors hawking their evening papers, the sharp clanging of the trams, beggars with their crutches and balding dogs, drunks swerving from bar to bar. Stella walked purposefully toward the tram stop, her bright clothes moving with the breeze, as though she were some garish hothouse flower.

I gripped Kitten's arm as a stream of scrambled questions ran through my head. Was Stella also in love with Beckett? Did she want him for herself? Had she . . . ? Had they . . . ? Did Beckett feel anything for Stella? Was this why Stella had been so contrary, so unsupportive of Kitten's suggestions?

"Stella has a crush on Beckett?" I whispered to Kitten.

And then Stella whipped around. "I heard that, Lucia. There's nothing between me and Sam Beckett. Nothing at all. I just want you to exercise some . . . Oh, never mind!" She gave an angry shake of her head.

"It's just a misunderstanding." Kitten looped her arm through Stella's so the three of us were walking in a line. "All my fault. I've got the perfect man for you, Stella. A friend of my new beau. Why don't we make up a foursome? Go to the movies? Or a sixsome with you and Sam, Lucia?"

There was no time to respond. We'd reached the tram stop and Stella's tram was reeling toward us. I watched her board, her glossy black curls bobbing beneath her crimson hat. And then I crossed her off my list of wedding guests. Yes, I thought, it's time to take Kitten's advice.

* * *

I HURRIED BACK to Robiac Square, my head full of wedding plans. When I got home, I knew instantly something was amiss. I heard Mama's raised voice from the hall, and when I got to the parlor she was pacing around and around, her face black and pinched. Babbo was slumped on the couch, eyes closed, white-lipped.

"She's too old! She's got a child and a husband! Why can't she be leavin' Giorgio alone?" Mama's voice was hard and angry.

"Her divorce has come through. That's the point." Babbo sounded weary, and there were red patches beneath his eyes.

"What's happened?" I sat beside him on the couch and took his ringed hand in mine. He gave me a wan smile before explaining that Giorgio and Mrs. Fleischman had been around for tea and announced their engagement. "And that was the meaning of the two nuns and the rat that crossed my path last night," he croaked. "Your mother is distraught."

"Giorgio engaged to a divorced woman! Sure she should be ashamed of herself! It's not that I'm not wanting him to marry." A slight note of contrition crept into Mama's voice.

"But why can't he be marrying someone of his own age? Someone without a babby and a fella?"

"At least she has wealth, Nora. And she *is* divorced now." Babbo sighed heavily.

"Oh, Jim, you always have an eye for the money. And no doubt you're thinking how her rich folk in America can help with your books."

Babbo coughed awkwardly but said nothing.

"You encouraged it, Jim, letting her come to the house to do your typing and your reading. She was such a brazen hussy, to be sure. Making eyes at you and when that didn't work, making eyes at our Giorgio—and him just a wee lad. Only seventeen! And her married with a babby of her own. And to think she's nearly my age! 'Tis a disgrace!"

Babbo shot Mama a reproachful look—a warning sign, as if she'd gone too far and overstepped the mark in some way.

"She comes strutting around with her money and her jewels like she's some sort of duchess, lording it over me. And then she steals him away, me only son, *our* only son, our Giorgio." Mama's voice cracked and her eyes brimmed. "What about the family, Jim?" She flopped into a chair, limp and defeated.

"We'll be a family of five now. They won't live far away," Babbo said soothingly. "And aren't you pleased they're intending to have a family? Wouldn't you like a grandchild?"

It was only at the mention of a grandchild that it hit me. Giorgio was actually leaving, to forge his own life, to write his own story. For the last ten months, he'd spent a grow-

ing amount of time with Mrs. Fleischman. Although we'd
grown used to his absence, the prospect of their marriage
simply hadn't occurred to us. But the thought of Giorgio and
Helen having a child made me realize, with a sudden shock,
that Giorgio was finally escaping, breaking free from the
clutches of Mama and Babbo.

"She's too old to have a babby. 'Tisn't healthy at her age."
Mama's lips tightened.

"She's still in her thirties. That's not too late."

"She's wormed her way into our home and stolen our Giorgio from us. And I'm betting they'll be off to America as fast
as you can say Dublin Bay. And her family are Jews! Why
couldn't he be marrying an Irish girl who could be a nice
daughter-in-law to me?"

Babbo flinched, fiddled with his lapel, said nothing.

"How can I be keeping up with her Jewish money? And
the way she's bossing him around. 'Tis a crying shame when
a woman has the gall to boss a fella like that. They say she's
had plenty o' lovers, so likely she'll tire o' Giorgio and send
him home with his tail between his legs. I'll not be speaking
to her. What about Stella Steyn? She's a nice young Irish
girl, to be sure. Or Kitten." Mama turned to me abruptly, as
if she'd just noticed my presence. "What about Kitten? She
was soft on him once."

Before I could open my mouth, Babbo told Mama that if
she carried on like this, she'd drive Giorgio away further and
faster into Mrs. Fleischman's arms. He then reminded her, in a
clipped voice, that Kitten was American and Stella was Jewish.

"Oh, what do I care! I'm losing my boy. To a vampire!" Mama's breath caught in her throat with a small sob.

"Just think of her . . ." Babbo stopped midsentence. A glazed look came into his eyes, and I knew he was on the verge of extolling her wealth, thinking of all the things that could be put right with Mrs. Fleischman's money, with Mrs. Fleischman's connections, with Mrs. Fleischman's family in America.

"Could they help make *Ulysses* legal, Babbo?"

He gave a thin-lipped smile. "Who knows, *mia bella bambina*? Who knows?"

I didn't sleep that night. I knew Giorgio's departure from Robiac Square would tighten the bars of my own cage. I asked myself, over and over, how my parents would spare me, now I was the only one left. As the gray light of morning pushed at the shutters, I knew it was time to move forward with my plan. I had nothing to lose.

NOVEMBER 1934
KÜSNACHT, ZURICH

"Why do you think Giorgio was your mother's favorite?" Doctor Jung pushes clumps of tobacco into his pipe. "Do you mind if I smoke, Miss Joyce?"

"He was an easy baby and I was always crying. Aunt Eileen told me that. She said Mama didn't know what to do with me. Everyone knew Mama preferred Giorgio. She even told me herself." I give an empty laugh and rub my hands up and down the sleeves of my fur coat. Coming across Lake Zurich on the ferry has made me cold, all those squalls of wind whisking over the lake, buffeting the ferry so that it rocked and seesawed.

"His departure from Robiac Square meant you had the full attention of your parents then?" The doctor sucks at his pipe and a small cloud of tobacco smoke rises and hovers above his head like a halo.

"I couldn't sleep for nights after that." I motion at my manuscript, spread out like a fan on the doctor's desk. "Giorgio and I had been through so much together. When we arrived in Paris—I was thirteen and he was fifteen—we stayed in a filthy, flea-ridden hotel in the Latin Quarter. We thought we were passing through on our way to a new life in London, but that never happened." I pause and look at my hands. How old and gnarled they look, the nails ragged and bitten, the skin beginning to wrinkle. I catch sight of the red, shiny scar on my thumb with its treacherous little puckers, but then my eye's drawn to the age spots on my wrists. "How old am I now, Doctor?"

"You are twenty-seven, Miss Joyce. What happened when you arrived in Paris?"

"We couldn't speak any French, and for three months, Giorgio and I spoke to no one except each other. We had no friends, no acquaintances of any sort. I had no room of my own. If I wanted privacy I went to Giorgio's room. I had no school to attend, no one to visit. Babbo demanded silence and darkness while he finished *Ulysses*, and so Giorgio and I spent hours in his bedroom doing Charlie Chaplin impressions." I lapse into silence. I can feel tears pooling in my eyes, even now, even after everything that has come between us. How did it come to pass that such friendship, such intimacy, could turn so quickly?

I swallow loudly and continue. "He got a job as a clerk

through one of Babbo's Flattering friends, but he loathed it, said it was menial and dull, and beneath him. His next job was at the American Trust Agency, where he was promised two hundred francs a month after a trial without pay. Babbo said it might lead to bigger things, but Giorgio didn't pass his trial. He found it boring and humiliating, pushing papers 'round a desk for no money." I pause and look up at the doctor. He's still puffing on his pipe and watching me, always watching me with his coin-bright eyes.

He pushes back his chair and stands up. The bones in his feet crack as he walks toward the window. "Carry on, Miss Joyce. I need to understand what caused the breach between you and your brother."

"I often knew what Giorgio was thinking. Sometimes I'd foresee his exact words." I gnaw distractedly at a torn cuticle and wonder if those were Cassandra moments or merely the result of a deep familiarity. As I ponder this, something floats up from a dark, cobwebby corner of my mind. I reach for it, but it slips away and I have a sudden sensation of insects crawling up my spine, tiny black ants moving in formation. I want to scratch my back but the doctor is pressing me to continue and I don't want to think about insects scuttling over my skin anymore. "When Babbo's Flatterers came to visit, they always hurried past us as if . . . as if we were invisible. We'd be called in to pour the tea. Giorgio would wink at me. That was our signal. We'd made up our own language—Italian and German and

English and the odd bit of French. And after he winked, we'd talk very loudly in our hodgepodge language. It always disarmed Babbo's Flatterers—not being able to understand us." The memory makes me smile and I forget the ants marching up my spine.

"So your bond was very deep, very close?" Doctor Jung stands at the window, looking out onto the hills and woods beyond the lake. Spatters of rain hit the glass. Over his shoulder I see black clouds swollen with rain.

"It was Mrs. Fleischman's money that gave him the strength and the . . ." I pause, searching for the right word. "The determination to escape Robiac Square. He never married for love."

"You think he married to escape your parents?"

"I know so." I drop my head into my hands. How can I explain what I now know to be true—that my parents' grip on me began to tighten, slowly and subtly, when Giorgio *first* met Mrs. Fleischman. They fought, of course, to keep Giorgio. But Mrs. Fleischman had been persistent. And rich. She fought back, using her charm and money to inveigle her return into Babbo's circle of Flatterers.

"I am very pleased with your progress, Miss Joyce. Miss Baynes tells me you have been calm and there are clearly no significant problems with your memory."

"So when can I go, Doctor?" I lift my head from my hands. "I'm feeling much better."

"When we have uncovered the memories you have blocked,

repressed. I am putting together my theory, which begins with your emotional abandonment as a baby. The way your family life revolved around a dominant father figure—"

"Babbo wasn't dominant! It was Mama who bossed me around and told me what to wear. You've got it all wrong!" I glare at Doctor Jung. The stupid man understands nothing.

"You are right, Miss Joyce. Your father is not authoritarian. But he controlled everything, did he not? You said that you worried about Mr. Beckett falling under his spell."

"So is that all you've come up with? I've been coming here for two months and *that* is all you've come up with!" I stand up and snatch my gloves and bag from the side table. I have to get back to the hotel. Babbo will be worried. All this rain, this wind. Doctor Jung is gesturing to the chair, asking me to sit down again. Now he's shouting at me, pushing me back into the chair. I swing my handbag, aim it at him, at his ruddy self-satisfied cheeks. He ducks, and I feel his thick arms on mine, pinioning me. My breath is coming in sharp little bursts, like the wind slapping at the window panes. My handbag falls to the floor and its contents spew out: a tin of shoe wax, a silver cake fork, a tea strainer, old tram tickets, a pink flamingo feather from Zurich Zoo, a lipstick, a bird's claw, a box of matches. And the great doctor is on his knees, scrabbling for my things, putting them carefully back into my bag.

"Miss Joyce." He looks up at me from the floor and for the first time I catch a glimpse of . . . of what? Is it tenderness?

"This is just the beginning." His eyes glide over the tea strainer as he returns it to my bag. "I believe you have a repressed complex, the result of something that happened to you as a child. A memory so hideous, so unacceptable, that you've buried it very, very deeply."

And when he says that, I feel everything inside me closing up, like a sea anemone jabbed with a stick. My insides rolling in, shutting down. And the air around me turns green and cold.

"The repression of such a memory results in the splitting of the personality and, sometimes, the development of a robust fantasy life. It is my hypothesis that you sublimated this memory into your dancing. When you stopped dancing, the memory started to resurface in your unconscious." He lets out a long sigh and stands up. "I am only telling you this because I believe you are intelligent enough to understand it."

Doctor Jung passes me my handbag and I stand up. "I need to go now," I say stiffly. "It's too chilly here. But there's something you should know, Doctor." I pause and chew my lips for a few long seconds. There is something I want to tell him, but I can't think what it is. I search for words—any words—but my mind feels blank and woolly and the ants have started moving up and down my spine again.

He looks expectantly at me.

"Next time," he says gently. "I think you've had enough for today." And as he ushers me to the door, he passes me a handkerchief. "Your lips, Miss Joyce. They are bleeding."

~~~~~~~

16

APRIL 1930

PARIS

Mama refused to speak to Mrs. Fleischman. I think we all knew it was too late, that Mrs. Fleischman had won and Giorgio had been liberated. But Mama preserved a dogged silence in her presence for several weeks.

In the meantime, I planned my own wedding, my own escape. I would wear white, of course, but I wanted a modern dress of the latest fashion with a dropped waist and short sleeves. I would wear a veil and carry pale-pink rosebuds and white lilac. The wedding would be very small—Mama and Babbo, Sandy, Kitten, perhaps some old friends from my disbanded dance troupe. We would invite Beckett's family, and McGreevy would have to come, but no other Flatterers. Giorgio would sing and Man Ray would take the photographs and I would perform a dance I'd been working on in my Margaret Morris lessons. And the reception would be at Fouquet's: champagne and cold chicken and alpine strawberries.

I would defer to Beckett on the thorny subject of *where* to get married. Although my grandparents were Catholic, Beckett's family were Protestant. I wanted to honeymoon in Ireland and see Beckett's childhood home. Then we'd go to Dublin and Galway and see my grandparents, aunts, uncles, and cousins. I saw it all in my mind's eye—he and I, arm in arm, our jaws sore from smiling. And their words as we left: "Hasn't Lucia done well! Aren't they both so beautiful together!"

And if Beckett didn't want to go to Ireland, perhaps we'd go to Germany and visit his aunt and uncle. We'd need somewhere to live afterward. Once we were settled in a little apartment of our own, I'd have the walls painted duck-egg blue and I'd buy a piano. He'd have a study with lots of pale oak shelves for his books and a mahogany desk where he'd write all day. I'd plant red geraniums on the balcony, to cheer us up when the weather was gloomy. I'd make our home so cozy and comfortable that Beckett would always come back at night. I'd play the piano and sing to him. And of course I'd dance onstage again. As Mrs. Samuel Beckett, I'd perform again!

I was shaken from my reverie by Mama, standing in front of me and waving a letter. "We have to go to Zurich, Lucia. We've a date for your father's eye operation—next week."

"I can't go! Miss Morris is over from England next week

and I won't become a dance teacher if she doesn't see me. It's an important week for me." I let my voice taper off, appalled at the thought of missing Miss Morris's visit, knowing she specifically wanted to watch me run a class.

"You don't need to come, Lucia," said Mama flatly. "You can be staying with Mrs. Fleischman."

"I don't want to stay with Mrs. Fleischman! Why can't I stay here? Anyway, you're not speaking to her, so how will you ask her?"

Mama grunted.

"Please let me stay here," I pleaded. "Can't Giorgio stay with me?"

"I'll talk to Jim about it, but I'll make no promises."

In that instant, I realized this was my chance. My chance to get engaged. With my parents away, Beckett and I would be free to discuss our marriage. Without Babbo breathing down our necks and scrutinizing our every move, our every glance, we could finally talk freely of our love. My mind whirred with boundless excitement as I decided how best to do this. I couldn't invite him to Robiac Square, in case Mama insisted I stay somewhere else or in case Giorgio was home. Theaters and cinemas wouldn't allow us enough time to talk. Dance halls and bars would be too busy, too full of people we knew.

What we needed was a quiet restaurant with dusky corners. An unfashionable, shadowy restaurant with indifferent waiters. Close to somewhere we could walk, talk, and kiss afterward, hidden from prying eyes. I ran through

the restaurants where we'd eaten with my family . . . too
expensive . . . not enough intimacy . . . no romance. I mentally ticked off Babbo's favorites: Fouquet's, Les Trianons,
Café Francis, le Closerie des Lilas. And then I remembered a little bistro, candlelit and low-ceilinged, beside
the southern exit to the Jardin du Luxembourg. We'd
all been there, my parents, Mrs. Fleischman and Giorgio, Beckett and I, just after Babbo's birthday in February. It hadn't been sufficiently swanky for my parents or
Mrs. Fleischman, and the waiters didn't bow and scrape as
they did at Fouquet's, but Beckett had loved it, said it was
the best steak-frites he'd ever had. It would be perfect for
our first declaration of love.

Beckett would speak of how he'd thought of nothing but
me for so long, of how he visited Robiac Square only to see
me. We'd whisper of how our bodies ached for each other
and how long we'd yearned for this moment. We'd reminisce
about those moments of passion in Mama's parlor and giggle
over her horrified expression when she discovered us. We'd
agree on a date for our marriage and we'd discuss his outfit
and the church and the flowers and the rings. I'd ask for his
thoughts on pink rosebuds and white lilac and he'd ask my
advice on what flower to wear in his buttonhole. Of course,
he'd want a wild Irish bloom. Perhaps a solitary rose from
the hedgerow. And we'd have a traditional Irish wedding
cake with three tiers, decorated with sugar roses. I'd suggest
Man Ray take the photographs. And then perhaps Beckett
would demur, saying he loves the pictures Berenice Abbott

took of me. We'd both laugh, and then Beckett would say, "No—if you want Man Ray, we must have Man Ray."

And when we'd agreed on our wedding, we'd discuss the honeymoon, our eyes still riveted, our knees caressing under the table. As I brushed aside the waiter, Beckett would tell me how he longed to take me to Ireland, to show me his garden, his dogs, his parents, the mountain hikes he did with his father, the attic bedroom he shared with his brother.

And then, our fingers laced together across the table, we'd talk about where to live. Should we find a small apartment near Babbo and Mama? Or should we move to the outskirts of Paris so we could have a garden with drifts of yellow daffodils, and a dog? I'd describe the plump cushions and the drapes I had in mind. I'd find out what he liked for breakfast and how he took his coffee.

Afterward we'd amble, hand in hand, through the Jardin du Luxembourg. The moon would cast stripes of pale shivering light on the paths and a soft spring breeze ripe with the perfume of tulips would cool our glowing cheeks. We'd stop and kiss under the horse chestnut tree by the fountain. It would be a wild, untamed kiss and we'd have to pull ourselves apart, panting and desperate. He'd beg to make love to me right there, against the ridged bark of the tree trunk. He'd tell me how he'd imagined and craved this moment . . . and I'd confess how I'd thought of nothing but him, for months and months and months. And his hands would creep beneath my dress. And my fingers would slip inside his shirt, inside his trousers . . .

I was so engrossed I didn't hear Mama banging on the door. Then the handle turned and there she was, standing in front of me, her mouth snapping.

"Lucia, it's after ten. You'll be late for your dance class, to be sure."

* * *

KITTEN, WITH WHOM I discussed everything, agreed my choice of restaurant was perfect. But she said I needed a new outfit and some new makeup. So I bought a pale-green dress and a new lipstick in strawberry red and a new eye shadow in a matching tone of mint green. The green showed off my clear skin and my dark hair. And green was, of course, the color of Ireland. I arranged to have my hair waved and I chose a necklace of jade beads to wear. By the time my parents had left for Zurich, I was ready. Giorgio had agreed to move back into Robiac Square while they were gone, but he was never at home, so I didn't need to fret about him. I telephoned Beckett and invited him to join me for dinner at eight o'clock. There was a pause, as if the line had gone dead; then he said, "Yes, that would be lovely, Lucia."

As I walked to the restaurant, my heart fluttered madly. I realized that not a day had gone by when I hadn't thought of him, hadn't imagined his arms around me and his lips on mine. And yet, on the brink of consummation, I was overcome with anxiety. I felt the palms of my hands, damp and clammy, and my throat, tight and crushed. I took deep breaths and said the words "Mrs. Samuel Beckett" over and over.

At the restaurant I was shown to a table for two in the corner. I positioned myself so Beckett would see me—and I him—as soon as he walked in. The surly waiter, to my relief, had no idea who I was. He lit the candle on the table and gave me a menu. I thought how blissful it was to be out incognito. After *Ulysses*, Babbo was so famous we were accosted or gawked at wherever we went. Being out, alone and unrecognized, brought a frisson of excitement.

As I waited I ran through the evening ahead of me. I'd planned the conversation for several days by then. I wasn't going to mention Sandy or Stella or Babbo, but I'd talk about Mrs. Fleischman and Giorgio and their wedding plans—just to set the scene. Beckett loved to talk about books, so I'd talk about *Lady Chatterley's Lover*—again, to set the scene. As usual I'd ask him what he was reading and what he was writing and who his favorite students were. But I didn't want to loiter on these subjects. So then we'd talk about our favorite parts of Paris, our favorite colors, our favorite artists, our favorite flowers. And Ireland, of course. I always wanted to hear about his mother and her garden. Knowing I was soon to meet her would add poignancy to our conversation. I had to be sure she'd welcome me into the Beckett family. I didn't want to be treated in the way Mama had treated Mrs. Fleischman, although that was entirely due to Mrs. Fleischman's blatant abduction of Giorgio. Beckett and I would be completely different. We were the same age;

neither of us was married or divorced; we were both Irish; and we were in love.

As I mulled over the differences between myself and Mrs. Fleischman, I looked up and saw the waiter heading toward me. I quickly patted my hair, for I could just make out Beckett behind him. Beckett waved to me over the waiter's shoulder and I was so overjoyed a huge smile spread across my face. As the waiter stepped to one side, Beckett leaned forward and kissed my cheek. It was only when he stepped back that I saw another man behind him. I paused for the waiter to guide the other guest to his table. But he didn't. Instead the waiter said he'd find another chair, lay another place.

I felt my face crumpling in confusion and bewilderment. I was about to tell the waiter we didn't need another chair when Beckett said, "I hope you don't mind, Lucia, but I've brought my pupil, Georges Pelorson. He was hungry." The two men laughed briefly, and in that moment, I felt a darkness within me, rising and churning. I struggled to conceal my feelings, to hold back the tide of anguish and disappointment. I felt my chest tightening and my breathing becoming labored and panicky. I was glad of the candlelight. Glad I was sitting down. I tried to focus on my breathing.

The waiter arrived with a third chair and two menus. Pelorson and Beckett discussed the wine, unable to agree on red or white.

Then Pelorson turned to me and said, "It's so nice to meet you. I've heard so much about your father. Can you reveal some of his secrets? We're all desperate to know the title of his new book, aren't we, Sam?"

My mouth fell open. I shook my head dumbly. I was so discomposed by the presence of Pelorson, by what it signified, I couldn't think straight. I kept asking myself why Beckett had brought his pupil. I replayed our telephone conversation over and over. When I telephoned and invited him to dinner, I'd said I had something very important to discuss, something personal, something pressing. Yes! Those were the very words I'd used . . . important, personal, and pressing. So why had he brought this man, with his interrogative questions?

I felt my breath, tattered and frayed. I felt my chest heaving. I closed my eyes and concentrated on my breath. In through the nose, out through the mouth. In through the nose, out through the mouth. When I opened my eyes I felt a little calmer, but then I saw Pelorson staring at me. He quickly looked down at his menu, but it was too late. I saw the distaste that crossed his face.

The waiter came to take our order. He looked expectantly at me. But the words on the menu dissolved into floating letters that ducked and dived before my eyes. Unable to read it, I threw the menu down and asked for the first thing that came into my head: a salad. But instead of taking my order, the waiter asked me a series of questions, none of which I could answer. What sort of salad? Would I like something with my salad? Would I like it as a starter or a main course? I looked at him blankly, unable to reply. I wanted the waiter to go away. I wanted him to take Pelorson and go away.

And then I heard Beckett tell him I'd like a large sal-
ade niçoise. While he and Pelorson ordered, I breathed. In
through the nose, out through the mouth. In through the
nose, out through the mouth. And while I breathed I looked
at Beckett, at his still face and his pale blue-green eyes flicking over the menu. And his hands. Oh God—his hands! I felt
all my love for him surging inside me, rolling and crashing.
But I was also filled with foreboding, for I knew why he'd
brought Pelorson with him. And it wasn't because Pelorson
was hungry.

I pushed my knees together under the table. I pushed
them so hard I felt the joints grinding. I straightened my
spine, made myself sit very upright, my back like a plank.
And I breathed. As I composed myself in this way, I listened
to Beckett and Pelorson talking about the food they'd ordered. I could see I'd disappointed Pelorson. No doubt he'd
expected a miniature literary genius capable of enlightening
him on the mysterious ways of the great James Joyce. No
doubt he'd told his friends he was dining with the daughter
of the celebrated writer. No doubt they were waiting to hear
all about it.

The waiter brought the wine and then our food. For the
next twenty minutes I pushed the limp lettuce leaves around
my plate and counted and re-counted the silvery anchovies
and the green beans. I was glad to have something to do
and somewhere to look. Pelorson asked me about my dancing but I ignored him. I was too busy counting the beans on
my plate—there seemed to be rather a lot of them slithering

around in a pool of oil, squeaking when I stabbed them with my fork. Beckett said very little, but he was squirming on his seat and his face was touched with color. I knew I was embarrassing him in front of his pupil.

I played with my salad, but I couldn't eat any of it, not a single bean, not a single slippery anchovy. When the waiter took my plate I looked up and caught Beckett's eye. He held my gaze, and for a minute, I thought I was at the top of the Eiffel Tower again—everything spread out before me, stretching away, bleeding into the horizon. And then the feeling of giddiness, the slow spinning in my head as I looked down. As I stared at Beckett, I was reminded of those sensations. But there was a wary look in his eyes and it was slowly dawning on me that perhaps he didn't feel the way I felt. Had I misunderstood something? Beckett turned to Pelorson and asked him if he'd like a dessert.

Should I raise the subject of our marriage now, regardless of Pelorson? Perhaps he'd take the hint and go away. After all, that's why I was there, in my new dress, with my coiffured hair, my reverting squint concealed beneath a sheen of newly purchased eye shadow. And suddenly I saw everything I'd hoped for and dreamed of splintering into a thousand little pieces. I saw my wedding bouquet exploding above my head, the pale-pink rosebuds falling listlessly to the ground. I saw the little home I'd imagined wrenched apart, the fat cushions ripped asunder. And Mrs. Samuel Beckett. I saw Mrs. Samuel Beckett dissolving like an apparition. Vanishing limb by limb. Until nothing but her head remained, dismembered and floating in the air, a single eye swerving before me.

I gasped for breath. Pushed the table away from me. Had to get out. Air! I needed air! As I stood up, shaking and awkward, I saw Beckett looking at me, his face taut with concern and embarrassment. Pelorson asked me if I was ill and tried to steady me by putting his hand on my arm. I thrust him away and floundered toward the restaurant door. Once outside, I took deep gulps of air and ran down the road in the direction of the Seine. Hot tears welled up—tears of shame and defeat and despair. Everything was black except the moon, which hung in the darkening sky like a cold silver coin. And then through the crouching dusk I heard Beckett's voice calling my name. I didn't look back. I ran and ran, tears tipping down my face, until I got to Robiac Square.

* * *

I'D BEEN HOME for no more than ten minutes when I heard the doorbell. I lay on the couch in the parlor, in the dark, listening, not moving. The bell rang again and again. And then I heard Beckett's voice calling my name from the street. My head whirred but eventually I got up, walked down the unlit hall, and let him in. I knew my eye makeup was smudged, and my face streaked with tears, but I no longer cared.

In the gloom, Beckett told me, his voice stuttering, that I'd misunderstood his intentions.

"Were you . . . were you . . . expecting . . . something else?" Beads of sweat had appeared where his forehead met his scalp.

I nodded mutely.

"I like your new outfit." Beckett's tone was diffident but kind. "And I think you're very beautiful. But I hope I haven't misled you in any way."

"You come to the house every day," I mumbled. "I hoped we'd get married." Once the words were out, hanging like flares between us, I felt a sense of relief.

"Oh, Lucia, I come to see your father, not you."

I recoiled instantly. "What?" I whispered.

"I come to help him with his work. That's the only reason I come." His words were cold and hard. His eyes had become flickering blue flames pushing me away, warning me off. I froze. And then a million questions started forming in my mind. Questions about the way he looked at me, the way he touched me in passing, all those moments of intimacy, our aborted lovemaking. He touched me where no man had touched me before. We had nearly made love. Had he forgotten all this? Had the whiskey wiped it from his memory? And all the walks, the trips to the cinema, the tea in his rooms. All just to see my father?

"If that's the only reason you come, what was everything else?" I asked bleakly.

Beckett looked at his feet, his shoulders stooped and hunched. "You're like a . . . like a sister to me," he stam-

mered. "But so . . . so beautiful . . . so full of life—sometimes
I couldn't . . . can't . . ." He paused, then lifted his head so
his shoulders rolled back. Sweat dripped down the side of
his face. "I'm not the marrying sort. It's your father I come
to see, Lucia."

I couldn't bear to be with him any longer. Betrayed, de-
ceived, humiliated, I pulled myself up to my full height,
feigned composure. "So I was nothing more than . . . than an
hors d'oeuvre?"

"I suppose not," he said quietly, wiping the back of his hand
across his face.

"I think you should go," I said. "Immediately."

"I'm sorry." Beckett seemed to wilt again, his shoulders
deflating and his eyes returning to the floor. "It's as though
I'm dead inside. I don't have human feelings . . . that's why I
can't fall in love with you. I tried . . ."

"Immediately," I repeated. I couldn't listen to any more of
his feeble excuses. He'd used me to get closer to Babbo. Just
another sycophantic Flatterer. I'd turned down Emile—
charming, sweet-natured Emile—for him. I'd been ready to
lose my virginity for him. And all the time, I'd been nothing more than a pawn in his game of "chase the genius."
Nothing more than James Joyce's daughter. A tasty little
hors d'oeuvre, chewed and swallowed in a second.

"Will you tell your father?" Beckett's eyes were glued to
the floor, but his voice was timorous, quivering.

I didn't answer him. He'd taken everything from me. I felt

like a husk, a thin brittle husk, empty and blundering—and all he could do was ask whether I'd tell my father. How could he be so cruel, so callous?

Beckett turned to go, shuffling down the hall like an old man. I heard the door of our apartment close behind him and the soft echo of his tread as he made his way down the stairs to the street.

I thought of the eighteen months I'd loved him, hungered for him. Eighteen months of waiting for him every day. Eighteen months of hallway talks and intimacies and family outings. I thought of our marriage bed—how he'd tumbled in my arms into that slice of honey-colored light, half-naked and panting with desire.

I turned the lights on, made my way to the telephone. The number of my parents' hotel in Zurich lay beside it. I picked up the receiver and asked the operator to put me through.

A few minutes later I spoke to Mama, told her everything. I told her what Beckett had said, that he'd broken my heart, that he'd left me to walk home alone in the dark, that he'd shamed and humiliated me. Mama was livid. I could hear the anger bubbling out of her as she relayed my words to Babbo. She said Babbo hadn't had his eye operation yet, but they'd be back as soon as they could. As I hung up, I heard her words loud and clear: "No one trifles with our daughter, Jim. No one!"

* * *

I STAYED IN bed for two days, talking to no one, eating nothing, hearing only the hoarse cries of the rag-and-bone men as they trundled their carts up and down the rue de Grenelle. I watched the hands of the clock move slowly and mercilessly past the hour of my dance class with Miss Morris. Still I couldn't move. I tried to tell myself how rude it was to miss an appointment, how long I'd waited to teach a class in front of her. But all I could think of was my curtailed evening with Beckett. I asked myself, repeatedly, how I could have gotten everything so wrong, how I could have misread so many signs. And yet, even in my darkest moments, I knew this was not all my fault. If his soft words and ardent embraces had been nothing more than a bid to ingratiate himself with the great James Joyce, then he had cruelly misled me.

I remembered Sandy's words, that all Paris thought Beckett and I were engaged. And, once again, the shame and humiliation reverberated through me until every inch of my body seemed shriveled and shrunken. How would I hold my head up now? Already I could imagine the whisperings in the Montparnasse cafés. The jilted Joyce girl . . . yes, the one with the squint . . . quite passed over.

And why had I behaved with such unnecessary drama in the restaurant? I asked myself what Kitten would have done. Would she have run out shaking and crying? No, she'd have remained seated, masking her shock and disappointment with a display of good manners. She would, I'm sure, have effaced her pain and hurt with a quiet acknowledgment of defeat. But I? What did I do? I went to pieces—spectacularly to pieces.

When my parents returned, I was still raw with grief and shame. My eyes were sunken and red from crying. My hair was unwashed and unbrushed. My face was pale and hollow. Mama bustled in, opening windows, picking up clothes from the floor, wiping lipstick off the mirror with a handkerchief. I saw her eyeing my new dress as she hung it in the wardrobe. Then she knelt on the floor and picked up each scattered jade bead and put them in a bowl on my dressing table.

"We can be getting them restrung," she said. She went to the bathroom and ran a bath for me, generously filling it with her favorite bath oil. As I lay in the lavender-scented water, watching the steam condense on the walls, I over-heard my parents talking. I'd forgotten to completely close the bathroom door and Mama's raised voice came floating in.

"I knew what was going on, Jim. I could see it with me own eyes. If you hadn't been so caught up in your own world, you'd have seen it too. Or maybe you did see it and you chose to ignore it—because it suited you having him here. But he took advantage, Jim. He led her on and then, when he had what he wanted with you, he dropped her. Just like that. She didn't even do her dancing for that Marga-ret Morris—the one that was so important she couldn't be coming to Zurich with us. And she looks something awful. Her squint's back with a vengeance for sure. What a lousy waste o' money that was!"

Her words hung momentarily in the air, then began circling and swarming in my head. I heard Babbo's voice and tried to push Mama's words to one side.

"What am I to do?" His voice dipped.

"Well now, isn't that blindingly obvious? Sure I want him banned from the house. All of them. Because it's me that's picking up the pieces. Not you, Jim, me!"

"Yes, you're right, Nora. I'll telephone him now."

"And not just him, Jim. You can telephone them all. All the unmarried men coming to help you with your bloody book."

"Even the pious and chaste McGreevy? Surely he can help me? Who'll help me now?"

"I don't give two straws, Jim. Your lady worshippers— Miss Beach, Miss Weaver. I don't want any more people upsetting my family when they're only interested in you. Mrs. Fleischman's no better, but at least she's marrying Giorgio. But Lucia's different—she needs our protection, Jim. And like I said, it's me that's picking up the pieces."

As their voices faded away, I realized the enormity of what had happened. Beckett was to be banned from the house. I was never going to see him again. My dreams of love and escape and freedom were over.

*　*　*

A WEEK LATER Stella came to tea. She wanted to take me to the Louvre to look at another painting, but I didn't feel ready to face Paris yet and I knew Beckett sometimes went to the Louvre, so we stayed at Robiac Square and talked. Stella had seen Beckett and she told me bluntly of his devastation. She said Babbo telephoned him at the École and told him never to set foot in Robiac Square again. She told me that Beckett worships Babbo and is lost without his daily meetings here. Her tone was frank and unrestrained. I wondered whose side she was on.

"Well, Stella," I said. "You can have him now."

Stella stood up, ignoring my words, and walked to the window. As if something had caught her eye. And then she said, "He's going back to Dublin, to teach."

I felt a spasm of pain. Was this my doing? Had I forced him out of France? I couldn't imagine Paris without Beckett. Everything was unraveling, coming apart.

"He looks terrible. Very thin and a rash on his face," Stella continued, her voice measured, as though she'd said these words before, practiced them on her way here perhaps. "He's working day and night on his study of Proust. And he's trying to finish his translation of your father's work."

"I thought they weren't doing anything together?" I said sharply.

"He promised to do that for your father before all this. He's lost without your father's good opinion, Lucia. Their relationship was very important to him." Stella kept her eyes fixed on the view from the window—the Paris sky, streaks of red and yellow and gray, blurring and smudging in a blaze of light. I wondered if she was admiring the view with her painterly eye or just avoiding me.

"Why are you telling me this?" I said. "You seem to forget he broke my heart!"

"Is it really necessary to break his in return?" She turned and looked straight at me. There was something flinty in her expression, in the square set of her jaw.

"That's not my doing! My father's angry. He doesn't want to see Beckett anymore. That's not my fault!" I could hear the indignation in my voice. Why was Stella saying this?

"I tried to warn you. I tried to tell you your plan wasn't going to work. But you'd only listen to Kitten. What does Kitten know about Irishmen or artists?"

"Kitten has lots of boyfriends," I said loyally. "She knows all about men!"

Stella turned back to the window, back to the receding sunset. "There's something else you should know." She paused and I heard her take a loud gulp of air. She seemed about to turn and look at me, but instead she carried on talking to the window. "Beckett already had a lover. Not now, but all of last year. When you thought he had eyes only for you, he was having a love affair with someone else. Mr. McGreevy told me. No one knew but Mr. McGreevy."

The noise in my head threatened to engulf me. Beckett's words, Mama's words, now Stella's words—all scrambling and flailing inside me.

"Who?" I whispered hoarsely.

Stella came to sit beside me on the couch. She took another deep breath before she answered. "His cousin. That's why he was always going to stay with his aunt and uncle in Germany. I'm sorry, Lucia. I thought you should know. Mr. McGreevy thinks it's over now, but he can't be sure because Beckett never talks about it. Mr. McGreevy said she wrote him millions of letters. That's how he guessed something was going on."

"That can't be true. It's not true. Mr. McGreevy's mistaken!" But even as I spoke I was remembering the letters under his bed . . . all those letters tied neatly into bundles.

"I don't think so, Lucia," said Stella gently.

I put my head in my hands and bit my lip to keep the tears back. Nothing had prepared me for this. How could I have been such a fool! I'd made myself the laughingstock of Paris. While everyone had been gossiping about our engagement, Beckett had been in love with his cousin! How could this have happened? And yet . . . and yet I didn't believe I was entirely at fault. I couldn't forget Beckett's affection. I couldn't forget the way he'd looked at me, touched me, kissed me. I couldn't forget his lover's gift or the way his hands had brushed mine at every opportunity. I couldn't forget the feel of his body pressing down on me, the feel of his lips on my neck, his tremulous voice as he told me I was beautiful. No—I was the wronged party and I wouldn't let Stella think otherwise.

"I don't care! He's a bastard! He's a fucking two-faced bastard!" I shouted. I saw the look of shock on Stella's face and heard the clattering of Mama's heels as she hurried down the hall toward the parlor.

"I hope you're not upsetting yourself again, Lucia?" Mama

peered at me, examining my left eye, my squint. "You need to calm yourself." She turned to Stella. "'Tis good of you to come, Stella. Lucia hasn't been out for days and days. Paris will be forgetting she exists."

"Shall we go out next week, Lucia? If you're not up to the Louvre, we could go somewhere else. Perhaps to some smaller galleries?" Stella sounded tentative, wary. I wondered if she would ask if she weren't under obligation to Babbo to instruct me in art history. Before I could respond, Mama replied for me.

"Yes, Stella, Lucia would love that. It would be just what she's needing right now. And she needs to meet some new people. Not writers. Not Irish. Not clever. Just normal. 'Tis what I've been saying to meself. Can you ask Kitten? She has lots of gentlemen friends."

17

SEPTEMBER 1930

PARIS

When I woke, I was panting slightly and out of breath, my
body covered in a thin film of sweat. Briefly, I thought
I was still onstage. I heard applause resounding all around
me. I felt the flood of exhilaration and relief that followed a
performance. For a few seconds I basked, like a fat lizard, in
the adulation and the glory. I smiled generously as I curtsied,
seeking out Babbo, Giorgio, and Beckett in the dark sea of
faces before me.

It was only when I opened my eyes and saw light easing reluctantly through the shutters that I knew I was in my room
at Robiac Square, that I hadn't performed for almost a year,
that I hadn't danced for several weeks. And the sour smell
that clung and rose in my nostrils was a sharp reminder that

Beckett was gone and Giorgio was gone and Babbo was so absorbed with *Work in Progress* he might as well be gone.

Since we'd returned from our summer tour of Wales, London, Dover, and Normandy, every night had been distorted and twisted by dreams. Frequently, I dreamed I was dancing again. Two nights ago, in my dream, I looked into the audience and found Beckett and Kitten and Stella standing and clapping enthusiastically. But as the dream progressed, they mutated into strange wire figures with wool hair and malevolent faces, and I saw they were being manipulated by a motor that Sandy was controlling in the wings. He changed the motor and they started belly dancing, their evil faces leering as they thrust and gyrated. In another dream, I ended my dance to jeers and catcalls from the audience. As I stood, bewildered, on the stage, Zelda Fitzgerald began jumping up and down in the front row, her hands cupped around her mouth. But the booing and hissing from the crowd was so loud I couldn't hear her. It was only when I looked down that I realized I was naked, I'd forgotten to put my costume on. As I fled from the stage in shame, I suddenly heard Mrs. Fitzgerald's voice, shrill and stentorian. She was trying to tell me both my eyes had crossed, that everyone could see. She didn't mention my nudity. When I woke, my face was wet and I was trembling with humiliation. I didn't get out of bed for two hours, because I couldn't face seeing myself in the mirror. Just in case.

Sometimes my dreams were so unpleasant, so perverse, that waking to my room and my life at Robiac Square was a relief. But sometimes waking up was like walking from warm sunlight into icy shadow. I had to think of things to look forward to, reasons to get out of bed. Today was good. Babbo was sitting for a portrait. Giorgio was coming for tea. Sandy was coming. Yes, Sandy was coming.

* * *

AFTER BECKETT, BABBO was more willing to let me go out alone. I don't think Mama wanted me moping around in the evenings, and I suspect they knew I'd never make friends or find a new boyfriend sitting in Fouquet's with them and their Flattering friends.

Just before we left for the summer, I was allowed to go to the Coupole with Sandy and his crowd. Sandy's friends were American and rich. We drank mint juleps, and when it got late, we went to a jazz club and danced for hours and hours while Sandy's friends cheered and pestered me for private dance classes. When I suggested a group lesson, they insisted the lessons should be private, all the time winking and nudging each other. The following morning, Babbo asked me about Sandy's crowd and a dark look of disapproval crossed his face. He and Mama exchanged an inscrutable glance, but neither said anything.

I didn't tell them what happened on the way home—how Sandy had kissed me on the lips, full and passionate. And while I was with Mama and Babbo on their summer tour, I wrote to him every week. Gradually, he helped anesthetize the pain that Beckett had left. He would never replace Beckett—no one could do that—but he distracted and amused me. Stella said Beckett had a girl in Dublin but she knew no more than that. When she told me, I thought I saw the brimming of a tear in her eye, but she turned away so quickly I couldn't be sure. Although I tried not to think of Beckett, he kept tiptoeing, insidiously, into my thoughts. Kitten said I would probably love him forever but that I had to move on and let myself fall in love with someone else now.

* * *

WHEN SANDY ARRIVED for our first drawing lesson after the summer break, I was flustered and on edge. He was wearing gray knickerbockers and bright red stockings and carrying an ivory-topped cane in one hand and his suitcase of circus figures in the other. He put his cane and suitcase down, then beamed at me for a long time, as though I was some rare and exotic creature he'd managed to trap with nothing more than his own skill. I closed the door to avoid Mama's prying eyes, and no sooner had I turned back than Sandy had scooped me into his arms and was covering my face with kisses and telling me how much he'd missed me. A few seconds later we heard footsteps and hastily disentangled ourselves.

"How about we have these lessons in my studio?" Sandy looked at me, his eyebrows raised.

A thrill ran through me as I imagined myself and Sandy

alone, every week, no one eavesdropping or interrupting. And then a memory of Beckett flashed before me—his hands clumsy with whiskey, searching beneath my dance tunic. What an intense, sweet ache had been induced in that simple brushing of my body. And from there my mind jumped back to Emile, and the odd resistance, almost disgust, I'd felt at his hands beneath my blouse. How distant those days seemed. But how far I'd come! I was now, finally, the fun-loving flapper, the modern Parisian girl I'd always wanted to be. Or was I? Would I need a bottle of whiskey before I made love to Sandy? No—this time I would get it right and go all the way, as Mama called it. Perhaps then I could stop loving Beckett.

"D'you reckon your pa would allow that?" Sandy pulled out a wire figure wearing a tutu made of hessian, her arms outstretched. I noticed her wire feet were on points. Before I could answer, Sandy passed me the figure.

"I made this for you, Lucia."

I looked at the figure's whimsical face and admired the grace and elegance of this ballet dancer made entirely of discarded wire and unwanted sacking.

"She's perfect," I whispered. "The arch of her feet. How did you do that?"

"You'll be amazed what you can do with a bit of old wire." Sandy chuckled. "I can't give her to you, though. She's in my next show. I'm going to call her the female aerialist. But she's in your honor." And then his face clouded over, and he asked me if I'd heard about Zelda Fitzgerald.

"Heard what?" I asked.

"Gone to the lunatic asylum, that's what I've heard. Gone crazy!" Sandy tapped the side of his head. "She always was wild. Scott's devastated, apparently. It was thinking of you both dancing that reminded me."

I looked at his lady aerialist, turning her over and over in my hand. And I thought of Mrs. Fitzgerald. The way she'd whirled into Madame Egorova's studio that day, her fierce determination to dance despite her age, her resolution to be more than just a bit part in her husband's story, her preoccupation with "genius." "Gone mad? Why? How?"

"Cheer up! She'll be back. Let's not draw this one, after all. I'll find you something funny." He gently took the lady aerialist from my hand and gave me a small woolly-haired clown playing a trumpet. He pulled his chair closer to mine, until he was so close I could feel the warmth of his body.

"I hope you were drawing over the summer?"

"A bit. It rained quite a lot," I said, evasively. "How did Mrs. Fitzgerald go mad?"

"It's probably just a nervous thing. Don't give it another thought. Can I see your sketchbooks?" He arranged the clown, bending its pipe-cleaner legs to make it more stable.

When I didn't answer, Sandy picked up a sketching pencil, pointing it impatiently at my stack of drawing books. "You're a damn fine artist, Lucia. I mean that. You have real talent."

"I like drawing." I looked down at the tiny clown in my hand and stroked its wool hair with my finger. "When I draw with full concentration, it reminds me of dancing. Mama says it calms me. She likes me sitting still. She never liked me dancing. But the focus is the same. The bad thoughts go away when I draw or paint."

Sandy nodded enthusiastically, but there was a blankness in his eyes, as if he didn't really understand what I was saying.

"When you talk like that, all thoughtful and sort of wistful, it makes me want to kiss you." He stopped nodding and brought his face toward mine. I dropped the clown, threw my arms around his neck, and pressed my mouth to his with a vehemence and force that surprised me. His smell, of scorched wool and oil paint and turpentine, filled my nose, and I felt his long moustache scouring my skin, his arms holding me so tightly I thought my ribs might crack. Images of Beckett and Giorgio and Stella appeared before me, as if etched onto my eyelids. And then they drifted from me, and I clung to Sandy, kissing him harder and harder, tugging his head into me as if I wanted to be swallowed up.

Sandy pulled away, and I heard the kitchen door open. We both recoiled, fixing our eyes innocently on the little clown. When Babbo came in, I breathed a sigh of relief. He was too blind to notice anything. Behind him was a man with a thick salt-and-pepper beard and piercing black eyes.

"This is my daughter, Lucia, having her drawing lesson with Mr. Calder," Babbo said, before turning to Sandy and me and saying, "This is Mr. Augustus John, who has come from England to draw me."

Sandy leapt from his chair, eyes shining, and rushed to shake Mr. John's hand.

"Mr. John is going to capture my likeness in the study. If Giorgio comes, ask him not to disturb us until five o'clock." Babbo gestured to Mr. John, who nodded to Sandy and me before turning and leaving.

Sandy was still glowing, and I couldn't tell if this was because of our kiss or because of meeting Mr. John. He paced distractedly around the table asking if he should invite Mr. John to his circus. When I suggested, tentatively, that Mr. John was too old for *Le Grand Cirque Calder*, Sandy laughed and said no one was too old for his circus. And then he said he couldn't kiss me while Mr. John was in the house. He was too distracted, too unsettled.

"Come to the Coupole tonight, Lucia. Quite a crowd of us going. And we can carry on where we left off." He winked at me. Then he put a hand theatrically to his chest and added, "You've stolen my heart, you naughty little creature."

But his words flew past me, as if a breeze had whipped them away.

"How does madness start, Sandy?" I picked up the little clown again, rubbed my thumb over its striped dungarees, cradled it in my palm.

"You're thinking about Zelda again? She'll be fine, I promise. Now, open your sketchbook. I'm not asking you again."

* * *

BABBO WAS POLISHING his spectacles and complaining about his portrait when Giorgio sauntered in, wearing a new velvet waistcoat with engraved silver buttons and the whitest spats I'd ever seen.

"Mr. John hasn't accurately captured the bottom half of my face. What am I to do, Giorgio?"

"Don't give out so, Jim." Mama picked up a cushion from the sofa and started pummeling it.

"It looks fine to me, Father. What I've actually come about is your marriage certificate." Giorgio slumped into an armchair, his gangly legs splayed out in front of him. "Helen needs to have a copy made, so if you could find it and let me borrow it for a couple of days, we'd really appreciate it."

Mama blanched. Babbo removed his glasses and started polishing them again. Silence fell over the room.

"You'll not be needing our wedding certificate to get married," said Mama finally.

"Oh, it's not for the wedding. As you know, Helen wants to have a child as soon as we're married. She's not so young now." Giorgio ran a preening hand over his oiled hair then laced his fingers together, placed his hands behind his head, and waited calmly for a response.

I looked at Mama, expecting a snide riposte on Mrs. Fleischman's age. But, oddly, she said nothing. Her face was very pale and she'd pulled her lips into a tight, thin line.

"When do you need it?" Babbo continued to polish his glasses with an exaggerated concentration.

"I suppose there's no rush," Giorgio drawled. "But when the child's born, naturally she wants it to be a Joyce."

"God save us!" Mama snapped. "And why wouldn't it be

a Joyce? What else would it be? If you're the father, 'tis a Joyce!"

"Actually, it's not that simple. It's only a Joyce if I'm a Joyce. And I'm only a Joyce if you're married. *We* all know you're married. *We* all know that Lucia and I are legitimate Joyces—we've been to enough of your wedding anniversaries, seen your rings—but the law only knows what's on paper. So I need to borrow your certificate." Giorgio eased a fingernail between his two front teeth, picked out something, inspected it, then relaced his hands behind his head. "I was hoping you'd have it to hand. If it's lost, Helen tells me we can get a copy made from whoever married you, but it might take some time and she wants to get it organized beforehand. These Jewish women are incredibly organized."

The room fell quiet again. So quiet I could hear the rattling chirp of next door's caged canary and the faraway whistle of a train. Mama sat on the sofa, her back rigid and upright. Her face, still bleached of color, was a mask—expressionless and immobile. Babbo's right leg twitched slightly, and his ringed hands continued to wipe his lenses with the little square of orange silk he kept in his spectacles case. I tried to catch Giorgio's eye, but he was gazing blandly at the ceiling.

"I think it's an inheritance thing too," he continued. "Helen knows all this stuff. Rich Jews—especially rich American Jews—have their affairs properly organized. If our child is to inherit, everything has to be legal. Otherwise it's just a little bastard with no rights at all." Giorgio laughed coarsely.

Mama gave a sharp intake of breath.

"That's enough, Giorgio," Babbo said firmly. He folded up the orange cloth, laid it carefully in his spectacles case, and put his glasses back on. Then he looked squarely at Giorgio and said he'd have the certificate in a week.

"What a lot o' fuss!" Mama got up from the sofa and walked over to stand beside Babbo. "She's not even expecting a babby yet. Maybe she won't even have one at her age. And you'll have put your father to all this work for nothing!"

"Oh, she'll have a baby, all right." Giorgio gave a short, dry laugh. "She's determined to have a Joycean offspring, a bit of Babbo's genius, as she puts it. She'll do it if she has to visit every doctor in the land. Anyway, she's already had a child, so we know *she* can breed. And I'm bound to be fertile. There'll be a baby Joyce, all right." There was something that struck me as boorish and lewd in Giorgio's words. How had the old Giorgio slipped so decisively away? How could one person metamorphose, so completely and wholly, into another? Giorgio turned and saw me contemplating him. For a second I imagined us sharing one of the old conspiratorial looks that had bound us so much to each other. I eased my facial muscles into an intimate smile, like the ones we shared when we wanted to silently ridicule our parents or their guests. But Giorgio's eyes were chilly, and he quickly looked away.

"Yes," he said. "There'll be a baby and it won't be a bastard."

* * *

WHEN SANDY ARRIVED to take me to the Coupole later that evening, he brought me a small package wrapped in tissue paper and laughingly told me it was for being such a good pupil. I assumed it was one of his circus people, perhaps the lady aerialist. But when I ran my fingers over the tissue paper, gently prodding and probing, I realized I was mistaken. I tore off the paper, unable to hide my excitement and pleasure. Inside was a brooch made entirely of wire, twisted into a simple concentric spiral and attached to a pin. It wasn't the sort of jewelry that Mama or Babbo would want me to wear. Indeed, it wasn't something I'd have chosen myself. But I loved the thought of Sandy making it, thinking of me as he hammered and molded the wire, anticipating my gratitude as his large fingers worked with the thin strands of metal.

"It's beautiful," I exclaimed. "I'll wear it every day so I can have a little bit of you with me wherever I go."

"Here, let me." Sandy took the brooch and held it up against me. "Where would it sit best? Near your long neck, I think. I like the idea of the roundness of it against the length of your neck."

"I can change my outfit," I said. "D'you think it would look better with a different neckline?"

"No, here is perfect." He pinned the brooch to the top of my dress, just below my throat. Then he stood back to admire me. I felt a lurch of happiness. Over the last five months, the pain of Beckett's rejection had slowly ebbed and I thanked Sandy for this. His boisterous kisses, his obvious desire for me, his faith and belief in me—he had redeemed me where

Beckett had diminished me. As he accompanied me around Montparnasse, kissing me publicly and passionately, the humiliation of Beckett's rebuff had slipped away. Sandy had let me glimpse a future again.

And so I'd started, very tentatively, to imagine myself as Mrs. Alexander Calder. But this time I knew it was real and nothing to do with my father. Sandy admired Babbo but had no interest in him or his work. He came to the house only to see *me*, to teach *me*. Sometimes I thought back to Beckett and laughed bitterly at how my love had blinded me to so much. How naïve I'd been! But it was different with Sandy. Where Beckett had been secretive and silent, Sandy was vocal and public. He didn't care who saw him kissing me. And when we bumped into his friends (and he had many), he introduced me as "Lucia, the light of my life," and told them what a great painter I was. Not a word about my father. And Sandy knew what had happened to Beckett, how my father had banned him from the house. Would he risk the wrath of Babbo if he wasn't serious about me?

Of course, Mrs. Alexander Calder would be very different from the exiled Mrs. Samuel Beckett, and her wedding bouquet would be completely different. The pale-pink rosebuds would have to be replaced with flame-colored gladioli and the white lilac swapped for deep red chrysanthemums. There'd be obstacles—America, for example. It would break Babbo's heart if I were to live in America. I'd have to insist on us living in Paris. I imagined myself helping Sandy with *Le Grand Cirque Calder*. So many things I could do. I could mend his figures and props when they broke, I could help with the gramophone, I could sell tickets and serve drinks.

Sandy stared at the brooch he'd just pinned to me, moving his head from side to side, taking a step back, then moving toward me until he was so close I could feel his breath on my neck. "How does it look?" I asked anxiously.

"I might need to borrow it. Think how great it would be with little springs on the back. Walk 'round the room for me, Lucia. As if you're modeling it in a fashion show."

Hips thrust forward, I shimmied around the room with Sandy loping along beside me, watching me and looking at his brooch. His face was alive and mobile, so unlike Beckett's. And in that moment, I recalled how my dancer's instincts had alerted me to Beckett's reticent body language, all those months ago. Why hadn't I trusted my instincts? Why had I been so blinkered by love? I'd known then that he was holding something back.

I stopped moving and looked at Sandy, examining him through my dancer's eyes. He moved with a looseness and energy that was entirely unlike Beckett's awkward caginess. I remembered the wooden feeling of Beckett when I tried to teach him the Charleston, before we started on Babbo's whiskey. I'd danced with Sandy numerous times—his movements were guileless and extravagant. And I knew then that our lovemaking would be unrestrained, abandoned, honest.

Sandy was oblivious to my sudden scrutiny. His eyes were shining and he was nodding his head with such vigor I thought it might fall off. "If I put tiny springs on the back of the spiral, between the spiral and the pin, it would move when you move. It would dance!" He put his hands on my shoulders to stop me walking and then unpinned the brooch. "Bad manners, I know, but think how much better it'll be with springs on. A dancing brooch for my dancing girl!" He hesitated, then moved his narrowed eyes to my ears. "Earrings!" There was such delight in his exclamation that I laughed out loud, despite knowing I was about to return my lover's gift within minutes of receiving it.

"Are you going to make me matching earrings?" I asked.

"Well, they wouldn't need springs, would they? They'd move naturally, with the wind, with your body. You shall have both! I'll fix springs to the brooch *and* make spiraling earrings." Sandy delicately rubbed my left earlobe between his thumb and forefinger. "I wonder what weight your ears could bear," he muttered. I smiled and stroked his forearm.

Then he picked up my hand, my left hand, and looked at it in a speculative way, as though he was assessing that too for its size and strength. "A brooch, a pair of earrings, and"—he paused mysteriously—"and a surprise." And with that, he pressed my hand to his mouth and kissed it.

"A surprise?" I was so startled, so overjoyed at the inherent meaning of his words that my voice came out as a croak.

"I'm not saying another word. Or it won't be a surprise, will it?" He dropped my hand and then put my brooch back in his pocket. "Come on, Lucia, light of my life. The Coupole calls!"

I felt a sudden urge to dance, to spin and turn and feel my

hair and dress skating out behind me. How quickly I was sloughing off my past. But Sandy was already jamming his hat onto his large head and making for the front door.

"Can't I show the brooch to Babbo?" I called after him. I wanted someone else to see how much Sandy loved me. It was as if a part of me didn't quite believe my good fortune, as if I needed someone else to see his gift and affirm its meaning.

"Not yet. When it's done, you can wear it and everyone will see it. I promise!" He grabbed my hand and together we left Robiac Square and headed down the rue de Grenelle and onto Avenue Bosquet. And that was when I remembered Stella's crazy words on our trip around the Louvre, when she'd told me Sandy was engaged.

"Sandy," I said, as I looped my gloved hand through his arm. "Stella Steyn thinks you have a fiancée." I didn't have time to say any more. He stopped right there, with the bleating of motorcar horns and the rumbling of distillery carts all around us. And he pulled me into him with such force I felt my breath seize in my throat. Then his mouth was on mine, warm and wet and pressing, his tongue prying at the corners of my mouth, pushing into my throat.

"You're driving me crazy, Lucia." He tucked my hand back into the crook of his arm. "Have you asked your parents about having lessons in my studio yet, you bewitching little creature?"

"I will. I promise." And I gave a small skip in anticipation. I suddenly felt released, like a boat that had been unmoored. By making his feelings for me so clear, Sandy had set me free. An image of myself and Sandy naked on the floor of his studio, his circus figures cheering us on as we flipped and rolled and devoured each other, floated before my eyes. How different this was from Emile, or Beckett. And how wrong serpent-tongued Stella had been. Yes, Mrs. Alexander Calder was gradually taking shape, developing and filling out like one of Sandy's sculptures.

"You're something else, Lucia." And Sandy gave such a bellow of laughter, I could feel his body shake against mine. "Ask them tomorrow, promise?"

* * *

OF COURSE, MAMA and Babbo didn't agree to me having lessons in Sandy's studio. And Sandy didn't mention the subject again. So we carried on my drawing classes in the kitchen at Robiac Square.

One day, after a long evening kissing me in a dark corner of the Coupole, Sandy arrived very late for my class and breathless with excitement. He'd come straight from Piet Mondrian's studio and talked so fast I couldn't keep up with him. His words fizzed and bubbled and overflowed as he walked around and around the kitchen table, too intoxicated to sit down.

"His studio's all white. There's hardly any furniture. Only the bare essentials, and he's painted them white too. He had nothing ornamental. Just a single tulip in a vase—and guess what? Yes, you got it! He'd painted that white too! There was one thing that wasn't white—his gramophone. But guess what? He'd painted that red. The gramophone—can you imagine?" Sandy paused to draw breath and then carried on, gesticulating wildly and shaking his head with amazement. "The studio has windows on either side so light comes in from the left and right but on the wall in between the windows he'd tacked up large rectangles of painted cardboard, in primary colors. And he moves them around according to how he's feeling. I've never seen anything like it!"

"He painted a tulip white? Why didn't he just buy a white tulip?" I reached out to stroke Sandy's arm. But Sandy ignored my question, disregarding its pertinence entirely, and carried on striding so fast around the kitchen I was unable to touch him.

"Mondrian only believes in lines and colors, says they're the purest form of expression and nothing else matters. But his rectangles gave me a brilliant idea—the idea of things floating in space, all different sizes and colors. Some moving and some still. So I asked if I could have a play with his rectangles, make them jiggle." Sandy was almost running around the table now, his arms waving and his fists opening and closing.

"What did he say?"

"He refused. Point-blank. Said his work was already fast enough. And his ideas on color . . . Wow! He only uses black and white and sometimes red. That's how his studio was, everything white, a black vase, and a red gramophone. No green or pink or purple. He thinks all those colors just confuse and muddle."

"So does he just dress in white too? Has he dyed his hair a primary color?" My question was serious but Sandy didn't hear me. I wondered if he was talking to me at all, or whether he'd notice if I quietly left the room.

"He kept talking about 'The How.' His work is all about the *how* of position, the *how* of dimension, the *how* of color. Damned inspiring!" Sandy was almost bouncing on the soles of his feet now. I glanced nervously at the open window. What if he were to accidentally propel himself out? Surely he would die?

"What about my drawing lesson?" I asked, reaching again for his arm, wishing he would come away from the open window.

Sandy looked cursorily at his pocket watch. "No time. I need to get back to my studio. I want to make a start this afternoon. Shall we meet at the Coupole later?"

I nodded and hoped I could think of some intelligent questions on space and volume before I got there.

"How's my brooch? And my earrings?" I called out. "And my surprise!" But there was no answer from Sandy, just the sound of his feet clattering down the stairs.

* * *

THE COUPOLE WAS busier than usual that night. Theatergoers, tourists, and artists stood in packs at the bar. And at the tables, flamboyantly dressed diners gossiped and argued and flirted, all through a thick blue haze of cigarette smoke.

I quickly spotted Sandy and some of his "gang," as he called them—Waldo Peirce surrounded by young girls with freshly shingled hair, Ivy Trautman (Waldo's placid, pretty wife), and Joan Miró. I was glad I'd brought Stella for support. Sandy's friends intimidated me with their brash, self-assured ways.

Sandy bought us each a gin fizz and Waldo started hectoring me, wanting to know when I could give him a private dance class. The girls hanging around him found this very funny and simpered and giggled, but Ivy told me to take no notice. She wore an extraordinary dress of beaded orange silk with a black velvet cape slung over her shoulders. She smoked through an orange cigarette holder, knocking the ash on the floor as though she hadn't seen the ashtray right in front of her. I thoughtfully pushed the ashtray a little nearer, so it sat immediately beside her glass of champagne, but she carried on flicking the ash to the floor.

Sandy could talk of nothing except Piet Mondrian's studio. He repeated what he'd told me earlier, about Mondrian's painted white tulip and painted red gramophone, to anyone who'd listen. Waldo and Miró, both artists, found it interesting the first time around. Even Stella was intrigued by Mondrian's home decoration skills. Funnily, no one asked why Mondrian didn't *buy* a white tulip and I didn't have the bravado to ask again, in case everyone thought I was stupid. When Sandy had told his friends twice about his day with Mondrian, they refused to listen anymore. So he started approaching perfect strangers at the bar and telling them about the white studio. When they got bored and moved away, he began regaling Gaston, the kindly head barman. Waldo ordered more gin fizzes and then champagne and then more champagne.

When Stella said she wanted to go home, I told her, confidingly, that Sandy had made me a brooch and was now making me matching earrings that would dance as I walked. I said I'd wear them for her next week. And then I told her he was making me a surprise, and I fluttered my left hand in front of her face. She looked at me askance, as if I'd just confessed to murder.

"Guess! What piece of jewelry will Sandy make me next?" My words were slurred and I could feel the warm fug of the bar folding itself around me, tucking me into its smoke and clamor.

"What on earth are you talking about, Lucia?"

"First a brooch. Then earrings. And now he wants to make me something for my left hand. Isn't it obvious, Stella? Haven't you got eyes in your head?" I chortled to myself. Some people were so slow!

"He's your drawing instructor," said Stella in a voice spiny with disapproval.

"Not just my drawing instructor." I turned to look at Sandy. He was leaning on the bar, his hair in messy spires and his fingers rubbing distractedly at the cleft in his chin. Something about the spread of his shoulders made me want to go over and touch him, run my hands down his back. But then everything started to swerve and blur. And I saw Stella glaring at me. She took the glass from my hand and yanked me from the banquette where I'd been comfortably slouched.

"We're going home. Now," she hissed. "You've had far too much to drink." She tugged me toward the door, and before I had time to protest, we were standing on the pavement, the chill autumnal wind in our hair.

"He's kissed me for hours and hours and he's going to make me a ring and we're going to make love before we marry, the modern way," I said, trying to keep my balance.

"We need someone to see us home," said Stella curtly. "Wait here. I'll ask Waldo."

"No, get Sandy." I could feel myself gently swaying and the lids of my eyes getting heavier and heavier. But Stella came back with Waldo, a cigar clamped between his moustachioed lips. We each took an arm and reeled down the boulevard Montparnasse, Waldo doing his infamous impression of a braying donkey, Stella stony-faced and silent.

* * *

AT MY NEXT drawing lesson, Sandy told me how cross he was that Stella and I had "scuttled home with Waldo." He asked me why I hadn't waited for him, and then, before I could reply, he told me how much he'd been looking forward to kissing me on the way home. He grinned and laughed as he spoke, so I knew he wasn't really cross.

He didn't mention Mondrian's studio, but he did say Mondrian had been to his circus the day before and loved it.

Sandy's circus had become quite famous, with artists traveling from far and wide to see it. Whenever Sandy told me about the celebrated people in the audience, I felt a deep swell of pride and started imagining myself as his circus assistant, crouched on the floor overseeing the gramophone or collecting tickets at the door. But then Sandy said something that made me freeze.

"*Le Grand Cirque Calder* has probably gotten to the end of its life. I don't know how much longer I'm going to run it."

"No!" I shouted.

Sandy looked at me, startled.

"You can't," I said, trying to sound calm and firm, trying to hide the panic in my voice. "What would Paris be without your circus?"

"Oh, Paris would be Paris, but I love your enthusiasm, Lucia." Sandy leaned over as if to look at my drawing, but then, suddenly and without warning, he cupped my face in his large paint-stained hands and pulled my face toward his, kissing me on the lips, his tongue lapping my mouth, circling my tongue, vigorously prodding and nudging at my teeth and gums. I dropped my sketchpad and reached my arms around his neck to pull him tighter into me, but, unexpectedly, he pulled back and wiped his mouth on his sleeve.

"The thing is, Lucia, I've gotten some fantastic ideas from Mondrian. The circus takes up so much time, I can't do the things I really want to do. I want to push the boundaries of sculpture. I want to work on a much bigger scale. The circus has been great but I need to move on."

The thought of relinquishing Mrs. Alexander Calder, circus assistant, left me feeling slightly dislocated. Having spent the last few nights imagining myself putting up posters, selling tickets, mending his figurines, it took me a few seconds to recalibrate. What would I do in a white house with painted tulips and floating blocks of color? Sandy must have detected my apprehension because he looked oddly at me, then backed away, frowning so that his eyebrows met in a single line.

"What about making the circus bigger? Bigger figures, bigger props, bigger everything. You love the motors and the mechanics of it. Why can't you do that?"

"Because I want to do something else now. I don't really know what, but if I don't make time to explore it, I'll never know." Sandy sucked his index finger thoughtfully and then turned and looked out the window.

As Sandy's words sunk in, I felt a sense of dread, as if something dark and vinegary was crawling and turning inside me. I tried to follow his gaze, out over the slated rooftops and crooked chimney pots to the Eiffel Tower. But everything was distorted and obscured. "Will you still teach me?"

"Of course I will. You're my favorite pupil, you know that. D'you think I kiss my other students?" Sandy bellowed with laughter and instantly my mood changed. I took a deep gulp of air, feeling the lurch of anxiety subsiding. There would, I told myself, be a role for Mrs. Alexander Calder with or without the circus. And then a flash of inspiration struck.

"Couldn't someone run the circus without you? It could

still be your circus, of course, but you wouldn't have to be there."

Sandy looked at me curiously. "D'you have someone in mind?"

"I might do," I said. Then I turned to my sketchpad and concentrated on my drawing, sucking my lips in to cover up my smile. Inside my head I wrote a small piece for the newspapers: *Mrs. Alexander Calder has taken over the running of Paris's legendary* Grand Cirque Calder, *relieving her husband to focus on the next chapter in his career as France's foremost sculptor. Asked his thoughts on this, Mr. Calder said such devotion from a wife was rare and he thanked her from the bottom of his heart.*

"That sketch is great, Lucia." Sandy looked over my shoulder, stooped, pressed his lips to my neck, ran his tongue up to my ear. I leaned into him and smiled quietly to myself.

* * *

LATER ON, AS I was showing Kitten the dance moves I'd been learning at Miss Morris's dance school, I mentioned my idea.

"I thought you wanted to get back to full-time dancing. If you end up running his circus, how will you have time to dance?" Kitten stood poised on one leg, her arms crossed above her head.

"I can do both." I adjusted her arms, prodded her hands. "Spread your fingers more."

"Anyway, I think it'd be very difficult for anyone other than Sandy to run the circus. His personality is such a big part of it. All those animal noises he makes, and blowing that tin whistle." Kitten rose up on the ball of her foot. Looked down on me. "Would you really want to be doing that?"

There was a tinge of disapproval in Kitten's expression, as if she didn't think I should be squeaking like a monkey or roaring like a lion in public. Certainly, this wouldn't show me at my most elegant or my most alluring. And what she said was true. I didn't have Sandy's huge personality, his lack of inhibitions, whatever it was that made his circus a success. I'd be anxious, unsteady, flustered. Why had I not realized this before? Whatever made me think I could step into Sandy's shoes? But surely I could still marry him? I could still be Mrs. Alexander Calder, but perhaps I'd have to let *Le Grand Cirque Calder* go. After all, I'd need to support him in any way he saw fit. He would, inevitably, need me to help with his painting and sculpture. And of course, there would be our children, our brood of little Calders.

"Now lift your other leg. Slowly. Hold it there." I stepped back and checked her position, smiling at the thought of a posse of baby Calders.

"Are you sure he's the marrying type?" Kitten asked, no doubt recalling what happened with me and Beckett and the stories I'd told her about Sandy's orange bicycle and his gang of crazy friends. "I mean, he does live a very bohemian sort of life, doesn't he? Why are you smiling, Lucia?"

"Lots of people in Paris live like that. I know we don't but lots do. He's not going to ask me to ride an orange bicycle, is he?"

Kitten laughed, wobbled, regained her balance. "I hope not, darling! I guess you know Stella's convinced he's engaged to someone else?"

"Oh, I know. She probably wants him for herself, like she did with Beckett." I felt my upper lip curling scornfully, of its own accord. "But this is different. He kisses me all the time and he's given me a brooch and he's making me earrings and I think he's making me an engagement ring."

"An engagement ring? Are you sure?"

I told Kitten how Sandy had assessed my left hand and then promised me a surprise. "I saw him looking at my wedding finger, so it can't be a bracelet, can it? Now drop your leg . . . arms back in port de bras . . . lovely."

Kitten lowered her arms and took a deep breath, making her flat stomach bulge just a fraction. "How romantic he is. Can I see the brooch?"

"You'll be the first to see it, dearest Kitten. But he's rebuilding it so that it moves when I walk. It's going to be beautiful." I sighed contentedly. "Take another deep breath. Miss Morris believes the lungs, abdomen, and feet are the most important parts of the body."

Kitten frowned. "How can a brooch move?"

"He's putting a spring on the back. He's obsessed with movement. Everything has to move and rotate and turn upside down."

Kitten shook out her legs and arms and laughed. "Oh, darling, why can't you choose a normal man to fall in love with?

A regular beau who works behind a desk and saves up for an automobile."

"That sounds like your new boyfriend." I sidestepped to the sofa, twirled once, and sat down. Kitten's boyfriend worked in the finance office at the Michelin tire factory and was always buying her red roses and chocolates.

Kitten rolled her shoulders, smiling. "Richard's been promoted so many times, I've lost track."

"Babbo would never accept someone like that as his son-in-law. How would they make conversation? Babbo can't talk about tires."

"But he'd be marrying you, not your father. So would it matter if they couldn't converse?" Kitten lifted each pale foot and shook it out.

I looked at her despairingly. How could I explain my life as the daughter of a genius? How could I tell her of Babbo's disappointment if I were to marry a suited-and-booted clerk? I shook my head and said nothing. I didn't want to hurt Kitten's feelings. She was the only friend I had left. I didn't count snake-eyed Stella anymore.

"Have you had any more of your psychic dreams or intuitions, Lucia?"

I gave a short, sardonic laugh. "Well, they weren't exactly accurate with Beckett, were they? It's more of a physical thing with Sandy."

"Perhaps the force of your emotions crowded out your psychic powers. I've heard that mediums can only work in certain conditions, like when it's quiet or they're very calm inside."

"Well, if that's the case, Sandy's definitely drowned them out. When he's around it's as if the air's vibrating with his presence." Even as I spoke, I felt a sharp twist of desire in the base of my stomach.

Kitten came over to the sofa, sat down beside me, and took my hand in hers. "I think you should be dancing more, Lucia. You were so happy when you were dancing all day. Why don't you get back in touch with Madika? She was desperate to teach you."

"I can't. I'm too ashamed after my failure at ballet. And my parents made it quite clear that dancing onstage isn't an appropriate career for the daughter of a literary genius."

"Well, perhaps we can do something together? Audition for the talkies as a pair. Or set up another dance troupe. It's the right time for me too. Will you think about it?"

"I'm too busy at the moment," I said. "I'm just about to qualify as a fully-fledged Margaret Morris dance teacher and I've got my drawing lessons and I have to help Mama and Babbo all the time and Giorgio's wedding's coming up." My voice trailed off at the thought of Giorgio's wedding. Mama was still not talking to Mrs. Fleischman, and so perhaps I wouldn't even be invited to the wedding.

"I'm just not sure teaching movement is enough for you. I don't mean to sound disparaging, but it's not like the dancing we used to do, is it?"

"No, I'm not performing," I said, choosing my words carefully. "But it's very helpful to lots of people." I hesitated, unsure how to articulate my thoughts. "And Miss Morris is very inspiring. Her method helps pregnant ladies and invalids and children and sports people. It's useful. And I want a useful life, Kitten."

"But you will think about my suggestion, won't you? To do something with me, either something creative or something where we're in control of our own lives. Promise me you'll think about it?" Kitten coaxed.

"Oh, Kitten, I promise." I liked her idea and I knew Sandy wouldn't object. He loved to see me dancing. Once or twice I'd caught him sketching me on a napkin at the Coupole as I tried out new steps or jumps. But was I ready to go back onstage? Was I ready to face Mama's wrath? Of course, if I married first . . . if I was Mrs. Alexander Calder . . .

I squeezed Kitten's hand. "Let me finish my Margaret Morris training and get through Giorgio's wedding. My life is going to be very different soon—you'll see."

* * *

BABBO HAD A new slave. Paul Leon, a refugee from Bolshevik Russia, was the brother-in-law of Babbo's Russian tutor, Alex Ponisovsky. After Beckett was banned from Robiac Square, Mr. Leon started appearing and inveigling himself into our home. Just like all the others.

Babbo liked him because his middle name was Leopold (like the main character in *Ulysses*) and his wife's name was Lucie, rather like mine. Mama was impressed by Mrs. Lucie Leon because she gave fashion tours to American tourists. Mr. Leon would do anything for Babbo and he treated Robiac Square as his own personal shrine. Mr. Leon was probably the most slavish slave Babbo had ever had. He was often at Robiac Square all day, typing and reading and translating and running Babbo's errands. Recently, Mr. Leon had arrived clutching huge leather-bound tomes on the laws of Italy, France, and England. The elevator was invariably broken, so when he arrived, lanky and stooped, he panted like a dog, under the weight of several enormous volumes.

I didn't think anything of Babbo's new reading material. He read obscure books all the time. The previous week he'd made Mr. Leon scour Paris for books of English nursery rhymes. When we were in Torquay, Babbo had become obsessed with English schoolgirl magazines and made one of the Flatterers order him back issues of *Poppy's Paper* and *Schoolgirl's Own*.

It was only later, after Mr. Leon had left one night, I began to wonder about the law books. While I was sitting at the piano, silently admiring the black and white keys and wondering if Sandy would want the piano painted red, I overheard snatches of Babbo's and Mama's conversation in the study. They appeared to be talking about the law books, which was odd, because Mama rarely read and never discussed Babbo's work with him. Babbo's fluty voice dipped and rose, and that was also peculiar because he so rarely raised his voice.

As I strained my ears, I heard Babbo saying that something (and I didn't catch what it was) had to be done legally in England and that it couldn't be done anywhere else. Mama said this was all his fault, after which there was a silence. I leaned my body toward the wall, stretched out my neck, and listened. Then Mama said something that surprised me. She said her family would never speak to her again. And her voice was caustic and bitter, quite unlike her usual tone. At this point, Babbo's voice dropped and I couldn't hear anything. Then Mama's voice chimed in, loud and clear and angry, asking what they were to do about the newspapermen. I heard Babbo saying he'd manage everything, that it could all be done quietly and legally in London. Mama replied that she bloody well hoped so, and then I heard the door handle turning, and Mama walked out of Babbo's study and into the parlor where I was sitting at the piano. I quickly looked down at the keyboard and played a scale. I heard her marching past, breathing loudly through her flared nostrils.

I decided to ask Sandy's advice. We had a drawing lesson the next day and I was expecting my brooch back, and perhaps my new earrings too and maybe even a ring. I tried not to think about the ring but couldn't help imagining how it might look. Perhaps it too would contain a miniature spring, so that when my left hand moved, the ring would dance and shimmer, as I did.

* * *

SANDY ARRIVED PUNCTUALLY at ten o'clock, cane in one hand
and suitcase in the other. He told me I was to draw the entire
circus as an exercise in perspective. He opened his case and
started setting up little poles and hanging wires for the trapeze and tightrope acts and then he unrolled small swatches
of red carpet. As he did so, I told him about the conversation
I'd overheard between my parents and asked him what he
made of it. He laughed so much he knocked over the trapeze
wires and had to set them up all over again.

"What's so funny?" I frowned.

"It's obvious," Sandy spluttered. "You're so naïve, Lucia."

"What d'you mean?" I drew back, inclined my head,
watched Sandy struggling to set up the trapeze wire as his
hands shook with laughter.

"Forgive me if I'm too blunt, but your pa writes books most
people consider dirty. Brilliant but dirty. Worse than dirty—
filthy." Sandy hesitated, pushed the trapeze wire into place,
and attached the lady aerialist. "You do know that, don't you,
Lucia? Don't tell me you haven't read *Ulysses*."

"He's the greatest writer of the twentieth century. Everyone says so!" I plucked the lady aerialist from her wire, studied her, tried to keep the truculence from my voice. Tried to
still the tremor in my hand. Failed.

"*Ulysses* is banned in almost every country in the world.
Back in America, they burn it. You can go to prison for selling it. Isn't that why you're all here in Paris?"

I nodded. I knew all about Babbo's decade of tribulations
trying to get *Ulysses* published but I didn't want to think

about that. "What's this got to do with newspapermen and people not talking to my mother?"

Sandy started laughing again, his body shaking with mirth. "The next book must be even filthier. He must be working on a real corker in that study of his." He stopped laughing and paused. "The funny thing is, he looks so respectable and he's so quiet and well-mannered and he always calls me Mr. Calder. I can't make it out, I really can't. Don't grip the lady aerialist so tightly—you're gonna snap her in two."

I blinked and tried to stop the muscles around my eyes from convulsing. Truth to tell, I had no idea what *Work in Progress* was about. Something to do with "the dark night of the soul," rivers, Ireland. The pieces I'd heard Babbo read aloud were beautiful and meandering and musical. But what did they mean? Was I a muse for something dirty? For something filthier, more scandalous than *Ulysses*? No, that simply wasn't possible. And so I told Sandy he was wrong, that *Work in Progress* had nothing dirty in it whatsoever.

But, at the same time, I welcomed Sandy's explanation of the broken overheard conversation between my parents. After all, what else would involve law books, and going to England, and newspapermen? Was it possible that *Work in Progress* was so disgusting we'd be forced to leave France? Although why it could be published legally in England but not in France made no sense to me. I shook my head in bewilderment as I set out my pencils and sketching paper. This train of thought brought me quickly to Mrs. Alexander Calder.

If my parents moved to England (and Mama had made it very clear England was her favorite country and London her favorite city), Sandy and I might need to settle there too.

"Sandy, have you finished my brooch yet?"

"Oh, shucks! I *have* finished it but I left it in my studio. I'll bring it next time. Promise." He kissed me absentmindedly on the side of my head.

"And . . . and . . . the earrings? The ones that'll sway when I walk and dance?"

"Still a Work in Progress!" Sandy started laughing at his own wit.

And what about the surprise he'd promised me? My surprise ring? I thought about asking him but then decided not to. It might look a bit presumptuous. A little rude, even. He kissed me several times during our lesson but with an air of distraction. Perhaps he too was worrying about my family going to England.

When I'd finished my drawing and he'd praised my understanding of perspective and packed up his circus, he suddenly and unexpectedly asked if I could get away for a whole night. He said he wanted to take me dancing and then home to his studio. "You'd be my first," I whispered, head bowed, eyes on my sketchbook. I felt a hot, rosy flush creeping up my throat, whether of excitement or bashfulness I wasn't sure.

"You're still a virgin?" Sandy reached out, took a strand of my hair, wound it around his finger. "Can you get away, then? For a whole night?"

"Yes." My heart was racing. Who could cover for me? It would have to be Kitten. Only Kitten would lie for me.

"Let's hatch a plan when I come next week." He moved away, snapped the lid of his suitcase shut, picked up his cane, and gave it an extravagant twirl. "You could drive a man to distraction, you little minx."

"Can't I see you before that?" I tried to speak calmly but my words gushed out. A whole week without him? Yes—a long, empty week—but then Mrs. Alexander Calder would rise, like a phoenix, from the ashes of my past.

"Next week gives us plenty of time to hatch a plan, my little Irish virgin." He smiled flirtatiously, his eyebrows going up and down. Then he tilted my chin with his thumb and kissed me so heavily and feverishly on the lips, my insides seemed to rise and plunge and spin and I could feel the blood rampaging around my heart. When I eventually opened my eyes he'd gone, leaving behind the residue of his smell, his energy, his warmth.

* * *

I SPENT THE next week drifting around Robiac Square smiling to myself, much to Mama's irritation. Babbo, however, noticed nothing. He was full of his own success at getting the famous conductor, Sir Thomas Beecham, to attend one of John Sullivan's recitals. I ignored his ramblings about Sullivan's "amazing tenor voice," for my mind was full of its own ramblings. I imagined my night with Sandy over and over again. I made a hundred decisions—what shoes, dress, and jewelry to wear, how my hair should be set, what color lipstick, where to dab my perfume, whether to buy new underwear.

While my parents were out, I telephoned Kitten and told her Sandy had asked to sleep with me and I'd agreed. I couldn't quite gauge her response. I sensed a reluctance, an unwillingness perhaps, but then she agreed to cover for me. It was only when I hung up I saw how absurd it was that I, at the age of twenty-three, should be resorting to such deception. I could name any number of girls in Paris who were in and out of abortionists' parlors. But of course none of them lived at home, with old-fashioned Irish parents from whom they couldn't escape.

When the day of my drawing lesson arrived, I was so tense with anticipation I couldn't sit still. I paced the flat, then chasséd around my room, pausing frequently to check my face and hair, to touch up my lipstick or repowder my cleavage. I changed my necklace and earrings several times before remembering Sandy was bringing jewelry for me. I discarded my beads, leaving myself ready to be adorned by his quaking, quivering brooch and swinging earrings. I put my lips to the mirror and kissed myself, but the glass was cold and hard against my tongue, and not like Sandy's vigorous mouth at all. So I did a couple more turns of the flat, swiping at bluebottles, checking the clocks had been wound up, pushing back the shutters to see if I could see him walking up the rue de Grenelle. Until Mama decided she couldn't bear my restlessness any longer and went out. Mr. Leon and Babbo were ensconced in the study. I heard the typewriter rattling and Babbo dictating in his mellifluous, bell-like voice.

Finally, the clock chimed the hour. It was time. I gathered up my sketching books and pencils and arranged them on the kitchen table. I tried to calm myself by sketching Mama's butter knife with the mother-of-pearl handle, but I was fidgeting so much it was impossible. I walked around the kitchen table mouthing the words "Mrs. Alexander Calder." And when I got tired of that, I started imagining the night ahead—his large hands unrolling my (new) garters and then peeling off my (new, silk) stockings, his face nuzzling my (perfumed) neck, that way he had of thrusting his tongue into my (brushed and rebrushed) mouth and lapping like a thirsty dog. I slipped my hands inside my blouse, ran them over my ribs, my breasts, my stomach. I swabbed the dampness from my armpits, ran my tongue along my teeth and gums, told myself I had a body made for love, and wished he would hurry up.

After fifteen minutes, when Sandy still hadn't arrived, I went to the hallway and waited for him there, pacing up and down, watching the clock, flicking at the lucky Greek flag, and thinking about Sandy's smile, Sandy's hands, Sandy's breath.

Another fifteen minutes passed. Tired of the dark airlessness of our hall, I went to the parlor, drew back the shutters, and sat at the piano. I ran my quivering fingers over the keys a few times until Mr. Leon stuck his head out of the study and asked me if I wouldn't mind doing something quieter. I was too anxious to point out that it was after five o'clock and I was allowed to make a noise. Instead I nodded dumbly and walked back to the kitchen.

As time ticked by, my nervousness ebbed away, for it became obvious Sandy wasn't coming. Instead I felt the creeping listlessness of disappointment and thwarted hope. When Mama walked in carrying a basket of vegetables, I was sitting at the kitchen table, my head on my unopened sketchbook, my arms curled protectively around my skull.

She started unpacking muddy potatoes from a bag. "Didn't Mr. Calder come today?"

"No," I muttered into the table.

"Likely he's ill. Have you telephoned him?"

"He doesn't have a telephone." I raised my head from the table and my shoulders felt suddenly lighter. Of course! He must be ill! He'd never yet missed a drawing class.

"Why don't you walk over to his studio and see if he's needing anything? Only yesterday I was hearing about some poor bugger found dead of meningitis in his hotel room. Not a soul noticed. He lay dead and rotting for three days. If you hurry, you'll be back in time to come to Fouquet's. And it'll be doing you good to get some fresh air."

* * *

THE TREES WERE beginning to shed their autumn leaves and there was a sharp chill in the air. I hurried through Montparnasse toward Sandy's studio, imagining him prostrate with meningitis, perhaps already dead, with vermin nesting in his hair. The streetlamps were coming on, sending cones of warm light onto the pavement. On every corner stood carts selling paper twists of sugared almonds, or braziers where old men scooped blackened chestnuts into squares of newspaper. I stumbled on, seeing images of Sandy dying, gasping for water, calling weakly for help. What if I was too late?

By the time I reached his studio at the Villa Brune, I was running and hot with sweat. I hammered on the door but there was no reply. When I looked up at the windows, they stared back at me, black and gaping. I kept banging my fists against the door until a wizened old woman put her head out of a nearby window and shouted at me, *"Arrêtez-vous! Que voulez-vous?"* I asked her if she'd seen the man who owned the studio, but she told me to go away and slammed her shutters so hard flakes of old paint fluttered to the pavement.

Sandy must have forgotten. Perhaps he'd gotten his days muddled up and would come tomorrow. I had enough time to check some of his favorite bars, so I retraced my steps until I got to the boulevard Montparnasse and then I pushed open the doors, one by one, of the Select, the Dôme, the Rotonde, and the Coupole. It was early and they were all quiet: no sign of Sandy. I was just leaving the Coupole, when Gaston, the head barman, called to me from behind the bar where he was polishing glasses. He'd seen me several times with Sandy, so I smiled bleakly at him and explained I was looking for Monsieur Calder.

His eyes lit up, then flickered with surprise.

"Ah, Mam'selle Joyce, Monsieur Calder was here last night. I never saw him drink so much. Never!" Gaston slapped his thigh to make the point. "You could not come? I've not been so busy since Pascin killed himself. *Quelle tragédie!*" He paused to pick up a new glass, then looked at me quizzically. "You were Monsieur Calder's friend—no?"

I stared at Gaston, confused. "No, I'm talking about Alexander Calder, the artist. You've seen me here with him lots of times. Often wears an orange suit, loud voice, always laughing, hands always covered in glue and paint."

"Yes, of course! Monsieur Calder!" Gaston paused, eyed me over his linen cloth, started polishing again. "We gave him a good party. Very sad that you missed it. I don't know how he caught his boat today. He must have felt terrible this morning."

"Boat?" I echoed dumbly.

"Yes, home to America. Oh, what a man of mystery! No one knew he was engaged. But his fiancée came last night too." Gaston saw the shock on my face and gestured to a chair behind me. "I think you need a drink, Mam'selle Joyce. Have something on the house. A brandy?"

I gaped at him, my mouth hanging open, limp and lifeless. His words churned in my head. Sandy—engaged, gone home to be married. On the day he and I were supposed to . . . No! It wasn't possible!

I reached out, took the brandy glass from Gaston, tipped it down my throat, felt it burning, stinging. The rising panic and darkness ebbing. Dizzy. Giddy.

"He was engaged to you too, Mam'selle Joyce?" Gaston shook his head sadly. "These artists are very bad. I am just a simple barman. Another brandy?"

He refilled my glass as I struggled with what he'd told me, that there *was* to be a Mrs. Alexander Calder but it *wasn't* to be me, that Sandy must have known this for ages, that he'd had a leaving party and not invited me. Not invited me! Said nothing—not a word. Not a single word! I gulped the brandy down, felt my insides scalding, my eyes watering, my temples beginning to throb.

"Who is she?" My voice was barely a whisper and Gaston had to bend down to hear me.

"American lady. Nobody knew her." Gaston refilled my glass, shaking his head and making sympathetic clicking sounds with his tongue.

"What did she look like?" My voice was stronger and louder now, and I slowly released the grip on my brandy glass.

"Not beautiful like you, Mam'selle Joyce." His kind eyes raked over me, full of solicitude and concern. "You are a real Irish beauty."

"I asked him, Gaston. I asked him if he had a fiancée." I drained the brandy from my glass, relishing the heat running through me, the tingling feeling behind my eyes, the lightness in my head. Stella's words were swimming in my brain, sinking then surfacing like flotsam. "He's engaged to someone in America." And I had asked him! And he had answered me with a kiss so full of passion he'd almost squeezed the breath from my body.

"He made her a beautiful ring. Made it himself. My wife would not like it, but it was beautiful." Gaston shook his head sadly again.

"The bastard! We were about to be married. I can't believe it!" And then I remembered my brooch. Sandy never gave back the brooch he made for me! The bloody bastard! I imagined the American fiancée, with her straight eyes and pockets full of Yankee money, sashaying around in *my* brooch, *my* earrings. I stood up and staggered to the bar, full of anger and fury and outrage. I slammed my glass onto the marble top and demanded another brandy.

Gaston narrowed his gentle eyes and said he thought I should go home.

"She's wearing *my* jewelry. Don't you see, Gaston? And she's got *my* fiancé. He's a bastard but he's mine!" A table of chomping tourists turned to stare at me, their forkfuls of steak poised midair. The room was starting to spin. Tilting and turning as though the world had come loose from its axis. "*I* am Mrs. Alexander Calder!" I swayed toward the chomping tourists, my voice becoming louder, coarser.

"I'll take you home now, Mam'selle Joyce." Gaston called to one of the waiters, walked out from behind the bar, and propelled me firmly toward the door. He had one hand on my elbow and one on my back, steadying and maneuvering me as he flagged down a taxicab. I didn't resist. At that moment I felt all my bravado and anger slip into self-pity and all the vigor of fury slide into wretched exhaustion. I leaned heavily on Gaston and wished the throbbing in my head would stop.

"We were in love, Gaston." Bile was rising, sharp and rancid, in my throat. "We were in love! How could he do this to me?"

"I know, I know. You must forget him, Mam'selle Joyce. You must forget all about Monsieur Calder." As a taxicab pulled over, I heard Gaston tell the driver to take us to Robiac Square.

"How d'you know where I live?" My words slurred and frothed as I stumbled onto the back seat.

"Everyone knows where the great Monsieur Joyce lives. Now give me your hand, Mam'selle Joyce, and hold on to me. You will feel better in the morning."

I lay back on the leather seat. Everything was swaying— the trees, the buildings, the streetlamps, the driver. A slick of nausea wound its way through my insides.

"I will leave you on the doorstep," said Gaston when we arrived at Robiac Square. "The great Monsieur Joyce must not think I made his daughter drunk." He had one arm around my shoulder while his other arm held my hand, securely and comfortingly.

"Don't leave me, Gaston," I mumbled. "I'll fall if you leave me. Please don't leave me."

"I won't leave you, Mam'selle Joyce. I will take you to your apartment, knock on the door, and then I will hide until your papa or maman let you in. You will not be alone, not for one second, I promise. If no one opens the door, I will take you back to the Coupole. I promise."

He did exactly as he said. He asked the taxi driver to wait and then he gently pulled me from the back seat. At Robiac Square, the elevator was still broken, so we lumbered up the five flights of stairs, me swaying on buckled knees, he pulling, cajoling, and chivying. At the top, he arranged me like a pile of laundry, folding me up and placing me by the door. Then he knocked loudly, turned, and bolted down the first flight of stairs. I sat slumped for what seemed forever, my arms neatly placed on top of each other. And then the door opened and there was lanky Mr. Leon peering at me. And Mrs. Leon in a bright pink hat with a feather on it. I heard Mama calling to Babbo, "Mercy me! Jim, come and see what the cat brought in. 'Tis not a pretty sight. Thank the Lord you're half blind." And through it all I heard Gaston's footsteps pounding down the stairs. And I thought of the people who had loved me and left me, their departing footsteps all singing and ringing in my ears.

* * *

I NEVER TOLD my parents or Giorgio about Sandy. After my evening with Gaston, I went to bed for ten days, feigning illness. Babbo was completely distracted by his legal investigations (Mr. Leon was still coming and going with law books) and his forthcoming eye operation. He'd barely written eight pages of *Work in Progress* in the last six months and the only thing that cheered him was news of Sullivan's operatic successes. Mama could think of nothing but the forthcoming marriage of Giorgio and Helen Fleischman, and how best to stop it.

While I lay in bed with a "cold," I cried and cried, always soundlessly under the quilt. Sometimes I'd get up and look in the mirror, and if I saw my squint slipping back, I returned to bed and cried longer and harder. I wept for Sandy's silent deception, his unthinkingly cruel words and promises. And when I had no tears left for Sandy, I'd think of Beckett and more tears would spring forth. I wept for all my stillborn hopes and dreams—of love and affection, of liberation, of wedding bouquets, of little houses with fat cushions, of gardens with drifts of yellow daffodils. All dashed, smashed into thousands of tiny shards. But most of all I wept for the premature deaths of Mrs. Samuel Beckett and Mrs. Alexander Calder.

After ten days, I made myself get up and go back to my classes at the Margaret Morris school. As I spiraled and spun, looped and leapt, twisted and twirled, I felt the darkness within me slowly falling away, the pain and humiliation gradually receding into the far pockets of my mind.

And that was when I remembered Kitten's words about dancing together, doing something of our own, something creative. How had she put it? Something that would give us control of our own lives. Yes, that was it! I would call Kitten. I would take control of my life, not as someone's wife but as myself—as Miss Lucia Joyce.

* * *

ONE MORNING, NOT long after I'd recovered from my "cold," Babbo told me he'd had a letter from Mr. Calder.

I froze, mid-pirouette.

"Sends his apologies. Says he had to return home on family business. Regrets he can't teach you anymore." Babbo offered me the letter, but I waved it away, saying I'd known all along of Sandy's plans to go home. My voice cracked as I spoke and my legs shook beneath me, but Babbo was too distracted to notice. When he asked, through the leather spine of his huge book, if I'd like another drawing instructor, I thought for a minute and then said, "No thank you."

"Mr. Calder held your artistic abilities in high esteem." Babbo glanced at me over the top of his law tome, his eyes covered in a milky film. "I cannot dispel my dream of you and me working together, *mia bella bambina*."

"Me illustrating your work instead of Stella?" I asked, and a small sob rose in my throat. No doubt Stella had heard about Sandy's departure. No doubt she thought me a gullible fool.

"Of course." He spoke impassively into the musty pages of his book. "Miss Steyn is no longer under any obligation to me."

When Mama came into the parlor holding a new hat with

a matching hat pin, Babbo told her Mr. Calder had gone and I didn't want another drawing teacher. She looked at me, her face tight and guarded, and said she didn't want me moping around all winter. And as her thin, painted lips closed over her teeth, the image of an animal trap came to me. I felt a swell of fury. I felt the bubbling of coarse and dreadful words, low in my throat. The rage I'd felt, inarticulate and uncontrollable, when I discovered Giorgio and Mrs. Fleischman, flashed before me.

I clamped my mouth shut, forced myself to move, took deep and long breaths. I had to keep dancing! I triple-stepped stiffly around the couch, arms trembling above my head.

"I'll carry on drawing. And I'll carry on training at the Margaret Morris school. I won't be moping around." And then I thought of Kitten and our secret scheme, and my rage dissipated, leaving just a dull hum of pain at Sandy's letter, like the low drone of a mosquito in the night.

I thought of telling my parents that Kitten and I were about to start working together, that we were planning to dance again, like the old days. And perhaps if Mama hadn't been there I might have said something. But her eyes were cold and weary, and I was barely in control of my emotions. I didn't want that demon voice to rise inside me again. So I said nothing.

"You need some more friends, to be sure." Mama looked at her hat, stabbed it with the hat pin. "Why can't you be more like Kitten? She has lots of gentlemen friends." She turned to the mirror, angled her hat, adjusted the brim. "All this cavorting around. They say Miss Morris is half naked when she gads about."

Babbo left Sandy's letter on the table and slid quietly into his study, where Mr. Leon was waiting slavishly. Mama picked up Sandy's letter, cast her eye quickly over it, and said she never liked Mr. Calder anyway. Too bohemian, too wild, mixed with the wrong crowd. She dropped the letter back on the table and announced that she was off for a fitting for a new coat.

Alone, with Sandy's letter in front of me, tears started welling in my eyes. Why hadn't he written to me? Why had he written such a stiff, formal letter to Babbo? Wasn't I owed some explanation, an apology? My body wilted, but instead of collapsing onto the sofa or crawling back into bed, I made myself go to the telephone, dial the operator, ask to be put through to Kitten's number. And when her mother answered and said Kitten was out, I asked her through stifled sobs if Kitten could telephone me as soon as possible as I had something urgent to discuss. And then I dried my eyes, choked back my sobs, and vowed to rise again. Not like a phoenix this time, but like a snowdrop that pushes its green spire through earth stiff with frost. Yes, I would rise again.

NOVEMBER 1934

KÜSNACHT, ZURICH

"Two rejections in the space of a year." Doctor Jung strokes his moustache with his index finger. "That must have been very difficult, Miss Joyce."

"Beckett is in psychoanalysis too, Doctor. Just like me. Right now. Three times a week, in London. Isn't that a coincidence? Both of us doing the talking cure at the same time." All week I have been thinking of Beckett, dreaming of Beckett. *Is Beckett discussing me, as I discuss him? Thinking of me, as I think of him? Is his sleep haunted by me, as mine is still haunted by him? Is this yet another omen?*

"Your belief in yourself as clairvoyant—was that affected by Mr. Beckett's departure?" Doctor Jung gets up and starts his habitual circling of the room. A bluebottle buzzes angrily at the window. "Did you question your Cassandra powers at this stage?"

"Beckett may yet be my destiny." My voice flounders, and then I remember what happened yesterday, how Babbo had reminded me again of my clairvoyance. I'd suggested he take up pipe smoking. More distinguished than cigarettes, more appropriate for a man of his erudition. After I'd gone back to the sanatorium, Babbo had gone to the park and sat on a bench. When he stood up to leave, he saw a pipe on the bench next to him. *But I can't tell Doctor Jung this, because he's not to know Babbo's still in Zurich. No, that is our little secret, mine and Babbo's.*

"How important was dancing to your state of mind at this point?"

"Dancing let me speak without words. I didn't realize it at the time, but it was my life jacket, Doctor." I look at the window where the bluebottle is hitting the glass with mounting rage. Every now and then a ray of light catches its shiny blue body, and its drone gets louder and more insistent.

"I believe you to be a very creative woman, Miss Joyce. It seems to me that your dancing was how you expressed your creativity. Perhaps it was also when you danced that your mother most envied you?"

"Envied me what? She had everything . . . beauty, Babbo, children, a life that gave her meaning. Why would she envy me?"

"Your father told me he suspected Mrs. Joyce of harboring envious feelings toward you. You had youth and talent and beauty. Could she dance or sing or paint or play the piano? Was she the muse for his new book? Tell me that, Miss Joyce."

The buzzing of the fly has become frenzied and furious. I look away from the doctor to the window, where the fly has become entangled in a spider's web and is beating its thin wings hopelessly against the threads that surround it.

"Oh, what does it matter! All I do now is talk, talk, talk. Why don't you look after physical things? Why is there no sport or movement in your so-called cure?" I stand up and move toward Doctor Jung. He steps back, a wary look in his eyes. And all the time the fly is buzzing, buzzing.

"Miss Joyce, my assistants have been watching you for several weeks now and they see no reason why you should not get back into life." The doctor moves behind his desk and motions me back to the armchair. "But for psychoanalysis to work, we must explore the depths of your unconscious. Can you face your unconscious? Can you accept what you might find there? However disturbing? However shocking? Are you ready to pass through the shadow of the valley of death?"

"The valley of death?" I echo, blinking rapidly. *Why won't that fly stop buzzing? I can't concentrate on the doctor's words . . . Buzzing . . . buzzing . . . in my skull . . . voices . . . buzzing . . .*

"Indeed. Facing the secrets of your unconscious is not easy. Some cannot do it. But it is essential if we are to get you back into life. I need to know if you have the stamina for it." He pauses and strokes his moustache again.

Why is the buzzing of the fly not distracting him, not making him lose his flow?

"And there is something else that must happen if psycho-analysis is to work. I believe you are caught in your father's psychic system. I have asked him to leave Zurich so that the transference process necessary for my cure to work is not inhibited."

"He *has* left." I put my hands over my ears to block out the sound of the fly. *When will it stop buzzing? My head is full of its febrile buzzing . . .*

"Do not lie to me, Miss Joyce. He has locked himself away in the Hotel Carlton Elite in Zurich, and I cannot carry on treating you if you both behave like this. I have asked him, again, to leave. If he does not do so, I will have to terminate your treatment." The doctor picks up his notebook from his desk, walks to the window, and slams the book against the glass. He flicks the crushed fly from his book onto the floor. "It is imperative that your father leave Zurich."

Panic ripples through me. *If Babbo leaves Zurich, how can I inspire him? How can I give him the ideas he so badly needs? And who will visit me? I will be incarcerated and friendless—again. His great work will stall—again.* I cast my eyes around the room and then catch sight of the fly on the floor, partially flattened. One leg is still twitching . . . twitching.

"You are indeed your father's *femme inspiratrice*, his anima. I cannot deny that."

"Anima?" I can't stop staring at the fly, on the floor, below the window. *Why won't its leg stop twitching? Why didn't the doctor kill it properly, cleanly? Twitching . . . twitching . . . When will it stop twitching?*

"Every man carries within him the eternal image of woman . . . a feminine image . . . unconscious, of course, and always projected upon a woman he loves. That is the anima and it acts as a bridge to creativity, to the unconscious." Doctor Jung pauses. "Are you listening, Miss Joyce?" He walks over to the window, bends down, and picks up the fly by one of its torn wings. He drops it in a wastepaper basket beneath his desk and sits down heavily on his swivel chair, his knees creaking loudly. "So, let us talk about your father."

I stare mistily at Doctor Jung sitting behind his desk, drumming his fingers on his notebook, watching me with his slitty eyes.

"No," I say. "It's not Babbo who lives in the valley of death. He is the only one who understands me. And the only person I trust." I slip off my chair and squat down, peering into the wastepaper basket. *Is the fly's leg still twitching? I must know if the fly is dead or alive . . .* I crawl across the floor until the wastepaper basket is immediately in front of me. *Where is the fly? Where is it?*

"Who lives in the valley of death, Lucia? Who is with you in the valley of death?" Doctor Jung bends from his chair so that his face hangs upside down, batlike, beneath his desk.

Why is he calling me Lucia? Where is the fly? Where is it?

"Who is with you in the valley of death?" he asks again, his voice urgent and insistent.

And then I see the fly, its flattened body still, its legs unmoving. And the blue of its body muted by the shadows of the wastepaper basket. And I remember who is with me in the valley of death.

Doctor Jung has slid from his swivel chair and is crouching beside me, under his desk, his great frame stooped and hunched. It's dim and gloomy under the desk, like the old hallway at Robiac Square, like Babbo's study. All the shutters closed, the blinds pulled down, the curtains drawn. All those apartments, all so dark and lightless. *The doctor smells of pine trees and soap and pipe tobacco. How nice he smells* . . .

"He's dead," I say.

"Who is dead?"

"The fly. His leg's stopped twitching."

"What happened in the valley of death, Lucia?"

But it's too late. I've locked myself away, far away, where the doctor can't get me. Where no one can get me. Where no one can pick at me, scratch at me, chip away at me as though I'm an old scab. *No, I'm not ready to be bloodied and inflamed.*

"Miss Joyce? Miss Joyce, can you hear me?"

Everything is becoming shadowy and blurred. And now darkness is pouring into my head, filling it like black smoke from a burning house. And words won't form in my throat. And I can hear nothing, see nothing, feel nothing. Nothing left . . . *just the smell of wet pine needles . . . such a nice scent . . . such a lovely scent . . .*

18

MARCH 1931

PARIS AND LONDON

know you don't feel ready to go back onstage, darling." Kitten leaned over and touched my arm. "So I've had another idea, a better idea."

"I'll go back onstage when my squint's gone. I need another operation, that's all. Mama says it's worse than it was before." We were sitting on a bench in the Jardin du Luxembourg, looking out at the daffodils and the first green leaves of spring. It had rained earlier and now everything looked clean and shiny.

"I think we should start our own dance school, darling." Kitten paused and looked at me, her eyes all bright and gleaming like the wet leaves in the trees. "I think we should set up our own physical training program. We can choreograph it ourselves and call it the Joyce Neel Method. What d'you say, Lucia?"

Yes! Of course! I leapt up from the bench, shook out my damp coat, and started pacing, swinging my umbrella as I went. "We can start by offering private lessons. And when we've got enough pupils we can be the Joyce Neel School. Or the Joyce Neel Institute of Dance and Physical Culture!"

"Exactly, darling!" Kitten jumped up and joined me, walking up and down the path, our boots crunching on the gravel. Shafts of grainy sunlight fell across the grass and the daffodils. And reflected in the puddles was the pale blue of the sky.

"Once we have enough private students, we can rent a dance studio. I've got so many ideas for our method, Kitten." I reached out for her hand and held it tightly as we walked. "It should be a combination of gymnastics, eurythmics, and jazz dance." I rose up onto the balls of my feet and pirouetted, pulling Kitten with me.

"We can use everything we know." She drew me to her as if about to lead me in a waltz across the Jardin. "Ballet, jazz, free form, everything we've learned. I've already started devising a program and I reckon if we get it finished in the next week or so we could be ready to start taking pupils in May. What d'you think, darling?"

"We need a trading card! What shall we put on it?"

"I think it should say 'Physical Training' and under that, 'Private Lessons.' And then a telephone number. We can do the lessons at my house."

I twirled my umbrella and then waved it in the air, as though it were a victory flag. A flurry of raindrops fell from its furled panels, and when I looked up I saw a fragile, gauzy rainbow reaching across the bowl of the sky.

"I'll ask Mama if I can put our telephone number on the card. There's always someone in at our house. Oh, Kitten, I'm so excited!"

"Imagine if our method is really successful, Lucia. We'd be running our own dance school. Wouldn't that be divine?"

"Yes," I agreed. Already I was thinking of my independence and freedom. And this time I wouldn't fail. I was determined not to fail. I would be Miss Lucia Joyce, founder of the Joyce Neel Institute of Dance and Physical Culture. Not Mrs. Calder or Mrs. Beckett or Mrs. Fernandez. Not someone's muse. Just me, myself. And I would not fail.

Kitten and I spent the next two weeks working on our method, creating sequences of movement and chains of positions for strengthening and toning and improving balance. And when we were happy with our program I asked Mama if we could use the Robiac Square telephone number for all the inquiries that we would, inevitably, receive.

* * *

SHE WAS SITTING at the kitchen table hunched over a piece of paper. Spread out before her were all Mrs. Fleischman's gifts from the last year: a porcelain tea set; several silk scarves; four cut-glass bottles of perfume; eleven books for Babbo.

"This lot comes to more than two hundred pounds, and that," she said smugly, "is without the cigarettes or wine."

"What are you doing, Mama?"

"Adding up the value of that vampire's presents. She must have given you some things."

"Only her cast-off clothes and that scarf." I pointed to the silk Coco Chanel scarf, which Mama had draped over the teapot.

"I'm thinking that if the gifts keep rolling in like this, I might be able to go to the wedding after all." Mama gouged at the air with her pencil. "I'll be letting you go to the wedding too, Lucia."

But I didn't want to think about Giorgio's impending marriage, so I just nodded and said, "Mama, please can I use our telephone number for my trading cards?"

"What trading cards?" She surveyed the table of gifts again and made a smacking noise with her lips.

"Kitten and I want to take private pupils for dance lessons and we need a telephone number so we can be contacted."

"So that's what the two of you have been up to! All that whispering and disappearing into your bedroom. You can use our number, but be sure to put a time. I'm not wanting to be answering the telephone day and night, or taking messages when Jim's trying to work. And what does your father have to say about this daft idea?"

"I haven't told him yet. He's too preoccupied with his law books."

Mama gave her wedding ring a quick twist and then looked up at me. "Yes, best to leave him out o' this. He'll only start harping on about bookbinding again."

"I'll ask people to telephone between two o'clock and three o'clock and I'll sit by the telephone every day for that hour. I promise."

"And what about your dancing at the Margaret Morris school? I don't want you hanging around here, getting under me feet all day."

"I've told them I'm leaving. I need to concentrate on my work with Kitten." I started edging toward the door. I didn't have time to chat. A new chapter in my life was opening and I needed to get to the printers—before Mama changed her mind.

* * *

FOUR DAYS LATER our cards arrived. How smart they looked! Little oblongs of stiff white card with our names in black. At the bottom was the Robiac Square telephone number and a polite request to telephone between 2 and 3 P.M. And it was my name on it, not Mrs. Alexander Calder or Mrs. Samuel Beckett, but me, Lucia Joyce, dance instructor for private pupils. Inventor of the Joyce Neel Method. Creator and founder of the Joyce Neel School of Dance. I put the box of cards—two hundred of them—inside my wardrobe. Then I remembered Mama and Babbo and slipped a few into my pocket. I'd present them with a card each, and a few for their friends. But first I'd telephone Kitten and tell her how marvelously divine our cards looked.

"They look so sophisticated and modern," I gushed into the receiver. "The font we chose is perfect. When can you come and get some? And when shall we start giving them out?"

"I'll come tomorrow morning, darling. I think I've already gotten us our first pupil." Kitten's voice squeaked with excitement.

"That's wonderful! Who?" I held the receiver tightly against my ear, not wanting to miss a single syllable. Ahead of me, through the window, I could see the lights of the Eiffel Tower coming on, floor by floor, lighting up the Paris sky.

"A friend of your mother? She wants to learn to dance? Well, she's coming to the right place. The Joyce Neel Method is ready to take Paris by storm!"

Kitten's laughter seemed to ripple down the telephone wires toward me, like some joyous contagion. I laughed back and then said I had to go. I wanted Mama and Babbo to be the first official recipients of our glorious new cards.

I had just put the receiver down when Babbo called me into the dining room. I knew immediately something was amiss. Mama sat at the table, her face long and her mouth screwed up like a drawstring purse. She had her hands in her lap and was breathing loudly through her nostrils.

Babbo motioned me to a chair and cleared his throat. My eyes flickered from him to Mama and back again. I put my hand into my pocket and curled my fingers around the sheaf of cards. This was *my* new chapter and nothing my parents said could change that.

"Lucia, I've written to the landlord to give notice on Robiac Square." Babbo's words were slow and measured.

"You can't," I said, my voice barely audible. "Our cards have been printed with this telephone number on. You have to tell the landlord—straightaway. Look!" I brought the cards from my pocket and gave one to Babbo and one to Mama. Babbo looked at it and frowned.

"Yes . . . well . . . you won't be needing those," Mama said dryly, passing the card back to me. She looked at Babbo in a deliberate way, and I saw his lips move and the dark pouches beneath his eyes tremble.

"W-what d'you mean?" I stammered, looking wildly from one parent to the other.

"We have to leave for a while. All three of us. We'll spend the summer in London." Babbo paused and looked helplessly at Mama, but she was staring at the table again and refusing to meet his eye.

"But I don't want to go to London. I want to stay here at Robiac Square!" My voice grew louder as his words sunk in. "My pupils will be calling here. This is the only place where I've lived for more than a few months. I'm not going!"

"I'm afraid you have to, Lucia. Your mother and I have to go to London and you have to come too." Babbo sighed heavily and closed his eyes.

"I tell you I'm not bloody going!" I slammed my fist onto the table. "I'll stay with Kitten or Mrs. Fleischman or any of your obsequious slaves that'll have me."

"Lucia! Don't be talking to your father like that!" Mama's eyes were like granite. But then she turned to Babbo and said, "This'll be all your fault, Jim. Dragging us all 'round Europe from pillar to post. What on earth d'ye expect?"

"What about Giorgio? Is he coming too?"

"He'll be staying with Mrs. Fleischman now they're as good as married. It's just us that's needed, isn't that right, Jim?"

I looked, bewildered, at Babbo. His eyes were still shut but his Adam's apple was going up and down and his ringed hands were twisting in his lap.

"What aren't you telling me?" I said suspiciously. "Why do we have to go to London? Is this something to do with your new book?" I remembered Sandy's words about my father and his dirty books, and glared at Babbo with undisguised disgust.

"No, no, not really." He opened his milky, bloodshot eyes and looked pleadingly at Mama.

Mama tutted, then rubbed her palm across her forehead. "We have to go to London to get married. There. I've said it. It's a legal thing and nothing more."

I sat, stunned and motionless, as I took in her words. Nothing they were saying made any sense. Had they both finally gone mad?

"I don't think you understand," I said. "My pupils will be calling here. *Here!* I'm starting a dance school. Kitten and I have come up with a whole program. That's all we've been doing for the last month, and we've spent all our savings on these cards. I can't go. Anyway, you're already married so you're talking nonsense."

"We're not properly married," Mama said sharply. "I don't know why you're leaving this to me, Jim, I really don't." She looked at Babbo's white face and shook her head in disbelief.

"Your mother and I have to get married. In London." Babbo took a cigarette from his pocket, jammed it between his lips, lit it, and inhaled deeply.

Confused, I glanced at Mama's left hand. Her gold wedding band gleamed dully on her fourth finger. Memories of all the wedding anniversaries we'd celebrated, every eighth of October, raced through my mind. I recalled, vividly, the twenty-fifth anniversary party Miss Beach threw for them. Mama had bought me a new dress in pea green and I'd worn a daring purple turban and an opera cloak borrowed from Kitten.

"What d'you mean, not *properly* married? Why d'you have to get married *again*? Why do we have to leave? I don't understand." I crossed my arms stoutly over my chest and raised my eyebrows questioningly.

Babbo took a long drag on his cigarette and looked beseechingly at Mama again. But she shook her head and kept her lips pressed tightly together.

"You got married on the eighth of October, 1904. Everyone knows that. That's why we always celebrate then. That's why you're Mr. and Mrs. Joyce. That's why Mama wears a wedding ring."

"It's not that simple," said Babbo. He paused, and I watched the cylinder of ash fall from his cigarette onto his flowered waistcoat.

"Oh, spit it out, Jim, for goodness sake, or we'll be here all day! Just tell her, will you?" Mama said with irritation.

"You and Giorgio are illegitimate. We have to make you legitimate so that any child of Giorgio and Helen's can legally take the Joyce name." Babbo wearily stubbed out his cigarette and finally turned to look at me. "The eighth of October is when your mother and I left Dublin."

I stared at his pallid face, trying to understand the full meaning of his words. Inside me, feelings of shock and horror and disbelief were crashing and colliding. "So I'm a bastard? Is that it?" I put my head in my hands. I felt humiliated, degraded, filthy. I was nothing but a bastard. And they had lied and lied. For years and years.

"We have to marry in London in order to become British residents and make you both properly legitimate. And to become British residents, we have to look as though we're planning to stay for some time. So I've taken a five-month lease on a flat in London. We can come back to Paris after that." Babbo lit another cigarette, his hands trembling as he struck the match.

"So I'm not Lucia Joyce?" I glared at Babbo. "I'm Lucia Barnacle, aren't I? Just a bastard Barnacle!"

Babbo closed his eyes and said, "You'll be Lucia Joyce as soon as we're married."

"And you've lied to everyone for all these years! What the hell were we celebrating if we were bastards all along?" Spittle flew from my mouth as I shouted. "And what was all that shit about marriage first and mischief after? The fucking Irish way!"

"Sweet Jesus! Calm yourself, Lucia. It's not the end o' the world. We're just going to London for a bit." Mama stood up and pushed her chair back. "Anyway, it'll be worse for me. Me own mother won't speak to me now, let alone the rest o' me family in Ireland."

"What?" I shrieked. "You've destroyed my dream of a business with Kitten! You've told me I'm a bastard—no better than some whore's unwanted brat! I find out you've lied to me—to everyone—all my life! You're getting rid of the only home I've ever known! And you say it's not the end of the world? You say it's worse for you? It may not be the end of your world, but it's the end of my damn world!" I took the cards out of my pocket and hurled them at her. Then I scraped back my chair with such ferocity that it fell on its side. I kicked it out of the way and shoved past Mama, pushing her so hard I felt her tip sideways.

As I opened the door, I glared back at Babbo. His face was drained of color and there was a distant look in his pink-rimmed eyes. I paused for a second. Then I remembered this was his fault, that he and Mama had destroyed my life.

"Don't worry about me," I shouted as I walked out. "I'm just a bastard!" I slammed the door with all my strength and ran to my room. I took the box of cards from my wardrobe, opened my bedroom window, and tossed them out. They fluttered and swirled to the ground like oversized pieces of confetti. A passing man in a top hat looked up curiously. And through choked sobs, I shouted, "Don't worry about me—I'm just a bastard!" The man averted his eyes, quickened his pace, disappeared around the corner. "Nothing more than a bastard!" I heard my voice carrying over the crooked rooftops and chimney pots of Paris, the wind taking my words far, far away.

When my heart stopped hammering and my anger subsided, I crawled into bed, pulled the covers over my head, and wept inconsolably. I hadn't been Mrs. Samuel Beckett, I hadn't been Mrs. Alexander Calder, and now I wasn't even Miss Lucia Joyce. I was a bastard Barnacle, bereft and plundered.

And then I thought of all the lies, all the deceit, from those I thought had loved me. Giorgio had lied to me. Beckett had lied to me. Sandy had lied to me. And now my own parents had lied to me—all my life. And I thought my tears would never end.

Later on, much later on, I heard my mother packing up the china and Babbo taking down the ancestral portraits and I knew it was real. We were going to London.

19

~~~~

MAY 1931

LONDON

But you promised no one would know, Jim. You promised!" Mama peered through the grimy lace curtains at the line of reporters waiting outside. Some had brought blankets and small cushions, as if they were planning to camp out on our doorstep. She began pacing around our tiny, fetid sitting room in Campden Grove, Kensington, wringing her hands. Every now and then her eyes developed a watery glaze and I thought she might cry—but she didn't.

The doorbell had been ringing all day. The first journalist arrived two hours after Babbo had applied for his special marriage licence (which he did a mere twenty-four hours before the wedding in a pathetic attempt at secrecy). Then they came, one after another, ringing and ringing, shouting through the letterbox, throwing pebbles at the window. Finally, when we thought they'd left for the night, Babbo insisted we go out for dinner, just the three of us. But when we returned at midnight we found another reporter sitting on the doorstep, a blanket over his peaked knees. We had to step across him while he fired a volley of questions at us.

"What are we going to do, Jim?" Mama implored. "It'll be all over the papers tomorrow, that Nora Barnacle, aged forty-seven and mother of two bastards, is finally getting married!"

"Well, I'm the bastard," I snarled. "I'll be all over the papers as a Joyce bastard. And then I have to go to some art school and sit in a roomful of people I don't know pointing and whispering and jeering. That's much worse. And it's not even my fault!"

"We should get some sleep." Babbo fidgeted nervously with his earlobe, his expression aloof and indecipherable.

"How on earth d'ye expect us to sleep with reporters all around us? And there's fungus growing in the bedroom. That's no way to spend the night before your wedding! I should never have run off with you like that. Foolish, downright stupid I was. Let this be a lesson to you, Lucia. Don't even touch a man 'til he's put a ring on your finger. They're slippery buggers, all of them!"

"You know I'm not coming to the wedding, don't you?" I watched my parents' faces closely, hoping they wouldn't try and make me go, like they tried to make me do so many other things I didn't want to do.

"Of course not, Lucia," said Babbo gently. "Go shopping. Buy yourself something nice. It's not a big story, a couple of lines in a couple of the less salubrious papers, but nothing more."

"Oh, you think so, do you? A couple o' lines in a couple of the less salubrious papers! Well, I'll be hoping you're right. It's not like we're film stars or nothing. Although you, Jim, you might think you're some sort o' star for sure. But you're not—you're really not worth a couple o' lines in a couple o' rags."

"Babbo's always right," I said staunchly.

"Oh, look at you. Always so loyal. Always hanging on your father's every word. Even after you know you're a bastard." Mama gave a shrill laugh and tossed her head.

"Well, if I am one, it's because you made me one!" I shouted. "Perhaps if you'd been a bit nicer, he might have married you!"

"Come, come, Lucia. I've already told you we had a wedding of sorts in Trieste. When we arrived off the boat." Babbo fiddled with the top button of his shirt, avoiding our eyes.

"For pity's sake, can you be stopping that story, Jim! Putting a blarney gold ring on someone's finger in a louse-ridden hotel room with not enough room to swing a rat is not what most people's calling a wedding!" She glared at Babbo, the whites of her eyes shining in the gloom.

"Now, now." Babbo sighed deeply. "We'll all be legitimate and married and legal tomorrow. Good night, Lucia." He took Mama's hand and they left me, curled up in the stained blue chair, listening to the scratching mice and the clock as it struck one—a single, solitary chime that echoed around the damp, empty flat where we were to start our lives as a respectable, legitimate family.

* * *

THE NEXT MORNING I woke early to the rumbling of the London underground train, which ran immediately behind our apartment. Mama was already up, dressing for her "wedding day." She'd bought an expensive new outfit of the latest fashion—a swirling skirt that barely covered her knees and a figure-hugging coat with the latest cuffs. Even though it was a warm summer's day, she insisted on wearing her favorite fox fur around her neck and a cloche hat, which she pulled very low. "So as no one can see me," she said with a tight smile.

When the lawyer arrived, he said the story was all over the *Daily Mirror* and that there were crowds of Fleet Street photographers, not only outside the Kensington Register Office, but up and down Campden Grove.

"I can get us past the newspapermen, but unless you have a back door, I don't advise Miss Joyce leaving the house," he said. So I agreed to stay home, besieged and imprisoned.

"Do some of your drawing. That calms your nerves," said Mama as she powdered her nose for the third time.

"Prepare for the worst, though," the lawyer added. "All the

Sunday newspapers will be there and they've a lot of pages to fill." And then he handed his rolled-up copy of the *Daily Mirror* to Babbo and told him to look at page three.

"Oh, Jim, read it out," squeaked Mama.

"'Notice has been given at a London register office of the forthcoming marriage of Mr. James Augustine Aloysius Joyce, aged forty-nine, of Campden Grove, Kensington.'" Babbo paused and cast his eyes over us all, as though he were onstage and we were his eager audience. "'The bride's name has been given as Nora Joseph Barnacle, aged forty-seven, of the same address. Mr. Joyce is the author of *Ulysses*. According to *Who's Who*, he was married in 1904 to Miss Nora Barnacle of Galway.'" He hesitated, his lips twitching slightly as though he was trying to suppress a smile. "'Mr. Joyce's solicitor stated yesterday, "For testamentary reasons, it was thought well that the partners should be married according to English law."'"

"What on earth does 'testamentary' mean?" Mama asked.

"Ah." Babbo paused and straightened his bow tie. "That was my idea. It doesn't mean anything but it reads well, don't you think?" He sounded smug and arrogant, and for a minute it occurred to me he was enjoying all this—the legal wrangling and wordplay, the attention and publicity.

"Mr. Joyce thought it was vague but important and legal-sounding enough to throw them off the scent. We'll see if it works." The lawyer sounded uncertain but Mama nodded vigorously in agreement and Babbo smiled to himself.

"I like that line about 'the bride's name.'" Mama tittered. "Miss Nora Barnacle of Galway—in the *Daily Mail* along with the film stars!"

"Time to sally forth, my bonny bride." Babbo smirked at Mama and tucked his cane carefully under his arm. I stood scowling at them as they prepared to do battle with the newspapermen and the photographers. But neither of them noticed me as they left the flat, Mama adjusting the rake of her hat and tucking away stray hairs, Babbo very upright and experimenting with the angle of his head.

* * *

I AWOKE THE following morning to hear my parents laughing. I found them sitting in the parlor, surrounded by newspapers.

"How grumpy you look in this picture, Jim." My mother chuckled as she raised a copy of the *Evening Standard* in the air. "And do you see how shapely me legs look! I *am* glad I bought that skirt. I was thinking it might be too short at the time. You know, too short to get married in!" She giggled girlishly.

"Have a look at this, Nora. They call you Nora Barnacle, spinster." Babbo pushed a copy of the *Sunday Express* toward my mother, his eyes lit with pleasure.

"You naughty boy!" My mother wagged her index finger suggestively at Babbo. "You're thinking you might sell more books now, I'll bet."

Babbo said nothing but carried on beaming.

"Or are you thinking o' the days when I was Nora Barnacle, spinster, of Galway—oh, you naughty, naughty boy! Well, I'm just plain old Mrs. Joyce now and there's nothing you can do about it." She simpered and reached eagerly for the newspaper.

"Rejoice, Mrs. Joyce, no longer joyless or juiceless but joyful juicy Mrs. Joyce." Babbo was chortling, his shoulders shaking with laughter.

"Oh, I did feel a fool," my mother squealed.

"And have you seen this telegram from Giorgio?" Babbo passed her a thin envelope. "In Paris they're saying the wedding is nothing more than a stunt to publicize my books!" He slapped his thigh in mirth. "We are wedicizing my work, Nora, my flora."

As I stood in the doorway, soundless, unnoticed, I felt only revulsion and bitterness at their ridiculous enjoyment of themselves. Anger began to surge through me. How swiftly their sense of shame was ebbing away.

I went back to my room, slamming the door with all the force I could muster.

* * *

IT WAS WARM under the covers, dark and comforting. I felt like a seed dibbled deep into the dark earth. Or a truffle, warty and scabrous, lying curled and silent among rotting beech leaves.

As I lay there I could feel something inside me spluttering

into life. I tried to imagine it as a shoot preparing to burst forth from a seed or a bulb. But at night it felt like something else. Something I didn't understand and couldn't name. It scratched and gnawed at me. It frightened me. And beneath my eiderdown with the sprays of pink roses, I breathed and breathed and breathed.

* * *

I STOOD IN the dank and gloomy hall of Campden Grove, waiting for the bell to ring. Beckett was in London and was coming to dine out with us. Babbo kindly asked if I'd mind him joining us. I demurred but then thought it might help me to see him, to show him what he'd lost through his own foolishness. And I had no friends in London, no one of my own age with whom to converse or reminisce.

When the bell pealed, I opened the door and there he was. Beckett—his blue-green eyes behind his wire-rimmed glasses, his beaky nose, his gaunt face that still looked as though it had been chiseled from stone. When he saw me he stepped back in surprise, as though he wasn't expecting me, as though he'd been tricked in some way. And then he recovered himself and said how grand it was to see me.

"Weren't you expecting me to be here?" I asked in a faltering voice. I suddenly felt the air around me compressing and buffeting me, pushing at my lungs.

"Oh yes, Mr. Joyce said you would be joining us and I was very pleased." Beckett's fingers strayed to a boil on his neck, then to his hair, then back to the boil. "But you look—you look different. You look tired, Lucia. That's all."

I exhaled in relief, then gave a short laugh that was meant to sound joyful, even a little coquettish. But it came out more like the bark of a nervous dog.

"It's been a difficult time for us all," I said. Then I remembered how much my parents enjoyed the newspaper coverage of their wedding, how outraged Babbo was that the *Times* hadn't covered it and that the *New York Times* had hidden it away in its "Marriages, Deaths and Births" column. So I added, "Difficult for some of us, at any rate."

"I imagine you're looking forward to being an aunt?" Beckett's voice was stiff and formal, as though I were someone he barely knew.

"Oh, that," I said carelessly. "I suppose so. Babbo is pleased his lineage is to be continued. Let's hope it's a boy, hey?" I gave a little trill of laughter but stopped abruptly when I saw Beckett eyeing me oddly. "Anyway, welcome to Campden Grave. More like a grave than a grove, don't you think? Come and have a drink and then we'll go out. I want to hear all your news." I kept my voice bright and took a long, deep breath at every opportunity. I wasn't sure if I wanted to hear his news or not. Seeing him again agitated me and my stomach seemed to be full of skittish sliding eels. I suddenly longed to be in my bed, deep under the covers. Why had he come? Why had I agreed to dine with him?

Instead, I said, "We're going to eat at Slater's. It's just 'round the corner."

"Grand," said Beckett.

I realized I hadn't taken his coat or hat or led him into the apartment. We were still standing in the dimly lit hallway with its stained wallpaper that rippled and bubbled with damp, and its odor of cooked cabbage and fungus.

And then Babbo's voice rang out. "Beckett, is that you? Come through, come through and have a drink."

* * *

OVER DRINKS, AND then dinner, Babbo and Beckett discussed their work. My mother crowed about the excellent roast chicken she bought around the corner every day, and her wedding, and Giorgio and Helen's expected baby. I pushed a veal cutlet around my plate and tried to hide how dejected and desolate I felt. I tried to laugh in the right places and look serious and sad at the appropriate moments. But I seemed to get my timings all wrong. When Babbo talked of his struggles with *Work in Progress*, I laughed manically, and when my mother tried to lighten the mood by making jokes about the English, strange whimpering sounds came up from my throat.

"Won't you eat something, Lucia?" My mother jabbed her fork at my plate with its pile of mangled food.

"I don't feel hungry," I said. "I had a big lunch today." She knew, of course, that I'd had no lunch, but how could I explain the nausea that lay like a coiled snake in the pit of my stomach?

Beckett asked me, carefully and politely, how Stella and Kitten were and whether I was enjoying London. I told him I had no idea how Kitten and Stella were because Stella had gone to study at the Bauhaus in Germany and had no address for me, and Kitten was very upset when I destroyed our dream of a dance school, and she had no address for me either. I could hear my voice becoming clamorous and sharp and I could see my mother glowering at me, but I continued. Since he asked.

"No, I don't like London. The apartment's horrid. I have no friends at art school. They won't talk to me because I'm a bastard. I have no life of my own here. I hate it! I want to go back to Paris—as soon as possible. I hate the English. They're all donkeys! I just can't escape them in London. They're everywhere, always staring at me. They know I'm a fucking bastard." The words tripped and fell from my lips, each one louder than the one before. I frowned, puzzled at how my larynx was talking—no, shouting—of its own accord.

People at the next table stared at me. Babbo stared at me. Beckett looked at his plate and concentrated very hard on cutting up his steak. My mother glared at me. And then Babbo started talking in Italian, telling me everything was going to be all right, that I could go home whenever I wanted, that I could stay with Giorgio in Paris. I didn't say much after that. And Beckett, sensibly, didn't ask me any more questions.

When we left the restaurant I was talking quite normally again. Babbo asked Beckett if he'd like to join us the follow-

ing week for dinner, before his return to Dublin. Only I saw
the look in Beckett's eyes, for it was the look of a man corralled. Only I saw the pleading, soft-soaping look in Babbo's
eyes. Only I knew that Beckett couldn't refuse my father.

"Just tell my father you don't want to come, Beckett. Go
on—just say it! Tell him the truth! You don't want to be with
me. You don't want to dine out with a cross-eyed bastard. I
don't care. Just say it!" And Beckett looked at me in surprise
and then his cheeks flooded with color and he quickly looked
away.

"Come on, Lucia." Babbo put his spidery hands on my
shoulders and wheeled me around, toward Campden Grove.
And when I looked down I saw the pavement of Kensington High Street, littered with small mounds of dog shit. And
when I looked up at the darkening sky, it seemed unsteady
and trembling, as though it could fall in at any moment. And
when I turned my head, there was Beckett, walking up Kensington Church Street, his shoulders all bent and hunched.
Oh, Beckett. My Beckett . . .

*　*　*

THAT NIGHT I knew there was something dark and monstrous inside me, lurking, waiting, biding its time. I couldn't
explain or describe it, but it scared me. Sometimes it jumped
into my throat and took control of me. I said nothing to my
mother. And I couldn't bother Babbo. He had his great *Work
in Progress* to complete. Nothing must come between him

and *Work in Progress.* And so tired. I was so tired. I couldn't dance anymore. I had no energy. And my mother said the flat was too small. Just climbing the stairs made my breath come harder. The simple act of dragging air into my lungs exhausted me. I concentrated on my drawing—my drawing and my breathing.

20

AUTUMN 1931

PARIS

t was Babbo's idea. Ever since I started drawing lessons, he'd talked of us embarking on a project together. After returning from London, I was at a loss. I didn't have the energy to start a new dance class and I seemed to have no friends left in Paris. Only Kitten, and she was always busy with her fiancé. We no longer lived in Robiac Square. Instead we had a small, airless apartment in Passy with moss growing in the bathroom and dark stains all over the ceiling. More and more I felt like a husk, empty and helpless. I took to sitting in my room and staring into the mirror, asking how I could scratch out a life for myself now. Asking who I was and who I was to become. But my reflection gave no answers, and my mother became more and more irritated by my inertia.

So Babbo asked me to design illuminated letters to accompany each of the thirteen poems that the Oxford University Press was publishing, in a special edition to be called *The Joyce Book*. The editor asked thirteen composers to write musical settings for each poem. I was to be a part of this illustrious crowd of artistic brilliance.

The Book of Kells must inspire me, Babbo said. And so it did. On good days. But on bad days I saw serpents, and when I looked at my lettrines later on, I saw the serpent's head plain and clear, tangled in the strokes of dove gray, smoke blue, and softest rose pink.

* * *

FOR THREE MONTHS I worked on Babbo's lettrines. All day and every day. Slowly and painstakingly. Babbo said they were beautiful. My mother said nothing. Finally, they were parceled up and sent by special delivery to Oxford. But at the beginning of December, as the Paris air turned chill and brittle, the lettrines were returned. They had arrived too late. The poems had already been typeset.

Babbo said he had another idea, a better idea. He got straight to work touting my lettrines all over Paris. A week later he told me the Black Sun Press had agreed to print twenty-five special editions of his poems with my illustrated letters. They were to be printed on thick ribbed paper and bound in raw green silk the color of a tart apple. Each page was to be interleaved with green tissue paper. My name was to be embossed, alongside Babbo's, on the front cover. My illustrations would leap from every page. They would be works of art, collectors' editions of James Joyce's poems.

But a week later Caresse Crosby of the Black Sun Press called. I heard Babbo talking to her on the telephone. I heard the long silences as he listened. I heard the despondency in his voice as he said, "Thank you, Mrs. Crosby" and "Goodbye, Mrs. Crosby." When he hung up and came into the parlor, he couldn't look me in the eye. He stood awkwardly by the window, looking out at the cloudless, colorless sky. He lit a cigarette, blew out a long plume of smoke, and told me Mrs. Crosby could find no American buyers for our work. I felt an undertow of defeat, of stillbirth, flowing around me, pressing in on me. Babbo quickly regained his composure. He told me he had another idea and I must give him time.

* * *

MY JANUS-FACED MOTHER visited Helen Fleischman-Joyce every day. If she wasn't at Giorgio and Helen's apartment, she was out and about in their car, with their chauffeur. I didn't care. I never liked her anyway.

* * *

"SHE FRIGHTENS ME, Jim. There, I've said it."

"You mustn't let her King Lear scenes intimidate you,

Nora. No doubt it's a simple hormone imbalance that can be resolved with a good doctor."

"That's not what Giorgio's thinking. He knows her better than we do. Those two were always thick as thieves."

"And what is Giorgio saying, as poor Lucia sits a glooming so gleaming in the gloaming?"

"That she's going mad and should be locked up, Jim. In a lunatic asylum."

I saw Babbo's stockinged feet twitching on the sofa and heard the strike of a match. Then Mama moved toward the door and closed it, and all I could hear was my heart stumbling against my ribs.

* * *

JANUARY 1932. A light snow fell over Paris. I sat at the window, the blind raised just a few inches, watching the snow as it drifted and settled. I thought of Alex Ponisovsky and how much time we'd been spending together. He no longer gave Babbo Russian lessons. Now he came to the house only to see me. He was gentle and kind, courteous and well-meaning. As I thought of Alex, smiling quietly to myself and watching the snow, my mother said something that made me freeze, that made every muscle and sinew in my body stiffen with shock.

"Lucia," she said. "I think you should know something. I think it's better you're hearing it from me before you're discovering it for yourself. Mr. Beckett has left his position in Dublin and come back to live in Paris. He's living on the rue de Vaugirard." She looked at me as though she was expecting a response. But I had nothing to say. I slowly turned my head back to the window, and as I watched the snow, pale and feathery against the black sky, a single word circled inside my head. Why? Why? Why?

"I'm glad you're all right with that. Likely you'll bump into him someplace or other—you know how 'tis in Paris. Haven't you anything to do, Lucia? Why don't you do some o' your drawing? Just look at this snow. If it don't stop soon we'll be snowed in, just before His Lordship's big birthday. That won't do. No, that won't do at all."

* * *

SOMETIMES I STRANGLED my mother, my two gloved hands wrenching her flabby neck. Sometimes I force-fed her with Babbo's morphine, spooning it expertly down her throat. Sometimes it was nothing more than a casual push that sent her toppling from our balcony. Whatever the method, the dream was the same. But recently others had entered my dreams too. Babbo, Giorgio, Helen Fleischman. I frantically measured the morphine, but there wasn't enough to go around. I pushed my mother over the balcony, but Babbo or Giorgio saw me and so I had to push them over too. I saw the terror in their eyes as I cast them to their death. One by one, the people in my life were killed, swiftly, efficiently, without mercy. Each dream ended in the same way. Once I'd murdered, I left the apartment with a skip in my step. I went to the quayside stalls on the Seine, where the caged birds were sold. I opened every cage and let every crested canary, every blue-eyed cockatoo, every peach-faced lovebird, every scarlet macaw fly freely into the air. And when the last bird was wheeling in the sky above me, and my ears were flooded with the sound of birdsong, I woke up, sweating and shaking.

* * *

BECAUSE IT WAS her fault. She gave me my squint. She made Babbo ban Beckett from Robiac Square. She stopped me dancing. She gave birth to me out of wedlock. She made me a bastard. Other things too. Things I couldn't understand. And all this time something was fluttering at the edges of my memory. Something unspeakably vile. Yes, it was her fault. She was to blame . . . in the beginning . . .

* * *

FEBRUARY 2, 1932. Babbo's fiftieth birthday and the tenth anniversary of the publication of *Ulysses*. Everyone was scurrying around, adjusting waistcoats and skirts, answering the telephone, hunting for hats and gloves and mislaid tiepins. One of Babbo's Flatterers was hosting a small party. There was to be a cake with fifty candles and a fondant replica of *Ulysses* in blue and gold. I wore a new dress my mother had bought me, with a beaded bodice and a matching headband and patent leather shoes with T-bars studded with rhinestones, all the color of a ripe mulberry.

I didn't think to ask about the other guests until a few minutes before we were due to leave. My mother was standing in the kitchen powdering her nose when I asked who else would be coming to the party. Giorgio, who had brought the car and chauffeur for us, was reading the newspaper. Babbo was in the bathroom combing his hair back so that it lay flat and smooth against his head.

"Sure it's very small this year," said my mother. "Did you invite Mr. Ponisovsky? Such a nice man."

I shook my head. "He had a prior engagement. So who's coming?"

"Helen will come for a bit, won't she, Giorgio?" Mama turned to Giorgio, who nodded and went back to the newspaper. "And Mr. and Mrs. Gilbert and Mr. and Mrs. Sullivan. And Mr. Beckett's coming too. So there'll only be a few of us. Nice and small."

"Beckett?" I said, incredulous. "Beckett's coming?"

"Yes, whyever not? We're all friends now." She snapped her powder compact shut and started humming to herself.

And in that moment a torrent of fury rushed through me, so strong, so decisive, that without thinking I lunged for the nearest thing—a wooden kitchen chair—and picked it up as though it were as light as a soap bubble. I raised the chair high above my head and hurled it at my mother. She saw the chair sweeping through the air and dodged it, her eyes, face, lips white with panic and fear.

As the chair left my hands, I realized I was shaking uncontrollably. But before I had time to respond, to apologize, to understand what had happened, Giorgio leapt up and grabbed my wrists. He held them so tightly I cried out in pain. He pulled me from the kitchen, dragging me down the hall and toward the elevator. As he pulled me, I heard him calling out to my mother, telling her that this time I had gone too far, that he was taking matters into his own hands. As I heard the elevator cranking its way toward us and Giorgio shouting, I caught sight of Babbo's bloodless face in the hall. He cried out to Giorgio, telling him to stop, to leave me alone. But it was too late. The door opened and Giorgio shoved me roughly inside. As the doors closed on us, all I could see were the rhinestones on my shoes and the beads on my dress, all winking and glinting with malice in the dim cage of the elevator. Then Giorgio grabbed my arms from behind, my wrists pinned in his bony hands. His nails dug so hard into my flesh, I was sure there must be a trail of crimson blood behind me.

When I cried out in pain, he put a hand over my mouth. He told me, in a low and violent voice, that he wouldn't let me ruin Babbo's fiftieth birthday, that he wouldn't let me hurt Mama—ever. "People are saying you've lost your wits. That you're bringing shame on us, after everything we've worked so hard for. How dare you! How dare you try and hurt Mother. You've gone too far, Lucia." He pushed me out of the elevator, one hand still over my mouth, the other still gripping my wrists.

Outside the apartment block, the Buick sat gleaming in the thin winter light. I saw the surprise in the chauffeur's eyes as he jumped out and opened the back door for us. Giorgio maneuvered me into the rear seat, thrusting me back against the leather. I shook my head so vigorously in protest that my silk headband slipped down my face until it lay nooselike around my neck.

"*Où?*" asked the chauffeur, bewildered. "*Pas la rue de Sévigné?*"

I saw Giorgio's eyes flit from left to right, as if he was trying to decide what direction we should take. Then he told the chauffeur to drive as fast as he could. He gave an address that was unfamiliar to me, but I heard the words "Maison de Santé" and I knew exactly where he was taking me. It struck me, like an unwanted echo from the past, that this was what had happened to Mrs. Zelda Fitzgerald. I recalled, with sudden clarity, Sandy's words two years before. First you go to a Maison de Santé. From there it's one small step to being locked up as a lunatic, like Mrs. Fitzgerald, like Nijinsky. I opened my eyes wide and started to wriggle and struggle. I wanted to tell Giorgio that I didn't mean to throw the chair, that it wasn't me who threw it, that someone else had taken control of my body, my arms. I tried to twist my head and look back at the apartment, to see if Babbo was coming for me. But my neck was jammed against Giorgio's chest and I could see nothing.

Giorgio stared grimly out the window. After a while, I felt the pressure from his hand over my mouth easing. I tried to shake my head free. I couldn't breathe. I needed to speak. But when he felt the movement in my head, he tightened his hand again, pushing it hard against my mouth, forcing me to inhale and exhale heavily and noisily through my nostrils.

Eventually, we arrived at a pair of heavy iron gates. The chauffeur was dispatched to open them while Giorgio kept me pinioned in the back seat, still unable to speak. By then, I had no resistance left. I slumped, motionless, feeling shudders run sporadically over my body. Once through the gates, we drove along a narrow winding track until we reached a large white house surrounded by gravel and laurel bushes. We pulled up at the front door and Giorgio removed his hands from my arms and my face and climbed out of the motorcar. He told the chauffeur to watch me and walked into the building. A few minutes later, he returned with two burly men and I saw him gesturing to the Buick.

The chauffeur opened the door so I could get out. But instead I cowered on the back seat, whimpering like a frightened dog. Giorgio told me to get out of the motorcar. But I was unable to move. I felt as though I'd been soldered to the leather, my legs and arms lifeless and heavy. And then I found my tongue and stopped whimpering. I begged Giorgio to take me home. I pleaded with him for forgiveness. I beseeched him to give me another chance. I swore never to spill our secrets. He just shook his head and said if I didn't move the two men would have to pull me out. Slowly, I climbed out of the car. One man took my right arm and the other took my left. Gently but firmly they led me toward the large white building. I turned and saw Giorgio smoothing his hair as he slid calmly into the motorcar.

"I didn't do it!" I shouted. But he didn't look back and I heard the wheels of the Buick crunching over the gravel as they drove slowly, inexorably, away.

* * *

FOR A WEEK I lay in bed or walked the dank, dripping grounds of the Maison de Santé. I thought of Beckett's hands, his fingers like twigs, thin and ridged at the knuckles, the veins that stood up like twisting tree roots. And when I managed to put Beckett's hands to one side, I thought of Alex Ponisovsky. Alex wrote to me every day, hoping I was feeling better, hoping I was resting. And saying how much he wanted to see me and hold me and kiss me again.

And all the time something dug and troweled in my stomach, as though another person were growing inside me—such an angry person, a beast, a monster, pawing and gnawing at me, full of rage and fury.

And when the beast retreated to its cage and I had her firmly chained to the bars, I wrote to Babbo.

Dear Babbo,

Please come and collect me. I'm fully rested now and I want to apologize to everyone. And I want to see Giorgio and Helen's new baby.

I'm very sorry, Babbo, but I won't be coming back to live with you and Mama in Passy. It's too cramped and dingy and I need to live away from you. I know this will be hard for you and Mama but it's something I have to do. Perhaps I could live with Mr. and Mrs. Leon for a bit until I've found my own apartment? I want to choose my own clothes and my own furnishings. I'll be twenty-five in July, and as you know, I am determined to be married by then!

Anyway, you chuckle all night as you work on your book and it keeps me awake. I know you'll agree how important rest is for my health now.

Come and collect me as soon as you can.
Your own bella bambina,
Lucia

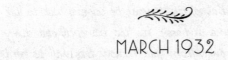

21

MARCH 1932

PARIS

So. I was to be married to Alex Ponisovsky. Exiled Russian Jew. Brother-in-law of Babbo's slave, Paul Leon. Lucie Leon's brother. Babbo's Russian teacher for several years at Robiac Square. Degree in economics from the University of Cambridge. Safe, secure job at the Banque Franco-Americaine. Charming. Kind. Clever. Quite possibly the nicest man in Paris. Very good friend of Giorgio and Helen. Friend and relative of Peggy Guggenheim. Oh—and Hazel Guggenheim.

It was all arranged. I was to have a dowry. Our engagement party was to be at Restaurant Drouant in the Place Gaillon. Everyone approved. Well, perhaps not quite everyone. My mother liked him and thought I'd finally found a man worthy of me. Babbo liked him. The many Flatterers were happy that my little "crise de nerfs" was over, happy that now I could be married off, leaving Babbo to finish his masterpiece undisturbed. Helen was thrilled and sent me a congratulatory telegram from the South of France where she, Giorgio, and their new baby were holidaying.

Only one person was disapproving. When Babbo telegraphed Giorgio and Helen to tell them the news, Giorgio took the first train to Paris and went straight to the little apartment in Passy, where he berated Babbo. Later, my mother told me that Giorgio had said I shouldn't be allowed to marry Alex, that I should be kept under lock and key with all the other lunatics of Paris.

* * *

WHEN KITTEN TOLD me Sandy Calder was back in Paris, that he was living in his old studio with his new wife, I sat perfectly calmly on Mrs. Leon's perfectly upholstered sofa. No chairs were thrown, no signs of madness or anger displayed. Instead, I looked at Kitten, my hands curled serenely in my lap.

"Is she wearing *my* earrings and *my* brooch?"

"Well, it's possible, I suppose. I haven't seen her personally." Kitten frowned and turned her head away.

"I shall pray I don't run into him." I didn't tell Kitten I was now going to church, slipping through the huge carved doors under the cover of darkness, kneeling on the stone floor, praying for the beast within me—praying for her execution, her termination, however bloody that might be.

"At least you have Alex now. He seems marvelous in every way."

"Yes, thank goodness I have Alex."

"And once you're married you'll feel more yourself."

"Myself?" I frowned, unsure who "myself" was now. And I felt the she-beast twinge and shift, as if rousing herself again, shaking off her lethargy, protesting at my uncertainty.

"You'll be Mrs. Ponisovsky," said Kitten brightly. "And perhaps we can dance again."

"Dance again?" I echoed. But as Kitten's words settled inside me, a feeling of lightness entered my body. My blood, so thick and heavy, seemed to turn to air. "You mean set up our dance school?"

"Why not? We'll both feel more settled when we're married. And there'll be some time before babies come along."

"Yes," I cried. "Yes!" And as I reached out for Kitten's hands, as I gripped them between mine, I felt the she-beast crawl back to her cage, routed and sullen.

"Once our weddings are over, we should put together a plan. Can you remember all those Margaret Morris sequences? Some of them were terribly complicated. And Monsieur Borlin's routines. Wasn't he funny!"

I leapt up and lifted myself onto the balls of my feet. Could I remember? Could I really dance again? I began to spin in slow deliberate circles, back arched, arms outstretched, just as Babbo liked me. And the stiffness slipped from my limbs and the hardened marrow of my bones seemed to melt away.

"You still move so beautifully, Lucia." Kitten fingered the ends of her hair and gazed appreciatively at me. "Promise you won't stop dancing again?"

"I promise." And I spoke so loudly I drowned out the soft snarling of the she-beast. I lengthened my neck, raised my arms above my head, splayed my fingers, and slid out my right leg. Why shouldn't I dance again? Yes, once I'd left home I would dance again!

* * *

A WEEK LATER, I sat in Restaurant Drouant opposite Babbo and Paul Leon, their faces ruddy with wine. Everyone was there. Everyone except Kitten, who was ill. Oh—and Giorgio. Everyone was drinking champagne, eating Russian caviar on blinis with sour cream, toasting my engagement to Alex. The waiters brought bottle after bottle and plate after plate. Babbo's face grew more and more flushed. Thank goodness he'd made his short speech early on! Mr. Leon was telling bad jokes and Babbo was humming an Irish ballad in an increasingly loud voice.

I felt ostracized from Alex, who'd spent most of the evening at the other end of the table, corralled by my mother and Lucie Leon. What were they saying to him? I wondered. I took the opportunity to examine Alex. Again. His thick, dark hair, soft and mossy. His face, as round and soft as a peach. His eyes, the color of burnt umber, brown and flecked, open and guileless. Quite unlike Beckett's craggy features, I thought. And when the image of Beckett floated freely before my eyes, and my pulse quickened, I felt a lurch of guilt. I hadn't been completely open with Alex. My own deceit was weighing down on me like water, forcing the air out of my lungs, making my breath come in short, sharp bursts. But when I cast Beckett away, when I pushed him back into the little box where he belonged, I looked again at Alex's open and guileless eyes—and I knew that he too was hiding something, that he too hadn't been completely open with me. Alex looked up, caught my eye, and gave me a little fluttering wave. I waved back with a bright, sculpted smile. My husband-to-be.

* * *

IT WAS AGREED. Alex would walk me back to the Leons' apartment after the party. I dawdled, letting Mr. and Mrs. Leon go ahead. When they were out of earshot I asked Alex why exactly he'd proposed to me. He said he proposed because he wanted me to be his wife, of course. I asked him to tell me the truth. I asked him whose idea it was. I asked him who encouraged it. And why he'd proposed now, and not before.

Alex was silent for a moment. I felt his arm stiffen beneath my hand. And then he told me that Paul Leon suggested it, that Paul and Lucie Leon told him he had to propose. They told him I wasn't a "bohemian American-in-Paris" type but a well-raised, bourgeois girl from a family with traditional Irish values. The sort of family that expected a man who'd walked out with their daughter to propose marriage. They told him I wasn't the sort of girl whose affections could be toyed with and that he owed me a proposal of marriage after what had passed between us.

When I asked him if he loved me, Alex said of course he loved me. He stooped to kiss my cheek. I didn't ask if he was *in* love with me. Nor did I tell him that my heart still belonged to Beckett.

* * *

AFTER ALEX AND I had kissed good night, I climbed the stairs to the Leons' apartment. Paul Leon had gone to bed. "Too much to drink," said Lucie crisply. I walked to the couch and dropped onto it, tired and confused. Alex's words were ricocheting around inside my head, pounding at my skull. I closed my eyes and tried to concentrate on my breathing. But instead of the customary respite, I felt myself falling, falling into blackness. I tried to lift my leg, but I couldn't. I tried to move my fingers, but they wouldn't obey my brain's instruction. I tried to turn my head, but nothing happened. I couldn't move.

Lucie came toward me and I heard her offer me a cup of tea. I tried to open my mouth but my lips stayed glued together. I stared blankly at her. Not one muscle in my face moved. I saw Lucie looking at me anxiously, her brow deeply creased, her eyebrows drawn tightly together. Still I couldn't respond. I felt the stiffness of my face, like an alabaster mask. I felt my eyes, wide and unblinking. I heard my breath escaping in short gusts. Lucie came with blankets and a quilt. She wrapped them around me and tucked them in so that I lay there like a swaddled baby.

I waited, expecting to feel fear or panic. Would I move again? Would I dance again? Would I speak again? These questions drifted through my woolly mind. But when I couldn't answer them, I felt nothing—just numb. It was as though a sleeping gas had leaked into the room, stolen inside my flesh, my bones, my brain. I felt only emptiness and a peculiar sense of peace.

For four days I lay on the Leons' couch. I didn't move or speak or eat. Lucie gave me water through a straw and listened to my heartbeat, being very careful not to touch my skin or get too near my breath. Babbo came and sang to me. Helen brought the baby to make me laugh. Kitten arrived with chocolates. Alex came with jonquils, his eyes brimming with alarm. I could just make out their dim and ragged outlines, as though they were on the other side of a thick gauze curtain. Their voices came to me as though they were speaking down an elevator shaft.

I heard the dread in Alex's voice as he waved his flowers under my nose. But he seemed such a long way away, and his voice was like that of a ghost. Even through my torpor,

I noticed he didn't try and kiss me. As if he was frightened I had some sort of contagious sickness. No one except Mama touched me. She came to me and put her hand on my cheek, and her eyes were like silvery fish. The numbness lifted then, just for a few seconds. I felt her touch and wanted her hand to stay on my cheek forever. But when she moved back and turned her head away, the emptiness rose up in me again. And I no longer cared. At times I didn't know if I was awake or asleep, dead or alive. I wondered if it was all a dream. Or was I in Heaven? No matter. I couldn't respond. I could only watch. And wait.

After four days, I felt my body open up again. My muscles began to ache and twitch. When I asked Lucie what happened to me, she said she went to the library, looked up my symptoms, and diagnosed me with temporary catatonia. Nothing to worry about, she said. Just nerves due to the impending wedding. Very common. Everything would be better when I was married. When I was Mrs. Ponisovsky.

* * *

SEVERAL DAYS LATER, at dinner, Helen told us about a little party she and Giorgio had been to the previous night. She told us Hazel Guggenheim had been there, how beautifully Hazel Guggenheim had sung. I saw Alex's head turn sharply, involuntarily. I saw a light come into his eyes. Our eyes briefly locked. And he knew that I had seen. And that I knew.

* * *

AN APRIL WIND slapped at our cheeks, bringing a fresh pink
hue to our faces. Alex and I were walking in the Jardin du
Luxembourg, admiring the blaze of daffodils that stretched
across the grass. Ahead of us was the tree that once inspired
me to choreograph a dance about a plane tree and a sapling
that struggled to survive in its shadow. I remembered telling
Beckett about it. I remembered wondering if Zelda Fitzgerald would dance it with me. How long ago that all seemed.
So long ago . . .

The memory of Beckett brought me out of my reminiscing. For it was he I wanted to discuss with Alex. Oh, and Hazel Guggenheim, of course. I told Alex, as kindly as I could,
that I loved him, of course, but that I was *in love* with Sam
Beckett. I told him that it was unrequited love, that Beckett
broke my heart and that, truth to tell, my heart had not yet
mended.

Alex didn't speak. He just looked straight ahead, his lips
drawn and thin. But when I turned my head, I saw his eyes
were wet with tears. I pressed on, like a surgeon who needs
to complete his butchery as quickly as possible. I told him I
was aware of his feelings for Hazel Guggenheim, that I was
no fool, that I'd been honest with him and I wanted him to
be honest with me.

Alex took a deep breath and then told me about Hazel,
about the affair they had for three years. I could tell from
the tone of his voice that he still loved her. He said she was

already on her third husband, that she was expecting yet another baby, that she was still having affairs with other men. He told me about her two children who fell off the roof of a New York apartment block and died. He told me about her father, who drowned on the *Titanic*. She was not, he said, the sort of woman he would ever want as a wife.

* * *

OUR HONESTY AND our respective grief brought a new intimacy to our relationship. For two weeks we talked daily, often for hours on the telephone, sometimes walking the streets and parks of Paris, or over dinner in unfashionable restaurants where we wouldn't be recognized or overheard. We talked about love and sex. We mulled over the pros and cons of arranged marriages, for we were under no illusions now. Ours was an arranged marriage. We talked of what we both wanted—children, a calm home with a telephone, a dog with long ears. I told him I'd always wanted a garden with drifts of yellow daffodils that burst forth in spring. And he smiled. Yes, he said, he'd like that too.

I talked to everyone I knew about what I now termed "the holy trinity": love and sex and marriage. Was it necessary to marry? Was it essential to love your husband? How important was sex? Could you love two people at once? Could you love one person but be in love with another? Was it wrong to marry someone if you weren't in love with them? Could you sleep with someone but not love them? The questions came spilling out, to the Leons' maid, to Helen, to Kitten. I didn't say a word to my parents. Alex said they were best kept out of our ruminations.

And when I told him I wanted to dance again, perhaps open a dance school with Kitten, he said, "Of course." He said he would never stop his wife from dancing. Not like Mr. Fitzgerald . . .

* * *

"YOUR FATHER IS on the telephone, Lucia." Mrs. Leon gestured to the hall, where the mahogany-and-brass telephone sat upon its own marble plinth. I put down my paintbrush, pushed the hair back from my face, and nodded.

"Hello, Babbo. Is everything all right?"

"You need to pack, Lucia. We need you to accompany us to London. We have to spend a little time in Campden Grove to guarantee our British residency, which also guarantees your legitimacy." Babbo's voice floated into my ear, then settled somewhere deep in my head. London? Campden Grove? I didn't even know we still had Campden Grove. That squalid apartment with the underground rattling beneath it and the odor of stewed cabbage and mold in the lobby, and the coils of dog shit that lay all over the pavements. I was silent.

"Now you're on the verge of marriage and may even become a mother yourself, nothing must cast aspersions on your legitimacy. I'm sure you can understand that, Lucia."

"Why doesn't Giorgio have to go?" I asked suspiciously.

"We'd like *you* to accompany us, *mia bella bambina.* It's not a legal requirement for our offspring to be in residence with us, but it might strengthen our case."

"So I could stay here? Or with Helen and Giorgio?" I looked at the telephone wires and thought how easy it would be to cut them, to snip them in two and forget about Babbo, forget about this conversation.

"The Leons need your room for a visitor, and Helen and Giorgio no longer have a spare room. I believe the nurse sleeps in it. It won't be for long."

It crossed my mind then that I was being offered a choice, albeit a skewed one. I could accompany them for a few days or I could stay in Paris, but not at the Leons'. My heart sank as I considered packing and moving again. "I don't have anywhere to stay in Paris, Babbo. Will you give me some money for a hotel?"

"I have no spare money, Lucia. We're really not going for long. We'd like you with us and I'll make you a wee art studio in the parlor."

"Very well," I said with a small sigh. "I'll pack a valise. How long shall I tell Alex we'll be away?"

"Oh, just a very short time. Not long at all." Babbo sounded relieved, as though he'd just crossed a tightrope and discovered himself on the other side, intact and triumphant. "London in the spring will be an unexpected pleasure, Lucia. We shall have a joyce-ful time, I am sure."

* * *

IT WAS ONLY when we got to the Gare du Nord and I saw the huge number of trunks and suitcases and hatboxes sent on ahead by my parents that I felt a horrible sense of déjà vu. Two porters were hauling a series of trunks clearly marked "Joyce" onto the train. Rivulets of sweat poured from their shining faces as they strained and gasped. I watched, open-mouthed. And I felt a darkness within me, rising and rolling like a wave, and the she-beast rattling at the bars of her cage, angry and accusatory.

"Have you given notice on the apartment, Babbo?" I asked, contriving to keep my voice as measured as possible.

"You know we have," snapped my mother, struggling to refasten a hatbox that had come undone.

"We have no Paris home now?" I asked, breathing deeply.

"We do not. We have a home in London and that's where we're going. Just for a few months. We can't afford two houses. Now pick up that hatbox and take it with you."

As I looked at Babbo for confirmation, I saw him tip fifty francs to one of the porters, nodding ostentatiously as he did so. He blinked when he saw me watching him. Then he pushed his wallet back into his pocket and said, "Are we all ready to board?"

I stared at him, aghast. My breath was coming in stabs now, making rasping noises from deep within my throat. And suddenly the she-beast burst from her cage and I started howling like a wild animal. I threw my head back and howled so loudly people everywhere stopped and stared. I felt my eyes rolling in their sockets like the eyes of a startled horse, white and panicked. I didn't want to go to London. I didn't want to be with my parents. I didn't want to leave Paris. I didn't want to leave Alex . . . Alex, my husband-to-be.

After twenty minutes or so (I was told this later—I had no idea of time or space in the midst of my second crise de nerfs), my howling subsided and I started to weep copiously. Babbo stood helplessly in front of me, clutching his cane, his eyes lowered to avoid the stares of passersby. My mother, her face a scalded pink, instructed the porters to remove the luggage from the train. She watched as each trunk was pitched from the train and stacked on the platform.

When every trunk and every suitcase and every hatbox had been retrieved, I started to feel more myself. As if the she-beast were creeping back into her cage, spent and subdued. My body stopped shuddering, my shoulders stopped heaving, the tears slowed, and I was finally able to dry my eyes and survey the scene. My parents were huddled together behind the trunks. When they reappeared, Babbo took my elbow and steered me toward the exit. He told me we were all going out for lunch and then we'd check into a hotel. My mother's face was black. She loved London, and I knew she was furious our plans had been thwarted. When no one could see me, I permitted myself just the very smallest of smiles.

* * *

THAT NIGHT, IN our plush hotel on the rue de Bassano, I dreamed of Donizetti's *Lucia di Lammermoor.* Not the melody or the libretto, for my dream was entirely soundless. No, I dreamed of Lucia, my namesake, betrayed by her brother, forced to marry someone she didn't love, descending into madness, stabbing her unwanted husband. I held the knife high above my head and brought it down, repeatedly, into the heart of a faceless body. Over and over again, the knife came down and was plunged deep into the body. But still it twitched and jerked. Still the body wouldn't die. And then I woke, cold and damp and frightened.

* * *

WE—MY MOTHER, Babbo, and I—went back to the gloomy apartment in Passy. Luckily, the landlord hadn't had sufficient time to find a new tenant and so the apartment was still available. Unluckily, there was still no room for me at the Leons'. My mother's witterings drove me mad, and, after losing my temper three times in four weeks, I decided to move in with some Irish Flattering friends of my parents.

Alex came to see me one evening. I cooked dinner for everyone and afterward he asked if I'd like to go to the theater with him. I said yes and put on my hat and coat. We were about to leave when the Flattering friends appeared and forbade me to go out. Alex and I looked at them, stunned. I told them I was going out, with my fiancé, whether they liked it or not.

"I've promised not to let you out," said Mr. Flatterer sternly.

"Have I left my father's house to be ordered about by you?" I pulled my belt tightly around my waist and reached out for the door handle. How dare he presume to control me!

"You can't go out!" repeated Mr. Flatterer, raising his arms to reveal salty rings of sweat.

Alex stood in the hall, looking embarrassed and awkward. "Perhaps we should just stay here?" he said quietly. "We could play cards."

"I will go out! Alone, if I have to!" I opened the front door and started walking decisively down the stairs.

And then I heard Mr. Flatterer behind me, commanding me. "I can't let you out, Lucia. I won't let you out!"

I felt his hand on my shoulder. The she-beast stirred in her cage. I waited. Mr. Flatterer's fingers gripped harder and tighter. The she-beast gave a low moan deep inside me. I waited for the now-familiar spasm of fury. But nothing came. Nothing but a small, strangled sob of humiliation.

"You win," I said. I had no will to fight anymore. As the energy leached from my body, I thought of Lucia di Lammermoor and wondered if I was doomed to the same fate.

I walked slowly upstairs, my heart heavy, my spirit crushed. Mr. Flatterer stalked behind me, apologizing in his brisk, determined voice. I ignored him. When we got back to the apartment, there was no sign of Alex or Mrs. Flatterer. The smell of casserole loitered in the air, but the temperature had fallen as though a cool breeze had blown through the place, and when I looked at my arms they were covered in goose bumps. I sat down at the dining table and waited for Alex. I could hear Mrs. Flatterer closing a window and then the banging of a door. He must be coming out of the bathroom, I thought. I had a sudden longing to feel his arms around me, to lay my head in the hollow of his shoulder, to hear the steady beat of his heart. Everything would be better when we were married, when I could finally be free, when I could dance again.

Mrs. Flatterer appeared, looking flustered and officious at the same time. I wondered if she'd been looking for a pack of playing cards so Alex and I could play rummy.

"Where's Alex?" I asked, summoning up the energy to turn toward her.

"He's gone," she said, as she collected up the glasses from the table.

"What?" I frowned. The apartment only had one exit and that was through the front door, where I'd just come from with Mr. Flatterer.

"I found the window in the bathroom open," she said. "I think he must have climbed out." She put the glasses down and moved toward me but I sprang past her, out of the dining room, shoving past Mr. Flatterer as he stood winding his watch in the hall. Along the corridor to the bathroom, where the caged parakeet opened one sleepy eye and watched me from its perch. I pushed open the bath-room, window and scoured the slate roofs. I saw a flash of Alex's pale linen suit disappearing down a fire escape. I opened my mouth to call out, but the bells of Saint-Sulpice started their relentless pealing and from below came the mangled shrieks of cats fighting in the gutter. And Alex was gone.

I felt my blood rising through me in a huge wave of crimson. And then Mr. and Mrs. Flatterer were beside me, holding me down, stroking my hair. And the she-beast bared her teeth and bit down on the bars of her cage in such a burst of hatred I knew I could no longer control her.

I never saw Alex Ponisovsky again.

* * *

THREE DAYS LATER Giorgio came to the Flatterers' apartment. He told me there was a taxi outside to take us to lunch with Mama and Babbo. I got my hat and coat and followed him down the stairs.

"Where are we going?" I asked.

He hesitated and then said we were going to Pruniers, one of his favorite restaurants. Fifteen minutes later, I realized the taxi driver had taken a wrong turn. I pointed this out to Giorgio, who was looking stonily out of the window. He shook his head as if a wrong turn was really nothing to worry about. So I carried on looking at the view, admiring the waxy tulips in window boxes and the purple lilac hanging in heavy blooms.

After a while I noticed we were heading toward the outskirts of Paris. I looked suspiciously at Giorgio.

"We're nowhere near Pruniers. We've just passed the Parc Montsouris. Where are we going?"

"It's a surprise. We're going for lunch, as I said." He kept his eyes on the window but his fingers strayed to the starched collar of his shirt.

"But Mama and Babbo will be there?" I persisted.

"It's a surprise," he repeated, his breath clouding the glass.

"I don't trust you." My eyes narrowed. I shouted to the taxi driver to stop but he took no notice. Indeed, I felt the engine accelerating. I lunged for the door, but Giorgio was prepared. He pulled me toward him and held me clamped against the bones of his chest.

"You should never have been taken out of the Maison de Santé," he said in a voice stripped bare of all kindness, all feeling. "Tantrums in train stations . . . not speaking for four days after your so-called engagement party . . . Half the time you're in bed refusing to talk . . . the rest of the time you're willful and out of control. I know you slapped Mother last week, as if throwing a chair at her wasn't enough! Even Alex thinks you're not right in the head. Why else would he jump out a window to get away from you?" He paused and dug his fingers deeper into my wrists. "Unlike Father, I do not believe lunacy is curable. And I will not have you going mad in front of my friends and my family. I will not have you sullying my name, Mother's name, Father's name. I won't have it!" He turned back to the window, still gripping my arms. I looked at my brother, now my jailer, and felt something cold and sour creep up the curve of my spine. And in the darkest crevice of my memory something chopped and clawed.

Outside, everything was rushing past—trees, houses,

lampposts, ladies with perambulators, men with dogs, troughs of tulips. And it was as though all the color and brightness had been sucked from everything, and all the light sucked from the sky. I felt the energy seeping out of me. I couldn't fight anymore. There was nothing left of me but dregs. Even the she-beast had left me now. I was empty and exhausted. They had taken everything from me.

I felt a tear of defeat prickling at my eyelids. "You win," I whispered. "You win."

* * *

GIORGIO TOOK ME to L'Haÿ-les-Roses, an institution for the mentally ill. There I was prescribed solitary confinement. He committed me, which meant I lost all status as an adult with full legal rights. From that day, I became the legal ward of a doctor. From that day, only a doctor could determine my future. From that day on, I was watched, guarded, or locked up.

DECEMBER 1934

KÜSNACHT, ZURICH

And after that you went from doctor to doctor?" Doctor Jung drums his fingertips on the last page of my manuscript.

"Yes, you're the twentieth. And I've had twelve nurses and eight 'companions,' as Babbo calls them. I call them guards, spies." *Why are his fingernails so dirty? What has he been doing? There are crescents of black grime in all his nails . . . smiling at me, laughing at me . . .*

"And no consistent diagnosis, according to your father." The doctor pushes his spectacles up his nose and frowns.

"No." *So many diagnoses . . . premature dementia, hebephrenia, schizophrenia, syphilis, hormone imbalance, manic depressive disorder, cyclothymia, catatonia, neurosis. And all those injections . . .*

daily injections of seawater . . . injections of serum made from the tissues of embryonic calves. All for what?

"The only thing they all agree on, according to your father's report, is your dislike of confinement and restraint." Doctor Jung peers at me over the top of his glasses that have fallen down his nose again.

"I'm a dancer!" *Am I still a dancer? Am I still an artist? Am I anything now? An insect? A prisoner . . . is that all I am now?* I pause and wipe my hands over my face. And as I do so I catch sight of the red welt on my thumb, its thin shiny puckers standing in angry ridges. The doctor says nothing, so I continue.

"To restrain a dancer is a crime. Is it any wonder I was driven to the very edge?" *All those straitjackets and leather mittens and the solitary confinement and the barred windows and the endless keys turning in locks and all those eyes, watching, observing, checking, snooping, spying . . .*

"Indeed." Doctor Jung looks at his notes. "And several doctors thought there was nothing wrong with you. Mild neurosis, according to one. No signs of any psychosis whatsoever, according to another."

"Doctors!" I stand up and move slowly to the window. *How stiff I am . . . how unyielding my body has become . . . I, who danced on some of the great stages of Paris . . . I, who danced with the most celebrated dancers in the world . . . What am I now?*

"Do you mind if I smoke my pipe?" He doesn't wait for my response but puts his pipe into the corner of his mouth and puffs at it. "I can cure you, Miss Joyce. But only if your father leaves Zurich. One cannot force a transference, but without it, I cannot cure you." The smoke from his pipe curls into the air above him, like the tendrils of a vine.

"Why is everything about my father?" *My father—who slurped the energy, the lifeblood, from us all, from everything around him. Even now, he's saying it's his gift, his spark that's been transmitted to me and kindled a fire in my brain. What nonsense!* I turn my head away from Doctor Jung and stare out the window at the little jetty where the doctor's boat is moored. The snow is falling more heavily now, drifting down over the lake before melting into the black water.

"It is possible that Giorgio had you locked in an asylum as a way of overthrowing his father. By removing you, he removed your father's muse, the very source of your father's creativity. No doubt that is what Doctor Freud would say. He would call it an Oedipus complex. That would also explain why your father's having trouble writing at the moment." I hear the doctor sucking noisily on his pipe and when I turn to look at him, he's staring distractedly at the ceiling.

"All his Flatterers are saying it's my fault his book isn't progressing. They're saying I've distracted him from it." *How I loathe those Flatterers . . . the way they dip their heads so reverently, fawning and obsequious . . .*

"Your father is indeed determined to cure you. He cannot accept that you have any illness of the mind. To accept that, he would have to accept that he too has an illness of the mind. But let us come back to Giorgio." He bats at the fog of tobacco smoke that now hangs between us.

Yes, Giorgio—turncoat, betrayer, Judas. It was he who turned me over to the doctors, it was he who pronounced me incurably mad, who changed my fate. But not to deny Babbo his muse. Oh no! That was never the reason . . . How mistaken you are, Doctor Jung! And inside, I feel the she-beast shifting, stirring, awakening.

"So. Why did your mother stop you sharing a room with Giorgio, Miss Joyce?"

The she-beast is moving, shuddering, and writhing inside me, preparing to pounce. I feel her claws unfolding, her lips curling, her thin body twisting, the flick of her tail. And the darkness is there too . . . inching forward, coming for me . . . *I must speak . . . before it's too late. Speak!* I feel the she-beast open her jaws. I feel her roar swell and roll . . .

"We found some letters," I say haltingly, tentatively. I can see them now. Thin sheets of paper folded into small squares, spattered with ink spots. *Why has this memory returned? Why am I saying this?* "They were in a white leather box . . . lined with white satin . . . Giorgio found them. He was looking for something and Mama and Babbo were out." I stop and look at the window. Squalls of snow blow against the panes.

"How old were you, Miss Joyce?"

"Nine or ten, I think." I stare at the snow collecting on the window. *How cold it looks, so cold.*

"Did you read the letters, Miss Joyce?"

I close my eyes and push my knees hard together, wrapping my arms around myself until I feel the jutting of my shoulder blades. *How thin I am now. Why am I so thin now? I*

*am insect-thin. Yes, mosquito-thin. Insect-thin. That word I saw
in the doctor's book. It wasn't "insect," was it?* I feel the heart of
the she-beast pounding inside its rib cage. Another flicker
of her tail. Impatient. Angry. *I am so thin. I must eat more . . .*

"The letters, Miss Joyce—who were they from?"

"My mother. They were from my mother to Babbo." There's
no turning back now. They are creeping and seeping back into
my memory, jumping in front of my eyes, taunting me, their
foul and filthy words filling my head. So obscene, so disgusting, they lodge in my throat like chicken bones. So vile and
lascivious and lewd I can't repeat them. *I will not repeat those
ugly, sordid words, those squalid, bestial desires. Not to Doctor Jung
in his tweed suit and his starched white shirt. Not to anyone. Ever!*

"Did you read them?"

"Giorgio read them. He read them aloud." And suddenly
Giorgio's shrill boy-voice is pealing in my head. I press my
hands over my ears but his voice is still there. Like a ghost-
voice returned to haunt me.

"Lucia, look what I've found! Letters from Mama to Babbo.
I found them in Babbo's drawer. Right at the very back! We
can see if we're going to live in Ireland." Giorgio had already unfolded a letter and was looking at it with his eyes all
screwed up tight, as if the sun was very bright.

"Does it say if we'll get birthday presents this year?"

"I can't . . . I don't . . . Oh!" Giorgio pulled back and wrinkled up his nose.

"I want a kitten. Does it say anything about a kitten?"

"It's . . . it's about . . ." He looked at me and stopped. Then he looked back at the letter and said, "It's about what grown-ups do."

"You mean cleaning the house and emptying the chamber pots and laying the fire? I help with those!"

"I think they do other things too." He frowned and pulled another letter out of the satin bag. "Do you know how babies come, Lucia?"

"From God. Can I read one? Is it about God?"

Giorgio shook his head. His eyes were very wide now, and startled. "It doesn't mention God. It's about peeing—and sh-shitting and—and sucking."

I put my hand over my mouth and giggled. "Yuck!"

He drew out another letter and read it with the same look of confusion. Every now and then he grimaced, as though he'd bitten into an unripe fruit. "Grown-ups do v-very s-strange things."

"What d'you mean? Read it out, Giorgio!" I was getting bored now. I could see my doll, lying undressed on Giorgio's bed. She needed to have her clothes and hat put on. She needed to take Baby Bear for a walk. "Show me!" And I reached for the letter.

Giorgio pulled back. He took a deep breath. "I am your b-brown-arsed f-fuckbird and I will sh-shit my drawers and then lie on my front and you can kiss my—my a-arse all over and then you can f-f-fuck me up behind like a h-hog riding a sow then I will squat on you and p-piss on your—" He stopped and blinked.

"That's disgusting!" I wanted to giggle again, but it no

longer seemed funny. And Giorgio wasn't laughing. "On your what? Chamber pot?"

"Cock." His voice was flat and expressionless. "And balls."

"Balls?" I knew a cock was a cockerel and why Mama wanted to piddle on a cockerel made no sense. Why she would dirty her drawers rather than use a chamber pot made no sense either. And why was she writing to Babbo about pigs? And what balls did she mean? The balls we threw in the park?

But Giorgio ignored my question and carried on reading, his lips moving silently and his forehead puckering.

"Nothing about my kitten, then?"

"D-do all grown-ups d-do this? Is that how Mama and Babbo made us?" he stuttered.

"We can try it with my doll." I gestured to Giorgio's bed. "She needs another baby. I can get your ball from the cupboard and piddle on it, like Mama does."

"Shall we try it?" His voice fell to a whisper. "Quick, Lucia. Lift up your nightdress."

"But I'll get in trouble if I dirty my drawers," I protested. "And the ball's not here."

"I have a piddle ready." He grabbed at my nightdress. "We can be like grown-ups."

"Can you make me get a baby with your piddle?" I lifted my nightdress eagerly. My own baby! Dolly and I would both have babies! I lay down with my nightdress up around my waist.

"Roll over, Lucia. I'll do you and then you can do me. Just like Mama and Babbo do."

I felt his lips against my naked bottom as he planted little chaste kisses across my buttocks. "Have you made the baby yet?"

"Not yet." I felt the heat of his body as he squatted over me and then the warm liquid of his pee-pee on my back. And under my tummy I felt Mama's letters, creasing and crumpling. "Turn over, Lucia."

"Not in my face . . . yuck!"

"To make the baby, stupid."

I rolled over quietly. My nightdress was sopping wet and the room smelled of urine, sharp and metallic. Giorgio had removed his nightshirt and was preparing to squat over my face.

"You need to suck this." He pointed at his small, pale penis.

"Do I? I thought I had to suck a ball." I looked over at Dolly. I'd had enough of this stupid game.

"This is my cock, stupid!"

"Cock-a-doodle-doo!" I crowed and snatched at his penis. It seemed larger than normal, slightly swollen and scalded, as though it was covered with insect bites. He lowered it toward my face and I noticed his body was shaking. And suddenly I didn't want to play anymore. Giorgio was frightening me with his peculiar insistence, and his eyes had become dark and glazed. And I didn't want to think about Mama's letters anymore. Or the things grown-ups do, or making babies. I wanted to dress Dolly in her best hat and take her far, far away. I closed my mouth and pegged up my nose with my thumb and forefinger. I would kiss his penis once and then I would play with Dolly. I felt something prodding, nuzzling, pushing at my mouth. I pursed my lips to kiss Giorgio's thingy and felt it slip against my gums.

I am too hot . . . too hot in the doctor's room! Must take my fur coat off . . . too hot . . . And the smell! The smell has followed me here . . . I need air! Clean air . . . mountain air. Why won't he open the window? The stench in here is unbearable . . . it's making me choke and gag . . . Why isn't he choking?

"Miss Joyce, why are you holding your nose? What can you smell? Miss Joyce? Miss Joyce? Can you hear me?"

The doctor's voice sounds as though it's traveling toward me through a very long tube, from a long, long way away. *From so far away, I can barely hear it . . . So far away . . .*

"Is that why your mother stopped letting you share a bed with Giorgio? Lucia? Lucia—can you hear me?"

And now I see her, Mama, on her knees, shouting and swearing and wiping up the mess. And she is so angry with me. So very, very angry. And I smell burning . . . and the bright flames of the fire are leaping in the grate. And she's burning everything—her letters, Giorgio's wet, stinking nightshirt, my soiled nightdress— and the room is full of smoke. And my hand is so hot, so very hot. Not my hand, Mama! Please not my hand! I wanted to get a baby, Mama . . . We were only playing, Mama . . . She's screaming at me . . . You did this, Lucia! You found private letters, you made Giorgio read them, you led Giorgio on like a strumpet, a hussy.

No, Mama, we were only playing . . . And Giorgio says nothing. Nothing at all.

"Lucia? Can you hear me?"

Babbo's in the doorway . . . screaming for Mama. Blood is coming from his head and he's screaming and holding his head in his hands and blood is dripping through his fingers to the floor. And through the smoke I see his eyes, huge and purple like plums. And he's crying now, saying he can't see, he's blind, and his life is over. And the blood is coming thick and fast from his skull. He says, in his blindness, he has walked into a lamppost, that he will never be able to walk alone—that his life is over.

"Lucia? Lucia? Can you hear me?"

And Mama is screaming too, calling him a perverted lunatic, saying he made her a pervert, his whoring and drinking have made perverts of us all. And his devilish desires have been passed to his own daughter, made her a slut and a trollop, made her defile her own brother. And she wants no more of his whore's diseases . . . and no more of his filthy ways . . . And my hand is stinging . . . so hot . . . my thumb shriveled and scorched. And it's all my fault . . . my wickedness has caused this . . . Because I wanted a baby . . . and I made Giorgio give me a baby . . . And still the room smells of burning and piss . . . and pools of blood lie on the floor . . . my fault . . . all my fault . . . All the time Mama stroking Giorgio's hair, screaming at Babbo. Him crying and bleeding. Me sucking my hand in the corner . . .

"Lucia? Look at me! Can you breathe?" The doctor is on his knees at my side, his fingers on my wrists.

My hands are clamped over my ears again. And now the

voices are receding and the smell has gone and the darkness is coming for me, swiping at my skin, closing in on me. Great waves of darkness washing over me. I reach out for my she-beast. But she is nowhere. Gone. Routed. Her cage empty.

I tilt my head toward the window and open my mouth. Nauseous. Need air. The doctor hurries over and throws open the casement so that a flurry of snow gusts into the room.

I look out, through the snow. Where is the lake? Where are the woods? Ah . . . the hills! I can just glimpse the blue-black hills in the distance, blurred and blue and thick with mountain flowers. And the snow is falling, falling. So soft, so silent.

The doctor is standing over me, his mouth opening and closing like a dying fish's. I hear his voice drifting toward me, its reverberative note of hope rising and falling. "I can cure you, Lucia. I can cure you. Your father must leave Switzerland and then I swear to God I will cure you."

His voice fades and for a few seconds I hear nothing. But then, from somewhere, I hear music. It comes from the open window, blown in with the snow . . . a single thread of music . . . I look past the doctor, past the lake and woods, past the blue-black hills with their mountain flowers, through the snow that falls like sifted sugar.

And far away at the edge of the horizon I see a thin belt of pale pink. Something is coming from it . . . carried in shafts of tremulous light. I move, I dance, toward the window. And in the pink of that distant sky, I catch a glimpse of them—my rainbow girls. See how they lift their feet . . . Look at the sweep of blue veins and soft bones that lie between their toes and their heels . . . like coiled springs . . . See how they move and sway . . . slipping like water toward me. Oh! Oh! Look at the twist of their waists. And the ripple of their shoulders. See how they bend their willowy backs. See how lithe their limbs are. See how they sheer toward me. My rainbow girls are coming . . . for me!

EPILOGUE

James Augustine Aloysius Joyce sat in the muffled silence of his thickly carpeted, heavily draped hotel room. He had his head in his hands. His loneliness seemed to stalk him these days, like a shadow he couldn't shake off. Or was it more like a growth, a tumor or goiter that swelled from the back of his neck? Perhaps the hotel staff laughed behind his back. Perhaps it was as obvious to everyone else as it was to him. Perhaps that charlatan, Doctor Jung, had seen it too.

He missed Nora. He missed the way she brushed the dust from his shoulders. He knew it was dandruff but she always said, "'Tis dust and nothing more, Jim." He missed the way she straightened his cuffs and fussed over his bow tie and made sure his shoelaces were securely tied. He missed the way she moved around him, her chin thrust out like the prow of a ship, steering and maneuvering him so he wouldn't bump into anything. And her voice. He would do anything to hear her voice. But he'd already telephoned her three times this morning and on the last occasion she had sounded distinctly irritated. He'd have to telephone her later. Perhaps he'd ask her again, one last time, to join him in Zurich.

He picked up the blue crayon he'd been trying to write with. He must write at least one more word this morning. Five words would be preferable. If he could do five words before Lucia visited, he would be happy. One short sentence. One short sentence a day. It would have to suffice. He took off his spectacles and wiped briskly at his eyes. He felt the tears standing in them. They were always there now. Everyone thought it was his eyes playing up again. But it wasn't.

Tears, ears, Mr. Earwicker, earwigger. It was all there in his book. The book he couldn't finish. *Finnegans Wake.* The title was still secret, of course. But yesterday he'd revealed it to Lucia, as they jigged around his hotel room. He'd explained all the puns, the layers of meaning, the double entendres. Of course she'd understood it all. Her response had been the very antithesis of his wife's. When he'd told Nora, all those years ago, she had looked at him quite blankly and then said, "You and yer words, Jim." And that had been that. But Lucia had understood it all. And when he said, "This book will keep the professors busy for three hundred years," she threw back her head and laughed with unbridled glee.

He felt a sudden spike of anger. Why did Doctor Jung talk of nothing but his, Jim's, effect on Lucia? At times he imagined putting his hands around the ignorant Doctor Jung's fat neck and throttling him. Why did no one understand about *her* effect on *him*? *Finnegans Wake*—this tightly woven tapestry of words, this spangled net of language—was *her* book. He couldn't have written it without her. Why did everyone talk of his genius, but never of hers? He looked up at the window, noticed the fresh snow drifting against the glass. The brightness hurt his eyes. He adjusted his spectacles, peered so hard he felt pain slice through his cornea. But something in the way the snow moved stopped him drawing the curtains. The way it floated, wafted, and then the sudden scampering as a few flakes caught the wind and seemed to tap, like the toenails of small children, upon the glass. As if the snow wanted to come in . . .

He opened the window a fraction. A clutch of snowflakes gusted straight into his face. He felt them hit his forehead, soften and melt, roll down the lenses of his spectacles. He closed the window and returned his gaze to the scene outside. It seemed to him the flakes were dancing, spinning and turning in a wild frenzy of abandonment. Lucia! She had come to him. And in that moment, words streamed into his head. He picked up his crayon and began writing.

For a second he saw himself not writing but dancing with words. He paused, looked back at the window. The snow swirled and sang. He felt it close around him. He shut his eyes. And there she was again. She was everywhere, in every snowflake, in every filament of his memory, in every fiber of his body, in every word of his execrable book. He started writing and the words seemed to fly from his crayon, from his fingers.

Such a rush of thoughts and words—like striking a vein of gold, he thought. Striking it so hard, shards of golden ore, bright ingots, flew into the air. And how adroitly, how nimbly, he had caught them. He put down his crayon and counted the words. But he couldn't concentrate. He kept miscounting, muddling words and sentences, confusing single and double digits. He felt his blood slow and his heart tighten and shrink. He stopped counting. Another thought was swimming just below the surface of his mind. Rising now. Assertive. Strident. He felt the thought still and coagulate, like the hardening of clay.

He sat motionless. He could feel the words nudging and creeping from his mouth. They wanted to be said aloud. "She will not be well until I finish this book." He removed his glasses, pushed the heels of his hands into his eyes. These perpetual tears . . . Would they never end? He put his glasses back on and sniffed. "When I leave this dark night, she too will be cured."

The air buckled around him. The snow beat against the window. He laid his hand carefully on the manuscript in front of him. He could cure her! He would cure her! But only by finishing this cursed book. He picked up his crayon again.

I am passing out. O bitter ending! I'll slip away before they're up. They'll never see. Nor know. Nor miss me.

AFTERWORD

$\mathcal{S}$amuel Beckett became one of the most influential writers of the twentieth century, receiving the 1969 Nobel Prize in Literature. He also received the French Croix de Guerre and Médaille de la Reconnaissance for his bravery as part of the French Resistance during the Second World War. One of the characters in his early novel *Dream of Fair to Middling Women* is thought to be based on Lucia.

Alexander Calder became one of the twentieth century's great sculptors and the originator of the mobile. His work can be seen at the Whitney Museum of American Art, New York; the Museum of Modern Art, New York; the Peggy Guggenheim Collection, Venice; and the Centre Georges Pompidou, Paris, among other places.

Zelda Fitzgerald was diagnosed with chronic schizophrenia and from 1930 on spent most of her remaining years in mental institutions, initially in France (including the same sanatorium supervised by the same doctor as Lucia), then in the United States. She died in a fire while at Highland Hospital in Asheville, North Carolina.

Stella Steyn left Paris to study at the Bauhaus in Germany. With the rise of fascism, she left Germany and spent the rest of her life living quietly in London. She painted, sporadically, and her paintings are now in many British and Irish collections, including that at No. 10 Downing Street.

Alex Ponisovsky narrowly missed being sued by the Joyce family for breaking his engagement contract to Lucia. He later helped extricate Peggy Guggenheim's art collection from Paris in 1940 but was picked up by the Nazis in Monte Carlo in 1942 and was never seen again.

Paul Leon was shot by the Nazis in 1942, having rescued Joyce's papers and belongings after the Joyce family fled their Paris apartment in 1939.

Emile Fernandez married, but after the collapse of his marriage, he fathered a child with a fifteen-year-old from the Ivory Coast. His musical career never reached the heights of that of his cousin, Darius Milhaud.

Margaret Morris's pioneering dance movement is still practiced across the world today.

The story of Lucia Joyce is undoubtedly sad, if not tragic. But Lucia's story has a sequel, a final act that is both uplifting and inspiring. Although this final act didn't take place within her lifetime, I like to think of her watching it unfold, from wherever she is.

After Lucia's death, details of her life began to trickle out, catching the imagination of numerous artists, in particular dancers, playwrights, and authors. At least ten writers have been inspired to write books and plays about Lucia, and several dancers have choreographed performances based on her life.

For me, Lucia's story has a special resonance. When I stumbled across her, I didn't intend to write a book. I'd given up an earlier career to raise my children, and after seven years at home, I'd enrolled at art college to study photography (for which I—truthfully—had very little talent!). The story of Lucia gripped me, and I couldn't get her out of my mind. I abandoned art college and decided to write my version of her story. I had no experience writing fiction but was inspired by authors like Therese Anne Fowler and Paula McLain, whose novels about Zelda Fitzgerald and Hadley Hemingway were published around this time. For three years I immersed myself in 1920s Paris and the Joyce circle. I spent weeks in Paris, my children reluctantly in tow, tracing Lucia's steps and reading every letter, account, biography of anyone who'd ever come in contact with her. She was elusive, but gradually her voice came to me, and eventually I had a novel. Unsure what to do with my manuscript, I entered a few writing competitions and was lucky enough to win one. Since then, I've written three more books, and I've been given what can only be called a new chapter. The credit must go to Lucia Joyce. Her moving and poignant story completely changed the trajectory of my life.

ACKNOWLEDGMENTS

am heavily indebted to the outstanding, seminal work done by Carol Loeb Shloss in her biography *Lucia Joyce: To Dance in the Wake*. Shloss spent sixteen years not only meticulously researching and writing her extraordinary biography of Lucia but fighting the Joyce Estate in a groundbreaking court case for the right to access Joyce family papers.

I am also indebted to the superb work of many other scholars and biographers too numerous to list here. But the following were the works I relied on most heavily: Gordon Bowker's *James Joyce*; Richard Ellmann's *James Joyce*; Brenda Maddox's *Nora* (including the censored final chapter, for which I thank the Joyce Centre in Zurich); Deirdre Bair's *Samuel Beckett*; James Knowlson's *Damned to Fame: The Life of Samuel Beckett*; Gerry Dukes's *Beckett*; Nancy Milford's *Zelda*; Conor Fennell's *A Little Circle of Kindred Minds: Joyce in Paris*; and Jane Lidderdale and Mary Nicholson's *Dear Miss Weaver.*

Alexander Calder's autobiography, *Calder: An Autobiography with Pictures*, was helpful, and his sculptures, drawings, and jewelry can all be seen online, as well as in many museums and galleries. His circus can be watched on YouTube.

The works of Joyce and Beckett were essential reading, in particular *Ulysses, Finnegans Wake*, and Beckett's early prose (*The Complete Short Prose*, ed. S. Gontarski).

For background information on Joyce, 1920s Paris, and dance, I am indebted to: Janet Flanner's *Paris Was Yesterday*; Robert McAlmon and Kay Boyle's *Being Geniuses Together*; Noel Riley Fitch's *Sylvia Beach and the Lost Generation: A History of Literary Paris in the Twenties and Thirties*; Peggy Guggenheim's autobiography, *Out of This Century*; Ernest Hemingway's *On Paris* and *A Moveable Feast*; William Wiser's *The Crazy Years*; Kevin Birmingham's *The Most Dangerous Book: The Battle for James Joyce's* Ulysses; Judith Mackrell's *Flappers*; Margaret Morris's *My Life in Movement*; Bev Trewhitt and Jim Hastie's *Margaret Morris, 1891–1980, Modern Dance Pioneer*; Kevin Jackson's *Constellation of Genius*; Vincent Bouvet and Gérard Durozoi's *Paris Between the Wars: Art, Style and Glamour in the Crazy Years*; Arlen Hansen's *Expatriate Paris*; Zelda Fitzgerald's *Save Me the Waltz*; and Gertrude Stein's *The Autobiography of Alice B. Toklas.*

For background information on Jung, I recommend John Kerr's *A Most Dangerous Method*; Vincent Brome's *Jung: Man and Myth*; and Jung's *Memories, Dreams, Reflections.*

On a lighter note, I must mention two graphic novels, the prizewinning *Dotter of Her Father's Eyes* by Mary and Bryan Talbot (without which I may never have come across Lucia) and *James Joyce: Portrait of a Dubliner* by Alfonso Zapico.

Because so much evidence (including letters to, from, and about Lucia; her medical notes; her novel and poems) has been destroyed or lost, I have imagined Lucia's thoughts and feelings throughout. Hence, this is a novel of the imagination, not a work of fact. However, where factual information was available, I adhered to it as closely as possible within the confines of the narrative.

Finally, I would like to thank all those who have supported me so generously with their time and expertise: Barbara Abbs, Pam Royds, Dr. Lisa Dart, Sarah Williams, Emma Darwin, Clare Stevenson-Hamilton, Annie Harris, Claire Baldwin, Stephanie Cabot, Douglas Matthews, and Thomasin Chinnery. I am particularly grateful to Sharon Galant at Zeitgeist Literary Agency, who believed in this novel from the beginning, and to David Lancett and Rachel Singleton at Impress Books, who gave me their prize, and proved to be excellent editors too. Thank you also to Natalie Clark and everyone else at Impress Books.

In the US, I would like to thank Lucia Macro and her talented team—Asanté Simons, Jeanie Lee, Mumtaz Mustafa, Diahann Sturge, Robin Barletta, Amelia Wood, and Andrew Gibeley—at William Morrow, for their faith, their eagle-eyed editing skills, their design skills, and for being such a delight to work with. And the very last thank-you must go to my New York agent, Claire Anderson-Wheeler, and the team at Regal Hoffmann, for finding such a good home for *The Joyce Girl*.

Thank you to everyone who answered my questions on subjects as diverse as Dublin dialects, Irish phraseology, ballerinas' feet, modern dance, and obscure Paris locations: Ali Mun-Gavin, Ann Marshall, Sandrine Marinho, Anna Carlisle, and Bernie Flynn. Thank you to the Margaret Morris dancers who bore with me as I learned to dance.

And thank you to my reading friends with whom I first discovered Lucia: Amy, Alison, Catherine, Isis, Nina, Rachel, and Susan.

The biggest thank-you, of course, goes to my husband, Matthew, and our children, Imogen, Bryony, Saskia, and Hugo.

Lastly, any mistakes made are mine—and mine alone!

About the author

About the book

Insights,
Interviews
& More . . .

Meet Annabel Abbs

Aaron Hargreaves

ANNABEL ABBS is a writer. Her first novel, *The Joyce Girl*, was published in 2016 to great acclaim and has sold across the world. It tells the fictionalized story of Lucia Joyce, forgotten daughter of James Joyce, and is currently being adapted for the stage. Her second novel, *Frieda*, was published in 2018 and immediately became a London *Times* Book of the Month and then a London *Times* Book of the Year, as well as being featured on BBC's *Woman's Hour* and in *Tatler, Good Housekeeping, Red*, and all UK national newspapers. It is currently being translated into several languages. The novel tells the dramatic story of Frieda von Richthofen, the woman who inspired D. H. Lawrence's Lady Chatterley and later became his wife. Abbs's first work of nonfiction, *The Age-Well Project*, was published in 2019 under the name Annabel Streets and coauthored with Susan Saunders. It explores the latest science of longevity. ❧

Historical Note

After four months in the sanatorium at Küsnacht, C. G. Jung refused to continue his treatment of Lucia, saying that continued psychoanalysis was possible but the outcome was uncertain and could even cause a deterioration. Joyce, who had always harbored misgivings about both psychoanalysis and Jung, removed Lucia from Küsnacht and installed her in his Zurich hotel with a nurse. Throughout Jung's analysis, he and his assistants probed for a "sexual secret" in her past, but she consistently clammed up at such questions. He later burned all his notes and files on Lucia, but maintained his opinion of Joyce as the cause of her troubles. Later, Jung said of them, "Both were going to the bottom of the ocean, he was diving and she was falling."

At the beginning of 1935, Joyce's patron, Harriet Weaver, and supporters were despairing of him ever completing *Finnegans Wake*. They regarded Lucia as a major obstacle to his work. Harriet Weaver and Joyce's assistant, Paul Leon, conspired to have her sent to London so that Joyce could continue writing. Lucia didn't protest—she was desperate to see Beckett again. She made her way, under supervision, to London, where Beckett was living and undergoing his own course of psychoanalysis after the death of his father. There is no record of what happened between them, except for a comment in one of

Beckett's letters: "The Lucia ember flared up and fizzled out."

From this time on, Nora Joyce refused to have Lucia in the house. After her stay in London with Harriet Weaver, Lucia made her way to Ireland, where she lived with her cousins for a few months. Here, according to her biographer, she became addicted to the barbiturate Veronal, which her father posted to her in large quantities, believing it would help her sleep. She also attempted suicide after reading an interview with Giorgio in *The New Yorker*.

Lucia ran away from her cousin's house and was eventually found living rough in Dublin, sleeping on those very streets her father had written and talked of throughout her life. In her pockets were dog-eared pages of *Finnegans Wake*, sent to her by Joyce. She told her cousins that she was the subject matter and muse for all the sections of *Finnegans Wake* that dealt with love, dancing, and madness. Rescued by a friend of Joyce's, she was returned to England, where she began another course of treatment with a doctor who prescribed seven weeks of solitary confinement. As before, the more Lucia was restrained, the more she struggled.

From then on, Lucia spent the rest of her life incarcerated in institutions, the last in Northampton, England. After numerous, differing diagnoses, she was eventually labeled as schizophrenic. Joyce spent much of his remaining life searching for possible cures, new ▶

Historical Note *(continued)*

doctors, better nurses, and sanatoriums for her. He wrote to her constantly, talked about her continuously, and regularly sent her gifts. He never balked at the fees required, despite them taking him to the verge of financial ruin. Meanwhile, Giorgio and Nora were united in their view that Lucia should be "shut in and left there to sink or swim" (noted in a letter from Paul Leon to Harriet Weaver, quoted in Carol Loeb Shloss, *Lucia Joyce: To Dance in the Wake*). Nora never visited Lucia.

According to the biography *James Joyce* by Richard Ellmann (published in 1958), Joyce always maintained that Lucia was clairvoyant, claiming that he and Nora had "seen hundreds of examples of her clairvoyance" and that her "intuitions" were "amazing."

Although Lucia didn't dance publicly again, her illuminated letters ("lettrines") were published as *Pomes Penyeach* in 1932, as *The Mime of Mick, Nick and the Maggies* in 1934, and as *A Chaucer ABC* on her birthday in 1936. Positive reviews appeared in a range of newspapers, including the *Daily Telegraph*, the *New York Herald*, *Paris-Midi*, and *Mercure de France*.

Lucia was last visited by her father in 1939. By 1940, Nazi Germany had annexed Austria and invaded Czechoslovakia, Poland, Norway, Denmark, the Netherlands, Belgium, Luxembourg—and France. In June 1940, the German army arrived in Paris, where Lucia was interned in a mental asylum. While many of the mentally ill and handicapped were killed by the Nazis as part of their euthanasia program, Lucia was lucky enough to escape and survive. She saw out the war from an asylum in northern France.

Joyce's letters demonstrate how, throughout this period, he worked tirelessly (but futilely) for her to be moved to Switzerland, where he, Nora, and Giorgio were now living in safety. When he died, all communication to Lucia ceased. It was Harriet Weaver who finally stepped in and arranged for Lucia to be relocated to England so that she could keep an eye on her.

From 1951 until she died in 1982, Lucia lived calmly (thanks to the availability of phenothiazine) at St. Andrew's Hospital in Northampton. Here, she continued to think constantly about marriage, going over and over her roster of former lovers, pondering whom she should have married. She also continued her crusade for freedom (even writing to General Charles de Gaulle at one stage) and maintained her loathing of imprisonment. Her only regular visitors were Joyce's patron, Harriet Weaver, and then Weaver's goddaughter, Jane Lidderdale, with the odd visit from a Joycean scholar interested in her father. But Samuel Beckett never forgot Lucia. He always sent her birthday presents and wrote to her regularly until she died. After his death, a picture of ▶

Lucia dressed as a mermaid at the International Dance Competition at the Bal Bullier was found among his personal belongings.

Lucia died on December 12 (the eve of St. Lucia's day), 1982. Despite there being a place for her in the Joyce family grave in Fluntern Cemetery, Zurich, she finally demonstrated her independence and chose her own burial place in Kingsthorpe Cemetery, Northampton.

In 1939, after seventeen years, Joyce penned the final lines of *Finnegans Wake*. According to Lucia's biographer, "Lucia's influence upon the life of her father and upon both the form and the substance of *Finnegans Wake* was profound." Joyce died two years later in Zurich, having not seen Lucia for well over a year and devastated by what had happened to her. Nora died in Zurich, with Giorgio at her side, in 1951. The infamous "dirty letters" she wrote to James Joyce were destroyed, but his were eventually made public. It has been speculated that Nora's participation in this infamous exchange of letters was her attempt to keep Joyce from revisiting the syphilis-ridden brothels of Dublin while he was attending to business in Ireland and she remained in Trieste.

Giorgio left his wife, Helen (Mrs. Fleischman), in 1939. She had been diagnosed as "markedly neurotic" after showing signs of early depression. Later, the diagnosis was changed to schizophrenia. He visited Lucia in England only once, in 1967.

The bulk of Lucia's letters were destroyed by her nephew, the last remaining descendant of James Joyce. These included letters to and from Samuel Beckett, allegedly destroyed at Beckett's request. Harriet Weaver had already destroyed all her letters from Lucia. An account of the destruction of Lucia's letters can be found in Lucia's biography (see Acknowledgments).

Although this novel is based on the life of Lucia Joyce, it is a work of fiction. I have imagined the thoughts and feelings of Lucia throughout. Although I took inspiration from actual events, I invented many scenes and most of the dialogue. The final scene was prompted by a single speculative line in Lucia's biography, some notes left by Jung's assistant, and a few cryptic lines in *Finnegans Wake*, but notwithstanding this, it is the product of my imagination—and no more. ∾

Reading Group Guide

1. To what extent does Lucia define herself through her relationships with men?

2. Do you think that Beckett was in love with Lucia?

3. How effective is the characterization of Lucia's madness as a beast?

4. How significant are Lucia's encounters with Zelda Fitzgerald?

5. How effective are the scenes between Lucia and Jung? Do you think Lucia is telling the truth in her memoir and in what she says to Doctor Jung?

6. Is James Joyce a main character in this novel? How does the nickname of "Babbo" separate James Joyce the character from James Joyce the writer?

7. Did the Historical Note and/or the Afterword change your perceptions of any of the characters?

8. Did Nora play a role in Lucia's mental deterioration?

9. Are there any early signs of Lucia's fragility that her friends or family could have spotted?

10. Does the novel offer any insights into father-daughter relationships? ❧